Yvonne

SO
b

The Complete Works of

NATHANAEL WEST

London : Secker & Warburg

This collection first published in England 1957 by
Martin Secker & Warburg Limited
14 Carlisle Street, London W1V 6NN

Re-issued 1968, 1974
Reprinted 1975

SBN: 436 56600 1

Printed in Great Britain by
REDWOOD BURN LIMITED
Trowbridge & Esher

The Dead Center:
An Introduction to Nathanael West

Writers, like seismographs, record the emotional charts of societies; so in the end, as obviously must happen, a period of time, with its behaviorisms and characteristics, conveys to our mental retina an instinctive pattern. The artist brings to the surface those x qualities that, mid-way between germs and tremors, lurk anonymously feeding on individual frustration. Once a society has been characterized or caricatured (has, in fact, been given a poetic or non-poetic name), it is freed. This release, which is pri-

marily given by the artist, acts as a standard for the dur-
ation of that social pattern—its people, like actors in a silent
film suddenly given words, move through the norms and
extremes of their lives with a new-found conviction. The
artistic truth, the "right" way of behavior for their time has
been established. So, looking at them through the wrong
end of a telescope, events appear as extensions or ab-
sorptions of those larger personalities that formalized them.

Yet, even when our patterns of culture appear to have
been established, new, sometimes uncomfortable, evi-
dences can materialize. A myth in the light of revaluation
is often destroyed. Similarly, and unspectacularly out of
seeming neglect, a myth can establish itself on the sole
basis of its truth. Our conception of periods of time naturally alters as our knowledge of them increases. What
seemed obvious to the point almost of stylization appears
curiously in a new key. It is like a gramophone record that,
having always been played on one side, is found to have
another that is equally acceptable.

The twenties and thirties in both England and America
have been meticulously documented. More nearly perhaps than in any previous era, literature became socially
representational. The mirror held up to humanity, its ec-
centricities and perversions, its social and political attitude,
disgorged a reflection that, if anything, was too close. The
heroic distaste for heroism, the intellectual's distaste for
himself and his embracing of his opposite, the divesting of
romance from illusions amongst those most in love with
illusions, all formed part of the dismantling of the human
personality that an age, out of love with itself, one moment
riding the waves, the next disembowelled at their base,
found necessary to save its face. One by one each writer
presented his or her case, then proceeded to destroy it—
*Eyeless in Gaza, The Woman Who Rode Away, To the
Lighthouse, Ulysses, The Memorial,* and in America, *Fiesta,*

The Great Gatsby, U.S.A., Appointment in Samarra—one by one these cancelled each other out. Each successive writer grew to know too much. Sophistication left the novelist dry.

Yet in general there remained a mixture of nostalgia and sadness, a residue of that good living which illumines prose, as it does a face, with a kind of dispassionate tenderness and which is the by-product of emotional prosperity, of a knowledge of good days. In England the class struggle of the thirties was reflected in literature by gestures of *avantgarde* idealism. The artistic truth in literary sympathies appeared also to be a political truth—but it was a conclusion English writers arrived at through a series of well-bred intellectual convictions, rather than a brute confronting with the facts of economic disaster. Their prototypes in the American slump—the inheritors of the Jazz Age débris, the sawn-off idealists who found themselves with not even an empty bomb in their pockets—had to learn the harder way. Their pessimism was not the reverse side of politico-literary idealism, it was a despair born from being witnesses of a suffering enormously outside their control. The wisecrack had frozen in their cynical mouths, the cocktail bravado of sexual indulgence gone flat like bad champagne. Somewhere hidden, Man was being anonymously pinned down with this weight of suffering on his back, this noisy civilized burden demanding a new martyrdom. It is this ruthless outline of collapse that Nathanael West created more savagely and poetically than any other contemporary writer in his two important novels *Miss Lonelyhearts* and *The Day of the Locust*—blueprints of the faithless Christ-symbols that in the end stood for the American common man, like bitter flowers, as he lay on the ground at the stockades of his own defeat.

Altogether, Nathanael West wrote four novels. Besides the two already mentioned, which were the second (1933) and fourth (1939) in point of time, there were *The Dream Life of Balso Snell,* printed in a limited edition in 1931, and *A Cool Million,* published in 1934. West was born in 1903 (his real name was Nathan Weinstein), educated at Brown University, and then consecutively was manager of a residential hotel in New York, and associate editor, with William Carlos Williams, of a magazine called *Contact.* His wife was Eileen McKenney, the original of the book *My Sister Eileen,* written by Ruth McKenney, and West's own sister married S. J. Perelman. So his links with the semi-fashionable, literary and stage world were fairly constant. until, after the publication of *Miss Lonelyhearts,* West went to Hollywood. He and his wife remained there till their death in a car accident in 1940. The last five years of his life West spent working on film scripts, among which were *Advice to the Lovelorn* (the adaptation of *Miss Lonelyhearts*), *Five Came Back, I Stole a Million, Spirit of Culver,* and *Men Against the Sky.* He was only thirty-seven at the time of his death. Perhaps the most remarkable things about West's career are its unevenness and its development. West's early writings are bitter, extremist, near surrealist and aggressive. The criticism underlying them is based on a disgust that is not far from hysteria: the language is obscure, extravagant, privately allusive and contemptuously scatalogical.

Yet after this unrelated little essay in intellectual gaucherie, West could suddenly strip his writing of all pretence, of all arrogant obscurantism, and produce a novel of the direct and economic intensity of *Miss Lonelyhearts,* in which every word is used exactly and functionally—and then again, in *A Cool Million,* forsake a personal style for mock-heroics and parody. Only several years later, when he had emerged from his incubatory period in Hollywood, and had written *The Day of the Locust,* was it apparent that West was somewhere on the way to integrating his gifts, to merging his bitterness and savagery into a wider, more organic pattern without losing his edge. *The Day of the Locust* marked his most important advance, the step from a political to a human view of drama. Basically, West was always a sociological writer, moved by the horrible emptiness of mass lives; and in this sense all his books are indictments, not so much of economic systems, but of life itself. *Life is terrible,* that was the despairing conclusion that led nowhere and which was the motive spring for his novels. For West there was no religious redemption to be found in human weakness, no transfiguring sense of good-and-evil, no compensation in the physical life. Seediness, apathy remained just seediness and apathy. The joke was on civilization, and West's own attitude was inexpressible through the perversion of great tides of compassion into relentless observation. So just as *Miss Lonelyhearts* is West's greatest book, because it is conceived most purely as a formal work of art, and is flawless within its structure, *The Day of the Locust* is his most mature because in it his criticism of life is not intruding between the characters, nor his pity confronting them. They exist simply in their relation to one another; the hidden reformer in West has contented himself with being an artist.

The Dream Life of Balso Snell, in any analysis of West's novels must, if it be considered at all, be subjected to a different sort of criteria—for the other three books, in the sense that they document from social, political, and what one might call "grotesque" angles, recognize symptoms of a disintegrating society, more or less hang together. *Balso Snell* analyses only the disintegration of the Self, and its illusion of superiority at its most pathetic moment of neurotic isolation. The story, since it is a dream, dispenses completely with plausibility. From its opening, when Balso Snell enters into the Trojan Horse, through his meetings in

its viscous landscape with various unrelated figures—an
art-loving guide, a naked man in a derby who calls himself
Maloney the Areopagite, and who is engaged on writing
the life of Saint Puce (a flea who lived in the armpit of
Christ), a psychotic twelve-year-old boy with a passion for
his schoolmistress whom he hopes to win by writing
pseudo-Russian journals, till the end, when the schoolmistress materializes and after two metamorphoses is had by
Balso Snell himself, the book is a piece of extreme exhibitionism. *Balso Snell* is a sneer in the bathroom mirror at
Art—cocksure, contemptuous, well-informed and rejecting
openly the object of its search. There is a revealing passage
in the middle of the book, where Balso is reading a pamphlet written by the young boy, in which West explains the
necessity for the extravagant bitterness of the book:

> All my acting has but one purpose, the attraction of
> the female. If it had been possible for me to attract by
> exhibiting a series of physical charms, my hatred would
> have been less, but I found it necessary to substitute
> strange conceits, wise and witty sayings, peculiar con-
> duct, Art, for the muscles, teeth, hair of my rivals.
> All this much exhibited intelligence is but a develop-
> ment of the instinct to please. My case is similar to that
> of a bird called the Amblyornis inornata. As his name
> indicates, the Inornata is a dull-colored, ugly bird. Yet
> the Inornata is cousin to the Bird of Paradise. Because he
> lacks his cousin's brilliant plumage, he has to exteriorize
> internal feathers. . . . Still more, the Bird of Paradise
> cannot be blamed for the quality of his tail—it just grew.
> The Inornata, however, is held personally responsible for
> his performance as an artist.
> There was a time when I felt that I was indeed a rare
> spirit. Then I had genuinely expressed my personality
> with a babe's delight in confessing the details of its inner

life. Soon, however, in order to interest my listeners, I found it necessary to shorten my long outpourings; to make them, by straining my imagination, spectacular. Oh! how much work goes into the search for the odd, the escape from the same!

Because of women like Saniette, I acquired the habit of extravagant thought. I now convert everything into fantastic entertainment and the extraordinary has become an obsession. . . .

West's natural reticence, the laughing at his own laugh rather than be laughed at, the savage defensive attack he employs as arguments against what he really wishes to believe in, are all explained in *Balso Snell*. It is the clue to all his later books; yet, despite its moments of brilliant writing, its poetic economy, it is the one book West wrote in which private despair is not related to a social condition.

Miss Lonelyhearts, which has been called a 'modernized, faithless, Pilgrim's Progress', is the formalizing and objectifying of the rebellious vision of *Balso Snell*. West has accepted the fact that an audience exists, and that art is communication. Preoccupation with the self has given way to an identification with society, and the stone that *Balso Snell* dropped into the middle of the pond has now reached the outer banks.

Ostensibly, *Miss Lonelyhearts* tells the story of a reporter, who, detailed to write an agony column and answer daily the letters desperate with human misery addressed to his paper, finds the panacea he has to offer turning sour in his hand.

Although the deadline was less than a quarter of an hour away, he was still working on his leader. He had gone as far as: "Life is worth while, for it is full of dreams and peace, gentleness and ecstasy, and faith that

burns like a clear white flame on a grim dark altar." But
he found it impossible to continue. The letters were no
longer funny. He could not go on finding the same joke
funny thirty times a day for months on end. And on most
days he received more than thirty letters, all of them
alike, stamped from the dough of suffering with a heart-
shaped cookie knife.

Throughout the book, which interweaves Miss Lonelyhearts' own life with the episodic relations he has with his
editor's wife, involvements with his correspondents, and
his gradual conviction that Christian love alone can ad-
equately soften this mass hopelessness, there is a constant
counterpointing of Miss Lonelyhearts' struggle for some
sort of solution to the human equation and his editor,
Shrike's, destruction of it. Miss Lonelyhearts comes to
stand for Intention, Shrike for Reality. From the very beginning, when Shrike, looking over Miss Lonelyhearts'
typewriter, says: "The same old stuff. Why don't you give
them something new and hopeful? Tell them about art.
Here, I'll dictate: *Art is a Way Out,*" it is apparent that
there can be no serious attempt to grapple with the problem (for there is no answer), but merely an attempt to
sugar the pill in as hard-boiled, efficient and calculated a
way as possible. Later in the book, when Miss Lonelyhearts
himself has reached a position where he is as much in need
of salvation as his most desperate reader, Shrike elaborates
and then punctures the various fantasy escapes with which
men dupe themselves. Shrike takes over Miss Lonelyhearts'
rôle in real life, but instead of feeling bound to offer a
remedy, his own frustration compels him to make any
solution—Christ, Art, the reclusive life—appear phony because he himself refuses to accept their premises; speaking
as one who no longer has illusions, he cannot bear to allow
others the benefits of self-deception. *Miss Lonelyhearts* is

short and brilliantly authentic. The newspaper background, the alternation of self-pity, ineffectual love-making, clinical disgust, and the hopeless efforts at a normal life, are contrived and pointed with a bare passion that charges the whole book with a hallucinatory fever. Though the properties of the story are extremely commonplace, little different from a hundred film-scripts or stories with a journalist-martyr theme, West's succinct handling of them and his approach through a central character that is neither aggressive nor successful, raise the story to the intensive level of a poem. Every word is part of a pattern and rhythm whose water-tight structure is so exactly balanced that a phrase too much or out of key would destroy the breathless control of the whole book. West is writing no longer with brilliant intellectual exhibitionism, but out of bitter necessity. The curious religious strain in West's writing, a sort of pessimistic Messianism in whose aura America becomes a glorified Oxford Street, dirty, haphazard, doped, reaches its fullest expression towards the end of *Miss Lonelyhearts*. The final scene, where the cripple husband of one of the column's correspondents (a beefy nymphomaniac who has seduced Miss Lonelyhearts) calls on him and Miss Lonelyhearts thinks in his delusion that he is now one with Christ and that the cripple is a test of his love, culminates in a tragedy of miscomprehension which symbolizes terrifyingly and finally the unreality of the Christian myth. Miss Lonelyhearts runs down the stairs with his arms open to receive the cripple, who, imagining he is being attacked, shouts out. But Miss Lonelyhearts, interpreting the shout as a "cry for help from Desperate, Harold S., Catholic Mother, Broken-hearted, Broad-shoulders, Sick-of-it-all, Disillusioned-with-tubercular-husband. He was running to succour them with love," falls on the cripple as he turns to get away. A gun in the cripple's hand goes off and they both roll part of the way down the stairs.

That is the end of the book. West says nothing more—
there is in fact no more to be said. But already in this book
certain Westisms that remain constant in all four books,
begin to emerge. Perhaps most important is West's view of
character and his treatment of it. For none of his people
are seen "in the round," as individuals created for their
own distinctiveness; nor yet are they exactly "types" or
vehicles for ideas in the Aldous Huxley manner. West uses
subsidiary characters as an architect uses windows—to let
in light on a central character and to show, but not offer him,
escape. They exemplify modes of living that are never
developed beyond the point where they become absurd;
and at one point or another they all become absurd. These
are West's primary characters: Beagle Darwin in *Balso
Snell*, Shrike, Miss Lonelyhearts in *Miss Lonelyhearts*,
Shagpoke Whipple in *A Cool Million*, Homer, Faye
Greener and Tod in *The Day of the Locust*. But around
them, and though they are main characters they never
"come off" in the sense that West makes them succeed in
their lives, there are a host of abnormal minor figures,
whose abnormality and pathos act as a series of reservoirs,
almost in the form of a Greek chorus, for West's savagery
and inverted violence. As in the freak shows in Oxford
Street, their deformity is a mockery of normality rather
than vice versa. In *Balso Snell* it is the beautiful hunchback with whom Balso falls in love ("The lobby was
crowded with the many beautiful girl-cripples who congregate there because Art is their only solace, most men
looking upon their strange forms with distaste. But it was
otherwise with Balso Snell. He likened their disarranged
hips, their short legs, their humps, their splay feet, their
wall-eyes, to ornament. Their strange fore-shortenings,
hanging heads, bulging spinesacks, were a delight. . . ."),
in *Miss Lonelyhearts* the cripple, Doyle, in *A Cool Million* nearly everyone; in *The Day of the Locust* it is no

more than an awful horror at the blind forces of ignorance.
—symbolized in the riot at the end—that make escape from
their decontamination impossible. In the end one has to live
and die with the mob. But West's political satire is con-
cerned with the way in which the sheeplike dependence of
the mob, their malleableness, is made use of for ulterior
political ends.

A *Cool Million* tackles this problem overtly. Written as a
burlesquing, melodramatic parody of the Horatio Alger
best-seller, it describes, in prose that is like a long heavy
wink, the adventures of a country bumpkin called Lemuel
Pitkin in search of success on the American pattern of free
enterprise. By the time he has finished he has been in jail,
lost his teeth, his eyes, a leg, his scalp, witnessed an infinite number of rapes, riots, and been the tool for both
Communist and Fascist organizations. Finally, he is shot by
a political assassin and made a martyr.

In its awareness of political technique, its devastatingly
true analysis of unrestricted Capitalist method, its fore-
shadowing of Americanism turned into a possible Fascism,
A *Cool Million* is brilliantly successful. Unfortunately, having decided on a mock-melodramatic style ("when our
hero regained consciousness," "In the half-gloom of the
cabin, Lem was horrified to see the Pike man busily tearing off Betty's sole remaining piece of underwear. She was
struggling as best she could, but the ruffian from Missouri
was too strong for her," etc.), West sacrificed the stylistic
hallmark that makes a writer's work compact and homo-
geneous.

The villain of the story is "Shagpoke" Whipple, an ex-
President of the United States, and a believer in American
opportunism. Whipple now lives in retirement in Rat River,
where he is President of the National Bank: here he is visited one day by Lemuel Pitkin in search of advice. Whipple,
citing his own past as precedent, tells Pitkin to go out into

the world and make his fortune. Pitkin meets with one misfortune after the other, is duped, robbed and wrongfully imprisoned. In jail he finds Whipple, convicted of fraud after the failure of his bank. "My boy," says Whipple, when Pitkin meets him in the prison carrying a bedpan, "there are two evils undermining this country which we must fight tooth and nail. These two arch-enemies of the American spirit, the spirit of fair play and open competition, are Wall Street and the Communists." The next time Pitkin meets Whipple, some weeks after he is out of jail, he finds him in the process of starting his new political party—the National Revolutionary movement, "because," as he tells Pitkin, "how could I, Shagpoke Whipple, ever bring myself to accept a program which promised to take from American citizens their inalienable birthright, the right to sell their labor and their children's labor without restrictions as to either price or hours?" Pitkin is enrolled in the movement, made a Commander, and then when the first party meeting is broken up by international Jewish bankers and Communists, beaten up.

In the course of the book, almost every popular American bogy is caricatured. Pitkin is victimized in a series of near-slapstick episodes which, despite their rather labored telling, are extremely funny. Beneath them lurk a very real horror and an acute feeling of sinister inevitability. The epilogue describes a future national holiday, with the youth of America parading up and down Fifth Avenue in Pitkin's honor and singing the Lemuel Pitkin song:

A million hearts for Pitkin, oh!
To do and die with Pitkin, oh!

Reviewing them from a special stand is Shagpoke Whipple. When the paraders have marched past him and gathered round his reviewing stand, Whipple addresses them in a remarkable closing speech that ends the book.

"What," he says, "made Lemuel Pitkin great? Let us examine his life. First we see him as a small boy, light of foot, fishing for bullheads in the Rat River of Vermont. Later, he attends the Ottsville High School, where he is captain of the nine and an excellent outfielder. Then he leaves for the big city to make his fortune. All this is in the honorable tradition of his country and its people and he has the right to expect certain rewards. Jail is his first reward. Poverty his second. Violence is his third. Death is his last."

Whipple goes on to analyze Pitkin's greatness, and then winds up with: "But he did not live or die in vain. Through his martyrdom the National Revolutionary Party triumphed, and by that triumph this country was delivered from sophistication, Marxism and International Capitalism. Through the National Revolution its people were purged of alien diseases and America became again American. Hail, Lemuel Pitkin! All Hail, the American Boy!"

West's last book, *The Day of the Locust*, written after he had been in Hollywood for three years, is by far his most ambitious and mature. It is the most objective of his novels, and the one in which his own personal integration most nearly coincides with the form of his book. Its deficiencies, such as they are, come from a slight slowness in the narrative's momentum, and a series of sub-plots whose interrelation is never developed quite closely enough. Once the real theme emerges, West's confident astringency of language seems to return and the last two-thirds of the book contain some of his very best writing.

Primarily, *The Day of the Locust* is about middle-aged, middle-class discontent—a discontent that is dangerous because it has developed from illusions of security, from a sense of betrayal, and now waits to feed on the misfortunes of individuals. Reactions are so dulled that only abnormality has the power to stimulate: abnormality and the drug of

mob action. The background is Hollywood—not the Hollywood of film stars, but the Hollywood exemplified by unimportant hangers-on fighting unsuccessfully for a little lime-
light: Faye Greener, a small-time blonde, and her father
Harry, a faded music-hall star; an ex-undergraduate artist
lured by a talent scout to learn scenery design (Tod
Hackett, the *Miss Lonelyhearts* symbol of the book); a retired clerk ordered to Hollywood for his health (Homer
Simpson), and around these the men whom Faye attracts
on the different levels of their lust—a Mexican cock-
fighter, a cowboy tailor's dummy, and a bookmaking
dwarf. Like a chorus around them, in a yet wider circle,
are the unnamed crowd extras—people "whose clothing
was sombre and badly cut, bought from mail-order houses.
They loitered on the corners or stood with their backs to
the shop windows and stared at everyone who passed.
When their stare was returned, their eyes filled with
hatred. At this time Tod knew very little about them except that they had come to California to die."

It is these people, an endless procession of loiterers, of
grown-up embittered Pitkins and Doyles, whom West
makes potentially capable of mass riot, blood-letting and
lynching, such as, in fact, takes place in the last chapter, at
a *première;* most of the crowd, if asked the reason for their
frenzy, would not have been able to answer. It was enough
that their frustration had found an outlet: the provoking
incident was not of consequence.

The tension and atmosphere of the novel, its tortured pity
and hatred, are summed up in West's description of the
crowd:

New groups, whole families, kept arriving. He could
see a change come over them as soon as they had become part of the crowd. Until they reached the line,
they looked diffident, almost furtive, but the moment

they had become part of it, they turned arrogant and pugnacious. It was a mistake to think them harmless curiosity seekers. They were savage and bitter, especially the middle-aged and the old, and had been made so by boredom and disappointment.

All their lives they had slaved at some kind of dull, heavy labor, behind desks and counters . . . dreaming of the leisure that would be theirs when they had enough. Where else should they go but California, the land of sunshine and oranges?

Once there, they discover that sunshine isn't enough. They get tired of oranges, even of avocado pears and passion fruit. Nothing happens. . . . Did they slave so long just to go to an occasional Iowa picnic? What else is there? They watch the waves come in at Venice. There wasn't any ocean where most of them came from, but after you've seen one wave, you've seen them all. The same is true of the airplanes at Glendale. If only a plane would crash once in a while so that they could watch the passengers being consumed in a "holocaust of flame," as the newspapers put it. But the planes never crash.

Their boredom becomes more and more terrible. They realize that they've been tricked and burn with resentment. Every day of their lives they read the newspapers and went to the movies. Both fed them on lynchings, murder, sex crimes, explosions, wrecks, love nests, fires, miracles, revolutions, wars. This daily diet made sophisticates of them. The sun is a joke. Oranges can't titillate their jaded palates. Nothing can ever be violent enough to make taut their slack minds and bodies.

West's Hollywood is made up of degeneracy and brothels, of failure and sexual desire, of cock-fighting and third-rate boarding houses. But more than anything it is made up of significant boredom, of an etiolated ennui: the whole canvas on which the motiveless actions take place acquires a Breughel-like stillness, as if all the monstrous things going on were part of a very ordinary pattern. And, indeed, the pattern of all West's books is ordinary; it is only the extraordinary stylized grotesques on the edge, the narrative logic that touches the rim of fantasy, that charge it with the nervous garishness, the disproportionate perspective that, like the beautiful hunchbacks in *Balso Snell,* mock normality with their own freakishness.

West's slightness of reputation is not easy to understand, for *Miss Lonelyhearts* and *The Day of the Locust* rank almost with any novels that came out of America in the thirties—more condensed, penetrating and poetic than many, that with much larger scope and subsequent recognition, purported to give the lie to the American scene.

Perhaps the ruthlessness of West's portrait, his making of the whole political and economic racket so undisguisedly repulsive and meaningless, was too near the bone for an American audience with a mass neurosis, and a guilty conscience. There were, of course, other factors; the fact that the publisher of *The Dream Life of Balso Snell* went bankrupt almost immediately after the book was issued, and the shadow of an imminent war that took American thought beyond its own frontiers. Perhaps it is only now, when West's books are again being made available, that he will reach the wider audience, with a different view on both him and his times, of which he was originally deprived.

ALAN ROSS

1 9 3 1

The Dream Life of Balso Snell

To A. S.

"After all, my dear fellow,
life, Anaxagoras has said,
is a journey."

BERGOTTE

1

While walking in the tall grass that has sprung up around the city of Troy, Balso Snell came upon the famous wooden horse of the Greeks. A poet, he remembered Homer's ancient song and decided to find a way in.

On examining the horse, Balso found that there were but three openings: the mouth, the navel, and the posterior opening of the alimentary canal. The mouth was beyond his reach, the navel proved a cul-de-sac, and so, forgetting his dignity, he approached the last. O Anus Mirabilis!

Along the lips of the mystic portal he discovered writings which after a little study he was able to decipher. Engraved in a heart pierced by an arrow and surmounted by the initial N, he read, "Ah! Qualis . . . Artifex . . . Pereo!" Not to be outdone by the actor-emperor, Balso carved with his penknife another heart and the words "O Byss! O Abyss! O Anon! O Anan!" omitting, however, the arrow and his initial.

Before entering he prayed:

"O Beer! O Meyerbeer! O Bach! O Offenbach! Stand me now as ever in good stead."

Balso immediately felt like the One at the Bridge, the Two in the Bed, the Three in the Boat, the Four on Horseback, the Seven Against Thebes. And with a high heart he entered the gloom of the foyer-like lower intestine.

After a little while, seeing no one and hearing nothing, Balso began to feel depressed. To keep his heart high and yet out of his throat, he made a song.

Round as the Anus
Of a Bronze Horse
Or the Tender Buttons
Used by Horses for Ani

On the Wheels of His Car
Ringed Round with Brass
Clamour the Seraphim
Tongues of Our Lord

Full Ringing Round
As the Belly of Silenus
Giotto Painter of Perfect Circles
Goes . . . One Motion Round

Round and Full
Round and Full as

A Brimming Goblet
The Dew-Loaded Navel
Of Mary
Of Mary Our Mother

Round and Ringing Full
As the Mouth of a Brimming Goblet
The Rust-Laden Holes
In Our Lord's Feet.
Entertain the Jew-Driven Nails.

He later gave this song various names, the most successful of which were: *Anywhere Out of the World, or a Voy-
age Through the Hole in the Mundane Millstone* and *At
Hoops with the Ani of Bronze Horses, or Toe Holes for a
Flight of Fancy*.

But despite the gaiety of his song, Balso did not feel sure
of himself. He thought of the Phoenix Excrementi, a race of
men he had invented one Sunday afternoon while in bed,
and trembled, thinking he might well meet one in this
place. And he had good cause to tremble, for the Phoenix
Excrementi eat themselves, digest themselves, and give
birth to themselves by evacuating their bowels.

Hoping to attract the attention of an inhabitant, Balso
shouted as though overwhelmed by the magnificence of his
surroundings:

"O the Rose Gate! O the Moist Garden! O Well! O Fountain! O Sticky Flower! O Mucous Membrane!"

A man with "Tours" embroidered on his cap stalked out
of the shadow. In order to prove a poet's right to trespass,
Balso quoted from his own works:

"If you desire to have two parallel lines meet at once or
even in the near future," he said, "it is important to make
all the necessary arrangements beforehand, preferably by
wireless."

The man ignored his little speech. "Sir," he said, "you are

an ambassador from that ingenious people, the inventors and perfectors of the automatic water-closet, to my people who are the heirs of Greece and Rome. As your own poet has so well put it, 'The Grandeur that was Greece and the Glory that was Rome' . . . I offer you my services as guide. First you will please look to the right where you will see a beautiful Doric prostate gland swollen with gladness and an over-abundance of good cheer."

This speech made Balso very angry. "Inventors of the automatic water-closet, are we?" he shouted. "Oh, you stinker! Doric, bah! It's Baptist '68, that's what it is. And no prostate gland either, simply an atrophied pile. You call this dump grand and glorious, do you? Have you ever seen the Grand Central Station, or the Yale Bowl, or the Holland Tunnel, or the New Madison Square Garden? Exposed plumbing, stinker, that's all I see—and at this late date. It's criminally backward, do you hear me?"

The guide gave ground before Balso's rage. "Please sir," he said, "please . . . After all, the ages have sanctified this ground, great men have hallowed it. In Rome do as the Romans do."

"Stinker," Balso repeated, but less ferociously this time.

The guide took heart. "Mind your manners, foreigner. If you don't like it here, why don't you go back where you came from? But before you go let me tell you a story—an old tale of my people, rich in local color. And, you force me to say it, apropos, timely. However, let me assure you that I mean no offense. The title of the story is

"VISITORS

"A traveler in Tyana, who was looking for the sage Appolonius, saw a snake enter the lower part of a man's body. Approaching the man, he said:

" 'Pardon me, my good fellow, but a snake just entered your . . .' He finished by pointing.

" 'Yes sir, he lives there,' was the astounding rejoinder.

" 'Ah, then you must be the man I'm looking for, the philosopher-saint, Appolonius of Tyana. Here is a letter of introduction from my brother George. May I see the snake please? Now the opening. Perfect!' "

Balso echoed the last word of the story. "Perfect! Perfect! A real old-world fable. You may consider yourself hired."

"I have other stories to tell," the guide said, "and I shall tell them as we go along. By the way, have you heard the one about Moses and the Burning Bush? How the prophet rebuked the Bush for speaking by quoting the proverb, 'Good wine needs no bush'; and how the Bush insolently replied, 'A hand in the Bush is worth two in the pocket.' "

Balso did not consider this story nearly as good as the other; in fact he thought it very bad, yet he was determined to make no more breaks and entered the large intestine on the arm of his guide. He let the guide do all the talking and they made great headway up the tube. But, unfortunately, coming suddenly upon a place where the intestine had burst through the stomach wall, Balso cried out in amazement:

"What a hernia! What a hernia!"

The guide began to splutter with rage and Balso tried to pacify him by making believe he had not meant the scenery. "Hernia," he said, rolling the word on his tongue. "What a pity childish associations cling to beautiful words such as hernia, making their use as names impossible. Hernia! What a beautiful name for a girl! Hernia Hornstein! Paresis Pearlberg! Paranoia Puntz! How much more pleasing to the ear [and what other sense should a name please?] than Faith Rabinowitz or Hope Hilkowitz."

But Balso had only blundered again. "Sirrah!" the guide cried in an enormous voice, "I am a Jew! and whenever

anything Jewish is mentioned, I find it necessary to say that
I am a Jew. I'm a Jew! A Jew!"

"Oh, you mistake me," Balso said, "I have nothing against
the Jews. I admire the Jews; they are a thrifty race. Some
of my best friends are Jews." But his protests availed him
little until he thought to quote C. M. Doughty's epigram.
"The semites," Balso said with great firmness, "are like to a
man sitting in a cloaca to the eyes, and whose brows touch
heaven."

When Balso had at last succeeded in quieting the guide,
he tried to please him further by saying that the magnificent tunnel stirred him to the quick and that he would be
satisfied to spend his remaining days in it with but a few
pipes and a book.

The guide tossed up his arms in one of those eloquent
gestures the latins know so well how to perform and said:

"After all, what is art? I agree with George Moore. Art is
not nature, but rather nature digested. Art is a sublime
excrement."

"And Daudet?" Balso queried.

"Oh, Daudet! Daudet, c'est de bouillabaisse! You know,
George Moore also says, 'What care I that the virtue of
some sixteen-year-old maiden was the price paid for Ingres'
La Source?' Now . . ."

"Picasso says," Balso broke in, "Picasso says there are no
feet in nature . . . And, thanks for showing me around. I
have to leave."

But before he was able to get away, the guide caught
him by the collar. "Just a minute, please. You were right to
interrupt. We should talk of art, not artists. Please explain
your interpretation of the Spanish master's dictum."

"Well, the point is . . ." Balso began. But before he
could finish the guide started again. "If you are willing to
acknowledge the existence of points," he said, "then the
statement that there are no feet in nature puts you in an

untenable position. It depends for its very meaning on the fact that there are no points. Picasso, by making this assertion, has placed himself on the side of monism in the eternal wrangle between the advocates of the Singular and those of the Plural. As James puts it, 'Does reality exist distributively or collectively—in the shape of *eaches, everys, anys, eithers* or only in the shape of an *all* or *whole?*' If reality is singular then there are no feet in nature, if plural, a great many. If the world is one [everything part of the same thing—called by Picasso nature] then nothing either begins or ends. Only when things take the shapes of *eaches, everys, anys, eithers* [have ends] do they have feet. Feet are attached to ends, by definition. Moreover, if everything is one, and has neither ends nor beginnings, then everything is a circle. A circle has neither a beginning nor an end. A circle has no feet. If we believe that nature is a circle, then we must also believe that there are no feet in nature.

"Do not pooh-pooh this idea as mystical. Bergson has . . ."

"Cezanne said, 'Everything tends toward the globular.'" With this announcement Balso made another desperate attempt to escape.

"Cezanne?" the guide said, keeping a firm hold on Balso's collar. "Cezanne is right. The sage of Aix is . . ."

With a violent twist, Balso tore loose and fled.

Balso fled down the great tunnel until he came upon a man, naked except for a derby in which thorns were sticking, who was attempting to crucify himself with thumb tacks. His curiosity got the better of his fear and he stopped.

"Can I help you?" he asked politely.

"No," the man answered with even greater politeness, tipping his hat repeatedly as he spoke. "No, I can manage, thank you . . .

"My name is Maloney the Areopagite," the man continued, answering the questions Balso was too well-bred to word, "and I am a catholic mystic. I believe implicitly in that terrible statement of Saint Hildegarde's, 'The lord dwells not in the bodies of the healthy and vigorous.' I live as did Marie Alacoque, Suso, Labre, Lydwine of Schiedam, Rose of Lima. When my suffering is not too severe, I compose verses in imitation of Notker Balbus, Ekkenard le Vieux, Hucbald le Chauve.

"In the feathered darkness
Of thy mouth,
O Mother of God!
I worship Christ
The culminating rose.

"Get the idea? I spend the rest of my time marveling at the love shown by all the great saints for even the lowliest of God's creatures. Have you ever heard of Benedict Labre? It was he who picked up the vermin that fell out of his hat and placed them piously back into his sleeve. Before calling in a laundress, another very holy man removed the vermin from his clothes in order not to drown the jewels of sanctity infesting them.

"Inspired by these thoughts I have decided to write the biography of Saint Puce, a great martyred member of the vermin family. If you are interested, I will give you a short précis of his life.

"Please do so, sir," Balso said. "Live and learn is my motto, Mr. Maloney, so please continue."

"Saint Puce was a flea," Maloney the Areopagite began in a well-trained voice. "A flea who was born, lived, and died, beneath the arm of our Lord.

"Saint Puce was born from an egg that was laid in the flesh of Christ while as a babe He played on the floor of the stable in Bethlehem. That the flesh of a god has been a stage in the incubation of more than one being is well known: Dionysius and Athene come to mind.

"Saint Puce had two mothers: the winged creature that laid the egg, and the God that hatched it in His flesh. Like most of us, he had two fathers: our Father Who art in Heaven, and he who in the cocksureness of our youth we called 'pop.'

"Which of his two fathers fertilized the egg? I cannot answer with certainty, but the subsequent actions of Saint Puce's life lead me to believe that the egg was fertilized by a being whose wings were of feathers. Yes, I mean the Dove or Paraclete—the Sanctus Spiritus. In defense of this belief antiquity will help us again: it is only necessary to remember Leda and Europa. And I must remind you, you who might plead a puce too small physically, of the nature of God's love and how it embraceth all.

"O happy, happy childhood! Playing in the curled brown silk, sheltered from all harm by Christ's arm. Eating the sweet flesh of our Saviour; drinking His blood; bathing in His sweat; partaking, oh how fully! of His Godhead. Having no need to cry as I have cried:

"Corpus Christi, salva me
Sanguis Christi, inebria me
Aqua lateris Christi, lave me.

"In manhood, fullgrown, how strong Saint Puce was, how lusty; and how his lust and strength were satisfied in one continuous, never-culminating ecstasy. The music of our Lord's skin sliding over His flesh!—more exact than the fugues of Bach. The pattern of His veins!—more intricate than the Maze at Cnossos. The odors of His Body!—more fragant than the Temple of Solomon. The temperature of His flesh!—more pleasant than the Roman baths to the youth Puce. And, finally, the taste of His blood! In this wine all pleasure, all excitement, was magnified, until with ecstasy Saint Puce's small body roared like a furnace.

"In his prime, Saint Puce wandered far from his birth-place, that hairsilk pocketbook, the armpit of our Lord. He roamed the forest of God's chest and crossed the hill of His abdomen. He measured and sounded that fathomless well, the Navel of our Lord. He explored and charted every crevasse, ridge, and cavern of Christ's body. From notes taken during his travels he later wrote his great work, *A Geography of Our Lord.*

"After much wandering, tired, he returned at last to his home in the savoury forest. To spend, he thought, his re-maining days in writing, worship, and contemplation. Happy in a church whose walls were the flesh of Christ, whose windows were rose with the blood of Christ, and on whose altars burned golden candles made of the sacred earwax.

"Soon, too soon, alas! the day of martyrdom arrived [O Jesu, mi dulcissime!], and the arms of Christ were lifted that His hands might receive the nails.

"The walls and windows of Saint Puce's church were broken and its halls flooded with blood.

"The hot sun of Calvary burnt the flesh beneath Christ's upturned arm, making the petal-like skin shrivel until it looked like the much-shaven armpit of an old actress.

"After Christ died, Saint Puce died, refusing to desert to lesser flesh, even to that of Mary who stood close under the cross. With his last strength he fought off the unconquerable worm. . . ."

Mr. Maloney's thin frame was racked by sobs as he finished, yet Balso did not spare him.

"I think you're morbid," he said. "Don't be morbid. Take your eyes off your navel. Take your head from under your armpit. Stop sniffing mortality. Play games. Don't read so many books. Take cold showers. Eat more meat."

With these helpful words, Balso left him to his own devices and continued on his way.

He had left Maloney the Areopagite far behind when, on turning a bend in the intestine, he saw a boy hiding what looked like a packet of letters in a hollow tree. After the boy had left, Balso removed the packet and sat down to read. First, however, he took off his shoes because his feet hurt.

What he had taken for letters proved on closer scrutiny to be a diary. At the top of the first page was written, "English Theme by John Gilson, Class 8B, Public School 186, Miss McGeeney, teacher." He read further.

Jan. 1st—at home

Whom do I fool by calling these pages a journal? Surely not you, Miss McGeeney. Alas! no-one. Nor is anyone fooled by the fact that I write in the first person. It is for this reason that I do not claim to have found these pages in a hollow tree. I am an honest man and feel badly about masks, cardboard noses, diaries, memoirs, letters from a Sabine farm, the theatre . . . I feel badly, yet I can do nothing. 'Sir!' I say to myself, 'your name is not Iago, but simply John. It is monstrous to write lies in a diary.'

However, I insist that I am an honest man. Reality troubles me as it must all honest men.

Reality! Reality! If I could only discover the Real. A Real that I could know with my senses. A Real that would wait for me to inspect it as a dog inspects a dead rabbit. But, alas! when searching for the Real I throw a stone into a pool whose ripples become of advancing less importance until they are too large for connection with, or even memory of, the stone agent.

Written while smelling the moistened forefinger of my left hand.

Jan 2nd—at home

Is this journal to be like all the others I have started? A large first entry, consisting of the incident which made me think my life exciting enough to keep a journal, followed by a series of entries gradually decreasing in size and culminating in a week of blank days.

Inexperienced diary-writers make their first entry the largest. They come to the paper with a constipation of ideas—eager, impatient. The white paper acts as a laxative. A diarrhoea of words is the result. The richness of the flow is unnatural; it cannot be sustained.

A diary must grow naturally—a flower, a cancer, a civilization . . . In a diary there is no need for figures of speech, honest Iago.

Sometimes my name is Raskolnikov, sometimes it is Iago. I never was, and never shall be, plain John Gilson—honest, honest Iago, yes, but never honest John. As Raskolnikov, I

keep a journal which I call *The Making of a Fiend.* I give
the heart of my Crime Journal:

Crime Journal

I have been in this hospital seven weeks. I am under observation. Am I sane? This diary shall prove me insane.
This entry gives me away.

Crime Journal

My mother visited me today. She cried. It is she who is
crazy. Order is the test of sanity. Her emotions and
thoughts are disordered. Mine are arranged, valued, placed.

Man spends a great deal of time making order out of
chaos, yet insists that the emotions be disordered. I order
my emotions: I am insane. Yet sanity is discipline. My
mother rolls on the hospital floor and cries: "John darling
. . . John sweetheart." Her hat falls over face. She clutches
her absurd bag of oranges. She is sane.

I say to her quietly: "Mother, I love you, but this specta-
cle is preposterous—and the smell of your clothing de-
presses me." I am insane.

Crime Journal

Order is vanity. I have decided to discard the nonsense of
precision instruments. No more measuring. I drop the slide
rule and take up the Golden Rule. Sanity is the absence of
extremes.

Crime Journal

Is someone reading my diary while I sleep?

On reading what I have written, I think I can detect a
peculiar change in my words. They have taken on the quality of comment.

*You who read these pages while I sleep, please sign
your name here.*

John Raskolnikov Gilson

Crime Journal

During the night I got up, turned to yesterday's entry and signed my name.

Crime Journal

I am insane. I [the papers had it CULTURED FIEND SLAYS DISHWASHER] am insane.

When a baby, I affected all the customary poses: I "laughed the icy laughter of the soul," I uttered "universal sighs"; I sang in "silver-fire verse"; I smiled the "enigmatic smile"; I sought "azure and elliptical routes." In everything I was completely the mad poet. I was one of those "great despisers," whom Nietzche loved because "they are the great adorers; they are arrows of longing for the other shore." Along with "mon hysterie" I cultivated a "rotten, ripe maturity." You understand what I mean: like Rimbaud, I practiced having hallucinations.

Now, my imagination is a wild beast that cries always for freedom. I am continually tormented by the desire to indulge some strange thing, perceptible but indistinct, hidden in the swamps of my mind. This hidden thing is always crying out to me from its hiding-place: "Do as I tell you and you will find out my shape. There, quick! what is that thing in your brain? Indulge my commands and some day the great doors of your mind will swing open and allow you to enter and handle to your complete satisfaction the vague shapes and figures hidden there."

I can know nothing; I can have nothing; I must devote my whole life to the pursuit of a shadow. It is as if I were attempting to trace with the point of a pencil the shadow of the tracing pencil. I am enchanted with the shadow's shape and want very much to outline it; but the shadow is attached to the pencil and moves with it, never allowing me to trace its tempting form. Because of some great need, I am continually forced to make the attempt.

Two years ago I sorted books for eight hours a day in the public library. Can you imagine how it feels to be surrounded for eight long hours by books—a hundred billion words one after another according to ten thousand mad schemes. What patience, what labor are those crazy sequences the result of! What starving! What sacrifice! And the fervors, deliriums, ambitions, dreams, that dictated them! . . .

The books smelt like the breaths of their authors; the books smelt like a closet full of old shoes through which a steam pipe passes. As I handled them they seemed to turn into flesh, or at lest some substance that could be eaten.

Have you ever spent any time among the people who farm the great libraries: the people who search old issues of the medical journals for pornography and facts about strange diseases; the comic writers who exhume jokes from old magazines; the men and women employed by the insurance companies to gather statistics on death? I worked in the philosophy department. That department is patronized by alchemists, astrologers, cabalists, demonologists, magicians, atheists, and the founders of new religious systems.

While working in the library, I lived in a theatrical rooming house in the west Forties, a miserable, uncomfortable place. I lived there because of the discomfort. I wanted to be miserable. I could not have lived in a comfortable house. The noises [harsh, grating], the dirt [animal, greasy], the smells [dry sweat, sour mold], permitted me to wallow in my discomfort. My mind was full of vague irritations and annoyances. My body was nervous and jumpy, and demanded an extraordinary amount of sleep. I was a bundle of physical and mental tics. I climbed into myself like a bear into a hollow tree, and lay there long hours, overpowered by the heat, odor, and nastiness of I.

The only other person living on my floor, the top one,

was an idiot. He earned his living as a dishwasher in the kitchen of the Hotel Astor. He was a fat, pink and grey pig of a man, and stank of stale tobacco, dry perspiration, clothing mold, and oatmeal soap. He did not have a skull on the top of his neck, only a face; his head was all face—a face without side, back or top, like a mask.

The idiot never wore a collar, yet he kept both a front and a back collar button in the neckband of his shirt. When he changed his shirt he removed the collar buttons from the dirty shirt and placed them in the clean one. His neck was smooth, white, fat, and covered all over with tiny blue veins like a piece of cheap marble. His Adam's apple was very large and looked as though it might be a soft tumor in his throat. When he swallowed, his neck bulged out and he made a sound like a miniature toilet being flushed.

My neighbor, the idiot, never smiled, but laughed continually. It must have hurt him to laugh. He fought his laughter as though it were a wild beast. A beast of laughter seemed always struggling to escape from between his teeth.

People say that it is terrible to hear a man cry. I think it is even worse to hear a man laugh. [Yet the ancients considered hysteria a woman's disease. They believed that hysteria was caused by the womb breaking loose and floating freely through the body. The cure they practiced was to place sweet-smelling herbs to the vulva in order to attract the womb back to its original position, and foul-smelling things to the nose in order to keep the womb away from the head.]

One night at the movies, I heard a basso from the Chicago Opera Company sing the devil's serenade from Faust. A portion of this song calls for a long laugh. When the singer came to the laugh he was unable to get started. He struggled with the laugh, but it refused to come. At last he managed to start laughing. Once started, he was unable to stop. The orchestra repeated the transition that led from the laugh to the next bars of the song, but he was unable to stop laughing.

I returned home with my head full of the singer's laughter. Because of it I was unable to fall asleep. I dressed myself and went downstairs. On my way to the street I passed my neighbor the idiot. He was laughing to himself. His laughter made me laugh. When he detected the strain in my voice he grew angry. He thought that I was making fun of him. He said, "Who you laughing at?" I became frightened and offered him a cigarette. He refused it. I left him on the stairs, struggling with his laughter and his anger.

I knew that if I did not get my customary amount of sleep, I would suffer when the time came for me to get up. I was certain that if I went back to bed I would be unable to sleep. In order to tire myself as quickly as possible, I walked to Broadway and then started uptown. My shoes hurt me and at first I enjoyed the pain. Soon, however, the pain became so intense that I had to stop walking and return home.

On regaining my bed, I still found it impossible to fall asleep. I knew that I must become interested in something outside of myself or go insane. I plotted the death of the idiot.

I felt certain that it would be a safe murder to commit. Safe, because its motives would not be comprehensible to the police. Policemen are reasonable men; they do not consider the shape and color of a man's throat, his laugh or the fact that he does not wear a collar, reasonable motives for killing him.

You also, eh, doctor, consider these poor reasons for murder. I agree—they are literary reasons. Reasoning your way, dear doctor—like Darwin or a policeman—I am expected to trace my action back to some such things as the desire to live or create life. Because I want you to believe me, I shall say that in order to remain sane I had to kill this man, just as I had to kill, when a child, all the flies in my room before being able to fall asleep.

Nonsense, eh? I agree—nonsense. Please, please—here [please believe me] is why I killed Adolph. I killed the idiot because he disturbed my sense of balance. I killed him thinking his death would permit me to regain my balance. My beloved balance!

The fact that I had never killed made me uncomfortable. What was this enormous crime I had never committed? What were all the horrors attendant on this act? I killed a man and discovered the answers. I shall never kill another man. I shall never need to kill another man.

Let me continue with my confession. I decided not to plot an intricate killing. I was afraid that if I attempted a complicated crime I might get entangled in my own scheme. I decided to have the murder consist of only one act, the killing. I even resisted the desire to look up certain books in the library.

Because the idea of the killing involved the dishwasher's throat, I decided to do the job with a knife. As a child I always took pleasure in cutting soft, firm things. I purchased a knife about fifteen inches long. The knife had only one cutting edge; the other edge or the back of the knife was about half an inch thick. Its weight made it a perfect instrument for the job.

I did not want to commit the murder too soon after purchasing the knife; but on the very night that I brought it home, I heard the idiot come up the stairs drunk. As I listened to him fumble with his key, I realized, for the first time, that he locked his door at night. This unlooked-for obstacle almost made me give up the idea of killing him. I rid myself of my misgivings by thinking of the torture I would have to go through if I frustrated my desire to commit murder. I decided to do the job that very evening and have it over with. I put on my bathrobe and went into the hall. His door was ajar. I went to it carefully. The idiot was stretched out on his bed, drunk. I went back to my room and took off my bathrobe and pajamas. I planned to do the murder naked, so that I should have no blood-stained things to wash or destroy. What blood I got on my body I could easily wash off. Naked: I felt cold; and I noticed that my genitals were tight and hard, like a dog's, or an archaic Greek statue's—they were as though I had just come out of an ice-cold bath. I was aware of a great excitement; an excitement that seemed to be near, but not quite within me.

I crossed the hall and entered the dishwasher's room. He had left his light burning. I walked to him and cut his throat. I had intended to do the cutting with several rapid strokes, but he awoke at the touch of the steel and I became frightened and sawed at his throat in a panic. When he lay still I calmed down.

I went back to my room and stood the knife up in the sink, like one does a wet umbrella, letting what blood was on it run into the drain. I dressed quickly, obsessed by the need for getting rid of the knife. While dressing I became conscious of a growing fear. A fear that as it grew seemed likely to burst me open; a fear so large that I felt I could not contain it without rupturing my mind. Inside of my head this expanding fear was like a rapidly growing child inside the belly of a mother. I felt that I must get rid of the fear or burst. I opened my mouth wide, but I was unable to give birth to my fear.

Carrying this fear as an ant carries a caterpiller thirty times its size, I ran down the stairs and into the street. I hurried west toward the river.

I let the knife slip into the water. With the knife went my fear. I felt light and free. I felt like a happy girl. I said to myself: "You feel like a young girl—kittenish, cuneycutey, darlingey, springtimey." I caressed my breasts like a young girl who has suddenly become conscious of her body on a hot afternoon. I imitated the mannered walk of a girl showing off before a group of boys. In the dark I hugged myself.

On my way back to Broadway I passed some sailors, and felt an overwhelming desire to flirt with them. I went through all the postures of a desperate prostitute; I camped for all I was worth. The sailors looked at me and laughed. I wanted very much for one of them to follow me. Suddenly I heard the sound of footsteps behind me. The steps came close and I felt as though I were melting—all silk and perfumed, pink lace. I died the little death. But the man went past without noticing me. I sat down on a bench and was violently sick.

I sat on the bench for a long time, and then returned to my room, sick and cold.

Inside of my head the murder has become like a piece of sand inside the shell of an oyster. My mind has commenced to form a pearl around it. The idiot, the singer, his laugh, the knife, the river, my change of sex, all cover the murder just as the secretions of an oyster cover an irritating grain of sand. As the accumulations grow and become solidified, the original irritation disappears. If the murder continues to grow in size it may become too large for me to contain; then I am afraid it will kill me, just as the pearl eventually kills the oyster.

Balso put the manuscript back into the tree and continued on his way, his head bowed in thought. The world was getting to be a difficult place for a lyric poet. He felt old. "Ah youth!" he sighed elaborately. "Ah Balso Snell!"

Suddenly he heard a voice at his elbow.

"Well, nosey, how did you like my theme?"

Balso turned and saw the boy whose diary he had been reading. He was still in short pants and looked less than twelve years old.

"Interesting psychologically, but is it art?" Balso said timidly. "I'd give you B minus and a good spanking."

"What the hell do I care about art! Do you know why I wrote that ridiculous story—because Miss McGeeney, my English teacher, reads Russian novels and I want to sleep with her. But maybe you run a magazine. Will you buy it? I need money."

"No, son, I'm a poet. I'm Balso Snell, the poet."

"A poet! For Christ's sake!"

"What you ought to do, child, is to run about more. Read less and play baseball."

"Forget it. I know a fat girl who only sleeps with poets. When I'm with her I'm a poet, too. I won her with a poem.

"O Beast of Walls!
O Walled-in Fat Girl!
Your conquest was hardly worth
The while of one whom Arras and
Arrat, Pelion, Ossa, Parnassus, Ida,
Pisgah and Pike's Peak never in-
terested.

"Not bad, eh? But I'm fed up with poetry and art. Yet what can I do. I need women and because I can't buy or force them, I have to make poems for them. God knows how tired I am of using the insanity of Van Gogh and the adventures of Gauguin as can-openers for the ambitious Count Six-Times. And how sick I am of literary bitches. But they're the only kind that'll have me. . . . Listen, Balso, for a dollar I'll sell you a brief outline of my position."

Balso gave the dollar to get rid of him and received in return a little pamphlet.

THE PAMPHLET

Yesterday, while debating whether I should shave or not, news of the death of my friend Saniette arrived. I decided not to shave.

Today, while shaving, I searched myself for yesterday's emotions. Searched, that is, the pockets of my dressing gown and the shelves of the medicine closet. Not finding anything, I looked further. I looked [first smiling, of course] into the bowels of my compassion, the depths of my being, and even into the receding vistas of my memory. I came from my search, as was to be expected, empty-handed. My "Open, oh flood gates of feeling! Empty, oh vials of passion!" made certain and immediate the defeat of my purpose.

That I failed in my search was for me a sign of my intelligence. I am [just as children choose sides to play "cops and robbers" or "Indians and cowboys"] on the side of intellect against the emotions, on the side of the brain against the heart. Nevertheless, I recognized the cardboard and tin of my position [a young man, while shaving, dismisses Death with a wave of his hand] and did not give up my search for an emotion. I marshalled all my reasons for grief [I had lived with Saniette for almost two years], yet failed to find sorrow.

Death is a very difficult thing for me to consider sincerely because I find certain precomposed judgments awaiting my method of consideration to render it absurd. No matter how I form my comment I attach to it the criticisms sentimental, satirical, formal. With these judgments there goes a series of literary associations which remove me still further from genuine feeling. The very act of recognizing Death, Love, Beauty—all the major subjects—has become, from literature and exercise, impossible.

After admitting to myself that I had failed, I tried to cover my defeat by practicing a few sneers in the bathroom mirror. I remembered that yesterday I had used Saniette's death as an excuse for not shaving and added in a loud voice, "Just as more than one friend will use the occasion of my death as an excuse for breaking an undesired appointment."

Heartened by my sneering reflection in the mirror, I pictured the death of Saniette. Hiding under the blankets of her hospital bed and invoking the aid of Mother Eddy and Doctor Coué: "I won't die! I am getting better and better. I won't die! The will is master o'er the flesh. I won't die!" Only to have Death answer: "Oh, yes you will." And she had. I made Death's triumph my own.

The inevitability of death has always given me pleasure, not because I am eager to die, but because all the Saniettes must die. When the preacher explained the one thing all men could be certain of—all must die—the King of France became angry. When death prevailed over the optimism of Saniette, she was, I am certain, surprised. The thought of Saniette's surprise pleases me, just as the King's anger must have pleased the preacher.

Only a portion of my dislike for Saniette is based on the natural antipathy pessimists feel for optimists, cowboys for Indians, cops for robbers. For a large part it consists of that equally natural antipathy felt by the performer for his audience. My relations with Saniette were exactly those of performer and audience.

While living with me, Saniette accepted my most desperate feats in somewhat the manner one watches the

marvelous stunts of acrobats. Her casualness excited me
so that I became more and more desperate in my per-
formances. A tragedy with only one death is nothing in the
theatre—why not two deaths? Why not a hundred? With
some such idea as this in mind I exhibited my innermost
organs: I wore my heart and genitals around my neck. At
each exhibition I watched carefully to see how she received my performance—with a smile or with a tear.
Though I exhibited myself as a clown, I wanted no mis-
takes to be made; I was a tragic clown.

I have forgotten the time when I could look back at an
affair with a woman and remember anything but a sequence of theatrical poses—poses that I assumed, no matter
how aware I was of their ridiculousness, because they were
amusing. All my acting has but one purpose, the attraction
of the female.

If it had been possible for me to attract by exhibiting
a series of physical charms, my hatred would have been
less. But I found it necessary to substitute strange con-
ceits, wise and witty sayings, peculiar conduct, Art, for
the muscles, teeth, hair, of my rivals.

All this much-exhibited intelligence is but a development
of the instinct to please. My case is similar to that of a
bird called the Amblyornis inornata. As his name indicates,
the Inornata is a dull-colored, ugly bird. Yet the Inornata is
cousin to the Bird of Paradise. Because he lacks his cousin's
brilliant plumage, he has to exteriorize internal feathers.
The Inornata plants a garden and builds a house of
flowers as a substitute for the gay feathers of his relative.
Of course the female Inornata loves her shabby artist
dearly; yet when a friend passes, Mrs. Bird of Paradise
can say, "Show your tail, dear," while Mrs. Inornata, to her
confusion, has no explanation to give for her love. If she
is in a temper she might even ask Mr. Inornata to exteriorize a few internal feathers. Still more, the Bird of

Paradise cannot be blamed for the quality of his tail—it just grew. The Inornata, however, is held personally responsible for his performance as an artist.

There was a time when I felt that I was indeed a rare spirit. Then I had genuinely expressed my personality with a babe's delight in confessing the details of its inner life. Soon, however, in order to interest my listeners, I found it necessary to shorten my long outpourings; to make them, by straining my imagination, spectacular. Oh, how much work goes into the search for the odd, the escape from the same!

Because of women like Saniette, I acquired the habit of extravagant thought. I now convert everything into fantastic entertainment and the extraordinary has become an obsession. . . .

An intelligent man finds it easy to laugh at himself, but his laughter is not sincere if it is thorough. If I could be Hamlet, or even a clown with a breaking heart 'neath his jester's motley, the role would be tolerable. But I always find it necessary to burlesque the mystery of feeling at its source; I must laugh at myself, and if the laugh is "bitter," I must laugh at the laugh. The ritual of feeling demands burlesque and, whether the burlesque is successful or not, a laugh. . . .

One night, while in a hotel bedroom with Saniette, I grew miserably sick of the mad dreams I had been describing to amuse her. I began to beat her. While beating her, I was unable to forget that strange man, John Raskolnikov Gilson, the Russian student. As I beat her, I shouted: "O constipation of desire! O diarrhoea of love! O life within life! O mystery of being! O Young Women's Christian Association! Oh! Oh!"

When her screams brought the hotel clerk to our door,

I attempted to explain my irritation. In part I said: "This evening I am very nervous. I have a sty on my eye, a cold sore on my lip, a pimple where the edge of my collar touches my neck, another pimple in the corner of my mouth, and a drop of salt snot on the end of my nose. Because I rub them continually my nostrils are inflamed, sore and angry.

"My forehead is wrinkled so hard that it hurts, yet I cannot unwrinkle it. I spend many hours trying to unwrinkle my forehead. I try to catch myself by surprise; I try to smooth my forehead with my fingers; I try to concentrate my whole mind to this end, but I am unable to make smooth my brow. The skin over my eyebrows is tied in an aching, unbreakable knot.

"The wood of this table, the glasses on it, this girl's woollen dress, the skin under it, excites and annoys me. It seems to me as though all the materials of life—wood, glass, wool, skin—are rubbing against my sty, my cold sore and my pimples; rubbing in such a way as not to satisfy the itch or convert irritation into active pain, but so as to increase the size of the irritation, magnify it and make it seem to cover everything—hysteria, despair.

"I go to a mirror and squeeze the sty with all my strength. I tear off the cold sore with my nails. I scrub my salt-encrusted nostrils with the rough sleeve of my overcoat. If I could only turn irritation into pain; could push the whole thing into insanity and so escape. I am able to turn irritation into active pain for only a few seconds, but the pain soon subsides and the monotonous rhythm of irritation returns. O how fleeting is pain!—I cry. I think of sandpapering my body. I think of grease, of sandalwood oil, of saliva; I think of velvet, of Keats, of music, of the hardness of precious stones, of mathematics, of the arrangements of architecture. But, alas! I can find no relief."

Both Saniette and the clerk refused to understand. Saniette said that she understood the irritation I was talking about was one of the spirit; yet, she added, the only conclusion she could arrive at—a gentleman would never strike a lady—was that I no longer loved her. The clerk murmured something about the police.

In order to get him away from the door, I asked him if he had ever heard of the Marquis de Sade or of Gilles de Rais. Fortunately, we were in a Broadway hotel whose employees are familiar with the world. When I mentioned these names, the clerk bowed and left us with a smile. Saniette was also of the world; she smiled and went back to bed.

The next morning, remembering their smiles, I thought it advisable to explain my actions again. Not that it was necessary for me to differentiate between the kind of a beating alcohol inspires a temperance-cartoon drunkard to give his hard-working spouse, and the beating I had given Saniette; but, rather, that I found it difficult to illustrate the point I desired to make clear.

"When you think of me, Saniette," I said, "think of two men—myself and the chauffeur within me. This chauffeur is very large and dressed in ugly ready-made clothing. His shoes, soiled from walking about the streets of a great city, are covered with animal ordure and chewing gum. His hands are covered with coarse woollen gloves. On his head is a derby hat.

"The name of this chauffeur is The Desire to Procreate.

"He sits within me like a man in an automobile. His heels are in my bowels, his knees on my heart, his face in my brain. His gloved hands hold me firmly by the tongue; his hands, covered with wool, refuse me speech for the emotions aroused by the face in my brain.

"From within, he governs the sensations I receive through my fingers, eyes, tongue and ears.

"Can you imagine how it feels to have this cloth-covered
devil within one? While naked, were you ever embraced
by a fully clothed man? Do you remember how his button-
covered coat felt, how his heavy shoes felt against your
skin? Imagine having this man inside of you, fumbling and
fingering your heart and tongue with wool-covered hands,
treading your tender organs with stumbling soiled feet."

Because of the phrasing of my complaint, Saniette was
able to turn my revenge into a joke. She weathered a
second beating with a slow, kind smile.

Saniette represents a distinct type of audience—smart,
sophisticated, sensitive yet hardboiled, art-loving frequenters
of the little theatres. I am their particular kind of a performer.

Some day I shall obtain my revenge by writing a play
for one of their art theatres. A theatre patronized by the
discriminating few: art-lovers and book-lovers, school
teachers who adore the grass-eating Shaw, sensitive young
Jews who adore culture, lending librarians, publisher's
assistants, homosexualists and homosexualists' assistants,
hard-drinking newpaper men, interior decorators, and the
writers of advertising copy.

In this play I shall take my beloved patrons into my
confidence and flatter their difference from other theatre-
goers. I shall congratulate them on their good taste in
preferring Art to animal acts. Then, suddenly, in the midst
of some very witty dialogue, the entire cast will walk to
the footlights and shout Chekov's advice:

"It would be more profitable for the farmer to raise rats
for the granary than for the bourgeois to nourish the artist,
who must always be occupied with undermining institutions."

In case the audience should misunderstand and align

31

itself on the side of the artist, the ceiling of the theatre
will be made to open and cover the occupants with tons
of loose excrement. After the deluge, if they so desire,
the patrons of my art can gather in the customary charming groups and discuss the play.

When he had finished reading, Balso threw the pamphlet
away with a sigh. In his childhood, things had been
managed differently; besides, shaving had not been permitted before the age of sixteen. Having no alternative,
Balso blamed the war, the invention of printing, nineteenth-century science, communism, the wearing of soft
hats, the use of contraceptives, the large number of
delicatessen stores, the movies, the tabloids, the lack of
adequate ventilation in large cities, the passing of the
saloon, the soft collar fad, the spread of foreign art, the
decline of the western world, commercialism, and, finally,
for throwing the artist back on his own personality, the
renaissance.

"What is beauty saith my sufferings then?" asked Balso
of himself, quoting Marlowe.

As though in answer to his question, he saw standing
naked before him a slim young girl busily washing her
hidden charms in a public fountain. Through the wood
of his brain there buzzed the saw of desire.

She called to him, saying:

"Charge, oh poet, the red-veined flowers of suddenly re-

membered intimacies—the foliage of memory. Feel, oh
poet, the warm knife of thought swift stride and slit in the
ready garden.

"Soon the hot seed will come to thwart the knife's
progress. The hot seed will come in a joyous burst-birth of
reeking undergrowth and swamp forest.

"Walk toward the houses of the city of your memory,
oh poet! Houses that are protuberances on the skin of
streets—warts, tumors, pimples, corns, nipples, sebaceous
cysts, hard and soft chancres.

"Like the gums of false teeth, red are the signs imploring you to enter the game paths lit by iron flowers.
Like ants under a new-turned stone, hysterical are the
women who run there clad in the silk tights of pleasure,
oiled with fish slime. Women whose only delight is to
rub the jaded until it becomes irritated and grows new
things, pimples of a . . ."

Throwing his arms around her, Balso interrupted her
recitation by sticking his tongue into her mouth. But
when he closed his eyes to heighten the fun, he felt that
he was embracing tweed. He opened them and saw that
what he held in his arms was a middle aged woman
dressed in a mannish suit and wearing hornrimmed glasses.

"My name is Miss McGeeney," she said. "I am a writer
as well as a school teacher. Let's discuss something."

Balso wanted to bash her jaw in, but he found that he
could not move. He tried to curse, but could only say:
"How interesting. On what are you working?"

"At present I am writing a biography of Samuel Perkins.
Stark, clever, disillusioned stuff, with a tenderness devoid
of sentiment, yet touched by pity and laughter and irony.
Into this book I hope to put the whimsical humor, the
kindly satire of a mellow life.

"On the surface *Samuel Perkins: Smeller* [for so I call it]
is simply a delightful story for children. The discriminating

adult soon discovers, however, that it sprang from the brain of a kindly philosopher, that it is a genial satire on humanity.

"Under the title I intend placing as motto a verse from Juvenal: 'Who is surprised to see a goiter in the Alps? Quis tumidum guttur miratur in Alpibus?' I feel that this quotation strikes the keynote of the work.

"But who is Samuel Perkins, you are probably wondering. Samuel Perkins is the biographer of E. F. Fitzgerald. And who is Fitzgerald? You are of course familiar with D. B. Hobson's life of Boswell. Well, E. F. Fitzgerald is the author of a life of Hobson. The subject of my biography, Samuel Perkins, wrote a life of Fitzgerald.

"Sometime ago, a publisher asked me to write a biography, and I decided to do one of E. F. Fitzgerald. Fortunately, before commencing my study, I met Samuel Perkins who told me that he had written a biography of Fitzgerald the biographer of Hobson the biographer of Boswell. This news did not discourge me, but, on the contrary, made me determine to write a life of Perkins and so become another link in a brilliant literary chain. It seems to me that someone must surely take the hint and write the life of Miss McGreeney, the woman who wrote the biography of the man who wrote the biography of the man who wrote the biography of the man who wrote the biography of Boswell. And that, ad infinitum, we will all go rattling down the halls of time, each one in his or her turn a tin can on the tail of Doctor Johnson.

"But there are other good reasons for writing a life of Perkins. He was a great, if peculiar, genius with a character that lends itself most readily to biography.

"At an age when most men's features are regular, before his personality had been able to elevate any one portion of his physiognomy over the rest, Perkins' face was dominated by his nose. This fact I have ascertained from a collection of early photographs lent me by a profound admirer of Perkins and a fellow practitioner of his art. I refer to Robert Jones, author of a book called *Nosologie*.

"When I met Perkins for the first time, his face reminded me of the body of a man I had known at college. According to gossip current in the girls' dormitory this man abused himself. The source of these rumors lay in the peculiar shape of his body: all the veins, muscles and sinews flowed toward and converged at one point. In a like manner the wrinkles on Perkins' face, the contours of his head, the lines of his brow and chin, seemed to have melted and run into his nose.

"At this first meeting, Perkins said something that was later to prove very illuminating. He quoted Lucretius to the effect that 'his nose was quicker to scent a fetid sore or a rank armpit, than a dog to smell out the hidden sow.' Like most quotations, this one is only partially true. True, that is, of only one stage in Perkins' aesthetic development—the, what I have called quite arbitrarily, excrement period.

"It is possible to explain the powers of Perkins' magnificent sense of smell by the well-known theory of natural compensation. No one who has ever observed the acuteness of touch exhibited by a blind man or the gigantic shoulders of a legless man, will question the fact that Nature compensates for the loss of one attribute by lavishing her bounty on another. And Nature had made in the person of Samuel Perkins another attempt at justice. He was deaf and almost blind; his fingers fumbled stupidly; his mouth was always dry and contained a dull, insensitive tongue. But his nose! His nose was a marvelously sensitive and nice instrument. Nature had concentrated in his sense of smell all the abilities usually distributed among the five senses. She had strengthened this organ and had made it so sensitive that it was able to do duty for all the contact organs. Perkins was able to translate the sensations, sound, sight, taste, and touch, into that of smell. He could smell a chord in D minor, or distinguish between the tone-smell of a violin and that of a viola. He could smell the caress of velvet and the strength of iron. It has been said of him that he could smell an isosceles triangle; I mean that he could apprehend through the sense of smell the principles involved in isosceles triangles.

"In the ability to interpret the functions of one sense in terms of another, he is not alone. A French poet, in a sonnet of the vowels, called the letter I red and the letter U blue. Another symbolist, Father Castel, made a clavichord on which he was able to play melody and harmony by using color. Des Esseintes, Huysmans' hero, used a taste organ on which he composed symphonies for the palate.

"But can you imagine, new-found friend and esteemed poet, how horrible was the predicament of this sensitive and sensuous man forced to interpret the whole external world through conclusions reached by the sense of smell alone? If we have great difficulty in discovering the Real, how much greater must his difficulty have been?

"In my presence, Perkins once called the senses a tread-mill. 'A tread-mill,' he said, 'on which one can go only from the odors of Indian-grass baskets to the sour smells of Africa and the stinks of decay.'

"Rather than a tread-mill, I should call the senses a circle. A step forward along the circumference of a circle is a step nearer the starting place. Perkins went, along the circumference of the circle of his senses, from anticipation to realization, from hunger to satiation, from naïveté to sophistication, from simplicity to perversion. He went [speaking in Perkinsesque] from the smell of new-mown hay to that of musk and vervain [from the primitive to the romantic], and from vervain to sweat and excrement [from the romantic to the realistic]; and, finally, to complete the circuit, from excrement he returned to new-mown hay.

"There is, however, a way out for the artist and Perkins discovered it. The circumference of a circle infinite in size is a straight line. And a man like Perkins is able to make the circle of his sensory experience approach the infinite. He can so qualify the step from simplicity to perversion, for example, that the curve which makes inevitable the return to simplicity is imperceptible.

"One day Perkins told me that he was going to be married. I asked him if he thought his wife would understand him, and whether he thought he could be happy with a woman. He answered no to both questions, and said that he was marrying as an artist. I asked him to explain. He replied that the man who had numbered the smells of the human body and found them to be seven was a fool, unless the number was used in its mystic sense.

"After studying this strange conversation with the master, I discovered his meaning. He had found in the odors of a woman's body, never-ending, ever-fresh variation and change—a world of dreams, seas, roads, forests, textures, colors, flavors, forms. On my questioning him further, he confirmed my interpretation. He told me that he had built from the odors of his wife's body an architecture and an aesthetic, a music and a mathematic. Counterpoint, multiplication, the square of a sensation, the cube root of an experience—all were there. He told me that he had even discovered a politic, a hierarchy of odors: self-government, direct . . . "

By this time, Balso had gotten one of his hands free. He hit Miss McGeeney a terrific blow in the gut and hove her into the fountain.

The wooden horse, Balso realized as he walked on, was inhabited solely by writers in search of an audience, and he
was determined not to be tricked into listening to another
story. If one had to be told, he would tell it.

As he hurried down the seemingly endless corridor, he
began to wonder whether he would ever reach the Anus
Mirabilis again. His feet hurt badly and his head ached.
When he came to a café built into the side of the intestine,
he sat down and ordered a glass of beer. After drinking
the beer, he took a newspaper out of his pocket, put it
over his face and went to sleep.

Balso dreamt that he was a young man again, lurking in
a corner of the Carnegie Hall lobby among the assembled
friends and relatives of music. The lobby was crowded
with the many beautiful girl-cripples who congregate
there because Art is their only solace, most men looking
upon their strange forms with distaste. But it was otherwise with Balso Snell. He likened their disarranged hips,
their short legs, their humps, their splay feet, their wall-
eyes, to ornament. Their strange foreshortenings, hanging
heads, bulging spinesacks, were a delight, for he had ever
preferred the imperfect, knowing well the plainness, the
niceness of perfection.

Spying a beautiful hunchback, he suddenly became sick
with passion. The cripple of his choice looked like some
creature from the depths of the sea. She was tall and
extraordinarily hunched. She was tall in spite of her

enormous hump; but for her dog-leg spine she would
have been seven feet high. Moreover, he could be certain
that, like all hunchbacks, she was intelligent.

He tipped his hat to her. She smiled and he snatched her
from the throng, crying as he took her arm:

"O arabesque, I, Balso Snell, shall replace music in your
affections! Your pleasures shall no longer be vicarious. No
longer shall you mentally pollute yourself. For me, your
sores are like flowers: the new, pink, budlike sores, the full,
rose-ripe sores, the sweet, seed-bearing sores. I shall cherish them all. O deviation from the Golden Mean! O out of
alignment!"

The Lepi [for so did he instantly dub her] opened her
mouth to reply and exhibited one hundred and forty-four
exquisite teeth in rows of four.

"Balso," she said, "you are a villian. Do you love as do all
villains?"

"No," he answered, "I love only this." As he spoke, he
laid his cool white hands upon her beautiful, hydrocephalic forehead. Then, bending over her enormous hump, he
kissed her full on the brow.

Feeling his lips on her forehead, Janey Davenport, [the
Lepi] gazed out over the blue waves of the Mediterranean
and felt the delight of being young, rich, beautiful.
No-one had ever before forgotten her strange shape long
enough to realize how beautiful her soul was. She had
never before known the thrill of being subdued by a male
from a different land from that of her dreams. Now
she had found a wonderful poet; now she knew the thrill
she had never known before . . . had found it in the
strength of this young and tall, strangely wise man, caught
like herself in the meshes of the greatest net human hearts
can know: Love.

Balso took her home and, in the hallway of her house,
tried to seduce her. She allowed him one kiss, then broke

away. From her lips—overhung by a moist eye and under-hung by a heaving embonpoint—there came, "Love is a strange thing, is it not, Balso Snell?" He was afraid to laugh; he knew that if he even smiled the jig would be up. "Love," she said, "is beautiful. You, Balso, do not love. Love is sacred. How can you kiss if you do not love?" When he began to unbutton, she said with a desperately gay smile: "Would you want some one to ask of your sister what you ask of me? So this is why you invited me to dinner? I pre-fer music."

He made another attempt, but she fended him off. "Love," she began again, "Love, with me, Mr. Snell, is sacred. I shall never debase love, or myself, or the mem-ory of my mother, in a hallway. Act your education, Mr. Snell. Tumbling in hallways at my age! How can you? After all, there are the eternal verities, not to speak of the janitor. And besides, we were never properly introduced."

After half an hour's sparring, he managed to warm her up a bit. She held him to her tightly for a second, capsized her eyeballs, and said: "If you only loved me, Balso. If you only loved me." He looked her in the eye, stroked her hump, kissed her brow, protesting desperately: "But I do love you, Janey. I do. I do. I swear it. I must have you. I must! I must!" She shoved him away with a sad yet deter-mined smile. "First you will have to prove your love as did the knights of old."

"I'm ready," Balso cried. "What would you have me do?"

"Come inside and I'll tell you."

Balso followed her into the apartment and sat down be-side her on a couch.

"I want you to kill a man called Beagle Darwin," she said with great firmness. "He betrayed me. In this hump on my back I carry his child. After you have killed him, I shall yield up my pink and white body to you, and then commit suicide."

"A bargain," Balso said. "Give me but your stocking to wear around my hat and I'm off to earn the prize."

"Not so fast, my gallant; first I must explain a few things to you.

"After listening to Beagle Darwin recite some of his poetry, I slept with him one night while my folks were visiting friends in Plainfield, New Jersey. Unfamiliar as I was with the wiles of men, I believed him when he told me that he loved me and wanted to take me to Paris to live in an artistic studio. I was very happy until I received the following letter."

Here the Lepi went to a bureau and took out two letters, one of which she gave Balso to read.

Darling Janey:

You persist in misunderstanding me. Please understand this: It is for your own good that I am refusing to take you to Paris, as I am firmly convinced that such a trip can only result in your death.

Here is the way in which you would die:

In your pajamas, Janey, you sit near the window and listen to the gay clatter of Paris traffic. The highpitched automobile horns make of every day a holiday. You are miserable.

You tell yourself: Oh, the carnival crowds are always hurrying past my window. I'm like an old actor mumbling Macbeth as he fumbles in the garbage can outside the theatre of his past triumphs. Only I'm not old; I'm young. Young, and I never had any triumphs to mumble over; my only triumphs were those I dreamed of having. I'm Janey Davenport, pregnant, unmarried, unloved, lonely, watching the laughing crowds hurry past her window.

I don't fit into life. I don't fit into his life. He only tolerates me for my body. He only wants one thing from me, and I want, oh how I want, love.

The ridiculous, the ridiculous, all day long he talks of nothing else but how ridiculous this, that, or the other thing is. And he means me. I am absurd. He is never satisfied with calling other people ridiculous, with him everything is ridiculous—himself, me. Of course I can laugh at Mother with him, or at the Hearth; but why must my own mother and home be ridiculous? I can laugh at Hobey, Joan, but I don't want to laugh at myself. I'm tired of laugh, laugh, laugh. I want to retain some portion of myself unlaughed at. There is something in me that I won't laugh at. I won't. I'll laugh at the outside world all he wants me to, but I won't, I don't want to laugh at my inner world. It's all right for him to say: "Be hard! Be an intellectual! Think, don't feel!" But I want to be soft. I want to feel. I don't want to think. I feel blue when I think. I want to keep a hard, outside surface towards the world, and a soft, inner side for him. And I want him to do the same, so that we can be secure in each other's love. But with his rotten, ugly jokes he keeps me at arm's length just when I want to be confiding and tender. When I show him my soft side he laughs. I don't want to be always on my guard against his laughter. There are times when I want to put down my armor. I am tired of eternally bearing armor against the world. Love is a merging, not an occasion for intellectual warfare. I want to enjoy my emotions. I want, sometimes, to play the child, and to make love like a child—tenderly, confidingly, prettily. I'm sick of his taunts.

Pregnant, unmarried, and he won't marry me. If I ask him to, he will laugh his terrible horse-laugh: "Well, my little bohemian, you want to get out of it, do you? Life, however, is Life; and the Realities are the Realities. You can't have your cake and eat it too, you know." He'll tell his friends the story as a joke—one of his unexplainable jokes. All his smug-faced friends will laugh at me, especially the Paige girl.

They don't like me; I don't fit in. All my life I have been a misfit—misunderstood. The carnival crowds are always hurrying past my window. As a kid, I never liked to play in the streets with the other kids; I always wanted to stay in the house and read a book. Since my father's death, I have no one to go to with my misery. He was always willing to understand and comfort me. Oh, how I want to be understood by someone who really loves me. Mother, like Beagle, always laughs at me. If they want to be kind it is, "You silly goose!" If they are angry, "Don't be an idiot." Only father was sympathetic, and he is dead. I wish I were dead.

Joan Higgins would know what to do if she were in my position—pregnant and unmarried. Joan fits into the kind of a life he and his friends lead better than I do. Like the time Joan said she had gone back to live with Hobey because it was such a bore looking for healthy men to sleep with. Joan warned me against him; she said he wasn't my kind. I thought him just my kind, sad and a poet. He is sad, but with a nasty sadness—all jeers for his own sadness. "It's the war. Everybody is sad nowadays. Great stuff, pessimism." Still he is sad; if he would only stop acting we could be very happy together. I want so much to comfort him—mother him.

Joan's advice would probably be for me to make him marry me. How he would howl. "Make an honest girl of you, eh?"

You can see the Café Carcas from the window. You are living in the Rue de la Grande Chaumiere, at the Hotel Liberia.

Why don't I fit in well at the Carcas? Joan would go big there. Why don't they like me? I'm as good looking as she is, and as clever. It's because I don't let myself go the way she does. Well, I don't want to. There is something fine in me that won't let me degrade myself.

You see me come out of the café, laughing and waving my arms.

I hope he comes upstairs.

You see me turn, and come towards the hotel.

Just as soon as he comes in I'll tell him I'm pregnant. I'll tell him in a matter-of-fact voice—casually. As long as I keep my tone casual he won't be able to laugh.

"Hello darling, how are you this morning?"
"All right. Beagle, je suis enceinte."
"You're what?"
[Oh, damn my pronunciation, I spoilt it.] "I'm pregnant." Despite your desire to appear casual you let a note of heartbreak into your voice. You droop.
"We'll have a party tonight and celebrate." I leave the room, shutting the door behind me, carefully.
Perhaps he'll never come back . . . You run to the window—sick. You sit down and prepare to indulge your misery. Your misery, your misery—you roll, you grovel in it. I'm pregnant! I'm pregnant! I'm pregnant! You force the rhythm of this cry into your blood. After the first moments of hysterical anguish are over, you wrap your predicament around you, snuggling into it, letting it cover you completely like a blanket. Your big trouble shelters you from a host of minor troubles. You are so miserable.

You remember that "life is a prison without bars," and think of suicide.

No one ever listens to me when I talk of suicide. The night I woke up in bed with him, it was no different. He thought I was joking when I said that I had frightened myself by brooding on death. But I told the truth. Death and suicide are never far from my thoughts. I said that death is like putting on a wet bathing suit. Now death seems warm and friendly. No, death is still like putting on a wet suit—shivery.

If I do it, I won't leave a note behind for him to laugh at. Just end it, that's all. No matter how I word a farewell note he will find something to laugh at—something to show his friends as a joke . . .

Mother knows I'm living with a man in Paris. Sophie wrote that everybody is talking about me. If I were to go home—even if I were not pregnant—mother would make an awful stink. I don't want to go back to the States: a long dull trip followed by a long dull life teaching elementary school.

What can I expect from him? He'll want me to have an abortion. They say that on account of the decreasing birth rate it is hard to get a competent doctor to do the operation. The French police are very strict. If the doctor killed me . . .

If I kill myself, I kill my body. I don't want to destroy my body; it is a good body—soft, white, and kind to me—a beautiful, happy body. If he were a true poet he would love me for my body's beauty; but he is like all men; he wants only one thing. Soon my body will be swollen and clumsy. The milk spoils the shape of a woman's breasts after an abortion. When my body becomes ugly, he will hate me. I once hoped that having a child would draw him closer to me—make him love me as a mother. But mother

for him is always Mammy: a popular Broadway ballad,
Mammy, Mammy, my old Kentucky Home, put it all together, it spells Mother. He doesn't see that Mother can
mean shelter, love, intimacy. Oh, how much I want, I need,
love.

If I wanted to make a squawk, mother would force him
to marry me; but she would scold terribly and make a horrible scene. I'm too tired and sick to go through with a
shotgun wedding.

Maybe I passed my period because of the wine—no, I
know. Where did I read, "In my belly there is a tangled
forest of arms and legs." It sounds like his stuff. When he
left, he said he'd give a party tonight in honor of the occasion. I know what kind of a party it will be. He'll get
drunk and make a speech: "Big with child, great with
young—let me toast your gut, my dear. Here's to the pup!
Waiters, stand erect while I toast my heir." He and his
friends will expect me to join in the sport—to be a good
sport.

He claims that the only place to commit suicide is on
Chekov's grave. The Seine is also famous for suicide:
" 'midst the bustle of 'Gay Paree'—suicide." "She killed herself in Paris." There is something tragic in the very
thought. French windows make it easy; all you have to do
is open the window and walk out. Every window over the
third floor is a door into heaven. When I arrive there I can
plead my belly—oh, how bitterly cruel the jest is. "Jest?"
He would correct me—"not 'jest,' my dear, but joke; never,
never say 'jest.' "

Oh, how miserable I am. I need love; I can't live without someone to treasure and comfort me. If I jumped from
the third floor I might cripple myself—lucky this room is
on the fourth. Lucky? [Animals never commit suicide.]

And mother—what would mother say? Mother would

feel worse about my being unmarried than about my death. I could leave a note asking him, as a final favor, to write her and say that we were married. He would forget to write.

When I'm dead, I'll be out of it all. Mother, Beagle—they will leave me alone. But I can't blame my trouble on him. I got myself into this mess. I went to his room after he acted decently in mine. I was jealous of Joan; she had so much fun going to men's rooms, and all that sort of thing. How childish Joan and her follies seem to me now.

When I'm dead the whole world as far as I am con-cerned—Beagle, mother—will be dead also. Or aussi: I came to Paris to learn French. I certainly learnt French. I wasn't even able to tell him in French without turning my trouble into a joke.

What love and a child by the man I loved once meant to me—and to live in Paris. If he should come back suddenly and catch me like this, brooding at the window, he'd say: "A good chance for you to kill two birds with one stone, my dear; but remember, an egg in the belly is worth more than a bird in the bush." What a pig he is! He thinks I haven't the nerve to kill myself. He patronizes me as though I were a child. "Suicide," he says, "is a charming affectation on the part of a young Russian, but in you, dear Janey, it is absurd."

You scream with irritation: "I'm serious! I am! I am! I don't want to live! I'm miserable! I don't want to live!"

I'm only teasing myself with thoughts of suicide at an open window. I know I won't do it. Mother will call me away: "Go away from that window—fool! You'll catch your death-cold or fall out—clumsy!"

At the word "clumsy" you fall to your death in the gut-ter below the window.

Horrible, eh? Yes, Janey, it is a suicide's grave that I saved you from when I refused to take you to Paris.

Yours,

Beagle

When Balso had finished reading, she handed him the other letter.

Darling Janey:

You did not take offence, I hope, at my letter. Please believe me when I say that I tried to make my treatment of your suicide as impersonal as possible. I did my best to keep the description of both our characters scientific and just. If I treated you savagely, I treated myself no gentler. It is true that I concentrated on you, but only because it was your suicide. In this letter I shall try to show, and so even the score, how I would have received your death.

You once said to me that I talk like a man in a book. I not only talk, but think and feel like one. I have spent my life in books; literature has deeply dyed my brain its own color. This literary coloring is a protective one—like the brown of the rabbit or the checks of the quail—making it impossible for me to tell where literature ends and I begin.

I start where I left off in my last letter:

As Janey's half-naked body crashed into the street, the usual crowds were hurrying to lunch from the Academies Colorossa and Grande Chaumiere; the concierge was coming out of the hotel's side door. In order to avoid running over her body, the driver of a cab coming from the Rue Notre Dame des Champs and going toward the Square de la Grande Chaumiere, brought his machine to a stop with screaming brakes. The concierge, on seeing the cab stop suddenly, one wheel over the body of a tenant of his, ran up, caught the chauffeur by the arm, and called loudly for the police. No one had seen her fall but the driver of the cab; he, bursting with rage, called the concierge an idiot, and pointed to the open window from which she had jumped. A crowd gathered around the chauffeur and shouted at him angrily. A policeman arrived. He, too, refused to believe the cab-driver, although he noticed that the dead girl was in her pajamas. "What would she be doing in the street in her night-clothes if she hadn't fallen from the window?" He shrugged his shoulders: "These American art students."

Beagle, on his way to the Café Carcas for a drink, turned to see where so many people were running. He saw the gesticulating group around the cab and went back, grateful for any diversion on what had been such a dull morning. As he joined them he kept thinking of Janey's announcement. "I'm pregnant." It reminded him of another announcement of hers. "It's about time I took a lover." "I'm pregnant" demanded for an answer, Life, just as "It's about time I took a lover" had been worthy of no less a reply than Love. She made a habit of these startling declarations: a few words, but freighted with meaning.

He knew what "I'm pregnant" meant; it meant canvassing his friends for the whereabouts of a doctor willing to perform the operation and writing frantic letters to the States for the necessary money. Through it all, Janey, having thrown the responsibility on him, would sit in one corner of the room: "Do with me what you will"—the groaning, patient, all-suffering, all-knowing, what has to be will be, beast of many burdens.

As he pushed into the crowd, someone told him a girl had been killed. He looked where the chauffeur was pointing and saw the open window of their room. Then he saw

Janey under the cab; he could not see her face, but he recognized her pajamas.

This was indeed a solution. The problem had been solved for him with a vengeance. He turned away and hurried up the street, afraid of being recognized. It had become impossible for him to take his drink at the Carcas. If he went there some friend would surely come to him with the news: "Beagle! Beagle! Janey has killed herself." He wanted to go somewhere and prepare a reply. "Here today and gone tomorrow" would never do, even at the Carcas.

He went past the Carcas up the Rue Delambre to the Avenue de Maine. On this street he went into a café hardly ever visited by Americans and sat down at a table in the corner of an inside room. He called for some cognac and asked himself:

Of what assistance could I have been? Should I have gone down on my knees in the street and wept over her dead body? Torn my hair? Called on the Deity? Or should I gave gone calmly up to the policeman and said: "I'm her husband. Allow me to accompany you to the morgue."

He ordered another cognac—Beagle Darwin the Destroyer. He pulled his hat down over his eyes and tossed off his drink.

She did it because she was pregnant. I would have married her, the fool. I hurt her when I made believe I didn't understand her French. "Je suis enceinte." My "what" was one of the astonishment, not the "what" of interrogation. No, it was not. You said "what" in order to humiliate her. What is the purpose of all your harping on petty affectations? Why this continual irritation at the sight of other peoples' stupidities? What of your own stupidities and affectations? Why is it impossible for you to understand, except in terms of art, her action? She killed herself because she was afraid to face her troubles—an abortion or the birth of a bastard. Absurd; she never asked you to marry her. You do not understand.

He crouched over his drink, Tiger Darwin, his eyes half shut—desperate.

I wonder if she was able to avoid generalizing before she killed herself. I am sure it was not trouble, that was uppermost in her mind, but the rag-tag of some "philosophy." Although I did my best to laugh away finita la comedia, I am certain that some such catch-word of disillusion was in her mouth when she turned the trick. She probably decided that Love, Life, Death, all could be contained in an epigram: "The things which are of value in Life are empty and rotten and trifling; Love is but a flitting shadow, a lure, a gimcrack, a kickshaw. And Death?—bah! What, then, is there still detaining you in this vale of tears?" Can it be that the only thing that bothers me in a statement of this sort is the wording? Or is it because there is something arty about suicide? Suicide: Werther, the Cosmic Urge, the Soul, the Quest, and Otto Greenbaum, Phil Beta Kappa, Age seventeen— Life is unworthy of him; and Haldington Knape, Oxford, author, man-about-town, big game hunter—Life is too tiresome; and Terry Kornflower, poet, no hat, shirt open to the navel—Life is too crude; and Janey Davenport, pregnant, unmarried, jumps from a studio window in Paris —Life is too difficult. O. Greenbaum, H. Knape, T. Kornflower, J. Davenport, all would agree that "Life is but the span from womb to tomb; a sigh, a smile; a chill, a fever; a throe of pain, a spasm of volupty: then a gasping for breath, and the comedy is over, the song is ended, ring down the curtain, the clown is dead."

The clown is dead; the curtain is down. And when I say clown, I mean you. After all, aren't we all . . . aren't we all clowns? Of course, I know it's old stuff; but what difference does that make? Life *is* a stage; and *we* are clowns. What is more tragic than the role of clown? What more filled with all the essentials of great art?—pity and irony. Get it? The thousands of sweating, laughing, grimacing, jeering animals out front—you have just set them in the aisles, when in comes a messenger. Your wife has run away with the boarder, your son has killed a man, the baby has cancer. Or maybe you ain't married. Coming from the bathroom, you discover that you have gonorrhoea, or you get a telegram that your mother is dead, or your father, or your sister, or your brother. Now get the picture. Outside, after your turn, the customers are hollering and screaming: "Do your stuff, kid! We want Beagle! Let's have Beagle! He's a wow!" The clowns down front are laughing, whistling, belching, crying, sweating, and eating peanuts. And you—you are back-stage, hiding in the shadow of an old prop. Clutching your bursting head with both hands, you hear nothing but the dull roar of your misfortunes. Slowly there filters through your clenched fingers the cries of your brother clowns. Your first thought is to rush out there and cut your throat before their faces with a last terrific laugh. But soon you are out front again doing your stuff, the same superb Beagle: dancing, laughing, singing—*acting*. Finally the curtain comes down, and, in your dressing room before the mirror, you make the faces that won't come off with the grease paint—the faces you will never make down front.

Beagle ordered another cognac and washed it down with a small beer. The saucers had begun to pile up before him on the table.

Well, Janey's death is a joke. A young, unmarried woman on discovering herself to be pregnant commits suicide. A very old and well-known way out of a very old and stale predicament. The moth and the candle, the fly and the spider, the butterfly and the rain, the clown and the curtain, all could be cited as having prepared one [oh how tediously!] for her suicide.

Another cognac! After this cognac, he would go to the Café Carcas and wait for a friend to bring him news of Janey's death.

How shall I receive the devastating news? In order to arouse no adverse criticism, it will be necessary for me to bear in mind that I come of an English-speaking race and therefore am cold, calm, collected, almost stolid, in the face of calamity. And, as the death is that of a very intimate friend, it is important that I show, in some subtle way, that I am hard hit for all my pretence of coldness. Or perhaps because the Carcas is full of artists, I can refuse to stop dreaming, refuse to leave my ivory tower, refuse to disturb that brooding white bird, my spirit. A wave of the hand: "Yes, really. You don't say so?—quite dead." Or I can play one of my favorite roles, be the "Buffoon of the New Eternities" and cry: "Death, what is it? Life, what is it? Life is of course the absence of Death; and Death merely the absence of Life." But I might get into an argument unbecoming one who is lamenting the loss of a loved one. For the sake of the waiters, I will be a quiet, sober, gentle, umbrella-carrying Mr. B. Darwin, and out of a great sadness sob: "Oh, my darling, why did you do it? Oh why?" Or, best of all, like Hamlet, I will feign madness; for if they discover what lies in my heart they will lynch me.

MESSENGER

"Beagle! Beagle! Janey has fallen from the window and is no more."

PATRONS, WAITERS, ETC., AT THE CAFÉ CARCAS

"The girl you lived with is dead."

"Poor Janey. Poor Beagle. Terrible, terrible death."
"And so young she was, and so beautiful . . . in the cold street she lay."

B. HAMLET DARWIN
"Bromius! Iacchus! Son of Zeus!"

PATRONS, WAITERS, ETC.
"Don't you understand, man? The girl you lived with is dead. Your sweetheart is dead. She has killed herself. She is dead!"

B. HAMLET DARWIN
"Bromius! Iacchus! Son of Zeus!"

PATRONS, WAITERS, ETC.
"He's drunk."
"Greek gods!—does he think we don't know he's a Methodist?"
"This is no time for blasphemy!"
"A little learning goes to the heads of fools."
"Yes, drink deep of the Pierian spring or . . ."
"Very picturesque though, 'Bromius! Iacchus!' very picturesque."

B. HAMLET DARWIN
"'O esca vermium! O massa pulveris!' Where is the rich Dives? He who was always eating? He is no longer even eaten."

PATRONS, WAITERS, ETC.
"A riddle! A riddle!"
"He is looking for a friend."
"He has lost something. Tell him to look under the table."

MESSENGER

"He means the worms have eaten Dives; and that, in their turn dead, the worms have been eaten by other worms."

B. HAMLET DARWIN

"Or quick tell me where has gone Samson?—strongest of men. He is no longer even weak. And where, oh tell me, where is the beautiful Appollon? He is no longer even ugly. And where are the snows of yesteryear? And where is Tom Giles? Bill Taylor? Jake Holtz? In other words, 'Here today and gone tomorrow.' "

MESSENGER

"Yes, what he says is but too true. An incident such as the sad demise we are now considering makes one stop 'midst the hustle-bustle of our work-a-day world to ponder the words of the poet who says we are 'nourriture des vers!' Continue, dear brother in sorrow, we attend your every word."

B. HAMLET DARWIN

"I shall begin all over again, folks.

"While I sit laughing with my friends, a messenger stalks into the café. He cries: "Beagle! Beagle! Janey has killed herself!' I jump up, white as a sheet of paper, let us say, and shriek in anguish: 'Bromius! Iacchus! Son of Zeus!' You then demand why I call so loudly on Dionysius. I go into my routine.

"Dionysius! Dionysius! I call on the wine-god because his begetting and birth were so different from Janey's, so different from yours, so different from mine. I call on Dionysius in order to explain the tragedy. A tragedy that is not alone Janey's, but one that is the tragedy of all of us.

"Who among us can boast that he was born three times, as was Dionysius?—once from the womb of 'hapless Semele,' once from the thigh of Zeus, and once from the flames. Or who can say, like Christ, that he was born of a virgin? Or who can even claim to have been born as was Gargantua? Alas! none of us. Yet it is necessary for us to compete—as it was necessary for Janey to compete—with Dionysius the thrice born, Christ son of God, Gargantua born 'midst a torrent of tripe at a most memorable party. You hear the thunder, you see the lightning, you smell the forests, you drink wine—and you attempt to be as was Christ, Dionysius, Gargantua! You who were born from the womb, covered with slime and foul blood, 'midst cries of anguish and suffering.

"At your birth, instead of the Three Kings, the Dove, the Star of Bethlehem, there was only old Doctor Haasenschweitz who wore rubber gloves and carried a towel over his arm like a waiter.

"And how did the lover, your father, come to his beloved? [After a warm day in the office he had seen two dogs in the street.] Did he come in the shape of a swan, a bull, or a shower of gold? No! But with his pants unsupported by braces, came he from the bath-room." . . .

B. Hamlet Darwin towered over his glass of cognac, and, in the theatre of his mind, over a cringing audience —tempestuous, gallant, headstrong, lovable Beagle Dionysius Hamlet Darwin. Up into his giant heart there welled a profound feeling of love for humanity. He choked with emotion as he realized the truth of his observations. Terrible indeed was the competition in which his hearers spent their lives; a competition that demanded their being more than animals.

He raised his hand as though to bless them, and the customers and waiters were silent. Gently, yet with a sense of mighty love, he murmured, "Ah my children." Then, sweeping the Café Carcas with tear-dimmed, eagle's eyes, he cried: "Yet, ah yet, are you expected to compete with Christ whose father is God, with Dionysius whose father is God; you who were Janey Davenport, or one conceived in an offhand manner on a rainy afternoon."

"Cognac! Cognac!"

After building up his tear-jerker routine for a repeat, he blacked out and went into his juggling for the curtain. He climaxed the finale by keeping in the air an Ivory Tower, a Still White Bird, the Holy Grail, the Nails, the Scourge, the Thorns, and a piece of the True Cross.

Yours,

Beagle

"Well, what do you think of them?"

Balso awoke and saw Miss McGeeney, the biographer of Samuel Perkins, sitting beside him at the café table.

"Think of what?"

"The two letters you just read," Miss McGeeney said impatiently. "They form part of a novel I'm writing in the manner of Richardson. Give me your candid opinion: do you think the epistolary style too old-fashioned?"

Refreshed by the nap he had taken, Balso examined his interrogator with interest. She was a fine figure of a woman. He wanted to please her and said:

"A stormy wind blows through your pages, sweeping

the reader breathless . . . witchery and madness. Comparable to George Bernard Shaw. It is a drama of passion that has all the appeal of wild living and the open road. Comparable to George Bernard Shaw. There's magic in its pages, and warm strong sympathy for an alien race."

"Thank you," she said with precision.

How gracious is a woman grateful, thought Balso. He felt young again: the heel of a loaf, a piece of cheese, a bottle of wine and an apple. Clear speakers, naked in the sun. Young students: and the days are very full, and the nights burst with excitement, and life is a torrent roaring.

"Oh!" Balso exclaimed, carried away by these memories of his youth. "Oh!" His mouth formed an O with lips torn angry in laying duck's eggs from a chicken's rectum.

"Oh, what?" Miss McGeeney was obviously annoyed.

"Oh, I loved a girl once. All day she did nothing but place bits of meat on the petals of flowers. She choked the rose with butter and cake crumbs, soiling the crispness of its dainty petals with gravy and cheese. She wanted the rose to attract flies, not butterflies or bees. She wanted to make of her garden a . . ."

"Balso! Balso! Is it you?" cried Miss McGeeney, spilling what was left of his beer, much to the disgust of the waiter who hovered near.

"Balso! Balso! Is it you?" she cried again before he could answer. "Don't you recognize me? I'm Mary. Mary McGeeney, your old sweetheart."

Balso realized that she was indeed Mary. Changed, alas! but with much of the old Mary left, particularly about the eyes. No longer was she dry and stick-like, but a woman, warmly moist.

They sat and devoured each other with looks until the waiter suggested that they leave as he wanted to close the place and go home.

They left arm-in-arm, walking as in a dream. Balso did

the steering and they soon found themselves behind a thick clump of bushes. Miss McGeeney lay down on her back with her hands behind her head and her knees wide apart. Balso stood over her and began a speech the intent of which was obvious.

"First," he said, "let us consider the political aspect. You who talk of Liberty and cling to the protection of Dogma in the face of Life and the Army of Unutterable Physical Law, cast, I say, cast free the anchors, let go the moorings of your desires! Let to the breezes flap the standard of your revolt!

"Also we must consider the philosophical aspects of the proposed act. Nature has lent you for a brief time a few organs capable of giving pleasure. Among these are to be listed the sexual ones. The organs of sex offer in reward for their intelligent use a very intense type of pleasure. Pleasure, it is necessary to admit, is the only good. It is only reasonable to say that if pleasure is desirable—and who besides a few fanatics say it is not?—one should get all the pleasure possible. First it is important to dissociate certain commonplace ideas. As a thinking person, as an individualist—and you are both of these, are you not, love?—it is necessary to dissociate the idea of pleasure from that of generation. Furthermore, it is necessary to disregard one's unreasonable moral training. Sex, not marriage, is a sacrament. You admit it? Then why allow an ancient, inherited code to foist on you, a thinking being, the old, outmoded strictures? Sexual acts are not sins, errors, faults, weaknesses. The sexual acts give pleasure, and pleasure is desirable. So come, Mary, let us have some fun.

"And for the sake of Art, Mary. You desire to write, do you not, love? And you must admit that without knowing what all the shooting is about, a sincere artist is badly handicapped. How can you portray men if you have never known a man? How can you read and understand, see and understand, without ever having known the divine excitement? How can you hope to motivate a theft, a murder, a rape, a suicide, convincingly? And are you ever out of themes? In my bed, love, you will find new themes, new interpretations, new experiences. You will be able to judge for yourself whether love is only three minutes of rapture followed by a feeling of profound disgust, or the all-consuming fire, the divine principle, a foretaste of the joys of heaven? Come, Mary McGeeney, to bed and a new world.

"And now, finally, we come to the Time-argument. Do not confuse what I shall say under this head with the theories so much in vogue among the metaphysicians and physicists, those weavers of the wind. My 'Time' is that of the poets. In a little while, love, you will be dead; that is my burden. In a little while, we all will be dead. Golden lads and chimney-sweeps, all dead. And when dying, will you be able to say, I turn down an empty glass, having drunk to the full, lived to the full? Is it not madness to deny life? Hurry! Hurry! for all is soon over. Blown, O rose! in the morning, thou shalt fade ere noon. Do you realize the tune the clock is playing? The seconds, how they fly! All is soon over! All is soon over! Let us snatch, while yet we may, in this brief span, whose briefness merely gilds the bubble so soon destroyed, some few delights. Have you thought of the grave? O love! have you thought of the grave and of the change that shall come over your fair body? Your most beautiful bride—though now she be pleasant and sweet to the nose—will be damnably mouldy a hundred years hence. O how small a part of time they share, that are so wonderous sweet and fair. Ah, make the most of what we yet may spend before we too into the dust descend. Into the dust, Mary! Thy sweet plenty, in the dust. I tremble, I burn for thy sweet

embrace. Be not miserly with thy white flesh. Give your
gracious body, for such a short time lent you. Give, for in
the giving you shall receive and still have what you give.
Only time can rob you of your flesh, I cannot. And time
will rob you—it will, it will! And those who husbanded the
golden grain, and those who flung it to the wind like
rain . . ."

Here Balso threw himself to the ground beside his
beloved.

How did she receive him? At first, by saying no.

No. No! Innocent, confused. Oh Balso! Oh Balso! with
pictures of the old farm house, old pump, old folks at
home, and the old oaken bucket—ivy over all.

Sir! Stamping her tiny foot—imperative, irate. Sir, how
dare you, sir! Do you presume? Down, Rover, I say down!
The prying thumbs of insolent chauffeurs. The queen
chooses. Elizabeth of England, Catherine of Russia, Faus-
tina of Rome.

These two noes graded into two yes-and-noes.

No . . . Oh . . . Oh, no. Eyes aswim with tears. Voice
throaty, husky with repressed passion. Oh, how sweet,
sweetheart, sweetheart, sweetheart. Oh, I'm melting. My
very bones are liquid. I'll swoon if you don't leave me
alone. Leave me alone, I'm dizzy. No . . . No! You beast!

No: No, Balso, not tonight. No, not tonight. No! I'm
sorry, Balso, but not tonight. Some other time, perhaps
yes, but not tonight. Please be a dear, not tonight. Please!

But Balso would not take no for an answer, and he soon
obtained the following yeses:

Allowing hot breath to escape from between moist, open
lips: eyes upset, murmurs love. Tiger skin on divan. Spanish shawl on grand piano. Altar of Love. Church and
Brothel. Odors of Ind and Afric. There's Egypt in your eyes.
Rich, opulent love; beautiful, tapestried love; oriental,
perfumed love.

Hard-bitten. Casual. Smart. Been there before. I've had policemen. No trace of a feminine whimper. Decidedly revisiting well-known, well-plowed ground. No new trees, wells, or even fences.

Desperate for life. Live! Experience! Live one's own. Your body is an instrument, an organ or a drum. Harmony. Order. Breasts. The apple of my eye, the pear of my abdomen. What is life without love? I burn! I ache! Hurrah!

Moooompitcher yaaaah. Oh I never hoped to know the passion, the sensuality hidden within you—yes, yes. Drag me down into the mire, drag. Yes! And with your hair the lust from my eyes brush. Yes . . . Yes . . . Ooh! Ah!

The miracle was made manifest. The Two became One. The One that is all things and yet no one of them: the priest and the god, the immolation, the sacrificial rite, the libation offered to ancestors, the incantation, the sacrificial egg, the altar, the ego and the alter ego, as well as the father, the child, and the grandfather of the universe, the mystic doctrine, the purification, the syllable "Om," the path, the master, the witness, the receptacle, the Spirit of Public School 186, the last ferry that leaves for Weehawken at seven.

His body broke free of the bard. It took on a life of its own; a life that knew nothing of the poet Balso. Only to death can this release be likened—to the mechanics of decay. After death the body takes command; it performs the manual of disintegration with a marvelous certainty. So now, his body performed the evolutions of love with a like sureness.

In this activity, Home and Duty, Love and Art, were forgotten.

An army moved in his body, an eager army of hurrying sensations. These sensations marched at first methodically and then hysterically, but always with precision. The army of his body commenced a long intricate drill, a long involved ceremony. A ceremony whose ritual unwound and manoeuvred itself with the confidence and training of chemicals acting under the stimulus of a catalytic agent.

His body screamed and shouted as it marched and uncoiled; then, with one heaving shout of triumph, it fell back quiet.

The army that a moment before had been thundering in his body retreated slowly—victorious, relieved.

1933

Miss Lonelyhearts

Miss Lonelyhearts became the
portrait of a priest of our time
who has a religious experience

TO MAX

Miss Lonelyhearts, help me, help me

The Miss Lonelyhearts of The New York *Post-Dispatch* (Are-you-in-trouble? — Do-you-need-advice? — Write-to-Miss-Lonelyhearts-and-she-will-help-you) sat at his desk and stared at a piece of white cardboard. On it a prayer had been printed by Shrike, the feature editor.

"*Soul of Miss L, glorify me.*
Body of Miss L, nourish me
Blood of Miss L, intoxicate me.

Tears of Miss L, wash me.
Oh good Miss L, excuse my plea,
And hide me in your heart,
And defend me from mine enemies.
Help me, Miss L, help me, help me.
In sæcula sæculorum. Amen."

Although the deadline was less than a quarter of an hour away, he was still working on his leader. He had gone as far as: "Life *is* worth while, for it is full of dreams and peace, gentleness and ecstasy, and faith that burns like a clear white flame on a grim dark altar." But he found it impossible to continue. The letters were no longer funny. He could not go on finding the same joke funny thirty times a day for months on end. And on most days he received more than thirty letters, all of them alike, stamped from the dough of suffering with a heart-shaped cookie knife.

On his desk were piled those he had received this morning. He started through them again, searching for some clue to a sincere answer.

Dear Miss Lonelyhearts—
I am in such pain I dont know what to do sometimes I think I will kill myself my kidneys hurt so much. My husband thinks no woman can be a good catholic and not have children irregardless of the pain. I was married honorable from our church but I never knew what married life meant as I never was told about man and wife. My grandmother never told me and she was the only mother I had but made a big mistake by not telling me as it dont pay to be inocent and is only a big disapointment. I have 7 children in 12 yrs and ever since the last 2 I have been so sick. I was opera-tored on twice and my husband promised no more children on the doctors advice as he said I might die but when I got

back from the hospital he broke his promise and now I am
going to have a baby and I dont think I can stand it my kidneys hurt so much. I am so sick and scared because I cant
have an abortion on account of being a catholic and my husband so religious. I cry all the time it hurts so much and I
dont know what to do.

Yours respectfully,
Sick-of-it-all

Miss Lonelyhearts threw the letter into an open drawer
and lit a cigarette.

Dear Miss Lonelyhearts—
I am sixteen years old now and I dont know what to do
and would appreciate it if you could tell me what to do.
When I was a little girl it was not so bad because I got used
to the kids on the block makeing fun of me, but now I would
like to have boy friends like the other girls and go out on
Saturday nites, but no boy will take me because I was born
without a nose—although I am a good dancer and have a
nice shape and my father buys me pretty clothes.
I sit and look at myself all day and cry. I have a big hole
in the middle of my face that scares people even myself so
I cant blame the boys for not wanting to take me out. My
mother loves me, but she crys terrible when she looks at me.
What did I do to deserve such a terrible bad fate? Even
if I did do some bad things I didnt do any before I was a
year old and I was born this way. I asked Papa and he says
he doesnt know, but that maybe I did something in the other
world before I was born or that maybe I was being punished
for his sins. I dont believe that because he is a very nice
man. Ought I commit suicide?

Sincerely yours,
Desperate

The cigarette was imperfect and refused to draw. Miss Lonelyhearts took it out of his mouth and stared at it furiously. He fought himself quiet, then lit another one.

Dear Miss Lonelyhearts—
I am writing to you for my little sister Gracie because something awfull hapened to her and I am afraid to tell mother about it. I am 15 years old and Gracie is 13 and we live in Brooklyn. Gracie is deaf and dumb and biger than me but not very smart on account of being deaf and dumb. She plays on the roof of our house and dont go to school except to deaf and dumb school twice a week on tuesdays and thursdays. Mother makes her play on the roof because we dont want her to get run over as she aint very smart. Last week a man came on the roof and did something dirty to her. She told me about it and I dont know what to do as I am afraid to tell mother on account of her being liable to beat Gracie up. I am afraid that Gracie is going to have a baby and I listened to her stomack last night for a long time to see if I could hear the baby but I couldn't. If I tell mother she will beat Gracie up awfull because I am the only one who loves her and last time when she tore her dress they loked her in the closet for 2 days and if the boys on the blok hear about it they will say dirty things like they did on Pee-wee Conors sister the time she got caught in the lots. So please what would you do if the same hapened in your family.

Yours truly,
Harold S.

He stopped reading. Christ was the answer, but, if he did not want to get sick, he had to stay away from the Christ business. Besides, Christ was Shrike's particular joke. "Soul of Miss L, glorify me. Body of Miss L, save me. Blood of . . ." He turned to his typewriter.

Although his cheap clothes had too much style, he still looked like the son of a Baptist minister. A beard would become him, would accent his Old-Testament look. But even without a beard no one could fail to recognize the New England puritan. His forehead was high and narrow. His nose was long and fleshless. His bony chin was shaped and cleft like a hoof. On seeing him for the first time, Shrike had smiled and said, "The Susan Chesters, the Beatrice Fairfaxes and the Miss Lonelyhearts are the priests of twentieth-century America."

A copy boy came up to tell him that Shrike wanted to know if the stuff was ready. He bent over the typewriter and began pounding its keys.

But before he had written a dozen words, Shrike leaned over his shoulder. "The same old stuff," Shrike said. "Why don't you give them something new and hopeful? Tell them about art. Here, I'll dictate:

"*Art Is a Way Out.*

"Do not let life overwhelm you. When the old paths are choked with the débris of failure, look for newer and fresher paths. Art is just such a path. Art is distilled from suffering. As Mr. Polnikoff exclaimed through his fine Russian beard, when, at the age of eighty-six, he gave up his business to learn Chinese, 'We are, as yet, only at the beginning. . . .'

"*Art Is One of Life's Richest Offerings.*

"For those who have not the talent to create, there is appreciation. For those . . .

"Go on from there."

Miss Lonelyhearts and the dead pan

When Miss Lonelyhearts quit work, he found that the weather had turned warm and that the air smelt as though it had been artificially heated. He decided to walk to Delehanty's speakeasy for a drink. In order to get there, it was necessary to cross a little park.

[margin handwritten: striking bare imagery · symbolic level]

He entered the park at the North Gate and swallowed mouthfuls of the heavy shade that curtained its arch. He walked into the shadow of a lamp-post that lay on the path like a spear. It pierced him like a spear.

[margin handwritten: waste land imagery]

As far as he could discover, there were no signs of spring. The decay that covered the surface of the mottled ground was not the kind in which life generates. Last year, he remembered, May had failed to quicken these soiled fields. It had taken all the brutality of July to torture a few green spikes through the exhausted dirt.

What the little park needed, even more than he did, was a drink. Neither alcohol nor rain would do. To-morrow, in his column, he would ask Broken-hearted, Sick-of-it-all, Desperate, Disillusioned-with-tubercular-husband and the rest of his correspondents to come here and water the soil with their tears. Flowers would then spring up, flowers that smelled of feet.

"Ah, humanity . . ." But he was heavy with shadow and the joke went into a dying fall. He tried to break its fall by laughing at himself.

Why laugh at himself, however, when Shrike was waiting at the speakeasy to do a much better job? "Miss Lonelyhearts, my friend, I advise you to give your readers stones. When they ask for bread don't give them crackers as does the Church, and don't, like the State, tell them to eat cake. Explain that man cannot live by bread alone and give them stones. Teach them to pray each morning: 'Give us this day our daily stone.'"

He had given his readers many stones; so many, in fact, that he had only one left—the stone that had formed in his gut.

Suddenly tired, he sat down on a bench. If he could only throw the stone. He searched the sky for a target. But the gray sky looked as if it had been rubbed with a soiled eraser. It held no angels, flaming crosses, olive-bearing doves, wheels within wheels. Only a newspaper struggled in the air like a kite with a broken spine. He got up and started again for the speakeasy.

Delehanty's was in the cellar of a brownstone house that differed from its more respectable neighbors by having an armored door. He pressed a concealed button and a little round window opened in its center. A blood-shot eye appeared, glowing like a ruby in an antique iron ring.

The bar was only half full. Miss Lonelyhearts looked around apprehensively for Shrike and was relieved at not finding him. However, after a third drink, just as he was settling into the warm mud of alcoholic gloom, Shrike caught his arm.

"Ah, my young friend!" he shouted. "How do I find you? Brooding again, I take it."

"For Christ's sake, shut up."

Shrike ignored the interruption. "You're morbid, my friend, morbid. Forget the crucifixion, remember the renaissance. There were no brooders then." He raised his glass, and the whole Borgia family was in his gesture. "I give you the renaissance. What a period! What pageantry! Drunken popes . . . Beautiful courtesans . . . Illegitimate children. . . ."

Although his gestures were elaborate, his face was blank. He practiced a trick used much by moving-picture comedians—the dead pan. No matter how fantastic or excited his speech, he never changed his expression. Under the shining white globe of his brow, his features huddled together in a dead, gray triangle.

"To the renaissance!" he kept shouting. "To the renaissance! To the brown Greek manuscripts and mistresses with the great smooth marbly limbs. . . . But that reminds me, I'm expecting one of my admirers—a cow-eyed girl of great intelligence." He illustrated the word *intelligence* by carving two enormous breasts in the air with his hands. "She works in a book store, but wait until you see her behind."

Miss Lonelyhearts made the mistake of showing his annoyance.

"Oh, so you don't care for women, eh? J. C. is your only sweetheart, eh? Jesus Christ, the King of Kings, the Miss Lonelyhearts of Miss Lonelyhearts. . . ."

At this moment, fortunately for Miss Lonelyhearts, the young woman expected by Shrike came up to the bar. She had long legs, thick ankles, big hands, a powerful body, a slender neck and a childish face made tiny by a man's haircut.

"Miss Farkis," Shrike said, making her bow as a ventriloquist does his doll, "Miss Farkis, I want you to meet Miss Lonelyhearts. Show him the same respect you show me. He, too, is a comforter of the poor in spirit and a lover of God."

She acknowledged the introduction with a masculine handshake.

"Miss Farkis," Shrike said, "Miss Farkis works in a book store and writes on the side." He patted her rump.

"What were you talking about so excitedly?" she asked.

"Religion."

"Get me a drink and please continue. I'm very much interested in the new thomistic synthesis."

This was just the kind of remark for which Shrike was waiting. "St. Thomas!" he shouted. "What do you take us for—stinking intellectuals? We're not fake Europeans. We were discussing Christ, the Miss Lonelyhearts of Miss Lonelyhearts. America has her own religions. If you need a synthesis, here is the kind of material to use." He took a clipping from his wallet and slapped it on the bar.

"ADDING MACHINE USED IN RITUAL OF WESTERN SECT . . . *Figures Will be Used for Prayers for Condemned Slayer of Aged Recluse.* . . . DENVER, COLO., Feb. 2 (A. P.) Frank H. Rice, Supreme Pontiff of the Liberal Church of America has announced he will carry out his plan for a 'goat and adding machine' ritual for William Moya, condemned slayer, despite objection to his program by a Cardinal of the sect. Rice declared the goat would be used as part of a 'sack cloth and ashes' service shortly before and after Moya's execution, set for the week of June 20. Prayers for the condemned man's soul will be offered on an adding machine. Numbers, he explained, constitute the only universal language. Moya killed Joseph Zemp, an aged recluse, in an argument over a small amount of money."

Miss Farkis laughed and Shrike raised his fist as though to strike her. His actions shocked the bartender, who hurriedly asked them to go into the back room. Miss Lonelyhearts did not want to go along, but Shrike insisted and he was too tired to argue.

They seated themselves at a table inside one of the booths. Shrike again raised his fist, but when Miss Farkis drew back, he changed the gesture to a caress. The trick worked. She gave in to his hand until he became too daring, then pushed him away.

Shrike again began to shout and this time Miss Lonelyhearts understood that he was making a seduction speech.

"I am a great saint," Shrike cried, "I can walk on my own water. Haven't you ever heard of Shrike's Passion in the Luncheonette, or the Agony in the Soda Fountain? Then I compared the wounds in Christ's body to the mouths of a miraculous purse in which we deposit the small change of our sins. It is indeed an excellent conceit. But now let us consider the holes in our own bodies and into what these congenital wounds open. Under the skin of man is a wondrous jungle where veins like lush tropical growths hang along overripe organs and weed-like entrails writhe in squirming tangles of red and yellow. In this jungle, flitting from rock-gray lungs to golden intestines, from liver to lights and back to liver again, lives a bird called the soul. The Catholic hunts this bird with bread and wine, the Hebrew with a golden ruler, the Protestant on leaden feet with leaden words, the Buddhist with gestures, the Negro with blood. I spit on them all. Phooh! And I call upon you to spit. Phooh! Do you stuff birds? No, my dears, taxidermy is not religion. No! A thousand times no. Better, I say unto you, better a live bird in the jungle of the body than two stuffed birds on the library table."

His caresses kept pace with the sermon. When he had reached the end, he buried his triangular face like the blade of a hatchet in her neck.

Miss Lonelyhearts and the lamb

Miss Lonelyhearts went home in a taxi. He lived by himself in a roon that was as full of shadows as an old steel *monastic*

engraving. It held a bed, a table and two chairs. The walls were bare except for an ivory Christ that hung opposite the foot of the bed. He had removed the figure from the cross to which it had been fastened and had nailed it to the wall with large spikes. But the desired effect had not been obtained. Instead of writhing, the Christ remained calmly decorative.

He got undressed immediately and took a cigarette and a copy of *The Brothers Karamazov* to bed. The marker was in a chapter devoted to Father Zossima.

"Love a man even in his sin, for that is the semblance of Divine Love and is the highest love on earth. Love all God's creation, the whole and every grain of sand in it. Love the animals, love the plants, love everything. If you love everything, you will perceive the divine mystery in things. Once you perceive it, you will begin to comprehend it better every day. And you will come at last to love the whole world with an all-embracing love."

It was excellent advice. If he followed it, he would be a big success. His column would be syndicated and the whole world would learn to love. The Kingdom of Heaven would arrive. He would sit on the right hand of the Lamb.

But seriously, he realized, even if Shrike had not made a sane view of this Christ business impossible, there would be little use in his fooling himself. His vocation was of a different sort. As a boy in his father's church, he had discovered that something stirred in him when he shouted the name of Christ, something secret and enormously powerful. He had played with this thing, but had never allowed it to come alive.

He knew now what this thing was—hysteria, a snake whose scales are tiny mirrors in which the dead world takes on a semblance of life. And how dead the world is . . . a world of doorknobs. He wondered if hysteria were really too steep a price to pay for bringing it to life.

Repressed Conflict religious + Sexual

For him, Christ was the most natural of excitements.
Fixing his eyes on the image that hung on the wall, he
began to chant: "Christ, Christ, Jesus Christ. Christ, Christ,
Jesus Christ." But the moment the snake started to uncoil
in his brain, he became frightened and closed his eyes.

With sleep, a dream came in which he found himself on
the stage of a crowded theater. He was a magician who did
tricks with doorknobs. At his command, they bled, flowered, spoke. After his act was finished, he tried to lead his
audience in prayer. But no matter how hard he struggled,
his prayer was one Shrike had taught him and his voice
was that of a conductor calling stations.

"Oh, Lord, we are not of those who wash in wine, water,
urine, vinegar, fire, oil, bay rum, milk, brandy, or boric
acid. Oh, Lord, we are of those who wash solely in the
Blood of the Lamb."

The scene of the dream changed. He found himself in
his college dormitory. With him were Steve Garvey and
Jud Hume. They had been arguing the existence of God
from midnight until dawn, and now, having run out of
whisky, they decided to go to the market for some applejack.

Their way led through the streets of the sleeping town
into the open fields beyond. It was spring. The sun and
the smell of vegetable birth renewed their drunkenness and
they reeled between the loaded carts. The farmers took
their horseplay good-naturedly. Boys from the college on
a spree.

They found the bootlegger and bought a gallon jug of
applejack, then wandered to the section where livestock
was sold. They stopped to fool with some lambs. Jud
suggested buying one to roast over a fire in the woods.
Miss Loneyhearts agreed, but on the condition that they
sacrifice it to God before barbecuing it.

Steve was sent to the cutlery stand for a butcher knife,

while the other two remained to bargain for a lamb. After a long, Armenian-like argument, during which Jud exhibited his farm training, the youngest was selected, a little, stiff-legged thing, all head.

They paraded the lamb through the market. Miss Lonelyhearts went first, carrying the knife, the others followed, Steve with the jug and Jud with the animal. As they marched, they sang an obscene version of "Mary Had a Little Lamb."

Between the market and the hill on which they intended to perform the sacrifice was a meadow. While going through it, they picked daisies and buttercups. Halfway up the hill, they found a rock and covered it with the flowers. They laid the lamb among the flowers. Miss Lonelyhearts was elected priest, with Steve and Jud as his attendants. While they held the lamb, Miss Lonelyhearts crouched over it and began to chant.

"Christ, Christ, Jesus Christ. Christ, Christ, Jesus Christ."

When they had worked themselves into a frenzy, he brought the knife down hard. The blow was inaccurate and made a flesh wound. He raised the knife again and this time the lamb's violent struggles made him miss altogether. The knife broke on the altar. Steve and Jud pulled the animal's head back for him to saw at its throat, but only a small piece of blade remained in the handle and he was unable to cut through the matted wool.

Their hands were covered with slimy blood and the lamb slipped free. It crawled off into the underbrush.

As the bright sun outlined the altar rock with narrow shadows, the scene appeared to gather itself for some new violence. They bolted. Down the hill they fled until they reached the meadow, where they fell exhausted in the tall grass.

After some time had passed, Miss Lonelyhearts begged them to go back and put the lamb out of its misery. They

refused to go. He went back alone and found it under a
bush. He crushed its head with a stone and left the carcass
to the flies that swarmed around the bloody altar flowers.

Miss Lonelyhearts and the fat thumb

Miss Lonelyhearts found himself developing an almost insane sensitiveness to order. Everything had to form a
pattern: the shoes under the bed, the ties in the holder, the
pencils on the table. When he looked out of a window, he
composed the skyline by balancing one building against
another. If a bird flew across this arrangement, he closed
his eyes angrily until it was gone.

For a little while, he seemed to hold his own but one
day he found himself with his back to the wall. On that
day all the inanimate things over which he had tried to
obtain control took the field against him. When he touched
something, it spilled or rolled to the floor. The collar
buttons disappeared under the bed, the point of the
pencil broke, the handle of the razor fell off, the window
shade refused to stay down. He fought back, but with too
much violence, and was decisively defeated by the spring
of the alarm clock.

He fled to the street, but there chaos was multiple.
Broken groups of people hurried past, forming neither
stars nor squares. The lamp-posts were badly spaced and
the flagging was of different sizes. Nor could he do anything with the harsh clanging sound of street cars and the
raw shouts of hucksters. No repeated group of words

would fit their rhythm and no scale could give them meaning.

He stood quietly against a wall, trying not to see or hear. Then he remembered Betty. She had often made him feel that when she straightened his tie, she straightened much more. And he had once thought that if her world were larger, were *the* world, she might order it as finally as the objects on her dressing table.

He gave Betty's address to a cab driver and told him to hurry. But she lived on the other side of the city and by the time he got there, his panic had turned to irritation.

She came to the door of her apartment in a crisp, white linen dressing-robe that yellowed into brown at the edges. She held out both her hands to him and her arms showed round and smooth like wood that has been turned by the sea.

With the return of self-consciousness, he knew that only violence could make him supple. It was Betty, however, that he criticized. Her world was not the world and could never include the readers of his column. Her sureness was based on the power to limit experience arbitrarily. Moreover, his confusion was significant, while her order was not.

He tried to reply to her greeting and discovered that his tongue had become a fat thumb. To avoid talking, he awkwardly forced a kiss, then found it necessary to apologize.

"Too much lover's return business, I know, and I . . ." He stumbled purposely, so that she would take his confusion for honest feeling. But the trick failed and she waited for him to continue:

"Please eat dinner with me."

"I'm afraid I can't."

Her smile opened into a laugh.

She was laughing at him. On the defense, he examined

her laugh for "bitterness," "sour-grapes," "a-broken-heart,"
"the devil-may-care." But to his confusion, he found nothing at which to laugh back. Her smile had opened naturally, not like an umbrella, and while he watched her
laugh folded and became a smile again, a smile that was
neither "wry," "ironical" nor "mysterious."

As they moved into the living-room, his irritation increased. She sat down on a studio couch with her bare legs
under and her back straight. Behind her a silver tree
flowered in the lemon wall-paper. He remained standing.

"Betty the Buddha," he said. "Betty the Buddha. You
have the smug smile; all you need is the pot belly."

His voice was so full of hatred that he himself was
surprised. He fidgeted for a while in silence. and finally
sat down beside her on the couch to take her hand.

More than two months had passed since he had sat with
her on this same couch and had asked her to marry him.
Then she had accepted him and they had planned their
life after marriage, his job and her gingham apron, his
slippers beside the fireplace and her ability to cook. He
had avoided her since. He did not feel guilty; he was
merely annoyed at having been fooled into thinking that
such a solution was possible.

He soon grew tired of holding hands and began to
fidget again. He remembered that towards the end of his
last visit he had put his hand inside her clothes. Unable
to think of anything else to do, he now repeated the
gesture. She was naked under her robe and he found her
breast.

She made no sign to show that she was aware of his
hand. He would have welcomed a slap, but even when
he caught at her nipple, she remained silent.

"Let me pluck this rose," he said, giving a sharp tug.
"I want to wear it in my buttonhole."

Betty reached for his brow. "What's the matter?" she asked. "Are you sick?"

He began to shout at her, accompanying his shouts with gestures that were too appropriate, like those of an old-fashioned actor.

"What a kind bitch you are. As soon as any one acts viciously, you say he's sick. Wife-torturers, rapers of small children, according to you they're all sick. No morality, only medicine. Well, I'm not sick. I don't need any of your damned aspirin. I've got a Christ complex. Humanity . . . I'm a humanity lover. All the broken bastards . . ." He finished with a short laugh that was like a bark.

intellectual not emotional

She had left the couch for a red chair that was swollen with padding and tense with live springs. In the lap of this leather monster, all trace of the serene Buddha disappeared.

But his anger was not appeased. "What's the matter, sweetheart?" he asked, patting her shoulder threateningly. "Didn't you like the performance?"

Instead of answering, she raised her arm as though to ward off a blow. She was like a kitten whose soft helplessness makes one ache to hurt it.

"What's the matter?" he demanded over and over again. "What's the matter? What's the matter?"

Her face took on the expression of an inexperienced gambler about to venture all on a last throw. He was turning for his hat, when she spoke.

"I love you."

"You what?"

The need for repeating flustered her, yet she managed to keep her manner undramatic.

"I love you."

"And I love you," he said. "You and your damned smiling through tears."

"Why don't you let me alone?" She had begun to cry. "I felt swell before you came, and now I feel lousy. Go away. Please go away."

Miss Lonelyhearts and the clean old man

In the street again, Miss Lonelyhearts wondered what to do next. He was too excited to eat and afraid to go home. He felt as though his heart were a bomb, a complicated bomb that would result in a simple explosion, wrecking the world without rocking it.

He decided to go to Delehanty's for a drink. In the speakeasy, he discovered a group of his friends at the bar. They greeted him and went on talking. One of them was complaining about the number of female writers.

"And they've all got three names," he said. "Mary Roberts Wilcox, Ella Wheeler Catheter, Ford Mary Rinehart. . . ."

Then some one started a train of stories by suggesting that what they all needed was a good rape.

"I knew a gal who was regular until she fell in with a group and went literary. She began writing for the little magazines about how much Beauty hurt her and ditched the boy friend who set up pins in a bowling alley. The guys on the block got sore and took her into the lots one night. About eight of them. They ganged her proper. . . ."

"That's like the one they tell about another female writer. When this hard-boiled stuff first came in, she dropped the trick English accent and went in for scram and lam. She got to hanging around with a lot of mugs in a speak, gathering material for a novel. Well, the mugs didn't know they were picturesque and thought she was regular until the barkeep put them wise. They got her into the back room to teach her a new word and put the boots to her. They didn't let her out for three days. On the last day they sold tickets to niggers. . . ."

Miss Lonelyhearts stopped listening. His friends would go on telling these stories until they were too drunk to talk. They were aware of their childishness, but did not know how else to revenge themselves. At college, and perhaps for a year afterwards, they had believed in literature, had believed in Beauty and in personal expression as an absolute end. When they lost this belief, they lost everything. Money and fame meant nothing to them. They were not worldly men.

Miss Lonelyhearts drank steadily. He was smiling an innocent, amused smile, the smile of an anarchist sitting in the movies with a bomb in his pocket. If the people around him only knew what was in his pocket. In a little while he would leave to kill the President.

Not until he heard his own name mentioned did he stop smiling and again begin to listen.

"He's a leper licker. Shrike says he wants to lick lepers. Barkeep, a leper for the gent."

"If you haven't got a leper, give him a Hungarian."

"Well, that's the trouble with his approach to God. It's too damn literary—plain song, Latin poetry, medieval painting, Huysmans, stained-glass windows and crap like that."

"Even if he were to have a genuine religious experience, it would be personal and so meaningless, except to a psychologist."

"The trouble with him, the trouble with all of us, is that we have no outer life, only an inner one, and that by necessity."

"He's an escapist. He wants to cultivate his interior garden. But you can't escape, and where is he going to find a market for the fruits of his personality? The Farm Board is a failure."

"What I say is, after all one has to earn a living. We can't all believe in Christ, and what does the farmer care about art? He takes his shoes off to get the warm feel of the rich earth between his toes. You can't take your shoes off in church."

Miss Lonelyhearts had again begun to smile. Like Shrike, the man they imitated, they were machines for making jokes. A button machine makes buttons, no matter what the power used, foot, steam or electricity. They, no matter what the motivating force, death, love or God, made jokes.

"Was their nonsense the only barrier?" he asked himself. "Had he been thwarted by such a low hurdle?"

The whisky was good and he felt warm and sure. Through the light-blue tobacco smoke, the mahogany bar shone like wet gold. The glasses and bottles, their high lights exploding, rang like a battery of little bells when the bartender touched them together. He forgot that his heart was a bomb to remember an incident of his childhood. One winter evening, he had been waiting with his little sister for their father to come home from church. She was eight years old then, and he was twelve. Made sad by the pause between playing and eating, he had gone to the piano and had begun a piece by Mozart. It was the first time he had ever voluntarily gone to the piano. His sister left her picture book to dance to his music. She had never danced before. She danced gravely and carefully, a simple dance yet formal. . . . As Miss Lonelyhearts stood at the bar, swaying slightly to the remembered music, he thought of children dancing. Square replacing oblong and being replaced by circle. Every child, everywhere; in the whole world there was not one child who was not gravely, sweetly dancing.

He stepped away from the bar and accidentally collided with a man holding a glass of beer. When he turned to beg the man's pardon, he received a punch in the mouth. Later he found himself at a table in the back room, playing with a loose tooth. He wondered why his hat did not fit and discovered a lump on the back of his head. He must have fallen. The hurdle was higher than he had thought.

His anger swung in large drunken circles. What in Christ's name was this Christ business? And children gravely dancing? He would ask Shrike to be transferred to the sports department.

Ned Gates came in to see how he was getting along and suggested the fresh air. Gates was also very drunk. When they left the speakeasy together, they found that it was snowing.

Miss Lonelyhearts' anger grew cold and sodden like the snow. He and his companion staggered along with their heads down, turning corners at random, until they found themselves in front of the little park. A light was burning in the comfort station and they went in to warm up.

An old man was sitting on one of the toilets. The door of his booth was propped open and he was sitting on the turned-down toilet cover.

Gates hailed him. "Well, well, smug as a bug in a rug, eh?"

The old man jumped with fright, but finally managed to speak. "What do you want? Please let me alone." His voice was like a flute; it did not vibrate.

"If you can't get a woman, get a clean old man," Gates sang.

The old man looked as if he were going to cry, but

suddenly laughed instead. A terrible cough started under his laugh, and catching at the bottom of his lungs, it ripped into his throat. He turned away to wipe his mouth.

Miss Lonelyhearts tried to get Gates to leave, but he refused to go without the old man. They both grabbed him and pulled him out of the stall and through the door of the comfort station. He went soft in their arms and started to giggle. Miss Lonelyhearts fought off a desire to hit him.

The snow had stopped falling and it had grown very cold. The old man did not have an overcoat, but said that he found the cold exhilarating. He carried a cane and wore gloves because, as he said, he detested red hands.

Instead of going back to Delehanty's they went to an Italian cellar close by the park. The old man tried to get them to drink coffee, but they told him to mind his own business and drank rye. The whisky burned Miss Lonelyhearts' cut lip.

Gates was annoyed by the old man's elaborate manners. "Listen, you," he said, "cut our the gentlemanly stuff and tell us the story of your life."

The old man drew himself up like a little girl making a muscle.

"Aw, come off," Gates said. "We're scientists. He's Havelock Ellis and I'm Krafft-Ebing. When did you first discover homosexualistic tendencies in yourself?"

"What do you mean, sir? I . . ."

"Yeh, I know, but how about your difference from other men?"

"How dare you . . ." He gave a little scream of indignation.

"Now, now," Miss Lonelyhearts said, "he didn't mean to insult you. Scientists have terribly bad manners. . . . But you are a pervert, aren't you?"

The old man raised his cane to strike him. Gates

grabbed it from behind and wrenched it out of his hand. He began to cough violently and held his black satin tie to his mouth. Still coughing he dragged himself to a chair in the back of the room.

Miss Lonelyhearts felt as he had felt years before, when he had accidentally stepped on a small frog. Its spilled guts had filled him with pity, but when its suffering had become real to his senses, his pity had turned to rage and he had beaten it frantically until it was dead.

"I'll get the bastard's life story," he shouted, and started after him. Gates followed laughing.

At their approach, the old man jumped to his feet. Miss Lonelyhearts caught him and forced him back into his chair.

"We're psychologists," he said. "We want to help you. What's your name?"

"George B. Simpson."

"What does the B stand for?"

"Bramhall."

"Your age, please, and the nature of your quest?"

"By what right do you ask?"

"Science gives me the right."

"Let's drop it," Gates said. "The old fag is going to cry."

"No, Krafft-Ebing, sentiment must never be permitted to interfere with the probings of science."

Miss Lonelyhearts put his arm around the old man. "Tell us the story of your life," he said, loading his voice with sympathy.

"I have no story."

"You must have. Every one has a life story."

The old man began to sob.

"Yes, I know, your tale is a sad one. Tell it, damn you, tell it."

When the old man still remained silent, he took his arm and twisted it. Gates tried to tear him away, but he refused to let go. He was twisting the arm of all the sick and miserable, broken and betrayed, inarticulate and impotent. He was twisting the arm of Desperate, Brokenhearted, Sick-of-it-all, Disillusioned-with-tubercular-husband.

The old man began to scream. Somebody hit Miss Lonelyhearts from behind with a chair.

Miss Lonelyhearts and Mrs. Shrike

Miss Lonelyhearts lay on his bed fully dressed, just as he had been dumped the night before. His head ached and his thoughts revolved inside the pain like a wheel within a wheel. When he opened his eyes, the room, like a third wheel, revolved around the pain in his head.

From where he lay he could see the alarm clock. It was half past three. When the telephone rang, he crawled out of the sour pile of bed clothes. Shrike wanted to know if he intended to show up at the office. He answered that he was drunk but would try to get there.

He undressed slowly and took a bath. The hot water made his body feel good, but his heart remained a congealed lump of icy fat. After drying himself, he found a little whisky in the medicine chest and drank it. The alcohol warmed only the lining of his stomach.

He shaved, put on a clean shirt and a freshly pressed suit and went out to get something to eat. When he had finished his second cup of scalding coffee, it was too late for him to go to work. But he had nothing to worry about, for Shrike would never fire him. He made too perfect a butt for Shrike's jokes. Once he had tried to get fired by recommending suicide in his column. All that Shrike had said was: "Remember, please, that your job is to increase the circulation of our paper. Suicide, it is only reasonable to think, must defeat this purpose."

He paid for his breakfast and left the cafeteria. Some exercise might warm him. He decided to take a brisk walk, but he soon grew tired and when he reached the little park, he slumped down on a bench opposite the Mexican War obelisk.

The stone shaft cast a long, rigid shadow on the walk in front of him. He sat staring at it without knowing why until he noticed that it was lengthening in rapid jerks, not as shadows usually lengthen. He grew frightened and looked up quickly at the monument. It seemed red and swollen in the dying sun, as though it were about to spout a load of granite seed.

He hurried away. When he had regained the street, he started to laugh. Although he had tried hot water, whisky, coffee, exercise, he had completely forgotten sex. What he really needed was a woman. He laughed again, remembering that at college all his friends had believed intercourse capable of steadying the nerves, relaxing the muscles and clearing the blood.

But he knew only two women who would tolerate him. He had spoiled his chances with Betty, so it would have to be Mary Shrike.

When he kissed Shrike's wife, he felt less like a joke. She returned his kisses because she hated Shrike. But even there Shrike had beaten him. No matter how hard he begged her to give Shrike horns, she refused to sleep with him.

Although Mary always grunted and upset her eyes, she would not associate what she felt with the sexual act. When he forced this association, she became very angry.

He had been convinced that her grunts were genuine by the change that took place in her when he kissed her heavily. Then her body gave off an odor that enriched the synthetic flower scent she used behind her ears and in the hollows of her neck. No similar change ever took place in his own body, however. Like a dead man, only friction could make him warm or violence make him mobile.

He decided to get a few drinks and then call Mary from Delehanty's. It was quite early and the speakeasy was empty. The bartender served him and went back to his newspaper.

On the mirror behind the bar hung a poster advertising a mineral water. It showed a naked girl made modest by the mist that rose from the spring at her feet. The artist had taken a great deal of care in drawing her breasts and their nipples stuck out like tiny red hats.

He tried to excite himself into eagerness by thinking of the play Mary made with her breasts. She used them as the coquettes of long ago had used their fans. One of her tricks was to wear a medal low down on her chest. Whenever he asked to see it, instead of drawing it out she leaned over for him to look. Although he had often asked to see the medal, he had not yet found out what it represented.

But the excitement refused to come. If anything, he felt colder than before he had started to think of women. It was not his line. Nevertheless, he persisted in it, out of desperation, and went to the telephone to call Mary.

"Is that you?" she asked, then added before he could reply, "I must see you at once. I've quarreled with him. This time I'm through."

She always talked in headlines and her excitement forced him to be casual. "O. K.," he said. "When? Where?"

"Anywhere, I'm through with that skunk, I tell you, I'm through."

She had quarreled with Shrike before and he knew that in return for an ordinary number of kisses, he would have to listen to an extraordinary amount of complaining.

"Do you want to meet me here, in Delehanty's?" he asked.

"No, you come here. We'll be alone and anyway I have to bathe and get dressed."

When he arrived at her place, he would probably find Shrike there with her on his lap. They would both be glad to see him and all three of them would go to the movies where Mary would hold his hand under the seat.

He went back to the bar for another drink, then bought a quart of Scotch and took a cab. Shrike opened the door. Although he had expected to see him, he was embarrassed and tried to cover his confusion by making believe that he was extremely drunk.

"Come in, come in, homebreaker," Shrike said with a laugh. "The Mrs. will be out in a few minutes. She's in the tub."

Shrike took the bottle he was carrying and pulled its cork. Then he got some charged water and made two high-balls.

"Well," Shrike said, lifting his drink, "so you're going in for this kind of stuff, eh? Whisky and the boss's wife."

Miss Lonelyhearts always found it impossible to reply to him. The answers he wanted to make were too general and began too far back in the history of their relationship.

"You're doing field work, I take it," Shrike said. "Well, don't put this whisky on your expense account. However, we like to see a young man with his heart in his work. You've been going around with yours in your mouth."

Miss Lonelyhearts made a desperate attempt to kid back. "And you," he said, "you're an old meanie who beats his wife."

Shrike laughed, but too long and too loudly, then broke off with an elaborate sigh. "Ah, my lad," he said, "you're wrong. It's Mary who does the beating."

He took a long pull at his highball and sighed again, still more elaborately. "My good friend, I want to have a heart-to-heart talk with you. I adore heart-to-heart talks and nowadays there are so few people with whom one can really talk. Everybody is so hard-boiled. I want to make a clean breast of matters, a nice clean breast. It's better to make a clean breast of matters than to let them fester in the depths of one's soul."

While talking, he kept his face alive with little nods and winks that were evidently supposed to inspire confidence and to prove him a very simple fellow.

"My good friend, your accusation hurts me to the quick. You spiritual lovers think that you alone suffer. But you are mistaken. Although my love is of the flesh flashy, I too suffer. It's suffering that drives me into the arms of the Miss Farkises of this world. Yes, I suffer."

Here the dead pan broke and pain actually crept into his voice. "She's selfish. She's a damned selfish bitch. She was a virgin when I married her and has been fighting ever since to remain one. Sleeping with her is like sleeping with a knife in one's groin."

It was Miss Lonelyhearts' turn to laugh. He put his face close to Shrike's and laughed as hard as he could.

Shrike tried to ignore him by finishing as though the whole thing were a joke.

"She claims that I raped her. Can you imagine Willie Shrike, wee Willie Shrike, raping any one? I'm like you, one of those grateful lovers."

Mary came into the room in her bathrobe. She leaned over Miss Lonelyhearts and said: "Don't talk to that pig. Come with me and bring the whisky."

As he followed her into the bedroom, he heard Shrike

slam the front door. She went into a large closet to dress. He sat on the bed.

"What did that swine say to you?"

"He said you were selfish, Mary—sexually selfish."

"Of all the god-damned nerve. Do you know why he lets me go out with other men? To save money. He knows that I let them neck me and when I get home all hot and bothered, why he climbs into my bed and begs for it. The cheap bastard!"

She came out of the closet wearing a black lace slip and began to fix her hair in front of the dressing table. Miss Lonelyhearts bent down to kiss the back of her neck.

"Now, now," she said, acting kittenish, "you'll muss me."

He took a drink from the whisky bottle, then made her a highball. When he brought it to her, she gave him a kiss, a little peck of reward.

"Where'll we eat?" she asked. "Let's go where we can dance. I want to be gay."

They took a cab to a place called El Gaucho. When they entered, the orchestra was playing a Cuban rhumba. A waiter dressed as a South-American cowboy led them to a table. Mary immediately went Spanish and her movements became languorous and full of abandon.

But the romantic atmosphere only heightened his feeling of icy fatness. He tried to fight it by telling himself that it was childish. What had happened to his great understanding heart? Guitars, bright shawls, exotic foods, outlandish costumes—all these things were part of the business of dreams. He had learned not to laugh at the advertisements offering to teach writing, cartooning, engineering, to add inches to the biceps and to develop the bust. He should therefore realize that the people who came to El Gaucho were the same as those who wanted to write and live the life of an artist, wanted to be an engineer and wear leather puttees, wanted to develop a grip that would impress the boss, wanted to cushion Raoul's head on their swollen breasts. They were the same people as those who wrote to Miss Lonelyhearts for help.

But his irritation was too profound for him to soothe it in this way. For the time being, dreams left him cold, no matter how humble they were.

"I like this place," Mary said. "It's a little fakey, I know, but it's gay and I so want to be gay."

She thanked him by offering herself in a series of formal, impersonal gestures. She was wearing a tight, shiny dress that was like glass-covered steel and there was something cleanly mechanical in her pantomime.

"Why do you want to be gay?"

"Every one wants to be gay—unless they're sick."

Was he sick? In a great cold wave, the readers of his column crashed over the music, over the bright shawls and picturesque waiters, over her shining body. To save himself, he asked to see the medal. Like a little girl helping an old man to cross the street, she leaned over for him to look into the neck of her dress. But before he had a chance to see anything, a waiter came up to the table.

"The way to be gay is to make other people gay," Miss Lonelyhearts said. "Sleep with me and I'll be one gay dog."

The defeat in his voice made it easy for her to ignore his request and her mind sagged with his. "I've had a tough time," she said. "From the beginning, I've had a tough time. When I was a child, I saw my mother die. She had cancer of the breast and the pain was terrible. She died leaning over a table."

"Sleep with me," he said.

"No, let's dance."

"I don't want to. Tell me about your mother."

"She died leaning over a table. The pain was so terrible that she climbed out of bed to die."

Mary leaned over to show how her mother had died and

he made another attempt to see the medal. He saw that there was a runner on it, but was unable to read the inscription.

"My father was very cruel to her," she continued. "He was a portrait painter, a man of genius, but . . ."

He stopped listening and tried to bring his great understanding heart into action again. Parents are also part of the business of dreams. My father was a Russian prince, my father was a Piute Indian chief, my father was an Australian sheep baron, my father lost all his money in Wall Street, my father was a portrait painter. People like Mary were unable to do without such tales. They told them because they wanted to talk about something besides clothing or business or the movies, because they wanted to talk about something poetic.

When she had finished her story, he said, "You poor kid," and leaned over for another look at the medal. She bent to help him and pulled out the neck of her dress with her fingers. This time he was able to read the inscription: "Awarded by the Boston Latin School for first place in the 100 yd. dash."

It was a small victory, yet it greatly increased his fatigue and he was glad when she suggested leaving. In the cab, he again begged her to sleep with him. She refused. He kneaded her body like a sculptor grown angry with his clay, but there was too much method in his caresses and they both remained cold.

At the door of her apartment, she turned for a kiss and pressed against him. A spark flared up in his groin. He refused to let go and tried to work this spark into a flame. She pushed his mouth away from a long wet kiss.

"Listen to me," she said. "We can't stop talking. We must talk. Willie probably heard the elevator and is listening behind the door. You don't know him. If he doesn't hear us talk, he'll know you're kissing me and open the door. It's an old trick of his."

He held her close and tried desperately to keep the spark alive.

"Don't kiss my lips," she begged. "I must talk."

He kissed her throat, then opened her dress and kissed her breasts. She was afraid to resist or to stop talking.

"My mother died of cancer of the breast," she said in a brave voice, like a little girl reciting at a party. "She died leaning over a table. My father was a portrait painter. He led a very gay life. He mistreated my mother. She had cancer of the breast. She . . ." He tore at her clothes and she began to mumble and repeat herself. Her dress fell to her feet and he tore away her underwear until she was naked under her fur coat. He tried to drag her to the floor.

"Please, please," she begged, "he'll come out and find us." He stopped her mouth with a long kiss.

"Let me go, honey," she pleaded, "maybe he's not home. If he isn't, I'll let you in."

He released her. She opened the door and tiptoed in, carrying her rolled up clothes under her coat. He heard her switch on the light in the foyer and knew that Shrike had not been behind the door. Then he heard footsteps and limped behind a projection of the elevator shaft. The door opened and Shrike looked into the corridor. He had on only the top of his pajamas.

Miss Lonelyhearts on a field trip

It was cold and damp in the city room the next day, and Miss Lonelyhearts sat at his desk with his hands in his pockets and his legs pressed together. A desert, he was thinking, not of sand, but of rust and body dirt, surrounded by a back-yard fence on which are posters describing the events of the day. Mother slays five with ax, slays seven, slays nine. . . . Babe slams two, slams three. . . . Inside the fence Desperate, Broken-hearted, Disillusioned-with-tubercular-husband and the rest were gravely forming the letters MISS LONELYHEARTS out of white-washed clam shells, as if decorating the lawn of a rural depot.

He failed to notice Goldsmith's waddling approach until a heavy arm dropped on his neck like the arm of a deadfall. He freed himself with a grunt. His anger amused Goldsmith, who smiled, bunching his fat cheeks like twin rolls of smooth pink toilet paper.

"Well, how's the drunkard?" Goldsmith asked, imitating Shrike.

Miss Lonelyhearts knew that Goldsmith had written the column for him yesterday, so he hid his annoyance to be grateful.

"No trouble at all," Goldsmith said. "It was a pleasure to read your mail." He took a pink envelope out of his pocket and threw it on the desk "From an admirer." He winked, letting a thick gray lid down slowly and luxuriously over a moist, rolling eye.

Miss Lonelyhearts picked up the letter.

Dear Miss Lonelyhearts—

I am not very good at writing so I wonder if I could have a talk with you. I am only 32 years old but have had a lot of trouble in my life and am unhappily married to a cripple. I need some good advice bad but cant state my case in a letter as I am not good at letters and it would take an expert to state my case. I know your a man and am glad as I dont trust women. You were pointed out to me in Delehantys as a man who does the advice in the paper and the minute I saw you I said you can help me. You had on a blue suit and a gray hat when I came in with my husband who is a cripple.

I don't feel so bad about asking to see you personal because I feel almost like I knew you. So please call me up at Bugess 7-7323 which is my number as I need your advice bad about my married life.

An admirer,
Fay Doyle

He threw the letter into the waste-paper basket with a great show of distaste.

Goldsmith laughed at him. "How now, Dostoievski?" he said. "That's no way to act. Instead of pulling the Russian by recommending suicide, you ought to get the lady with child and increase the potential circulation of the paper."

To drive him away, Miss Lonelyhearts made believe that he was busy. He went over to his typewriter and started pounding out his column.

"Life, for most of us, seems a terrible struggle of pain and heartbreak, without hope or joy. Oh, my dear readers, it only seems so. Every man, no matter how poor or humble, can teach himself to use his senses. See the cloud-flecked sky, the foam-decked sea. . . . Smell the sweet pine and heady privet. . . . Feel of velvet and of satin. . . . As the popular song goes, 'The best things in life are free.' Life is . . ."

He could not go on with it and turned again to the imagined desert where Desperate, Broken-hearted and the others were still building his name. They had run out of sea shells and were using faded photographs, soiled fans, time-tables, playing cards, broken toys, imitation jewelry— junk that memory had made precious, far more precious than anything the sea might yield.

He killed his great understanding heart by laughing, then reached into the waste-paper basket for Mrs. Doyle's letter. Like a pink tent, he set it over the desert. Against

the dark mahogany desk top, the cheap paper took on rich
flesh tones. He thought of Mrs. Doyle as a tent, hair-covered
and veined, and of himself as the skeleton in a water closet,
the skull and cross-bones on a scholar's bookplate. When
he made the skeleton enter the flesh tent, it flowered at
every joint.

But despite these thoughts, he remained as dry and cold
as a polished bone and sat trying to discover a moral
reason for not calling Mrs. Doyle. If he could only believe
in Christ, then adultery would be a sin, then everything
would be simple and the letters extremely easy to answer.

The completeness of his failure drove him to the
telephone. He left the city room and went into the hall
to use the pay station from which all private calls had to
be made. The walls of the booth were covered with
obscene drawings. He fastened his eyes on two disembodied
genitals and gave the operator Burgess 7-7323.

"Is Mrs. Doyle in?"

"Hello, who is it?"

"I want to speak to Mrs. Doyle," he said. "Is this Mrs.
Doyle?"

"Yes, that's me." Her voice was hard with fright.

"This is Miss Lonelyhearts."

"Miss who?"

"Miss Lonelyhearts, Miss Lonelyhearts, the man who does
the column."

He was about to hang up, when she cooed, "Oh,
hello. . . ."

"You said I should call."

"Oh, yes . . . what?"

He guessed that she wanted him to do the talking. "When
can you see me?"

"Now." She was still cooing and he could almost feel
her warm, moisture-laden breath through the earpiece.

"Where?"

"You say."

"I'll tell you what," he said. "Meet me in the park, near the obelisk, in about an hour."

He went back to his desk and finished his column, then started for the park. He sat down on a bench near the obelisk to wait for Mrs. Doyle. Still thinking of tents, he examined the sky and saw that it was canvas-colored and ill-stretched. He examined it like a stupid detective who is searching for a clue to his own exhaustion. When he found nothing, he turned his trained eye on the skyscrapers that menaced the little park from all sides. In their tons of forced rock and tortured steel, he discovered what he thought was a clue.

Americans have dissipated their radical energy in an orgy of stone breaking. In their few years they have broken more stones than did centuries of Egyptians. And they have done their work hysterically, desperately, almost as if they knew that the stones would some day break them.

The detective saw a big woman enter the park and start in his direction. He made a quick catalogue: legs like Indian clubs, breasts like balloons and a brow like a pigeon. Despite her short plaid skirt, red sweater, rabbit-skin jacket and knitted tam-o'-shanter, she looked like a police captain.

He waited for her to speak first.

"Miss Lonelyhearts? Oh, hello . . ."

"Mrs. Doyle?" He stood up and took her arm. It felt like a thigh.

"Where are we going?" she asked, as he began to lead her off.

"For a drink."

"I can't go to Delehanty's. They know me."

"We'll go to my place."

"Ought I?"

He did not have to answer, for she was already on her

way. As he followed her up the stairs to his apartment, he watched the action of her massive hams; they were like two enormous grindstones.

He made some highballs and sat down beside her on the bed.

"You must know an awful lot about women from your job," she said with a sigh, putting her hand on his knee.

He had always been the pursuer, but now found a strange pleasure in having the rôles reversed. He drew back when she reached for a kiss. She caught his head and kissed him on his mouth. At first it ticked like a watch, then the tick softened and thickened into a heart throb. It beat louder and more rapidly each second, until he thought that it was going to explode and pulled away with a rude jerk.

"Don't," she begged.

"Don't what?"

"Oh, darling, turn out the light."

He smoked a cigarette, standing in the dark and listening to her undress. She made sea sounds; something flapped like a sail; there was the creak of ropes; then he heard the wave-against-a-wharf smack of rubber on flesh. Her call for him to hurry was a sea-moan, and when he lay beside her, she heaved, tidal, moon-driven.

Ironic style at its best

Some fifteen minutes later, he crawled out of bed like an exhausted swimmer leaving the surf, and dropped down into a large armchair near the window. She went into the bathroom, then came back and sat in his lap.

"I'm ashamed of myself," she said. "You must think I'm a bad woman."

He shook his head no.

"My husband isn't much. He's a cripple like I wrote you, and much older than me." She laughed. "He's all dried up. He hasn't been a husband to me for years. You know, Lucy, my kid, isn't his."

He saw that she expected him to be astonished and did his best to lift his eyebrows.

"It's a long story," she said. "It was on account of Lucy that I had to marry him. I'll bet you must have wondered how it was I came to marry a cripple. It's a long story."

Her voice was as hypnotic as a tom-tom, and as monotonous. Already his mind and body were half asleep.

"It's a long, long story, and that's why I couldn't write it in a letter. I got into trouble when the Doyles lived above us on Center Street. I used to be kind to him and go to the movies with him because he was a cripple, although I was one of the most popular girls on the block. So when I got into trouble, I didn't know what to do and asked him for the money for an abortion. But he didn't have the money, so we got married instead. It all came through my trusting a dirty dago. I thought he was a gent, but when I asked him to marry me, why he spurned me from the door and wouldn't even give me money for an abortion. He said if he gave me the money that would mean it was his fault and I would have something on him. Did you ever hear of such a skunk?"

"No," he said. The life out of which she spoke was even heavier than her body. It was as if a gigantic, living Miss Lonelyhearts letter in the shape of a paper weight had been placed on his brain.

"After the baby was born, I wrote the skunk, but he never wrote back, and about two years ago, I got to thinking how unfair it was for Lucy to have to depend on a cripple and not come into her rights. So I looked his name up in the telephone book and took Lucy to see him. As I told him then, not that I wanted anything for myself, but just that I wanted Lucy to get what was coming to her. Well, after keeping us waiting in the hall over an hour—I was boiling mad, I can tell you, thinking of the wrong he had done me and my child—we were taken into the parlor by the butler. Very quiet and lady-like, because money ain't everything and he's no more a gent than I'm a lady, the dirty wop—I told him he ought to do something for Lucy see'n' he's her father. Well, he had the nerve to say that he had never seen me before and that if I didn't stop bothering him, he'd have me run in. That got me riled and I lit into the bastard and gave him a piece of my mind. A woman came in while we were arguing that I figured was his wife, so I hollered, 'He's the father of my child, he's the father of my child.' When they went to the 'phone to call a cop, I picked up the kid and beat it.

"And now comes the funniest part of the whole thing. My husband is a queer guy and he always makes believe that he is the father of the kid and even talks to me about *our* child. Well, when we got home, Lucy kept asking me why I said a strange man was her papa. She wanted to know if Doyle wasn't really her papa. I must of been crazy because I told her that she should remember that her real papa was a man named Tony Benelli and that he had wronged me. I told her a lot of other crap like that—too much movies I guess. Well, when Doyle got home the first thing Lucy says to him is that he ain't her papa. That got him sore and he wanted to know what I had told her. I didn't like his high falutin' ways and said, 'The truth.' I guess too that I was kinda sick of see'n him moon over her. He went for me and hit me one on the cheek. I wouldn't let no man get away with that so I socked back and he swung at me with his stick but missed and fell on the floor and started to cry. The kid was on the floor crying too and that set me off because the next thing I know I'm on the floor bawling too."

She waited for him to comment, but he remained silent until she nudged him into speech with her elbow. "Your husband probably loves you and the kid," he said.

"Maybe so, but I was a pretty girl and could of had my pick. What girl wants to spend her life with a shrimp of a cripple?"

"You're still pretty," he said without knowing why, except that he was frightened.

She rewarded him with a kiss, then dragged him to the bed.

Miss Lonelyhearts in the dismal swamp

Soon after Mrs. Doyle left, Miss Lonelyhearts became physically sick and was unable to leave his room. The first two days of his illness were blotted out by sleep, but on the third day, his imagination began again to work.

He found himself in the window of a pawnshop full of fur coats, diamond rings, watches, shotguns, fishing tackle, mandolins. All these things were the paraphernalia of suffering. A tortured high light twisted on the blade of a gift knife, a battered horn grunted with pain.

He sat in the window thinking. Man has a tropism for order. Keys in one pocket, change in another. Mandolins are tuned G D A E. The physical world has a tropism for disorder, entropy. Man against Nature . . . the battle of the centuries. Keys yearn to mix with change. Mandolins strive to get out of tune. Every order has within it the germ of destruction. All order is doomed, yet the battle is worth while.

A trumpet, marked to sell for $2.49, gave the call to battle and Miss Lonelyhearts plunged into the fray. First

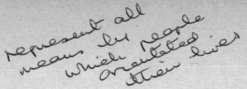

he formed a phallus of old watches and rubber boots, then a heart of umbrellas and trout flies, then a diamond of musical instruments and derby hats, after these a circle, triangle, square, swastika. But nothing proved definitive and he began to make a gigantic cross. When the cross became too large for the pawnshop, he moved it to the shore of the ocean. There every wave added to his stock faster than he could lengthen its arms. His labors were enormous. He staggered from the last wave line to his work, loaded down with marine refuse—bottles, shells, chunks of cork, fish heads, pieces of net.

Drunk with exhaustion, he finally fell asleep. When he awoke, he felt very weak, yet calm.

There was a timid knock on the door. It was open and Betty tiptoed into the room with her arms full of bundles. He made believe that he was asleep.

"Hello," he said suddenly.

Startled, she turned to explain. "I heard you were sick, so I brought some hot soup and other stuff."

He was too tired to be annoyed by her wide-eyed little mother act and let her feed him with a spoon. When he had finished eating, she opened the window and freshened the bed. As soon as the room was in order, she started to leave, but he called her back.

"Don't go, Betty."

She pulled a chair to the side of his bed and sat there without speaking.

"I'm sorry about what happened the other day," he said. "I guess I was sick."

She showed that she accepted his apology by helping him to excuse himself. "It's the Miss Lonelyhearts job. Why don't you give it up?"

"And do what?"

"Work in an advertising agency, or something."

"You don't understand, Betty, I can't quit. And even if I were to quit, it wouldn't make any difference. I wouldn't be able to forget the letters, no matter what I did."

"Maybe I don't understand," she said, "but I think you're making a fool of yourself."

"Perhaps I can make you understand. Let's start from the beginning. A man is hired to give advice to the readers of a newspaper. The job is a circulation stunt and the whole staff considers it a joke. He welcomes the job, for it might lead to a gossip column, and anyway he's tired of being a leg man. He too considers the job a joke, but after several months at it, the joke begins to escape him. He sees that the majority of the letters are profoundly humble pleas for moral and spiritual advice, that they are inarticulate expressions of genuine suffering. He also discovers that his correspondents take him seriously. For the first time in his life, he is forced to examine the values by which he lives. This examination shows him that he is the victim of the joke and not its perpetrator."

Although he had spoken soberly, he saw that Betty still thought him a fool. He closed his eyes.

"You're tired," she said. "I'll go."

"No, I'm not tired. I'm just tired of talking, you talk a while."

She told him about her childhood on a farm and of her love for animals, about country sounds and country smells and of how fresh and clean everything in the country is. She said that he ought to live there and that if he did, he would find that all his troubles were city troubles.

While she was talking, Shrike burst into the room. He was drunk and immediately set up a great shout, as though he believed that Miss Lonelyhearts was too near death to hear distinctly. Betty left without saying good-by.

Shrike had evidently caught some of her farm talk, for he said: "My friend, I agree with Betty, you're an escapist.

But I do not agree that the soil is the proper method for you to use."

Miss Lonelyhearts turned his face to the wall and pulled up the covers. But Shrike was unescapable. He raised his voice and talked through the blankets into the back of Miss Lonelyhearts' head.

"There are other methods, and for your edification I shall describe them. But first let us do the escape to the soil, as recommended by Betty:

"You are fed up with the city and its teeming millions. The ways and means of men, as getting and lending and spending, you lay waste your inner world, are too much with you. The bus takes too long, while the subway is always crowded. So what do you do? So you buy a farm and walk behind your horse's moist behind, no collar or tie, plowing your broad swift acres. As you turn up the rich black soil, the wind carries the smell of pine and dung across the fields and the rhythm of an old, old work enters your soul. To this rhythm, you sow and weep and chivy your kine, not kin or kind, between the pregnant rows of corn and taters. Your step becomes the heavy sexual step of a dance-drunk Indian and you tread the seed down into the female earth. You plant, not dragon's teeth, but beans and greens. . . .

"Well, what do you say, my friend, shall it be the soil?"

Miss Lonelyhearts did not answer. He was thinking of how Shrike had accelerated his sickness by teaching him to handle his one escape, Christ, with a thick glove of words.

"I take your silence to mean that you have decided against the soil. I agree with you. Such a life is too dull and laborious. Let us now consider the South Seas:

"You live in a thatch hut with the daughter of the king, a slim young maiden in whose eyes is an ancient wisdom. Her breasts are golden speckled pears, her belly a melon, and her odor is like nothing so much as a jungle fern. In the evening, on the blue lagoon, under the silvery moon, to your love you croon in the soft sylabelew and vocabelew of her langorour tongorour. Your body is golden brown like hers, and tourists have need of the indignant finger of the missionary to point you out. They envy you your breech clout and carefree laugh and little brown bride and fingers instead of forks. But you don't return their envy, and when a beautiful society girl comes to your hut in the night, seeking to learn the secret of your happiness, you send her back to her yacht that hangs on the horizon like a nervous racehorse. And so you dream away the days, fishing, hunting, dancing, swimming, kissing, and picking flowers to twine in your hair. . . .

"Well, my friend, what do you think of the South Seas?"

Miss Lonelyhearts tried to stop him by making believe that he was asleep. But Shrike was not fooled.

"Again silence," he said, "and again you are right. The South Seas are played out and there's little use in imitating Gauguin. But don't be discouraged, we have only scratched the surface of our subject. Let us now examine Hedonism, or take the cash and let the credit go. . . .

"You dedicate your life to the pursuit of pleasure. No over-indulgence, mind you, but knowing that your body is a pleasure machine, you treat it carefully in order to get the most out of it. Golf as well as booze, Philadelphia Jack O'Brien and his chestweights as well as Spanish dancers. Nor do you neglect the pleasures of the mind. You fornicate under pictures by Matisse and Picasso, you drink from Renaissance glassware, and often you spend an evening beside the fireplace with Proust and an apple. Alas, after much good fun, the day comes when you realize that soon you must die. You keep a stiff upper lip and decide to give a last party. You invite all your old mis-

tresses, trainers, artists and boon companions. The guests
are dressed in black, the waiters are coons, the table is
a coffin carved for you by Eric Gill. You serve caviar and
blackberries and licorice candy and coffee without cream.
After the dancing girls have finished, you get to your feet
and call for silence in order to explain your philosophy
of life. 'Life,' you say, 'is a club where they won't stand
for squawks, where they deal you only one hand and you
must sit in. So even if the cards are cold and marked by
the hand of fate, play up, play up like a gentleman and
a sport. Get tanked, grab what's on the buffet, use the
girls upstairs, but remember, when you throw box cars,
take the curtain like a dead game sport, don't squawk.' . . .

"I won't even ask you what you think of such an
escape. You haven't the money, nor are you stupid enough
to manage it. But we come now to one that should suit
you much better. . . .

"Art! Be an artist or a writer. When you are cold, warm
yourself before the flaming tints of Titian, when you are
hungry, nourish yourself with great spiritual foods by listening to the noble periods of Bach, the harmonies of
Brahms and the thunder of Beethoven. Do you think there
is anything in the fact that their names all begin with B?
But don't take a chance, smoke a 3 B pipe, and remember
these immortal lines: *When to the suddenness of melody
the echo parting falls the failing day.* What a rhythm!
Tell them to keep their society whores and pressed duck
with oranges. For you *l'art vivant,* the living art, as you
call it. Tell them that you know that your shoes are broken
and that there are pimples on your face, yes, and that you
have buck teeth and a club foot, but that you don't care,
for to-morrow they are playing Beethoven's last quartets
in Carnegie Hall and at home you have Shakespeare's
plays in one volume."

After art, Shrike described suicide and drugs. When he had finished with them, he came to what he said was the goal of his lecture.

"My friend, I know of course that neither the soil, nor the South Seas, nor Hedonism, nor art, nor suicide, nor drugs, can mean anything to us. We are not men who swallow camels only to strain at stools. God alone is our escape. The church is our only hope, the First Church of Christ Dentist, where He is worshiped as Preventer of Decay. The church whose symbol is the trinity new-style: Father, Son and Wirehaired Fox Terrier. . . . And so, my good friend, let me dictate a letter to Christ for you:

Dear Miss Lonelyhearts of Miss Lonelyhearts—
I am twenty-six years old and in the newspaper game. Life for me is a desert empty of comfort. I cannot find pleasure in food, drink, or women—nor do the arts give me joy any longer. The Leopard of Discontent walks the streets of my city; the Lion of Discouragement crouches outside the walls of my citadel. All is desolation and a vexation of the spirit. I feel like hell. How can I believe, how can I have faith in this day and age? Is it true that the greatest scientists believe again in you?

I read your column and like it very much. There you once wrote: 'When the salt has lost its savour, who shall savour it again?' Is the answer: 'None but the Saviour?'

Thanking you very much for a quick reply, I remain yours truly,

A Regular Subscriber"

Betty came to see Miss Lonelyhearts the next day and every day thereafter. With her she brought soup and boiled chicken for him to eat.

He knew that she believed he did not want to get well, yet he followed her instructions because he realized that his present sickness was unimportant. It was merely a trick by his body to relieve one more profound.

Whenever he mentioned the letters or Christ, she changed the subject to tell long stories about life on a farm. She seemed to think that if he never talked about these things, his body would get well, that if his body got well everything would be well. He began to realize that there was a definite plan behind her farm talk, but could not guess what it was.

When the first day of spring arrived, he felt better. He had already spent more than a week in bed and was anxious to get out. Betty took him for a walk in the zoo and he was amused by her evident belief in the curative power of animals. She seemed to think that it must steady him to look at a buffalo.

He wanted to go back to work, but she made him get Shrike to extend his sick leave a few days. He was grateful to her and did as she asked. She then told him her plan. Her aunt still owned the farm in Connecticut on which she had been born and they could go there and camp in the house.

She borrowed an old Ford touring car from a friend.

They loaded it with food and equipment and started out early one morning. As soon as they reached the outskirts of the city, Betty began to act like an excited child, greeting the trees and grass with delight.

After they had passed through New Haven, they came to Bramford and turned off the State highway on a dirt road that led to Monkstown. The road went through a wild-looking stretch of woods and they saw some red squirrels and a partridge. He had to admit, even to himself, that the pale new leaves, shaped and colored like candle flames, were beautiful and that the air smelt clean and alive.

There was a pond on the farm and they caught sight of it through the trees just before coming to the house. She did not have the key so they had to force the door open. The heavy, musty smell of old furniture and wood rot made them cough. He complained. Betty said that she did not mind because it was not a human smell. She put so much meaning into the word "human" that he laughed and kissed her.

They decided to camp in the kitchen because it was the largest room and the least crowded with old furniture. There were four windows and a door and they opened them all to air the place out.

While he unloaded the car, she swept up and made a fire in the stove out of a broken chair. The stove looked like a locomotive and was almost as large, but the chimney drew all right and she soon had a fire going. He got some water from the well and put it on the stove to boil. When the water was scalding hot, they used it to clean an old mattress that they had found in one of the bedrooms. Then they put the mattress out in the sun to dry.

It was almost sundown before Betty would let him stop working. He sat smoking a cigarette, while she prepared supper. They had beans, eggs, bread, fruit and drank two cups of coffee apiece.

After they had finished eating, there was still some light left and they went down to look at the pond. They sat close together with their backs against a big oak and watched a heron hunt frogs. Just as they were about to start back, two deer and a fawn came down to the water on the opposite side of the pond. The flies were bothering them and they went into the water and began to feed on the lily pads. Betty accidentally made a noise and the deer floundered back into the woods.

When they returned to the house, it was quite dark. They lit the kerosene lamp that they had brought with them, then dragged the mattress into the kitchen and made their bed on the floor next to the stove.

Before going to bed, they went out on the kitchen porch to smoke a last cigarette. It was very cold and he had to go back for a blanket. They sat close together with the blanket wrapped around them.

There were plenty of stars. A screech owl made a horrible racket somewhere in the woods and when it quit, a loon began down on the pond. The crickets made almost as much noise as the loon.

Even with the blanket around them it was cold. They went inside and made a big fire in the stove, using pieces of a hardwood table to make the fire last. They each ate an apple, then put on their pajamas and went to bed. He fondled her, but when she said that she was a virgin, he let her alone and went to sleep.

He woke up with the sun in his eyes. Betty was already busy at the stove. She sent him down to the pond to wash and when he got back, breakfast was ready. It consisted of eggs, ham, potatoes, fried apples, bread and coffee.

After breakfast, she worked at making the place more comfortable and he drove to Monkstown for some fresh fruit and the newspapers. He stopped for gas at the Aw-Kum-On Garage and told the attendant about the deer.

The man said that there was still plenty of deer at the pond because no yids ever went there. He said it wasn't the hunters who drove out the deer, but the yids.

He got back to the house in time for lunch and, after eating, they went for a walk in the woods. It was very sad under the trees. Although spring was well advanced, in the deep shade there was nothing but death—rotten leaves, gray and white fungi, and over everything a funereal hush.

Later it grew very hot and they decided to go for a swim. They went in naked. The water was so cold that they could only stay in for a short time. They ran back to the house and took a quick drink of gin, then sat in a sunny spot on the kitchen porch.

Betty was unable to sit still for long. There was nothing to do in the house, so she began to wash the underwear she had worn on the trip up. After she had finished, she rigged a line between two trees.

He sat on the porch and watched her work. She had her hair tied up in a checked handkerchief, otherwise she was completely naked. She looked a little fat, but when she lifted something to the line, all the fat disappeared. Her raised arms pulled her breasts up until they were like pink-tipped thumbs.

There was no wind to disturb the pull of the earth. The new green leaves hung straight down and shone in the hot sun like an army of little metal shields. Somewhere in the woods a thrush was singing. Its sound was like that of a flute choked with saliva.

Betty stopped with her arms high to listen to the bird. When it was quiet, she turned towards him with a guilty laugh. He blew her a kiss. She caught it with a gesture that was childishly sexual. He vaulted the porch rail and ran to kiss her. As they went down, he smelled a mixture of sweat, soap and crushed grass.

Miss Lonelyhearts returns

Several days later, they started to drive back to the city. When they reached the Bronx slums, Miss Lonelyhearts knew that Betty had failed to cure him and that he had been right when he had said that he could never forget the letters. He felt better, knowing this, because he had begun to think himself a faker and a fool.

Crowds of people moved through the street with a dream-like violence. As he looked at their broken hands and torn mouths he was overwhelmed by the desire to help them, and because this desire was sincere, he was happy despite the feeling of guilt which accompanied it.

He saw a man who appeared to be on the verge of death stagger into a movie theater that was showing a picture called *Blonde Beauty*. He saw a ragged woman with an enormous goiter pick a love story magazine out of a garbage can and seem very excited by her find.

Prodded by his conscience, he began to generalize. Men have always fought their misery with dreams. Although dreams were once powerful, they have been made puerile by the movies, radio and newspapers. Among many betrayals, this one is the worst.

The thing that made his share in it particularly bad was that he was capable of dreaming the Christ dream. He felt that he had failed at it, not so much because of Shrike's jokes or his own self-doubt, but because of his lack of humility.

He finally got to bed. Before falling asleep, he vowed to

make a sincere attempt to be humble. In the morning, when he started for his office, he renewed his vow.

Fortunately for him, Shrike was not in the city room and his humility was spared an immediate trial. He went straight to his desk and began to open letters. When he had opened about a dozen, he felt sick and decided to do his column for that day without reading any of them. He did not want to test himself too severely.

The typewriter was uncovered and he put a sheet of paper into the roller.

"Christ died for you.

"He died nailed to a tree for you. His gift to you is suffering and it is only through suffering that you can know Him. Cherish this gift, for . . ."

He snatched the paper out of the machine. With him, even the word Christ was a vanity. After staring at the pile of letters on his desk for a long time, he looked out the window. A slow spring rain was changing the dusty tar roofs below him to shiny patent leather. The water made everything slippery and he could find no support for either his eyes or his feelings.

Turning back to his desk, he picked up a bulky letter in a dirty envelope. He read it for the same reason that an animal tears at a wounded foot: to hurt the pain.

Dear Miss Lonelyhearts:—

Being an admirer of your column because you give such good advice to people in trouble as that is what I am in also I would appreciate very much your advising me what to do after I tell you my troubles.

During the war I was told if I wanted to do my bit I should marry the man I was engaged to as he was going away to help Uncle Sam and to make a long story short I was married to him. After the war was over he still had to remain in the army for one more year as he signed for it and naturaly I went to work as while doing this patriotic stunt he had only $18 dollars to his name. I worked for three years steady and then had to stay home because I became a mother and in the meantime of those years my husband would get a job and then would tire of it or want to roam. It was all right before the baby came because then I could work steady and then bills were paid but when I stopped everything went sliding backward. Then two years went by and a baby boy was added to our union. My girl will be eight and my boy six years of age.

I made up my mind after I had the second child that in spite of my health as I was hit by an auto while carrying the first I would get some work to do but debts collected so rapidly it almost took a derick to lift them let alone a sick woman. I went to work evenings when my husband would be home so as somebody could watch the baby and I did this until the baby was three years old when I thought of taking in a man who had been boarding with his sister as she moved to Rochester and he had to look for a new place. Well my husband agreed as he figured the $15 dollars per he paid us would make it easier for him as this man was a widower with two children and as my husband knew him for twelve years being real pals then going out together etc. After the boarder was with us for about a year my husband didn't come home one night and then two nights etc. I listed him in the missing persons and after two and a half months I was told to go to Grove St. which I did and he was arrested because he refused to support me and my kids. When he served three months of the six the judge asked me to give him another chance which like a fool I did and when he got home he beat me up so I had to spend over $30 dollars in the dentist afterwards.

He got a pension from the army and naturaly I was the one to take it to the store and cash it as he was so lazy I always had to sign his name and of course put per my name and through wanting to pay the landlord because he wanted to put us out I signed his check as usual but forgot to put per my name and for this to get even with me because he did three months time he sent to Washington for the copy of the check so I could be arrested for forgery but as the butcher knew about me signing the checks etc nothing was done to me.

He threatened my life many times saying no one solved the Mrs. Mills murder and the same will happen to you and many times when making beds I would find under his pillow a hammer, scissors, knife, stone lifter etc and when I asked him what the idea was he would make believe he knew nothing about it or say the children put them there and then a few months went buy and I was going to my work as usual as the boarder had to stay home that day due to the fact the material for his boss did not arrive and he could not go to work as he is a piece worker. I always made a habit of setting the breakfast and cooking the food the night before so I could stay in bed until seven as at that time my son was in the Kings County hospital with a disease which my husband gave me that he got while fighting for Uncle Sam and I had to be at the clinic for the needle to. So while I was in bed unbeknown to me my husband sent the boarder out for a paper and when he came back my husband was gone. So later when I came from my room I was told that my husband had gone out. I fixed the childs breakfast and ate my own then went to the washtub to do the weeks wash and while the boarder was reading the paper at twelve o'clock noon my mother came over to mind the baby as I had a chance to go out and make a little money doing house work. Things were a little out of order beds not dressed and things out of place and a little sweeping had to be done as I was washing all morning and I didn't have a chance to do it so I thought to do it then while my mother was in the house with her to help me so that I could finish quickly. Hurrying at break neck speed to get finished I swept through the rooms to make sure everything was spick and span so when my husband came home he couldn't have anything to say. We had three beds and I was on the last which was a double bed when stooping to put the broom under the bed to get at the lint and the dust when lo and behold I saw a face like the mask of a devil with only the whites of the eyes showing and hands' clenched to choke anyone and then I saw it move and I was so frighted that almost till night I was hystirical and I was paralised from my waist down. I thought I would never be able to walk again. A doctor was called for me by my mother and he said the man ought to be put in an asylum to do a thing like that. It was my husband lieing under the bed from seven in the morning until almost half past one o'clock lieing in his own dirt instead of going to the bath room when he had to be dirtied himself waiting to fright me.

So as I could not trust him I would not sleep with him and as I told the boarder to find a new place because I thought maybe he was jealous of something I slept in the boarders bed in an other room. Some nights I would wake up and find him standing by my bed laughing like a crazy man or walking around stripped etc.

I bought a new sowing machine as I do some sowing for other people to make both ends meet and one night while I was out delivering my work I got back to find the house cleaned out and he had pawned my sowing machine and also all the other pawnables in the house. Ever since he frighted me I have been so nervous during the night when I get up for the children that he would be standing behind a curtain and either jump out at me or put his hand on me before I could light the light. Well as I had to see that I could not make him work steady and that I had to be mother and housekeeper and wage earner etc and I could not let my nerves get the best of me as I lost a good job once on account of having bad nerves I simply moved away from him and anyway there was nothing much left in the house. But he pleaded with me for another chance so I thought seeing he is the father of my children I will and then he did more crazy things to many to write and I left him again. Four times we got together and four times I left. Please Miss Lonelyhearts believe me just for the childrens sake is the bunk and pardon me because I dont know how you are fixed but all I know is that in over three years I got $200 dollars from him altogether.

About four months ago I handed him a warrant for his arrest for non support and he tore it up and left the house and I havent seen him since and as I had pneumonia and my little girl had the flu I was put in financial embarasment with the doctor and we had to go to the ward and when we came out of the hospital I had to ask the boarder to come to live with us again as he was a sure $15 dollars a week and if anything happened to me he would be there to take care of the children. But he tries to make me be bad and as there is nobody in the house when he comes home drunk on Saturday night I dont know what to do but so far I didnt let him. Where my husband is I dont know but I received a vile letter from him where he even accused his inocent children of things and sarcasticaly asked about the star boarder.

Dear Miss Lonelyhearts please dont be angry at me for writing such a long letter and taking up so much of your time in reading it but if I ever write all the things which happened to me living with him it would fill a book and please forgive me for saying some nasty things as I had to give you an idea of what is going on in my home. Every woman is intitiled to a home isnt she? So Miss Lonelyhearts please put a few lines in your column when you refer to

*this letter so I will know you are helping me. Shall I take
my husband back? How can I support my children?*

Thanking you for anything you can advise me in I remain
yours truly—
Broad Shoulders

*P.S. Dear Miss Lonelyhearts dont think I am broad shoul-
dered but that is the way I feel about life and me I mean.*

Miss Lonelyhearts and the cripple

Miss Lonelyhearts dodged Betty because she made him
feel ridiculous. He was still trying to cling to his humility,
and the farther he got below self-laughter, the easier it
was for him to practice it. When Betty telephoned, he
refused to answer and after he had twice failed to call her
back, she left him alone.

One day, about a week after he had returned from the
country, Goldsmith asked him out for a drink. When he
accepted, he made himself so humble that Goldsmith was
frightened and almost suggested a doctor.

They found Shrike in Delehanty's and joined him at the
bar. Goldsmith tried to whisper something to him about
Miss Lonelyhearts' condition, but he was drunk and refused to listen. He caught only part of what Goldsmith
was trying to say.

"I must differ with you, my good Goldsmith," Shrike
said. "Don't call sick those who have faith. They are the
well. It is you who are sick."

Goldsmith did not reply and Shrike turned to Miss Lonelyhearts. "Come, tell us, brother, how it was that you first came to believe. Was it music in a church, or the death of a loved one, or mayhap, some wise old priest?"

The familiar jokes no longer had any effect on Miss Lonelyhearts. He smiled at Shrike as the saints are supposed to have smiled at those about to martyr them.

"Ah, but how stupid of me," Shrike continued. "It was the letters, of course. Did I myself not say that the Miss Lonelyhearts are the priests of twentieth-century America?"

Goldsmith laughed, and Shrike, in order to keep him laughing, used an old trick; he appeared to be offended. "Goldsmith, you are the nasty product of this unbelieving age. You cannot believe, you can only laugh. You take everything with a bag of salt and forget that salt is the enemy of fire as well as of ice. Be warned, the salt you use is not Attic salt, it is coarse butcher's salt. It doesn't preserve; it kills."

The bartender who was standing close by, broke in to address Miss Lonelyhearts. "Pardon me, sir, but there's a gent here named Doyle who wants to meet you. He says you know his wife."

Before Miss Lonelyhearts could reply, he beckoned to someone standing at the other end of the bar. The signal was answered by a little cripple, who immediately started in their direction. He used a cane and dragged one of his feet behind him in a box-shaped shoe with a four-inch sole. As he hobbled along, he made many waste motions, like those of a partially destroyed insect.

The bartender introduced the cripple as Mr. Peter Doyle. Doyle was very excited and shook hands twice all around, then with a wave that was meant to be sporting, called for a round of drinks.

Before lifting his glass, Shrike carefully inspected the

cripple. When he had finished, he winked at Miss Lonely-hearts and said, "Here's to humanity." He patted Doyle on the back. "Mankind, mankind . . ." he sighed, wagging his head sadly. "What is man that . . ."

The bartender broke in again on behalf of his friend and tried to change the conversation to familiar ground. "Mr. Doyle inspects meters for the gas company."

"And an excellent job it must be," Shrike said. "He should be able to give us the benefit of a different view-point. We newspapermen are limited in many ways and I like to hear both sides of a case."

Doyle had been staring at Miss Lonelyhearts as though searching for something, but he now turned to Shrike and tried to be agreeable. "You know what people say, Mr. Shrike?"

"No, my good man, what is it that people say?"

"Everybody's got a frigidaire nowadays, and they say that we meter inspectors take the place of the iceman in the stories." He tried, rather diffidently, to leer.

"What!" Shrike roared at him. "I can see, sir, that you are not the man for us. You can know nothing about humanity; you are humanity. I leave you to Miss Lonely-hearts." He called to Goldsmith and stalked away.

The cripple was confused and angry. "Your friend is a nut," he said. Miss Lonelyhearts was still smiling, but the character of his smile had changed. It had become full of sympathy and a little sad.

The new smile was for Doyle and he knew it. He smiled back gratefully.

"Oh, I forgot," Doyle said, "the wife asked me, if I bumped into you, to ask you to our house to eat. That's why I made Jake introduce us."

Miss Lonelyhearts was busy with his smile and accepted without thinking of the evening he had spent with Mrs.

Doyle. The cripple felt honored and shook hands for a
third time. It was evidently his only social gesture.

After a few more drinks, when Doyle said that he was
tired, Miss Lonelyhearts suggested that they go into the
back room. They found a table and sat opposite each
other.

The cripple had a very strange face. His eyes failed to
balance; his mouth was not under his nose; his forehead
was square and bony; and his round chin was like a forehead
in miniature. He looked like one of those composite photographs used by screen magazines in guessing contests.

They sat staring at each other until the strain of word-
less communication began to excite them both. Doyle
made vague, needless adjustments to his clothing. Miss
Lonelyhearts found it very difficult to keep his smile
steady.

When the cripple finally labored into speech, Miss
Lonelyhearts was unable to understand him. He listened
hard for a few minutes and realized that Doyle was making no attempt to be understood. He was giving birth to
groups of words that lived inside of him as things, a jumble of the retorts he had meant to make when insulted
and the private curses against fate that experience had
taught him to swallow.

Like a priest, Miss Lonelyhearts turned his face slightly
away. He watched the play of the cripple's hands. At first
they conveyed nothing but excitement, then gradually
they became pictorial. They lagged behind to illustrate a
matter with which he was already finished, or ran ahead
to illustrate something he had not yet begun to talk about.
As he grew more articulate, his hands stopped trying to
aid his speech and began to dart in and out of his clothing.
One of them suddenly emerged from a pocket of his coat,
dragging some sheets of letter paper. He forced these on
Miss Lonelyhearts.

Dear Miss Lonelyhearts—

I am kind of ashamed to write you because a man like me dont take stock in things like that but my wife told me you were a man and not some dopey woman so I thought I would write to you after reading your answer to Disillusioned. I am a cripple 41 yrs of age which I have been all my life and I have never let myself get blue until lately when I have been feeling lousy all the time on account of not getting anywhere and asking myself what is it all for. You have a education so I figured may be you no. What I want to no is why I go around pulling my leg up and down stairs reading meters for the gas company for a stinking $22.50 per while the bosses ride around in swell cars living off the fat of the land. Dont think I am a greasy red. I read where they shoot cripples in Russia because they cant work but I can work better than any park bum and support a wife and child to. But thats not what I am writing you about. What I want to no is what is it all for my pulling my god damed leg along the streets and down in stinking cellars with it all the time hurting fit to burst so that near quitting time I am crazy with pain and when I get home all I hear is money money which aint no home for a man like me. What I want to no is what in hell is the use day after day with a foot like mine when you have to go around pulling and scrambling for a lousy three squares with a toothache in it that comes from useing the foot so much. The doctor told me I ought to rest it for six months but who will pay me when I am resting it. But that aint what I mean either because you might tell me to change my job and where could I get another one I am lucky to have one at all. It aint the job that I am complaining about but what I want to no is what is the whole stinking business for.

Please write me an answer not in the paper because my wife reads your stuff and I dont want her to no I wrote to you because I always said the papers is crap but I figured

*maybe you no something about it because you have read a
lot of books and I never even finished high.*

> Yours truly,
> Peter Doyle

While Miss Lonelyhearts was puzzling out the crabbed
writing, Doyle's damp hand accidentally touched his under
the table. He jerked away, but then drove his hand back
and forced it to clasp the cripple's. After finishing the
letter, he did not let go, but pressed it firmly with all the
love he could manage. At first the cripple covered his
embarrassment by disguising the meaning of the clasp
with a handshake, but he soon gave in to it and they sat
silently, hand in hand.

Miss Lonelyhearts pays a visit

They left the speakeasy together, both very drunk and
very busy: Doyle with the wrongs he had suffered and
Miss Lonelyhearts with the triumphant thing that his humility had become.

They took a cab. As they entered the street in which
Doyle lived, he began to curse his wife and his crippled
foot. He called on Christ to blast them both.

Miss Lonelyhearts was very happy and inside of his
head he was also calling on Christ. But his call was not a
curse, it was the shape of his joy.

When the cab drew up to the curb, Miss Lonelyhearts
helped his companion out and led him into the house.
They made a great deal of noise with the front door and

Mrs. Doyle came into the hall. At the sight of her the cripple started to curse again.

She greeted Miss Lonelyhearts, then took hold of her husband and shook the breath out of him. When he was quiet, she dragged him into their apartment. Miss Lonely-hearts followed and as he passed her in the dark foyer, she goosed him and laughed.

After washing their hands, they sat down to eat. Mrs. Doyle had had her supper earlier in the evening and she waited on them. The first thing she put on the table was a quart bottle of guinea red.

When they had reached their coffee, she sat down next to Miss Lonelyhearts. He could feel her knee pressing his under the table, but he paid no attention to her and only broke his beatific smile to drink. The heavy food had dulled him and he was trying desperately to feel again what he had felt while holding hands with the cripple in the speakeasy.

She put her thigh under his, but when he still failed to respond, she got up abruptly and went into the parlor. They followed a few minutes later and found her mixing ginger-ale highballs.

They all drank silently. Doyle looked sleepy and his wife was just beginning to get drunk. Miss Lonelyhearts made no attempt to be sociable. He was busy trying to find a message. When he did speak it would have to be in the form of a message.

After the third highball, Mrs. Doyle began to wink quite openly at Miss Lonelyhearts, but he still refused to pay any attention to her. The cripple, however, was greatly disturbed by her signals. He began to fidget and mumble under his breath.

The vague noises he was making annoyed Mrs. Doyle. "What in hell are you talking about?" she demanded.

The cripple started a sigh that ended in a groan and

then, as though ashamed of himself, said, "Ain't I the pimp, to bring home a guy for my wife?" He darted a quick look at Miss Lonelyhearts and laughed apologetically.

Mrs. Doyle was furious. She rolled a newspaper into a club and struck her husband on the mouth with it. He surprised her by playing the fool. He growled like a dog and caught the paper in his teeth. When she let go of her end, he dropped to his hands and knees and continued the imitation on the floor.

Miss Lonelyhearts tried to get the cripple to stand up and bent to lift him; but, as he did so, Doyle tore open Miss Lonelyhearts' fly, then rolled over on his back, laughing wildly.

His wife kicked him and turned away with a snort of contempt.

The cripple soon laughed himself out, and they all returned to their seats. Doyle and his wife sat staring at each other, while Miss Lonelyhearts again began to search for a message.

The silence bothered Mrs. Doyle. When she could stand it no longer, she went to the sideboard to make another round of drinks. But the bottle was empty. She asked her husband to go to the corner drug store for some gin. He refused with a single, curt nod of his head.

She tried to argue with him. He ignored her and she lost her temper. "Get some gin!" she yelled. "Get some gin, you bastard!"

Miss Lonelyhearts stood up. He had not yet found his message, but he had to say something. "Please don't fight," he pleaded. "He loves you, Mrs. Doyle; that's why he acts like that. Be kind to him."

She grunted with annoyance and left the room. They could hear her slamming things around in the kitchen.

Miss Lonelyhearts went over to the cripple and smiled at him with the same smile he had used in the speakeasy.

The cripple returned the smile and stuck out his hand. Miss Lonelyhearts clasped it, and they stood this way, smiling and holding hands, until Mrs. Doyle reëntered the room.

"What a sweet pair of fairies you guys are," she said.

The cripple pulled his hand away and made as though to strike his wife. Miss Lonelyhearts realized that now was the time to give his message. It was now or never.

"You have a big, strong body, Mrs. Doyle. Holding your husband in your arms, you can warm him and give him life. You can take the chill out of his bones. He drags his days out in areaways and cellars, carrying a heavy load of weariness and pain. You can substitute a dream of yourself for this load. A buoyant dream that will be like a dynamo in him. You can do this by letting him conquer you in your bed. He will repay you by flowering and becoming ardent over you. . . ."

She was too astonished to laugh, and the cripple turned his face away as though embarrassed.

With the first few words Miss Lonelyhearts had known that he would be ridiculous. By avoiding God, he had failed to tap the force in his heart and had merely written a column for his paper.

He tried again by becoming hysterical. "Christ is love," he screamed at them. It was a stage scream, but he kept on. "Christ is the black fruit that hangs on the crosstree. Man was lost by eating of the forbidden fruit. He shall be saved by eating of the bidden fruit. The black Christ-fruit, the love fruit . . ."

This time he had failed still more miserably. He had substituted the rhetoric of Shrike for that of Miss Lonelyhearts. He felt like an empty bottle, shiny and sterile.

He closed his eyes. When he heard the cripple say, "I love you, I love you," he opened them and saw him kissing his wife. He knew that the cripple was doing this, not because of the things he had said, but out of loyalty.

"All right, you nut," she said, queening it over her husband. "I forgive you, but go to the drug store for some gin."

Without looking at Miss Lonelyhearts, the cripple took his hat and left. When he had gone Mrs. Doyle smiled. "You were a scream with your fly open," she said. "I thought I'd die laughing."

He did not answer.

"Boy, is he jealous," she went on. "All I have to do is point to some big guy and say, 'Gee, I'd love to have him love me up.' It drives him nuts."

Her voice was low and thick and it was plain that she was trying to excite him. When she went to the radio to tune in on a jazz orchestra, she waved her behind at him like a flag.

He said that he was too tired to dance. After doing a few obscene steps in front of him, she sat down in his lap. He tried to fend her off, but she kept pressing her open mouth against his and when he turned away, she nuzzled his cheek. He felt like an empty bottle that is being slowly filled with warm, dirty water.

When she opened the neck of her dress and tried to force his head between her breasts, he parted his knees with a quick jerk that spilled her to the floor. She tried to pull him down on top of her. He struck out blindly and hit her in the face. She screamed and he hit her again and again. He kept hitting her until she stopped trying to hold him, then he ran out of the house.

Miss Lonelyhearts attends a party

Miss Lonelyhearts had gone to bed again. This time his bed was surely taking him somewhere, and with great speed. He had only to ride it quietly. He had already been riding for three days.

Before climbing aboard, he had prepared for the journey by jamming the telephone bell and purchasing several enormous cans of crackers. He now lay on the bed, eating crackers, drinking water and smoking cigarettes.

He thought of how calm he was. His calm was so perfect that he could not destroy it even by being conscious of it. In three days he had gone very far. It grew dark in the room. He got out of bed, washed his teeth, urinated, then turned out the light and went to sleep. He fell asleep without even a sigh and slept the sleep of the wise and the innocent. Without dreaming, he was aware of fireflies and the slop of oceans.

Reborn

Later a train rolled into a station where he was a reclining statue holding a stopped clock, a coach rumbled into the yard of an inn where he was sitting over a guitar, cap in hand, shedding the rain with his hump.

He awoke. The noise of both arrivals had combined to become a knocking on the door. He climbed out of bed. Although he was completely naked, he went to the door without covering himself. Five people rushed in, two of whom were women. The women shrieked when they saw him and jumped back into the hall.

The three men held their ground. Miss Lonelyhearts recognized Shrike among them and saw that he, as well as the others, was very drunk. Shrike said that one of the women was his wife and wanted to fight Miss Lonelyhearts for insulting her.

Miss Lonelyhearts stood quietly in the center of the room. Shrike dashed against him, but fell back, as a wave that dashes against an ancient rock, smooth with experience, falls back. There was no second wave.

Instead Shrike became jovial. He slapped Miss Lonelyhearts on the back. "Put on a pair of pants, my friend," he said, "we're going to a party."

Miss Lonelyhearts picked up a can of crackers.

"Come on, my son," Shrike urged. "It's solitary drinking that makes drunkards."

Miss Lonelyhearts carefully examined each cracker before popping it into his mouth.

"Don't be a spoil-sport," Shrike said with a great deal of irritation. He was a gull trying to lay an egg in the smooth flank of a rock, a screaming, clumsy gull. "There's a game we want to play and we need you to play it.—'Everyman his own Miss Lonelyhearts.' I invented it, and we can't play without you."

Shrike pulled a large batch of letters out of his pockets and waved them in front of Miss Lonelyhearts. He recognized them; they were from his office file.

The rock remained calm and solid. Although Miss Lonelyhearts did not doubt that it could withstand any test, he was willing to have it tried. He began to dress.

They went downstairs, and all six of them piled into one cab. Mary Shrike sat on his lap, but despite her drunken wriggling the rock remained perfect.

The party was in Shrike's apartment. A roar went up when Miss Lonelyhearts entered and the crowd surged forward. He stood firm and they slipped back in a futile curl. He smiled. He had turned more than a dozen drunkards.

He had turned them without effort or thought. As he stood smiling, a little wave crept up out of the general welter and splashed at his feet for attention. It was Betty.

"What's the matter with you?" she asked. "Are you sick again?"

He did not answer.

When every one was seated, Shrike prepared to start the game. He distributed paper and pencils, then led Miss Lonelyhearts to the center of the room and began his spiel.

"Ladies and gentlemen," he said, imitating the voice and gestures of a circus barker. "We have with us to-night a man whom you all know and admire. Miss Lonelyhearts, he of the singing heart—a still more swollen Mussolini of the soul.

"He has come here to-night to help you with your moral and spiritual problems, to provide you with a slogan, a cause, an absolute value and a *raison d'être*.

"Some of you, perhaps, consider yourself too far gone for help. You are afraid that even Miss Lonelyhearts, no matter how fierce his torch, will be unable to set you on fire. You are afraid that even when exposed to his bright flame, you will only smolder and give off a bad smell. Be of good heart, for I know that you will burst into flame. Miss Lonelyhearts is sure to prevail."

Shrike pulled out the batch of letters and waved them above his head.

"We will proceed systematically," he said. "First, each of you will do his best to answer one of these letters, then, from your answers, Miss Lonelyhearts will diagnose your moral ills. Afterwards he will lead you in the way of attainment."

Shrike went among his guests and distributed the letters as a magician does cards. He talked continuously and read a part of each letter before giving it away.

"Here's one from an old woman whose son died last

week. She is seventy years old and sells pencils for a living. She has no stockings and wears heavy boots on her torn and bleeding feet. She has rheum in her eyes. Have you room in your heart for her?

"This one is a jim-dandy. A young boy wants a violin. It looks simple; all you have to do is get the kid one. But then you discover that he has dicated the letter to his little sister. He is paralyzed and can't even feed himself. He has a toy violin and hugs it to his chest, imitating the sound of playing with his mouth. How pathetic! However, one can learn much from this parable. Label the boy Labor, the violin Capital, and so on . . ."

Miss Lonelyhearts stood it with the utmost serenity; he was not even interested. What goes on in the sea is of no interest to the rock.

When all the letters had been distributed, Shrike gave one to Miss Lonelyhearts. He took it, but after holding it for a while, he dropped it to the floor without reading it.

Shrike was not quiet for a second.

"You are plunging into a world of misery and suffering, peopled by creatures who are strangers to everything but disease and policemen. Harried by one, they are hurried by the other. . . .

"Pain, pain, pain, the dull, sordid, gnawing, chronic pain of heart and brain. The pain that only a great spiritual liniment can relieve. . . ."

When Miss Lonelyhearts saw Betty get up to go, he followed her out of the apartment. She too should see the rock he had become.

Shrike did not miss him until he discovered the letter on the floor. He picked it up, tried to find Miss Lonelyhearts, then addressed the gathering again.

"The master has disappeared," he announced, "but do not despair. I am still with you. I am his disciple and I shall lead you in the way of attainment. First let me read you this letter which is addressed directly to the master."

He took the letter out of its envelope, as though he had not read it previously, and began: " 'What kind of a dirty skunk are you? When I got home with the gin, I found my wife crying on the floor and the house full of neighbors. She said that you tried to rape her you dirty skunk and they wanted to get the police but I said that I'd do the job myself you . . .'

"My, oh my, I really can't bring myself to utter such vile language. I'll skip the swearing and go on. 'So that's what all your fine speeches come to, you bastard, you ought to have your brains blown out.' It's signed, 'Doyle.'

"Well, well, so the master is another Rasputin. How this shakes one's faith! But I can't believe it. I won't believe it. The master can do no wrong. My faith is unshaken. This is only one more attempt against him by the devil. He has spent his life struggling with the arch fiend for our sakes, and he shall triumph. I mean Miss Lonelyhearts, not the devil.

"The gospel according to Shrike. Let me tell you about his life. It unrolls before me like a scroll. First, in the dawn of childhood, radiant with pure innocence, like a rain-washed star, he wends his weary way to the University of Hard Knocks. Next, a youth, he dashes into the night from the bed of his first whore. And then, the man, the man Miss Lonelyhearts—struggling valiantly to realize a high ideal, his course shaped by a proud aim. But, alas! cold and scornful, the world heaps obstacle after obstacle in his path; deems he the goal at hand, a voice of thunder bids him 'Halt!' 'Let each hindrance be thy ladder,' thinks he. 'Higher, even higher, mount!' And so he climbs, rung by weary rung, and so he urges himself on, breathless with hallowed fire. And so . . ."

Miss Lonelyhearts and the party dress

When Miss Lonelyhearts left Shrike's apartment, he found Betty in the hall waiting for the elevator. She had on a light-blue dress that was very much a party dress. She dressed for things, he realized.

Even the rock was touched by this realization. No; it was not the rock that was touched. The rock was still perfect. It was his mind that was touched, the instrument with which he knew the rock.

He approached Betty with a smile, for his mind was free and clear. The things that muddied it had precipitated out into the rock.

But she did not smile back. "What are you grinning at?" she snapped.

"Oh, I'm sorry," he said. "I didn't mean anything."

They entered the elevator together. When they reached the street, he took her arm although she tried to jerk away.

"Won't you have a soda, please?" he begged. The party dress had given his simplified mind its cue and he delighted in the boy-and-girl argument that followed.

"No; I'm going home."

"Oh, come on," he said, pulling her towards a soda fountain. As she went, she unconsciously exaggerated her little-girl-in-a-party-dress air.

They both had strawberry sodas. They sucked the pink drops up through straws, she pouting at his smile, neither one of them conscious of being cute.

"Why are you mad at me, Betty? I didn't do anything. It was Shrike's idea and he did all the talking."

"Because you are a fool."

"I've quit the Miss Lonelyhearts job. I haven't been in the office for almost a week."

"What are you going to do?"

"I'm going to look for a job in an advertising agency."

He was not deliberately lying. He was only trying to say what she wanted to hear. The party dress was so gay and charming, light blue with a frothy lace collar flecked with pink, like the collar of her soda.

"You ought to see Bill Wheelright about a job. He owns an agency—he's a swell guy. . . . He's in love with me."

"I couldn't work for a rival."

She screwed up her nose and they both laughed.

He was still laughing when he noticed that something had gone wrong with her laugh. She was crying.

He felt for the rock. It was still there; neither laughter nor tears could affect the rock. It was oblivious to wind or rain.

"Oh . . ." she sobbed. "I'm a fool." She ran out of the store.

He followed and caught her. But her sobs grew worse and he hailed a taxi and forced her to get in.

She began to talk under her sobs. She was pregnant. She was going to have a baby.

He put the rock forward and waited with complete poise for her to stop crying. When she was quiet, he asked her to marry him.

"No," she said. "I'm going to have an abortion."

"Please marry me." He pleaded just as he had pleaded with her to have a soda.

He begged the party dress to marry him, saying all the things it expected to hear, all the things that went with strawberry sodas and farms in Connecticut. He was just what the party dress wanted him to be: simple and sweet, whimsical and poetic, a trifle collegiate yet very masculine.

By the time they arrived at her house, they were discussing their life after marriage. Where they would live and in how many rooms. Whether they could afford to have the child. How they would rehabilitate the farm in Connecticut. What kind of furniture they both liked.

She agreed to have the child. He won that point. In return, he agreed to see Bill Wheelright about a job. With a great deal of laughter, they decided to have three beds in their bedroom. Twin beds for sleep, very prim and puritanical, and between them a love bed, an ornate double bed with cupids, nymphs and Pans.

He did not feel guilty. He did not feel. The rock was a solidification of his feeling, his conscience, his sense of reality, his self-knowledge. He could have planned anything. A castle in Spain and love on a balcony or a pirate trip and love on a tropical island.

When her door closed behind him, he smiled. The rock had been thoroughly tested and had been found perfect. He had only to climb aboard the bed again.

Miss Lonelyhearts has a religious experience

After a long night and morning, towards noon, Miss Lonelyhearts welcomed the arrival of fever. It promised heat and mentally unmotivated violence. The promise was soon fulfilled; the rock became a furnace.

He fastened his eyes on the Christ that hung on the wall opposite his bed. As he stared at it, it became a bright fly, spinning with quick grace on a background of blood velvet sprinkled with tiny nerve stars.

Everything else in the room was dead—chairs, table, pencils, clothes, books. He thought of this black world of things as a fish. And he was right, for it suddenly rose to the bright bait on the wall. It rose with a splash of music and he saw its shining silver belly.

Christ is life and light.

"Christ! Christ!" This shout echoed through the innermost cells of his body.

He moved his head to a cooler spot on the pillow and the vein in his forehead became less swollen. He felt clean and fresh. His heart was a rose and in his skull another rose bloomed.

The room was full of grace. A sweet, clean grace, not washed clean, but clean as the innersides of the inner petals of a newly forced rosebud.

Delight was also in the room. It was like a gentle wind, and his nerves rippled under it like small blue flowers in a pasture.

He was conscious of two rhythms that were slowly becoming one. When they became one, his identification with God was complete. His heart was the one heart, the heart of God. And his brain was likewise God's.

God said, "Will you accept it, now?"

And he replied, "I accept, I accept."

He immediately began to plan a new life and his future conduct as Miss Lonelyhearts. He submitted drafts of his column to God and God approved them. God approved his every thought.

Suddenly the door bell rang. He climbed out of bed and went into the hall to see who was coming. It was Doyle, the cripple, and he was slowly working his way up the stairs.

God had sent him so that Miss Lonelyhearts could perform a miracle and be certain of his conversion. It was a sign. He would embrace the cripple and the cripple

would be made whole again, even as he, a spiritual cripple, had been made whole.

He rushed down the stairs to meet Doyle with his arms
spread for the miracle.

Doyle was carrying something wrapped in a newspaper.
When he saw Miss Lonelyhearts, he put his hand inside
the package and stopped. He shouted some kind of a warning, but Miss Lonelyhearts continued his charge. He did
not understand the cripple's shout and heard it as a cry for
help from Desperate, Harold S., Catholic-mother, Broken-
hearted, Broad-shoulders, Sick-of-it-all, Disillusioned-with-
tubercular-husband. He was running to succor them with
love.

The cripple turned to escape, but he was too slow and
Miss Lonelyhearts caught him.

While they were struggling, Betty came in through the
street door. She called to them to stop and started up the
stairs. The cripple saw her cutting off his escape and tried
to get rid of the package. He pulled his hand out. The gun
inside the package exploded and Miss Lonelyhearts fell,
dragging the cripple with him. They both rolled part of
the way down the stairs.

1934

A Cool Million

or, The Dismantling of Lemuel Pitkin

To S. J. PERELMAN

"*John D. Rockefeller would give a cool million to have a stomach like yours.*"—OLD SAYING

1

The home of Mrs. Sarah Pitkin, a widow well on in years, was situated on an eminence overlooking the Rat River, near the town of Ottsville in the state of Vermont. It was a humble dwelling much the worse for wear, yet exceedingly dear to her and her only child, Lemuel.

While the house had not been painted for some time, owing to the straitened circumstances of the little family, it still had a great deal of charm. An antique collector, had one chanced to pass it by, would have been greatly inter-

ested in its architecture. Having been built about the time
of General Stark's campaign against the British, its lines
reflected the character of his army, in whose ranks several
Pitkins had marched.

One late fall evening, Mrs. Pitkin was sitting quietly in
her parlor, when a knock was heard on her humble door.

She kept no servant, and, as usual, answered the knock
in person.

"Mr. Slemp!" she said, as she recognized in her caller the
wealthy village lawyer.

"Yes, Mrs. Pitkin, I come upon a little matter of business."

"Won't you come in?" said the widow, not forgetting her
politeness in her surprise.

"I believe I will trespass on your hospitality for a brief
space," said the lawyer blandly. "Are you quite well?"

"Thank you, sir—quite so," said Mrs. Pitkin as she led
the way into the sitting room. "Take the rocking chair, Mr.
Slemp," she said, pointing to the best chair which the simple room contained.

"You are very kind," said the lawyer, seating himself
gingerly in the chair referred to.

"Where is your son, Lemuel?" continued the lawyer.

"He is in school. But it is nearly time for him to be
home; he never loiters." And the mother's voice showed
something of the pride she felt in her boy.

"Still in school!" exclaimed Mr. Slemp. "Shouldn't he be
helping to support you?"

"No," said the widow proudly. "I set great store by learning, as does my son. But you came on business?"

"Ah, yes, Mrs. Pitkin. I fear that the business may be unpleasant for you, but you will remember, I am sure, that
I act in this matter as agent for another."

"Unpleasant!" repeated Mrs. Pitkin apprehensively.

"Yes. Mr. Joshua Bird, Squire Bird, has placed in my

hands for foreclosure the mortgage on your house. That is, he will foreclose," he added hastily, "if you fail to raise the necessary monies in three months from now, when the obligation matures."

"How can I hope to pay?" said the widow brokenly. "I thought that Squire Bird would be glad to renew, as we pay him twelve per cent interest."

"I am sorry, Mrs. Pitkin, sincerely sorry, but he has decided not to renew. He wants either his money or the property."

The lawyer took his hat and bowed politely, leaving the widow alone with her tears.

(It might interest the reader to know that I was right in my surmise. An interior decorator, on passing the house, had been greatly struck by its appearance. He had seen Squire Bird about purchasing it, and that is why that worthy had decided to foreclose on Mrs. Pitkin. The name of the cause of this tragedy was Asa Goldstein, his business, "Colonial Exteriors and Interiors." Mr. Goldstein planned to take the house apart and set it up again in the window of his Fifth Avenue shop.)

As Lawyer Slemp was leaving the humble dwelling, he met the widow's son, Lemuel, on the threshold. Through the open door, the boy caught a glimpse of his mother in tears, and said to Mr. Slemp:

"What have you been saying to my mother to make her cry?"

"Stand aside, boy!" exclaimed the lawyer. He pushed Lem with such great force that the poor lad fell off the porch steps into the cellar, the door of which was unfortunately open. By the time Len had extricated himself, Mr. Slemp was well on his way down the road.

Our hero, although only seventeen years old, was a strong, spirited lad and would have followed after the lawyer but for his mother. On hearing her voice, he dropped the ax which he had snatched up and ran into the house to comfort her.

The poor widow told her son all we have recounted and the two of them sat plunged in gloom. No matter how they racked their brains, they could not discover a way to keep the roof over their heads.

In desperation, Lem finally decided to go and see Mr. Nathan Whipple, who was the town's most prominent citizen. Mr. Whipple had once been President of the United States, and was known affectionately from Maine to California as "Shagpoke" Whipple. After four successful years in office, he had beaten his silk hat, so to speak, into a ploughshare and had refused to run a second time, preferring to return to his natal Ottsville and there become a simple citizen again. He spent all his time between his den in the garage and the Rat River National Bank, of which he was president.

Mr. Whipple had often shown his interest in Lem, and the lad felt that he might be willing to help his mother save her home.

2

Shagpoke Whipple lived on the main street of Ottsville in a two-story frame house with a narrow lawn in front and a garage that once had been a chicken house in the rear. Both buildings had a solid, sober look, and, indeed, no one was ever allowed to create disorder within their precincts.

The house served as a place of business as well as a residence; the first floor being devoted to the offices of the bank and the second functioning as the home of the ex-President. On the porch, next to the front door, was a large bronze plate that read:

RAT RIVER NATIONAL BANK
Nathan "Shagpoke" Whipple
PRES.

Some people might object to turning a part of their dwelling into a bank, especially if, like Mr. Whipple, they had hobnobbed with crowned heads. But Shagpoke was not proud, and he was of the saving kind. He had always saved: from the first time he received a penny at the age of five, when he had triumphed over the delusive pleasures of an investment in candy, right down to the time he was elected President of the United States. One of his favorite adages was "Don't teach your grandmother to suck eggs." By this he meant that the pleasures of the body are like grandmothers, once they begin to suck eggs they never stop until all the eggs (purse) are dry.

As Lem turned up the path to Mr. Whipple's house, the sun rapidly sank under the horizon. Every evening at this time, the ex-President lowered the flag that flew over his garage and made a speech to as many of the town's citizenry as had stopped to watch the ceremony. During the first year after the great man's return from Washington, there used to collect quite a crowd, but this had dwindled until now, as our hero approached the house, there was but a lone Boy Scout watching the ceremony. This lad was not present of his own free will, alas, but had been sent by his father, who was desirous of obtaining a loan from the bank.

Lem removed his hat and waited in reverence for Mr. Whipple to finish his speech.

"All hail Old Glory! May you be the joy and pride of the American heart, alike when your gorgeous folds shall wanton in the summer air and your tattered fragments be dimly seen through clouds of war! May you ever wave in honor, hope and profit, in unsullied glory and patriotic fervor, on the dome of the Capitol, on the tented plain, on the wave-rocked topmast and on the roof of this garage!"

With these words, Shagpoke lowered the flag for which so many of our finest have bled and died, and tenderly gathered it up in his arms. The Boy Scout ran off hurriedly. Lem moved forward to greet the orator.

"I would like to have a few words with you, sir," said our hero.

"Certainly," replied Mr. Whipple with native kindness. "I am never too busy to discuss the problems of youth, for the youth of a nation is its only hope. Come into my den," he added.

The room into which Lem followed Mr. Whipple was situated in the back of the garage. It was furnished with extreme simplicity; some boxes, a cracker barrel, two brass spittoons, a hot stove and a picture of Lincoln were all it held.

When our hero had seated himself on one of the boxes, Shagpoke perched on the cracker barrel and put his congress gaiters near the hot stove. He lined up the distance to the nearest spittoon with a measuring gob of spittle and told the lad to begin.

As it will only delay my narrative and serve no good purpose to report how Lem told about his predicament, I will skip to his last sentence.

"And so," concluded our hero, "the only thing that can save my mother's home is for your bank to take over Squire Bird's mortgage."

"I would not help you by lending you money, even if it were possible for me to do so," was the surprising answer Mr. Whipple gave the boy.

"Why not, sir?" asked Lem, unable to hide his great disappointment.

"Because I believe it would be a mistake. You are too young to borrow."

"But what shall I do?" asked Lem in desperation.

"There are still three months left to you before they can sell your house," said Mr. Whipple. "Don't be discouraged. This is the land of opportunity and the world is an oyster."

"But how am I to earn fifteen hundred dollars (for that was the face value of the mortgage) here in such a short time?" asked Lem, who was puzzled by the ex-President's rather cryptic utterances.

"That is for you to discover, but I never said that you should remain in Ottsville. Do as I did, when I was your age. Go out into the world and win your way."

Lem considered this advice for a while. When he spoke again, it was with courage and determination.

"You are right, sir. I'll go off to seek my fortune." Our hero's eyes shone with a light that bespoke a high heart.

"Good," said Mr. Whipple, and he was genuinely glad. "As I said before, the world is an oyster that but waits for hands to open it. Bare hands are best, but have you any money?"

"Something less than a dollar," said Lem sadly.

"It is very little, my young friend, but it might suffice, for you have an honest face and that is more than gold. But I had thirty-five dollars when I left home to make my way, and it would be nice if you had at least as much."

"Yes, it would be nice," agreed Lem.

"Have you any collateral?" asked Mr. Whipple.

"Collateral?" repeated Lem, whose business education was so limited that he did not even know what the word meant.

"Security for a loan," said Mr. Whipple.

"No, sir, I'm afraid not."

"Your mother has a cow, I think?"

"Yes, Old Sue." The boy's face fell as he thought of parting with that faithful servitor.

"I believe that I could lend you twenty-five dollars on her, maybe thirty," said Mr. Whipple.

"But she cost more than a hundred, and besides she supplies us with milk, butter and cheese, the main part of our simple victuals."

"You do not understand," said Mr. Whipple patiently. "Your mother can keep the cow until the note that she will sign comes due in sixty days from now. This new obligation will be an added incentive to spur you on to success."

"But what if I fail?" asked Lem. Not that he was losing heart, be it said, but he was young and wanted encouragement.

Mr. Whipple understood how the lad felt and made an effort to reassure him.

"America," he said with great seriousness, "is the land of opportunity. She takes care of the honest and industrious and never fails them as long as they are both. This is not a matter of opinion, it is one of faith. On the day that Americans stop believing it, on that day will America be lost.

"Let me warn you that you will find in the world a certain few scoffers who will laugh at you and attempt to do you injury. They will tell you that John D. Rockefeller was a thief and that Henry Ford and other great men are also thieves. Do not believe them. The story of Rockefeller and of Ford is the story of every great American, and you should strive to make it your story. Like them, you were born poor and on a farm. Like them, by honesty and industry, you cannot fail to succeed."

It is needless to say that the words of the ex-President encouraged our young hero just as similar ones have heartened the youth of this country ever since it was freed

from the irksome British yoke. He vowed then and there
to go and do as Rockefeller and Ford had done.

Mr. Whipple drew up some papers for the lad's mother
to sign and ushered him out of the den. When he had gone,
the great man turned to the picture of Lincoln that hung
on the wall and silently communed with it.

3

Our hero's way home led through a path that ran along
the Rat River. As he passed a wooded stretch he cut a
stout stick with a thick gnarled top. He was twirling this
club, as a bandmaster does his baton, when he was startled
by a young girl's shriek. Turning his head, he saw a terrified figure pursued by a fierce dog. A moment's glance
showed him that it was Betty Prail, a girl with whom he
was in love in a boyish way.

Betty recognized him at the same moment.

"Oh, save me, Mr. Pitkin!" she exclaimed, clasping her
hands.

"I will," said Lem resolutely.

Armed with the stick he had most fortunately cut, he
rushed between the girl and her pursuer and brought the
knob down with full force on the dog's back. The attention of the furious animal—a large bulldog—was diverted
to his assailant, and with a fierce howl he rushed upon Lem.
But our hero was wary and expected the attack. He
jumped to one side and brought the stick down with great
force on the dog's head. The animal fell, partly stunned,
his quivering tongue protruding from his mouth.

"It won't do to leave him so," thought Lem; "when he
revives he'll be as dangerous as ever."

He dealt the prostrate brute two more blows which
settled its fate. The furious animal would do no more harm.

"Oh, thank you, Mr. Pitkin!" exclaimed Betty, a trace of

color returning to her cheeks. "I was terribly frightened."

"I don't wonder," said Lem. "The brute was certainly ugly."

"How brave you are!" the young lady said in admiration.

"It doesn't take much courage to hit a dog on the head with a stick," said Lem modestly.

"Many boys would have run," she said.

"What, and left you unprotected?" Lem was indignant. "None but a coward would have done that."

"Tom Baxter was walking with me, and he ran away."

"Did he see the dog chasing you?"

"Yes."

"And what did he do?"

"He jumped over a stone wall."

"All I can say is that that isn't my style," said Lem. "Do you see how the dog froths at the mouth? I believe he's mad."

"How fearful!" exclaimed Betty with a shudder. "Did you suspect that before?"

"Yes, when I first saw him."

"And yet you dared to meet him?"

"It was safer than to run," said Lem, making little of the incident. "I wonder whose dog it was?"

"I'll tell you," said a brutal voice.

Turning his head, Lem beheld a stout fellow about three years older than himself, with a face in which the animal seemed to predominate. It was none other than Tom Baxter, the town bully.

"What have you been doing to my dog?" demanded Baxter with a snarl.

Addressed in this tone, Lem thought it unnecessary to throw away politeness on such a brutal customer.

"Killing him," he answered shortly.

"What business have you killing my dog?" demanded the bully with much anger.

"It was your business to keep the brute locked up, where he wouldn't do any harm," said Lem. "Besides, you saw him attack Miss Prail. Why didn't you interfere?"

"I'll flog you within an inch of your life," said Baxter with an oath.

"You'd better not try it," said Lem coolly. "I suppose you think I ought to have let the dog bite Miss Prail."

"He wouldn't have bitten her."

"He would too. He was chasing her with that intention."

"It was only in sport."

"I suppose he was frothing at the mouth only in sport," said Lem. "The dog was mad. You ought to thank me for killing him because he might have bitten you."

"That don't go down," said Baxter coarsely. "It's much too thin."

"It's true," said Betty Prail, speaking for the first time.

"Of course you'll stand up for him," said the butcher boy (for that was Baxter's business), "but that's neither here nor there. I paid five dollars for that dog, and if he don't pay me what I gave, I'll mash him."

"I shall do nothing of the sort," said Lem quietly. "A dog like that ought to be killed, and no one has any right to let him run loose, risking the lives of innocent people. The next time you get five dollars you ought to invest it better."

"Then you won't pay me the money?" cried the bully in a passion. "I'll break your head."

"Come on," said Lem, "I've got something to say about that," and he squared off scientifically.

"Oh, don't fight him, Mr. Pitkin," said Betty, very much distressed. "He is much stronger than you."

"He'll find that out soon enough, I'm thinking," growled Lem's opponent.

That Tom Baxter was not only larger but stronger than our hero was no doubt true. On the other hand he did not know how to use his strength. It was merely undisciplined brute force. If he could have got Lem around the waist the latter would have been at his mercy, but our hero knew that well enough and didn't choose to allow it. He was a pretty fair boxer, and stood on his defense, calm and wary.

When Baxter rushed in, thinking to seize his smaller opponent, he was greeted by two rapid blows in the face, one of which struck him on the nose, the other in the eye, the effect of both being to make his head spin.

"I'll mash you for that," he yelled in a frenzy of rage, but as he rushed in again he never thought to guard his face. The result was a couple of more blows, the other eye and his mouth being assailed this time.

Baxter was astonished. He had expected to "chaw up" Lem at the first onset. Instead of that, there stood Lem cool and unhurt, while he could feel that his nose and mouth were bleeding and both his eyes were rapidly closing.

He stopped short and regarded Lem as well as he could through his injured optics, then surprised our hero by smiling. "Well," he said, shaking his head sheepishly, "you're the better man. I'm a rough customer, I expect, but I know when I'm bested. There's my hand to show that I don't bear malice."

Lem gave his hand in return without fear that there might be craft in the bully's offer of friendship. The former was a fair-dealing lad himself and he thought that everyone was the same. However, no sooner did Baxter have a hold of his hand than he jerked the poor boy into his embrace and squeezed him insensible.

Betty screamed and fainted, so great was her anxiety for Lem. Hearing her scream, Baxter dropped his victim to the ground and walked to where the young lady lay in a dead faint. He stood over her for a few minutes admiring her beauty. His little pig-like eyes shone with bestiality.

4

It is with reluctance that I leave Miss Prail in the lecherous embrace of Tom Baxter to begin a new chapter, but I cannot with propriety continue my narrative beyond the point at which the bully undressed that unfortunate lady.

However, as Miss Prail is the heroine of this romance, I would like to use this opportunity to acquaint you with a little of her past history.

On her twelfth brithday, Betty became an orphan with the simultaneous death of her two parents in a fire which also destroyed what little property might have been left her. In this fire, or rather at it, she also lost something which, like her parents, could never be replaced.

The Prail farm was situated some three miles from Ottsville on a rough dirt road, and the amateur fire company, to whose ministrations all the fires in the district were left, was not very enthusiastic about dragging their apparatus to it. To tell the truth, the Ottsville Fire Company consisted of a set of young men who were more interested in dirty stories, checkers and applejack than they were in fire fighting. When the news of the catastrophe arrived at the fire house, the volunteer firemen were all inebriated, and their chief, Bill Baxter (father to the man in whose arms we left our heroine), was dead drunk.

After many delays, the fire company finally arrived at the Prail farm, but instead of trying to quench the flames they immediately set to work and looted the place.

Betty, although only twelve years old at the time, was a well-formed little girl with the soft, voluptuous lines of a beautiful woman. Dressed only in a cotton nightgown, she was wandering among the firemen begging them to save her parents, when Bill Baxter noticed her budding form and enticed her into the woodshed.

In the morning, she was found lying naked on the ground by some neighbors and taken into their house. She had a bad cold, but remembered nothing of what Bill Baxter had done to her. She mourned only the loss of her parents.

After a small collection had been taken up by the minister to purchase an outfit, she was sent to the county orphan asylum. There she remained until her fourteenth year, when she was put out as a maid of all work to the Slemps, a prominent family of Ottsville, the head of which, Lawyer Slemp, we already know.

As one can well imagine, all was not beer and skittles in this household for the poor orphan. If she had been less beautiful, perhaps things would have gone better for her. As it was, however, Lawyer Slemp had two ugly daughters and a shrewish wife who were very jealous of their beautiful servant. They saw to it that she was badly dressed and that she wore her hair only in the ugliest possible manner. Yet despite these things, and although she had to wear men's shoes and coarse cotton stockings, our heroine was a great deal more attractive than the other women of the household.

Lawyer Slemp was a deacon in the church and a very stern man. Still, one would think that as a male he would have less against the poor orphan than his women folks. But, unfortunately, it did not work out this way. Mr. Slemp beat Betty regularly and enthusiastically. He had started these beatings when she first came from the asylum as a little girl, and did not stop them when she became a splendid woman. He beat her twice a week on her bare behind with his bare hand.

It is a hard thing to say about a deacon, but Lawyer Slemp got little exercise and he seemed to take a great deal of pleasure in these bi-weekly workouts. As for Betty, she soon became inured to his blows and did not mind

them as much as the subtler tortures inflicted on her by
Mrs. Slemp and her daughters. Besides, Lawyer Slemp, although he was exceedingly penurious, always gave her a
quarter when he had finished beating her.

It was with this weekly fifty cents that Betty hoped to
effect her escape from Ottsville. She had already obtained
part of an outfit, and was on her way home from town
with the first store hat she had ever owned when she met
Tom Baxter and his dog.

The result of this unfortunate encounter we already
know.

5

When our hero regained consciousness, he found himself
in a ditch alongside the path on which he had his set-to
with Tom Baxter. It had grown quite dark, and he failed to
notice Betty in some bushes on the other side of the path.
He thought that she must have got safely away.

As he walked home his head cleared and he soon recovered his naturally high spirits. He forgot his unfortunate encounter with the bully and thought only of his
coming departure for New York City.

He was greeted at the door of his humble home by his
fond parent, who had been waiting anxiously for his return.

"Lem, Lem," said Mrs. Pitkin, "where have you been?"

Although our hero was loth to lie, he did not want to
worry his mother unduly, so he said, "Mr. Whipple kept
me."

The lad then told her what the ex-President had said.
She was quite happy for her son and willingly signed the
note for thirty dollars. Like all mothers, Mrs. Pitkin was
certain that her child must succeed.

Bright and early the next morning, Lem took the note

to Mr. Whipple and received thirty dollars minus twelve per cent interest in advance. He then bought a ticket for New York at the local depot, and waited there for the arrival of the steam cars.

Our hero was studying the fleeting scenery of New England when he heard someone address him.

"Papers, magazines, all the popular novels! Something to read, mister?"

It was the news butcher, a young boy with an honest, open countenance.

Our hero was eager to talk, so he spoke to the newsboy.

"I'm not a great one for reading novels," he said. "My Aunt Nancy gave my ma one once but I didn't find much in it. I like facts and I like to study, though."

"I ain't much on story reading either," said the news butcher. "Where are you goin'?"

"To New York to make my fortune," said Lem candidly.

"Well, if you can't make money in New York, you can't make money anywhere." With this observation he began to hawk his reading matter farther down the aisle.

Lem again took up his study of the fleeting scenery. This time he was interrupted by a stylishly dressed young man who came forward and accosted him.

"Is this seat engaged?" the stranger asked.

"Not as I know of?" replied Lem with a friendly smile.

"Then with your kind permission I will occupy it," said the over-dressed stranger.

"Why, of course," said our hero.

"You are from the country, I presume," he continued affably as he sank into the seat alongside our hero.

"Yes, I am. I live near Bennington in the town of Ottsville. Were you ever there?"

"No. I suppose you are taking a vacation trip to the big city?"

"Oh, no; I'm leaving home to make my fortune."

"That's nice. I hope you are successful. By the way, the Mayor of New York is my uncle."

"My, is that so?" said Lem with awe.

"Yes indeed, my name is Wellington Mape."

"Glad to make your acquaintance, Mr. Mape. I'm Lemuel Pitkin."

"Indeed! An aunt of mine married a Pitkin. Perhaps we're related."

Lem was quite elated at the thought that he might be kin to the Mayor of New York without knowing it. He decided that his new acquaintance must be rich because of his clothing and his extreme politeness.

"Are you in business, Mr. Mape?" he asked.

"Well, ahem!" was that suave individual's rejoinder. "I'm afraid I'm rather an idler. My father left me a cool million, so I don't feel the need of working."

"A cool million!" ejaculated Lem. "Why, that's ten times a hundred thousand dollars."

"Just so," said Mr. Mape, smiling at the lad's enthusiasm.

"That's an awful pile of money! I'd be satisfied if I had five thousand right now."

"I'm afraid that five thousand wouldn't last me very long," said Mr. Mape with an amused smile.

"Gee! Where would anybody get such a pile of money unless they inherited it?"

"That's easy," said the stranger. "Why, I've made as much in one day in Wall Street."

"You don't say."

"Yes, I do say. You can take my word for it."

"I wish I could make some money," said Lem wistfully, as he thought of the mortgage on his home.

"A man must have money to make money. If now, you had some money . . ."

"I've got a little under thirty dollars," said Lem.

"Is that all?"

"Yes, that's all. I had to give Mr. Whipple a note to borrow it."

"If that's all the money you have, you'd better take good care of it. I regret to say that despite the efforts of the Mayor, my uncle, there are still many crooks in New York."

"I intend to be careful."

"Then you keep your money in a safe place?"

"I haven't hidden it because a secret pocket is the first place a thief would look. I keep it loose in my trousers where nobody would think I carried so much money."

"You are right. I can see that you are a man of the world."

"Oh, I can take care of myself, I guess," said Lem with the confidence of youth.

"That comes of being a Pitkin. I'm glad to know that we're related. You must call on me in New York."

"Where do you live?"

"At the Ritz. Just ask for Mr. Wellington Mape's suite of rooms."

"Is it a good place to live?"

"Why, yes. I pay three dollars a day for my board, and the incidentals carry my expenses up to as high as forty dollars a week."

"Gee," ejaculated Lem. "I could never afford it—that is, at first." And our hero laughed with the incurable optimism of youth.

"You of course should find a boarding house where they give you plain but solid fare for a reasonable sum. . . . But I must bid you good morning, a friend is waiting for me in the next car."

After the affable Mr. Wellington Mape had taken his departure, Lem turned again to his vigil at the car window.

The news butcher had changed his cap. "Apples, bananas, oranges!" he shouted as he came down the aisle with a basket of fruit on his arm.

Lem stopped his rapid progress to ask him the price of an orange. It was two cents, and he decided to buy one to eat with the hard-boiled egg his mother had given him. But when our hero thrust his hand into his pocket, a wild spasm contracted his features. He explored further, with growing trepidation, and a sickly pallor began to spread over his face.

"What's the matter?" asked Steve, for that was the train boy's name.

"I've been robbed! My money's gone! All the money Mr. Whipple lent me has been stolen!"

6

"I wonder who did it?" asked Steve.

"I can't imagine," answered Lem brokenly.

"Did they get much?"

"All I had in the world. . . . A little less than thirty dollars."

"Some smart leather must have gotten it."

"Leather?" queried our hero, not understanding the argot of the underworld with which the train boy was familiar.

"Yes, leather—pickpocket. Did anybody talk to you on the train?"

"Only Mr. Wellington Mape, a rich young man. He is kin to the Mayor of New York."

"Who told you that?"

"He did himself."

"How was he dressed?" asked Steve, whose suspicions were aroused. (He had been "wire"—scout—to a "leather" when small and knew all about the dodge.) "Did he wear a pale blue hat?"

"Yes."

"And looked a great swell?"

"Yes."

"He got off at the last station and your dough-re-me went with him."

"You mean he got my money? Well, I never. He told me he was worth a cool million and boarded at the Ritz Hotel."

"That's the way they all talk—big. Did you tell him where you kept your money?"

"Yes, I did. But can't I get it back?"

"I don't see how. He got off the train."

"I'd like to catch hold of him," said Lem, who was very angry.

"Oh, he'd hit you with a piece of lead pipe. But look through your pockets, maybe he left you a dollar."

Lem put his hand into the pocket in which he had carried his money and drew it out as though he had been bitten. Between his fingers he held a diamond ring.

"What's that?" asked Steve.

"I don't know," said Lem with surprise. "I don't think I ever saw it before. Yes, by gum, I did. It must have dropped off the crook's finger when he picked my pocket. I saw him wearing it."

"Boy!" exclaimed the train boy. "You're sure in luck. Talk about falling in a privy and coming up with a gold watch. You're certainly it. With a double t."

"What is it worth?" asked Lem eagerly.

"Permit me to look at it, my young friend, perhaps I can tell you," said a gentleman in a gray derby hat, who was sitting across the aisle. This stranger had been listening with great curiosity to the dialogue between our hero and the train boy.

"I am a pawnbroker," he said. "If you let me examine the ring, I can surely give you some idea of its value."

Lem handed the article in question to the stranger, who put a magnifying glass into his eye and looked at it carefully.

"My young friend, that ring is worth all of fifty dollars," he announced.

"I'm certainly in luck," said Lem. "The crook only stole twenty-eight dollars and sixty cents from me. But I'd rather have my money back. I don't want any of his."

"I'll tell you what I'll do," said the self-styled pawnbroker. "I'll advance you twenty-eight dollars and sixty cents against the ring, and agree to give it back for that sum and suitable interest if the owner should ever call for it."

"That's fair enough," said Lem gratefully, and he pocketed the money that the stranger tendered him.

Our hero paid for the piece of fruit that he had bought from the train boy and ate it with quiet contentment. In the meantime, the "pawnbroker" prepared to get off the train. When he had gathered together his meager luggage, he shook hands with Lem and gave him a receipt for the ring.

But no sooner had the stranger left than a squad of policemen armed with sawed-off shotguns entered and started down the aisle. Lem watched their progress with great interest. His interest, however, changed to alarm when they stopped at his seat and one of them caught him roughly by the throat. Handcuffs were then snapped around his wrists. Weapons pointed at his head.

7

"Begorra, we've got him," said Sergeant Clancy, who was in charge of the police squad.

"But I haven't done anything," expostulated Lem, turning pale.

"None of your lip, sweetheart," said the sergeant. "Will

you go quietly or will you go quietly?" Before the poor
lad had a chance to express his willingness to go, the police officer struck him an extremely hard blow on the head
with his club.

Lem slumped down in his seat and Sergeant Clancy
ordered his men to carry the boy off the train. A patrol
wagon was waiting at the depot. Lem's unconscious form
was dumped into the "Black Maria" and the police drove
to the station house.

When our hero regained consciousness some hours later,
he was lying on the stone floor of a cell. The room was full
of detectives and the air was foul with cigar smoke. Lem
opened one eye, unwittingly giving the signal for the detectives to go into action.

"'Fess up," said Detective Grogan, but before the boy
could speak he kicked him in the stomach with his heavy
boot.

"Faith now," interfered Detective Reynolds, "give the
lad a chance." He bent over Lem's prostrate form with a
kind smile on his face and said, "Me lad, the jig is up."

"I'm innocent," protested Lem. "I didn't do anything."

"You stole a diamond ring and sold it," said another detective.

"I did not," replied Lem, with as much fire as he could
muster under the circumstances. "A pickpocket dropped
it in my pocket and I pawned it with a stranger for thirty
dollars."

"Thirty dollars!" exclaimed Detective Reynolds, his voice
giving great evidence of disbelief. "Thirty dollars for a
ring that cost more than a thousand. Me lad, it won't
wash." So saying the detective drew back his foot and
kicked poor Lem behind the ear even harder than his col-
league had done.

Our hero lost consciousness again, as was to be ex-

pected, and the detectives left his cell, having first made
sure that he was still alive.

A few days later, Lem was brought to trial, but neither
judge nor jury would believe his story.

Unfortunately, Stamford, the town in which he had
been arrested, was in the midst of a crime wave and both
the police and the judiciary were anxious to send people
to jail. It also counted heavily against him that the man
who had posed as a pawnbroker on the train was in
reality Hiram Glazer, alias "The Pinhead," a notorius
underworld character. This criminal turned state's evidence and blamed the crime on our hero in return for a
small fee from the district attorney, who was shortly
coming up for re-election.

Once the verdict of guilty had been brought in, Lem
was treated with great kindness by everyone, even by the
detectives who had been so brutal in the station house. It
was through their recommendations, based on what they
called his willingness to cooperate, that he received only
fifteen years in the penitentiary.

Our hero was immediately transferred to prison, where
he was incarcerated exactly five weeks after his departure
from Ottsville. It would be hard to say from this that
justice is not swift, although, knowing the truth, we must
add that it is not always sure.

The warden of the state prison, Ezekiel Purdy, was a
kind man if stern. He invariably made all newcomers a
little speech of welcome and greeted Lem with the following words:

"My son, the way of the transgressor is hard, but at
your age it is still possible to turn from it. However, do
not squirm, for you will get no sermon from me."

(Lem was not squirming. The warden's expression was
purely rhetorical.)

"Sit down for a moment," added Mr. Purdy, indicating the chair in which he wanted Lem to sit. "Your new duties can wait yet awhile, as can the prison barber and tailor."

The warden leaned back in his chair and sucked meditatively on his enormous calabash pipe. When he began to talk again, it was with ardor and conviction.

"The first thing to do is to draw all your teeth," he said. "Teeth are often a source of infection and it pays to be on the safe side. At the same time we will begin a series of cold showers. Cold water is an excellent cure for morbidity."

"But I am innocent," cried Lem, when the full significance of what the warden had said dawned on him. "I am not morbid and I never had a toothache in my life."

Mr. Purdy dismissed the poor lad's protests with an airy wave of his hand. "In my eyes," he said, "the sick are never guilty. You are merely sick, as are all criminals. And as for your other argument; please remember that an ounce of prevention is worth a ton of cure. Because you have never had a toothache does not mean that you will never have one."

Lem could not help but groan.

"Be of good cheer, my son," said the warden brightly, as he pressed a button on his desk to summon a guard.

A few minutes later our hero was led off to the prison dentist, where we will not follow him just yet.

8

Several chapters back I left our heroine, Betty Prail, lying naked under a bush. She was not quite so fortunate as Lem, and did not regain consciousness until after he had returned home.

When she recovered the full possession of her faculties, she found herself in what she thought was a large box that was being roughly shaken by some unknown agency. In a little while, however, she realized that she was in reality lying on the bottom of a wagon.

"Could it be that she was dead?" she asked herself. But no, she heard voices, and besides she was still naked. "No matter how poor a person is," she comforted herself, "they wrap him or her up in something before burial."

There were evidently two men on the driver's seat of the wagon. She tried to understand what they were saying, but could not because they spoke a foreign tongue. She was able to recognize their language as Italian, however, having had some few music lessons in the orphan asylum.

"Gli diede uno scudo, il che lo rese subito gentile," said one of her captors to the other in a guttural voice.

"Si, si," affirmed the other. "Questa vita terrena e quasi un prato, che'l serpente tra fiori giace." After this bit of homely philosophy, they both lapsed into silence.

But I do not want to mystify my readers any longer. The truth was that the poor girl had been found by white slavers, and was being taken to a house of ill fame in New York City.

The trip was an exceedingly rough one for our heroine. The wagon in which she was conveyed had no springs to speak of, and her two captors made her serve a severe apprenticeship to the profession they planned for her to follow.

Late one night, the Italians halted their vehicle before the door of a Chinese laundry somewhere near Mott Street. After descending from their dilapidated conveyance, they scanned the street both up and down for a possible policeman. When they had made sure that it was deserted, they covered their captive with some old sacking and bundled her into the laundry.

There they were greeted by an ancient Chinaman, who

was doing sums on an abacus. This son of the Celestial Empire was a graduate of the Yale University in Shanghai, and he spoke Italian perfectly.

"Qualche cosa de nuovo, signori?" he asked.

"Molto, molto," said the older and more villainous looking of the two foreigners. "La vostra lettera l'abbiamo ricevuto, ma il danaro no," he added with a shrewd smile.

"Queste sette medaglie le trovero, compaesano," answered the Chinaman in the same language.

After this rather cryptic dialogue, the Chinaman led Betty through a secret door into a sort of reception room. This chamber was furnished in luxurious oriental splendor. The walls were sheathed in a pink satin that had been embroidered with herons in silver by some cunning workman. On the floor was a silk rug that must have cost more than a thousand dollars, the colors of which could well vie with the rainbow. Before a hideous idol, incense was burning, and its heady odor filled the air. It was evident that neither pains nor expense had been spared in the decoration of the room.

The old Chinaman struck a gong, and ere its musical note died away an oriental woman with bound feet came to lead Betty off.

When she had gone, Wu Fong, for that was the Chinaman's name, began to haggle with the two Italians over her purchase price. The bargaining was done in Italian, and rather than attempt to make a word-for-word report of the transaction I shall give only the result. Betty was knocked down to the Chinaman for six hundred dollars.

This was a big price, so far as prices went in the white slave market. But Wu Fong was set on having her. In fact it was he who had sent the two to scour the New England countryside for a real American girl. Betty suited him down to the ground.

The reader may be curious to know why he wanted an

American girl so badly. Let me say now that Wu Fong's establishment was no ordinary house of ill fame. It was like that more famous one in the Rue Chabanis, Paris, France—a "House of All Nations." In his institution he already had a girl from every country in the known world except ours, and now Betty rounded out the collection.

Wu Fong was confident that he would soon have his six hundred dollars back with interest, for many of his clients were from non-Aryan countries and would appreciate the services of a genuine American. Apropos of this, it is lamentable but a fact, nevertheless, that the inferior races greatly desire the women of their superiors. This is why the Negroes rape so many white women in our southern states.

Each one of the female inmates of Wu Fong's establishment had a tiny two-room suite for her own use, furnished and decorated in the style of the country from which she came. Thus, Marie, the French girl, had an apartment that was Directoire. Celeste's rooms (there were two French girls because of their traditional popularity) were Louis the Fourteenth; she being the fatter of the two.

In her suite, the girl from Spain, Conchita, had a grand piano with a fancy shawl gracefully draped over it. Her arm-chair was upholstered in horsehide fastened by large buttons, and it had enormous steer horns for arms. On one of her walls a tiny balcony had been painted by a poor but consummate artist.

There is little use in my listing the equipment of the remaining some fifty-odd apartments. Suffice it to say that the same idea was carried out with excellent taste and real historical knowledge in all of them.

Still wearing the sacking into which the Italians had bundled her, our heroine was led to the apartment that had been prepared against her arrival.

The proprietor of the house had hired Asa Goldstein to

decorate this suite and it was a perfect colonial interior. Antimacassars, ships in bottles, carved whalebone, hooked rugs—all were there. It was Mr. Goldstein's boast that even Governor Windsor himself could not have found anything wrong with the design or furnishings.

Betty was exhausted, and immediately fell asleep on the poster bed with its candlewick spread. When she awoke, she was given a hot bath, which greatly refreshed her. She was then dressed by two skillful maids.

The costume that she was made to wear had been especially designed to go with her surroundings. While not exactly in period, it was very striking, and I will describe it as best I can for the benefit of my feminine readers.

The dress had a full waist made with a yoke and belt, a gored skirt, long, but not too long to afford a very distinct view of a well-turned ankle and a small, shapely foot encased in a snowy cotton stocking and a low-heeled black slipper. The material of the dress was chintz—white ground with a tiny brown figure—finished at the neck with a wide white ruffle. On her hands she was made to wear black silk mitts with half-fingers. Her hair was worn in a little knot on the top of her head, and one thick short curl was kept in place by a puff-comb on each side of her face.

Breakfast, for so much time had elapsed, was served her by an old Negro in livery. It consisted of buckwheat cakes with maple syrup, Rhode Island Johnny cakes, bacon biscuits, and a large slice of apple pie.

(Wu Fong was a great stickler for detail, and, like many another man, if he had expended as much energy and thought honestly he would have made even more money without having to carry the stigma of being a brothel-keeper. Alas!)

So resilient are the spirits of the young that Betty did the breakfast full justice. She even ordered a second helping of pie, which was brought to her at once by the darky.

After Betty had finished eating, she was given some embroidery to do. With the reader's kind permission we will leave her while she is still sewing, and before the arrival of her first client, a pockmarked Armenian rug merchant from Malta.

9

Justice will out. I am happy to acquaint my readers with the fact that the real criminal, Mr. Wellington Mape, was apprehended by the police some weeks after Lem had been incarcerated in the state penitentiary.

But our hero was in a sorry state when the Governor's pardon arrived, and for a while it looked as though the reprieve had come too late. The poor lad was in the prison infirmary with a bad case of pneumonia. Weakened greatly by the drawing of all his teeth, he had caught cold after the thirteenth icy shower and the fourteenth had damaged his lungs.

Due to his strong physique, however, and a constitution that had never been undermined by the use of either tobacco or alcohol, Lem succeeded in passing the crisis of the dread pulmonary disease.

On the first day that his vision was normal, he was surprised to see Shagpoke Whipple go through the prison infirmary carrying what was evidently a bedpan and dressed in the uniform of a convict.

"Mr. Whipple," Lem called. "Mr. Whipple."

The ex-President turned and came towards the boy's bed.

"Hello, Lem," said Shagpoke, putting down the utensil he was carrying. "I'm glad to see that you're better."

"Thank you, sir. But what are you doing here?" asked Lem with bewildered surprise.

"I'm the trusty in charge of this ward. But what you really mean, I take it, is why am I here?"

The elderly statesman looked around. He saw that the guard was busy talking to a pretty nurse and drew up a chair.

"It's a long story," said Mr. Whipple with a sigh. "But the long and short of it is that the Rat River National failed and its depositors sent me here."

"That's too bad, sir," Lem said sympathetically. "And after all you had done for the town."

"Such is the gratitude of the mob, but in a way I can't blame them," Mr. Whipple said with all the horse sense for which he was famous. "Rather do I blame Wall Street and the Jewish international bankers. They loaded me up with a lot of European and South American bonds, then they forced me to the wall. It was Wall Street working hand in hand with the Communists that caused my downfall. The bankers broke me, and the Communists circulated lying rumors about my bank in Doc Slack's barber shop. I was the victim of an un-American conspiracy."

Mr. Whipple sighed again, then said in a militant tone of voice: "My boy, when we get out of here, there are two evils undermining this country which we must fight with tooth and nail. These two archenemies of the American Spirit, the spirit of fair play and open competition, are Wall Street and the Communists."

"But how is my mother?" interrupted Lem, "and whatever became of our house? And the cow—did you have to sell her?" Our hero's voice trembled as he asked these questions, for he feared the worst.

"Alas," sighed Mr. Whipple, "Squire Bird foreclosed his mortgage and Asa Goldstein took your home to his store in New York City. There is some talk of his selling it to the Metropolitan Museum. As for the cow, the creditors of my bank sheriffed her. Your mother disappeared. She wandered off during the foreclosure sale, and neither hair nor hide of her was seen again."

This terrible intelligence made our hero literally groan with anguish.

In an effort to cheer the boy up, Mr. Whipple kept on talking. "Your cow taught me a lesson," he said. "She was about the only collateral I had that paid one hundred cents on the dollar. The European bonds didn't bring ten cents on the dollar. The next bank I own will mortgage nothing but cows, good American cows."

"You expect to keep a bank again?" asked Lem, making a brave attempt not to think of his own troubles.

"Why, certainly," replied Shagpoke. "My friends will have me out of here shortly. Then I will run for political office, and after I have shown the American people that Shagpoke is still Shagpoke, I will retire from politics and open another bank. In fact, I am even considering opening the Rat River National a second time. I should be able to buy it in for a few cents on the dollar."

"Do you really think you can do it?" asked our hero with wonder and admiration.

"Why, of course I can," answered Mr. Whipple. "I am an American businessman, and this place is just an incident in my career. My boy, I believe I once told you that you had an almost certain chance to succeed because you were born poor and on a farm. Let me now tell you that your chance is even better because you have been in prison."

"But what am I to do when I get out?" asked Lem with ill-concealed desperation.

"Be an inventor," Mr. Whipple replied without a moment's hesitation. "The American mind is noted for its ingenuity. All the devices of the modern world, from the safety pin to four-wheel brakes, were invented by us."

"But I don't know what to invent," said Lem.

"That's easy. Before you leave here I will give you several of my inventions to work on. If you perfect them we will split fifty-fifty."

"That'll be great!" exclaimed Lem with increased cheerfulness.

"My young friend, you don't want me to think that you were in any way discouraged by the misfortunes that befell you?" asked Mr. Whipple with simulated surprise.

"But I didn't even get to New York," apologized Lem.

"America is still a young country," Mr. Whipple said, assuming his public manner, "and like all young countries, it is rough and unsettled. Here a man is a millionaire one day and a pauper the next, but no one thinks the worse of him. The wheel will turn, for that is the nature of wheels. Don't believe the fools who tell you that the poor man hasn't got a chance to get rich any more because the country is full of chain stores. Office boys still marry their employers' daughters. Shipping clerks are still becoming presidents of railroads. Why, only the other day, I read where an elevator operator won a hundred thousand dollars in a sweepstake and was made a partner in a brokerage house. Despite the Communists and their vile propaganda against individualism, this is still the golden land of opportunity. Oil wells are still found in people's back yards. There are still gold mines hidden away in our mountain fastnesses. America is . . ."

But while Shagpoke was still speaking, a prison guard came by and forced him hurriedly to resume his duties. He left with his bedpan before Lem had an opportunity to thank him properly for his inspiring little talk.

Helped not a little by the encouragement Mr. Whipple had given him, our hero mended rapidly. One day he was summoned to the office of Mr. Purdy, the warden. That official showed him the pardon from the Governor

As a parting gift, he presented Lem with a set of false teeth. He then conducted him to the prison gates, and stood there awhile with the boy, for he had grown fond of him.

Shaking Lem's hand in a hearty farewell, Mr. Purdy said:

"Suppose you had obtained a job in New York City that paid fifteen dollars a week. You were here with us in all twenty weeks, so you lost the use of three hundred dollars. However, you paid no board while you were here, which was a saving for you of about seven dollars a week or one hundred and forty dollars. This leaves you the loser by one hundred and sixty dollars. But it would have cost you at least two hundred dollars to have all your teeth extracted, so you're really ahead of the game forty dollars. Also, the set of false teeth I gave you cost twenty dollars new and is worth at least fifteen dollars in its present condition. This makes your profit about fifty-five dollars. Not at all a bad sum for a lad of your age to save in twenty weeks."

10

Along with his civilian clothes, the prison authorities turned back to Lem an envelope containing the thirty dollars he had had in his pockets on the day he was arrested.

He did not loiter in Stamford, but went immediately to the depot and bought a ticket for New York City. When the cars pulled into the station, he boarded them determined not to speak to any strangers. He was helped in this by the fact that he was not as yet used to his false teeth. Unless he exercised great care, they fell into his lap every time he opened his mouth.

He arrived in the Grand Central Station all intact. At first he was quite confused by the hustle and bustle of the great city, but when a Jehu standing by a broken-down Pierce Arrow hack accosted him, he had the presence of mind to shake his head in the negative.

The cabby was a persistent fellow. "Where do you want to go, young master?" he asked with sneering servility. "Is it the Ritz Hotel you're looking for?"

Lem took a firm purchase on his store teeth and asked, "That's one of those high-priced taverns, isn't it?"

"Yes, but I'll take you to a cheap one if you'll hire me."

"What's your charge?"

"Three dollars and a half, and half a dollar for your baggage."

"This is all the baggage I have," said Lem, indicating his few things tied in a red cotton handkerchief.

"I'll take you for three dollars, then," said the driver with a superior smile.

"No, thanks, I'll walk," said our hero. "I can't afford to pay your charge."

"You can't walk; it's over ten miles from this station to town," replied the Jehu without blushing, although it was evident that they were at that moment standing almost directly in the center of the city.

Without another word, Lem turned on his heel and walked away from the cab driver. As he made his way through the crowded streets, he congratulated himself on how he had handled his first encounter. By keeping his wits about him, he had saved over a tenth of his capital.

Lem saw a peanut stand, and as a matter of policy purchased a bag of the toothsome earth nuts.

"I'm from the country," he said to the honest-appearing merchant. "Can you direct me to a cheap hotel?"

"Yes," said the sidewalk vendor, smiling at the boy's candor. "I know of one where they charge only a dollar a day."

"Is that cheap?" asked our hero in surprise. "What then do they charge at the Ritz?"

"I have never stayed there, but I understand that it is as much as three dollars a day."

"Phew!" whistled Lem. "Think of that now. Twenty-one dollars a week. But I suppose they do you awfully well."

"Yes, I hear they set a very good table."

"Will you be so kind as to direct me to the cheap one of which you first spoke?"

"Certainly."

It was the Commercial House to which the peanut dealer advised Lem to go. This hostelry was located in a down-town street very near the Bowery and was not a stylish inn by any manner of means. However, it was held in good repute by many merchants in a small way of business. Our hero was well satisfied with the establishment when he found it. He had never before seen a fine hotel, and this structure being five stories above the offices seemed to him rather imposing than otherwise.

After being taken to his room, Lem went downstairs and found that dinner was ready, it being just noon. He ate with a country boy's appetite. It was not a luxurious meal, but compared with the table that Warden Purdy set it was a feast for the gods.

When he had finished eating, Lem asked the hotel clerk how to get to Asa Goldstein's store on Fifth Avenue. He was told to walk to Washington Square, then take the bus uptown.

After an exciting ride along the beautiful thoroughfare, Lem descended from the bus before a store, across the front of which was a sign reading

ASA GOLDSTEIN, LTD.
Colonial Exteriors and Interiors

and in the window of which his old home actually stood.

At first the poor boy could not believe his eyes, but, yes, there it was exactly as in Vermont. One of the things that struck him was the seediness of the old house. When he and his mother had lived in it, they had kept it in a much better state of repair.

Our hero stood gazing at the exhibit for so long that he attracted the attention of one of the clerks. This suave individual came out to the street and addressed Lem.

"You admire the architecture of New England?" he said, feeling our hero out.

"No; it's that particular house that interests me, sir," replied Lem truthfully. "I used to live in it. In fact I was born in that very house."

"My, this is interesting," said the clerk politely. "Perhaps you would like to enter the shop and inspect it at firsthand."

"Thank you," replied Lem gratefully. "It would give me a great deal of pleasure so to do."

Our hero followed after the affable clerk and was permitted to examine his old home at close range. To tell the truth, he saw it through a veil of tears, for he could think of nothing but his poor mother who had disappeared.

"I wonder if you would be so kind as to furnish me with a little information?" asked the clerk, pointing to a patched old chest of drawers. "Where would your mother have put such a piece of furniture had she owned it?"

Lem's first thought on inspecting the article in question was to say that she would have kept it in the woodshed, but he thought better of this when he saw how highly the clerk valued it. After a little thought, he pointed to a space next to the fireplace and said, "I think she would have set it there."

"What did I tell you!" exclaimed the delighted clerk to

his colleagues, who had gathered around to hear Lem's answer. "That's just the spot I picked for it."

The clerk then ushered Lem to the door, slipping a two-dollar note into the boy's hand as he shook it good-by. Lem did not want to take the money because he felt that he had not earned it, but he was finally prevailed upon to accept it. The clerk told Lem that he had saved them the fee an expert would have demanded, since it was very important for them to know exactly where the chest of drawers belonged.

Our hero was considerably elated at his stroke of luck and marveled at the ease with which two dollars could be earned in New York. At this rate of pay, he calculated, he would earn ninety-six dollars for an eight-hour day or five hundred and seventy-six dollars for a six-day week. If he could keep it up, he would have a million in no time.

From the store, Lem walked west to Central Park, where he sat down on a bench in the mall near the bridle path to watch the society people ride by on their beautiful horses. His attention was particularly attracted by a man driving a small spring wagon, underneath which ran two fine Dalmatians or coach dogs, as they are sometimes called. Although Lem was unaware of this fact, the man in the wagon was none other than Mr. Asa Goldstein, whose shop he had just visited.

The country-bred boy soon noticed that Mr. Goldstein was not much of a horseman. However, that individual was not driving his beautiful team of matched bays for pleasure, as one might be led to think, but for profit. He had accumulated a large collection of old wagons in his warehouse and by driving one of them in the mall he hoped to start a vogue for that type of equipage and thus sell off his stock.

While Lem was watching the storekeeper's awkward handling of the "leathers" or reins, the off horse, which was very skittish, took fright at a passing policeman and bolted. His panic soon spread to the other horse and the wagon went careening down the path wreaking havoc at every bound. Mr. Goldstein fell out when his vehicle turned over, and Lem had to laugh at the comical expression of mingled disgust and chagrin that appeared on his countenance.

But suddenly Lem's smile disappeared and his jaw became set, for he saw that a catastrophe was bound to occur unless something was immediately done to halt the maddened thoroughbreds.

11

The reason for the sudden disappearance of the smile from our hero's face is easily explained. He had spied an old gentleman and his beautiful young daughter about to cross the bridle path, and saw that in a few more seconds they would be trampled under the iron hooves of the flying beasts.

Lem hesitated only long enough to take a firm purchase on his store teeth, then dashed into the path of the horses. With great strength and agility, he grasped their bridles and dragged them to a rearing halt, a few feet from the astounded and thoroughly frightened pair.

"That lad has saved your lives," said a bystander to the old gentleman, who was none other than Mr. Levi Underdown, president of the Underdown National Bank and Trust Company.

Unfortunately, however, Mr. Underdown was slightly deaf, and, although exceedingly kind, as his many large charities showed, he was very short tempered. He entirely misunderstood the nature of our hero's efforts and thought that the poor boy was a careless groom who had let his charges get out of hand. He became extremely angry.

"I've a mind to give you in charge, young man," said the banker, shaking his umbrella at our hero.

"Oh, don't, father!" interfered his daughter Alice, who also misunderstood the incident. "Don't have him arrested. He was probably paying court to some pretty nursemaid and forgot about his horses." From this we can readily see that the young lady was of a romantic turn of mind.

She smiled kindly at our hero, and led her irate parent from the scene.

Lem had been unable to utter one word in explanation because, during his tussle with the horses, his teeth had jarred loose and without them he was afraid to speak. All he could do was to gaze after their departing backs with mute but ineffectual anguish.

There being nothing else for it, Lem gave over the reins of the team to Mr. Goldstein's groom, who came running up at this juncture, and turned to search for his oral equipment in the mud of the bridle path. While he was thus occupied, a man representing the insurance company with which Mr. Goldstein carried a public liability policy approached him.

"Here is ten dollars, my lad," said the claim adjuster. "The gentleman whose horses you so bravely stopped wishes you to have this money as a reward."

Lem took it without thinking.

"Please sign this for me," added the insurance man, holding out a legal form which released his company from any and all claim to damages.

One of Lem's eyes had been so badly injured by a flying stone that he could not see out of it, but nevertheless he refused to sign.

The claim adjuster had recourse to a ruse. "I am an autograph collector," he said slyly. "Unfortunately, I have not my album with me, but if you will be so kind as to sign this piece of paper which I happened to have in my pocket, you will make me very happy. When I return home, I will immediately transfer your autograph to a distinguished place in my collection."

Befuddled by the pain in his injured eye, Lem signed in order to be rid of the importunate fellow, then bent again to the task of finding his store teeth. He finally discovered them deep in the mud of the bridle path. After carefully prying the set loose, he went to a public drinking fountain for the dual purpose of bathing both it and his hurt eye.

12

While he busied himself at the fountain, a young man approached. This stranger was distinguished from the usual run by his long black hair which tumbled in waves over the back of his collar and by an unusually high and broad forehead. On his head he wore a soft, black hat with an enormously wide brim. Both his tie, which was Windsor, and his gestures, which were Latin, floated with the same graceful freedom as his hair.

"Excuse me," said this odd-appearing individual, "but I witnessed your heroic act and I wish to take the liberty of congratulating you. In these effete times, it is rare indeed for one to witness a hero in action."

Lem was embarrassed. He hurriedly replaced his teeth and thanked the stranger for his praise. He continued, however, to bathe his wounded eye, which was still giving him considerable pain.

"Let me introduce myself," the young man continued. "I am Sylvanus Snodgrasse, a poet both by vocation and avocation. May I ask your name?"

"Lemuel Pitkin," answered our hero, making no attempt to hide the fact that he was suspicious of this self-styled "poet." In fact there were many things about him that reminded Lem of Mr. Wellington Mape.

"Mr. Pitkin," he said grandly, "I intend to write an ode about the deed performed by you this day. You do not perhaps appreciate, having a true hero's modesty, the significance, the classicality—if I may be permitted a neologism—of your performance. Poor Boy, Flying Team, Banker's Daughter . . . it's in the real American tradition and perfectly fitted to my native lyre. Fie on your sickly Prousts, U.S. poets must write about the U.S."

Our hero did not venture to comment on these sentiments. For one thing, his eye hurt so much that even his sense of hearing was occupied with the pain.

Snodgrasse kept talking, and soon a crowd of curious people gathered around him and poor Lemuel. The "poet" no longer addressed our hero, but the crowd in general.

"Gentlemen," said he in a voice that carried all the way to Central Park South, "and ladies, I am moved by this youth's heroism to venture a few remarks.

"There have been heroes before him—Leonidas, Quintus Maximus, Wolfe Tone, Deaf Smith, to mention only a few —but this should not prevent us from hailing L. Pitkin as the hero, if not of our time, at least of the immediate past.

"One of the most striking things about his heroism is the dominance of the horse motif, involving, as it does, not one but two horses. This is important because the depression has made all us Americans conscious of certain spiritual lacks, not the least of which is the symbolic horse.

"Every great nation has its symbolic horses. The grandeur that was Greece is made immortal by those marvelous equines, half god, half beast, still to be seen in the corners of the Parthenon pediment. Rome, the eternal city, how perfectly is her glory caught in those martial steeds that rear their fearful forms to Titus's triumph! And Venice, Queen of the Adriatic, has she not her winged sea horses, kindred to both air and water?

"Alas, only we are without. Do not point to General

Sherman's horse or I will be angry, for that craven hack,
that crowbait, is nothing. I repeat, nothing. What I want is
for all my hearers to go home and immediately write to
their congressmen demanding that a statue depicting Pitkin's heroic act be erected in every public park throughout our great country."

Although Sylvanus Snodgrasse kept on in this vein for
quite some time, I will stop reporting his oration to acquaint you, dear reader, with his real purpose. As you
have probably surmised, it was not so innocent as it
seemed. The truth is that while he kept the crowd amused,
his confederates circulated freely among its members and
picked their pockets.

They had succeeded in robbing the whole crowd, includ-
ing our hero, when a policeman made his appearance.
Snodgrasse immediately discontinued his address and hurried off after his henchmen.

The officer dispersed the gathering and everyone moved
away except Lem, who was lying on the ground in a dead
faint. The bluecoat, thinking that the poor boy was drunk,
kicked him a few times, but when several hard blows in
the groin failed to budge him, he decided to call an ambulance.

13

One wintry morning, several weeks after the incident in
the park, Lem was dismissed from the hospital minus his
right eye. It had been so severely damaged that the physi-
cians had thought best to remove it.

He had no money, for, as we have recounted, Snodgrasse's henchmen had robbed him. Even the teeth that
Warden Purdy had given him were gone. They had been
taken from him by the hospital authorities, who claimed

that they did not fit properly and were therefore a menace to his health.

The poor lad was standing on a windy corner, not knowing which way to turn, when he saw a man in a coonskin hat. This remarkable headgear made Lem stare, and the more he looked the more the man seemed to resemble Shagpoke Whipple.

It was Mr. Whipple. Lem hastened to call out to him, and the ex-President stopped to shake hands with his young friend.

"About those inventions," Shagpoke said immediately after they had finished greeting each other. "It was too bad that you left the penitentiary before I could hand them over to you. Not knowing your whereabouts, I perfected them myself.

"But let us repair to a coffee place," he added, changing the subject, "where we can talk over your prospects together. I am still very much interested in your career. In fact, my young friend, America has never had a greater need for her youth than in these parlous times."

After our hero had thanked him for his interest and good wishes, Mr. Whipple continued to talk. "Speaking of coffee," he said, "did you know that the fate of our country was decided in the coffee shops of Boston during the hectic days preceding the late rebellion?"

As they paused at the door of a restaurant, Mr. Whipple asked Lem still another question. "By the way," he said, "I am temporarily without funds. Are you able to meet the obligation we will incur in this place?"

"No," replied Lem, sadly, "I am penniless."

"That's different," said Mr. Whipple with a profound sigh. "In that case we will go where I have credit."

Lem was conducted by his fellow townsman to an extremely poor section of the city. After standing on line for several hours, they each received a doughnut and a cup of coffee from the Salvation Army lassie in charge. They then sat down on the curb to eat their little snack.

"You are perhaps wondering," Shagpoke began, "how it is that I stand on line with these homeless vagrants to obtain bad coffee and soggy doughnuts. Be assured that I do it of my own free will and for the good of the state."

Here he paused long enough to skillfully "shoot a snipe" that was still burning. He puffed contentedly on his catch.

"When I left jail, it was my intention to run for office again. But I discovered to my great amazement and utter horror that my party, the Democratic Party, carried not a single plank in its platform that I could honestly endorse. Rank socialism was and is rampant. How could I, Shagpoke Whipple, ever bring myself to accept a program which promised to take from American citizens their inalienable birthright; the right to sell their labor and their children's labor without restrictions as to either price or hours?

"The time for a new party with the old American principles was, I realized, overripe. I decided to form it; and so the National Revolutionary Party, popularly known as the 'Leather Shirts,' was born. The uniform of our 'Storm Troops' is a coonskin cap like the one I am wearing, a deerskin shirt and a pair of moccasins. Our weapon is the squirrel rifle."

He pointed to the long queue of unemployed who stood waiting before the Salvation Army canteen. "These men," he said, "are the material from which I must fill the ranks of my party."

With all the formality of a priest, Shagpoke turned to our hero and laid his hand on his shoulder.

"My boy," he said, and his voice broke under the load of emotion it was forced to bear, "my boy, will you join me?"

"Certainly, sir," said Lem, a little unsurely.

"Excellent!" exclaimed Mr. Whipple. "Excellent! I herewith appoint you a commander attached to my general staff."

He drew himself up and saluted Lem, who was startled by the gesture.

"Commander Pitkin," he ordered briskly, "I desire to address these people. Please obtain a soapbox."

Our hero went on the errand required of him, and soon returned with a large box, which Mr. Whipple immediately mounted. He then set about attracting the attention of the vagrants collected about the Salvation Army canteen by shouting:

"Remember the River Raisin!

"Remember the Alamo!

"Remember the Maine!"

and many other famous slogans.

When a large group had gathered, Shagpoke began his harangue.

"I'm a simple man," he said with great simplicity, "and I want to talk to you about simple things. You'll get no highfalutin talk from me.

"First of all, you people want jobs. Isn't that so?"

An ominous rumble of assent came from the throats of the poorly dressed gathering.

"Well, that's the only and prime purpose of the National Revolutionary Party—to get jobs for everyone. There was enough work to go around in 1927, why isn't there enough now? I'll tell you; because of the Jewish international bankers and the Bolshevik labor unions, that's why. It was those two agents that did the most to hinder American business and to destroy its glorious expansion. The former because of their hatred of America and love for Europe and the latter because of their greed for higher and still higher wages.

"What is the role of the labor union today? It is a privileged club which controls all the best jobs for its members. When one of you applies for a job, even if the man who owns the plant wants to hire you, do you get it? Not if you haven't got a union card. Can any tyranny be greater? Has Liberty ever been more brazenly despised?"

These statements were received with cheers by his audience.

"Citizens, Americans," Mr. Whipple continued, when the noise had subsided, "we of the middle class are being crushed between two gigantic millstones. Capital is the upper stone and Labor the lower, and between them we suffer and die, ground out of existence.

"Capital is international; its home is in London and in Amsterdam. Labor is international; its home is in Moscow. We alone are American; and when we die, America dies.

"When I say that, I make no idle boast, for history bears me out. Who but the middle class left aristocratic Europe to settle on these shores? Who but the middle class, the small farmers and storekeepers, the clerks and petty officials, fought for freedom and died that America might escape from British tyranny?

"This is our country and we must fight to keep it so. If America is ever again to be great, it can only be through the triumph of the revolutionary middle class.

"We must drive the Jewish international bankers out of Wall Street! We must destroy the Bolshevik labor unions! We must purge our country of all the alien elements and ideas that now infest her!

"America for Americans! Back to the principles of Andy Jackson and Abe Lincoln!"

Here Shagpoke paused to let the cheers die down, then called for volunteers to join his "Storm Battalions."

A number of men came forward. In their lead was a very dark individual, who had extra-long black hair of an extremely coarse quality, and on whose head was a derby hat many sizes too small for him.

"Me American mans," he announced proudly. "Me got heap coon hat, two maybe six. By, by catchum plenty more coon maybe." With this he grinned from ear to ear.

But Shagpoke was a little suspicious of his complexion, and looked at him with disfavor. In the South, where he expected to get considerable support for his movement, they would not stand for Negroes.

The good-natured stranger seemed to sense what was wrong, for he said, "Me Injun, mister, me chief along my people. Gotum gold mine, oil well. Name of Jake Raven. Ugh!"

Shagpoke grew cordial at once. "Chief Jake Raven," he said, holding out his hand, "I am happy to welcome you into our organization. We 'Leather Shirts' can learn much from your people, fortitude, courage and relentless purpose among other things."

After taking down his name, Shagpoke gave the Indian a card which read as follows:

EZRA SILVERBLATT
Official Tailor
to the
NATIONAL REVOLUTIONARY PARTY
Coonskin hats with extra long tails, deerskin shirts with or without fringes, blue jeans, moccasins, squirrel rifles, everything for the American Fascist at rock bottom prices. 30% off for Cash.

But let us leave Mr. Whipple and Lem busy with their recruiting to observe the actions of a certain member of the crowd.

The individual in question would have been remarkable in any gathering, and among the starved, ragged men that surrounded Shagpoke, he stuck out like the proverbial sore thumb. For one thing he was fat, enormously fat. There were other fat men present to be sure, but they were yellow, unhealthy, while this man's fat was pink and shone with health.

On his head was a magnificent bowler hat. It was a beautiful jet in color, and must have cost more than twelve dollars. He was snugly encased in a tight-fitting Chesterfield overcoat with a black velvet collar. His stiff-bosomed shirt had light gray bars, and his tie was of some rich but sober material in black and white pin-checks. Spats, rattan stick and yellow gloves completed his outfit.

This elaborate fat man tiptoed out of the crowd and made his way to a telephone booth in a nearby drug store, where he called two numbers.

His conversation with the person answering his first call, a Wall Street exchange, went something like this:

"Operative 6384XM, working out of the Bourse, Paris, France. Middle-class organizers functioning on unemployed front, corner of Houston and Bleecker Streets."

"Thank you, 6384XM, what is your estimate?"

"Twenty men and a fire hose."

"At once, 6384XM, at once."

His second call was to an office near Union Square.

"Comrade R, please. . . . Comrade R?"

"Yes."

"Comrade R, this is Comrade Z speaking. Gay Pay Oo, Moscow, Russia. Middle-class organizers recruiting on the corner of Houston and Bleecker Streets."

"Your estimate, comrade, for liquidation of said activities?"

"Ten men with lead pipes and brass knuckles to cooperate with Wall Street office of the I.J.B."

"No bombs required?"

"No, comrade."

"Der Tag!"

"Der Tag!"

Mr. Whipple had just enrolled his twenty-seventh recruit, when the forces of both the international Jewish
bankers and the Communists converged on his meeting.
They arrived in high-powered black limousines and de-
ployed through the streets with a skill which showed long
and careful training in that type of work. In fact their
officers were all West Point graduates.

Mr. Whipple saw them coming, but like a good general
his first thoughts were for his men.

"The National Revolutionary Party will now go under-
ground!" he shouted.

Lem, made wary by his past experiences with the police,
immediately took to his heels, followed by Chief Raven.
Shagpoke, however, was late in getting started. He still
had one foot on the soapbox when he was hit a terrific
blow on the head with a piece of lead pipe.

14

"My man, if you can wear this glass eye, I have a job for
you."

The speaker was an exceedingly dapper gentleman in a
light gray fedora hat and a pince-nez with a black silk ribbon that fell to his coat opening in a graceful loop.

As he spoke, he held out at arm's length a beautiful glass
eye.

But the object of his words did not reply; it did not
even move. To anyone but a trained observer, he would
have appeared to be addressing a bundle of old rags that
someone had propped up on a park bench.

Turning the eye from side to side, so that it sparkled like

a jewel in the winter sun, the man waited patiently for the bundle to reply. From time to time, he stirred it sharply with the Malacca walking stick he carried.

Suddenly a groan came from the rags and they shook sightly. The cane had evidently reached a sensitive spot. Encouraged, the man repeated his original proposition.

"Can you wear this eye? If so, I'll hire you."

At this, the bundle gave a few spasmodic quivers and a faint whimper. From somewhere below its peak a face appeared, then a greenish hand moved out and took the glittering eye, raising it to an empy socket in the upper part of the face.

"Here, let me help you," said the owner of the eye kindly. With a few deft motions he soon had it fixed in its proper receptacle.

"Perfect!" exclaimed the man, standing back and admiring his handiwork. "Perfect! You're hired!"

He then reached into his overcoat and brought forth a wallet from which he extracted a five-dollar bill and a calling card. He laid both of these on the bench beside the one-eyed man, who by now had again become a quiescent bundle of greasy rags.

"Get yourself a haircut, a bath and a big meal, then go to my tailors, Ephraim Pierce and Sons, and they will fit you out with clothes. When you are presentable, call on me at the Ritz Hotel."

With these words, the man in the gray fedora turned sharply on his heel and left the park.

If you have not already guessed the truth, dear reader, let me acquaint you with the fact that the bundle of rags contained our hero, Lemuel Pitkin. Alas, to such a sorry pass had he come.

After the unfortunate termination of Shagpoke's attempt to recruit men for his "Leather Shirts," he had rapidly gone from bad to worse. Having no money and no way in which to obtain any, he had wandered from employment agency to employment agency without success. Reduced to eating from garbage pails and sleeping in empty lots, he had become progressively shabbier and weaker, until he had reached the condition we discovered him in at the beginning of this chapter.

But now things were looking up again, and just in time I must admit, for our hero had begun to doubt whether he would ever make his fortune.

Lem pocketed the five dollars that the stranger had left and examined the card.

ELMER HAINEY, ESQUIRE
RITZ HOTEL

This was all the bit of engraved pasteboard said. It gave no evidence of either the gentleman's business or profession. But this did not in any way bother Lem, for at last it looked as though he were going to have a job; and in the year of our Lord nineteen thirty-four that was indeed something.

Lem struggled to his feet and set out to follow Mr. Hainey's instructions. In fact he ate two large meals and took two baths. It was only his New England training that prevented him from getting two haircuts.

Having done as much as he could to rehabilitate his body, he next went to the shop of Ephraim Pierce and Sons, where he was fitted out with a splendid wardrobe complete in every detail. Several hours later, he walked up Park Avenue to wait on his new employer, looking every inch a prosperous young businessman of the finest type.

When Lem asked for Mr. Hainey, the manager of the Ritz bowed him into the elevator, which stopped to let him off at the fortieth floor. He rang the doorbell of Mr. Hainey's suite and in a few minutes was ushered into that gentleman's presence by an English personal servant.

Mr. Hainey greeted the lad with great cordiality. "Excellent! Excellent!" he repeated three or four times in rapid succession as he inspected the transformed appearance of our hero.

Lem expressed his gratitude by a deep bow.

"If there is anything about your outfit that you dislike," he went on to say, "please tell me now before I give you your instructions."

Emboldened by his kind manner, Lem ventured an objection. "Pardon me, sir," he said, "but the eye, the glass eye you gave me is the wrong color. My good eye is blue-gray, while the one you provided me with is light green."

"Exactly," was Mr. Hainey's surprising answer. "The effect is, as I calculated, striking. When anyone sees you I want to make sure that they notice that one of your eyes is glass."

Lem was forced to agree to this strange idea and he did so with all the grace he could manage.

Mr. Hainey then got down to business. His whole manner changed, becoming as cold as a steel trap and twice as formal.

"My secretary," he said, "has typed a set of instructions which I will give you tonight. I want you to take them home and study them carefully, for you will be expected to do exactly as they order without the slightest deviation. One slip, please remember, and you will be immediately discharged."

"Thank you, sir," replied Lem. "I understand."

"Your salary," said Mr. Hainey, softening a bit, "will be thirty dollars a week and found. I have arranged room and board for you at the Warford House. Please go there tonight."

Mr. Hainey then took out his wallet and gave Lem three ten-dollar bills.

"You are very generous," said Lem, taking them. "I shall do my utmost to satisfy you."

"That's nice, but please don't show too much zeal, simply follow instructions."

Mr. Hainey next went to his desk and took from it several typewritten sheets of paper. He gave these to Lem.

"One more thing," he said, shaking hands at the door, "you may be a little mystified when you read your instructions, but that cannot be helped, for I am unable to give you a complete explanation at this time. However, I want you to know that I own a glass eye factory, and that your duties are part of a sales-promotion campaign."

15

Lem restrained his curiosity. He waited until he was safely ensconced in his new quarters in the Warford House before opening the instructions Mr. Hainey had given him.

Here is what he read:

"Go to the jewelry store of Hazelton Frères and ask to see their diamond stickpins. After looking at one tray, demand to see another. While the clerk has his back turned, remove the glass eye from your head and put it in your pocket. As soon as the clerk turns around again, appear to be searching frantically on the floor for something.

"The following dialogue will then take place:

"*Clerk:* 'Have you lost something, sir?'

"*You:* 'Yes, my eye.' (Here indicate the opening in your head with your index finger.)

"*Clerk:* 'That's unfortunate, sir. I'll help you look, sir.'

"*You:* 'Please do. (With much agitation.) I must find it.'

"A thorough search of the premises is then made, but of course the missing eye cannot be found because it is safe in your pocket.

"*You:* 'Please may I see one of the owners of this store; one of the Hazelton Brothers?' (Note: Frères means brothers and is not to be mistaken for the storekeeper's last name.)

"In a few minutes the clerk will bring Mr. Hazelton from his office in the rear of the store.

"*You:* 'Mr. Hazelton, sir, I have had the misfortune to lose my eye here in your shop.'

"*Mr. Hazelton:* 'Perhaps you left it at home.'

"*You:* 'Impossible! I would have felt the draft for I walked here from Mr. Hamilton Schuyler's house on Fifth Avenue. No, I'm afraid that it was in its proper position when I entered your place.'

"*Mr. Hazelton:* 'You can be certain, sir, that we will make a thorough search.'

"*You:* 'Please do. I am, however, unable to wait the outcome of your efforts. I have to be in the Spanish embassy to see the ambassador, Count Raymon de Guzman y Alfrache (the y is pronounced like the e in eat) within the hour.'

"Mr. Hazelton will bow profoundly on hearing with whom your appointment is.

"*You* (continuing): 'The eye I have lost is irreplaceable. It was made for me by a certain German expert, and cost a very large sum. I cannot get another because its maker was killed in the late war and the secret of its manufacture was buried with him. (Pause for a brief moment, bowing your head as though in sorrow for the departed expert.) However (you continue), please tell your clerks that I will pay one thousand dollars as a reward to anyone who recovers my eye.'

"*Mr. Hazelton:* 'That will be entirely unnecessary, sir. Rest assured that we will do everything in our power to discover it for you.'

"*You:* 'Very good. I am going to visit friends on Long

Island tonight, but I will be in your shop tomorrow. If you have the eye, I will insist on paying the reward.'

"Mr. Hazelton will then bow you out of the shop.

"Until you receive further instructions from Mr. Hainey, you are to stay away from the near vicinity of Hazelton Frères.

"On the day following your visit to the shop call the Ritz Hotel and ask for Mr. Hainey's secretary. Tell him whether or not everything went off in accordance with these instructions. The slightest deviation on the part of Mr. Hazelton from the prescribed formula must be reported."

16

Lem's job was a sinecure. He had merely to enact the same scene over one morning a week, each time in a different store. He soon had his part by heart, and once he had lost his embarrassment over having to say that he knew the Spanish Ambassador, he quite enjoyed his work. It reminded him of the amateur theatricals he had participated in at the Ottsville High School.

Then, too, his position permitted him a great deal of leisure. He used this spare time to good advantage by visiting the many interesting spots for which New York City is justly famous.

He also made an unsuccessful attempt to find Mr. Whipple. At the Salvation Army post they told him that they had observed Mr. Whipple lying quietly in the gutter after the meeting of the "Leather Shirts," but that when they looked the next day to see if he were still there they found only a large blood stain. Lem looked himself but failed even to find this stain, there being many cats in the neighborhood.

He was a sociable youth and quickly made friends with several of the other guests of the Warford House. None of them were his age, however, so that he was pleased when a young man named Samuel Perkins spoke to him.

Sam worked in a furnishing goods store on lower Broadway. He was very fond of dress and indulged in a variety of showy neckties, being able to get them at reduced rates.

"What line are you in?" he asked our hero in the lobby one evening while they were waiting for the supper bell to ring.

"I'm in the glass business," Lem answered cautiously, for he had been warned not to explain his duties to anyone.

"How much do you get?" was the forward youth's next question.

"Thirty dollars a week and found," said Lem, honestly.

"I get thirty-five without keep, but it's too little for me. A man can't live on that kind of money, what with the opera once a week and decent clothes. Why, my carfare alone comes to over a dollar, not counting taxicabs."

"Yes, it must be rather a tight squeeze for you," said Lem with a smile as he thought of all the large families who lived on smaller incomes than Mr. Perkins'.

"Of course," Sam went on, "the folks at home allow me another ten dollars a week. You see the old gent has money. But I tell you it sure melts away in this town."

"No doubt," said Lem. "There are a good many ways to spend money here."

"Suppose we go to the theater tonight?"

"No," Lem replied, "I'm not as fortunate as you are. I have no wealthy father to fall back on and must save the little I earn."

"Well, then," said Sam, for that youth could not live without excitement of some sort, "what do you say we visit Chinatown? It'll only cost us carfare."

To this proposition Lem readily agreed. "I'd like very much to go," he said. "Perhaps Mr. Warren would like to join us."

Mr. Warren was another guest whose acquaintance Lem had made.

"What, that crank!" exclaimed Sam, who was by way of being somewhat of a snob. "He's soft in his upper story. Pretends that he's literary and writes for the magazines."

"He does, doesn't he?"

"Very likely, but did you ever see such shabby neckties as he wears?"

"He hasn't your advantages for getting them," said Lem with a smile, for he knew where the young man worked.

"How do you like the tie I have on? It's a stunner, isn't it?" asked Sam complacently.

"It's very striking," said Lem, whose tastes were much more sober.

"I get a new necktie every week. You see, I get them at half price. The girls always notice a fellow's necktie."

The supper bell sounded, and the two youths parted to go to their own tables. After eating, they met again in the lobby and proceeded to Chinatown.

17

Lem and his new friend wandered through Mott Street and its environs, observing with considerable interest the curious customs and outlandish manners of that neighborhood's large oriental population.

Early in the evening, however, an incident occurred which made our hero feel sorry that he had ventured out with Sam Perkins. When they came upon an ancient celestial, who was quietly reading a newspaper under an arc lamp, Sam accosted him before Lem could interfere.

"Hey, John," said the youth mockingly, "no tickee, no washee." And he laughed foolishly in the manner of his kind.

The almond-eyed old man looked up from his newspaper

and stared coldly at him for a full minute, then said with great dignity, "By the blessed beard of my grandfather, you're the lousiest pimple-faced ape I ever did see."

At this Sam made as though to strike the aged oriental. But that surprising individual was not in the least frightened. He took a small hatchet out of his pocket and proceeded to shave the hair from the back of his hand with its razor-sharp edge.

Sam turned quite pale and began to bluster until Lem thought it best to intervene.

But even his lesson in manners had no effect on the brash youth. He so persisted in his unmannerly conduct that our hero was tempted to part company with him.

Sam stopped in front of what was evidently an unlicensed liquor parlor.

"Come on in," he said, "and have a whisky."

"Thank you," said our hero, "but I don't care for whisky."

"Perhaps you prefer beer?"

"I don't care to drink anything, thank you."

"You don't mean to say you're a temperance crank?"

"Yes, I think I am."

"Oh, go to the devil, you prude," said Sam, ringing a signal button that was secreted in the door of the "blind pig."

To Lem's great relief, he at last found himself alone. It was still early, so he decided to continue his stroll.

He turned a corner not far from Pell Street, when, suddenly, a bottle smashed at his feet, missing his skull by inches.

Was it intentional or accidental?

Lem looked around carefully. The street was deserted and all the houses that faced on it had their blinds drawn. He noticed that the only store front on the block carried a sign reading, "Wu Fong, Wet Wash Laundry," but that meant nothing to him.

When he looked closer at the bottle, he was surprised to see a sheet of notepaper between the bits of shattered glass and stooped to pick it up.

At this the door of the laundry opened noiselessly to emit one of Wu Fong's followers, an enormous Chinaman. His felt slippers were silent on the pavement, and as he crept up on our hero, something glittered in his hand.

It was a knife.

18

Many chapters earlier in this book, we left our heroine, Betty Prail, in the bad house of Wu Fong, awaiting the visit of a pockmarked Armenian from Malta.

Since then numbers of orientals, Slavs, Latins, Celts and Semites had visited her, sometimes as many as three in one night. However, so large a number was rare because Wu Fong held her at a price much above that of the other female inmates.

Naturally enough, Betty was not quite as happy in her situation as was Wu Fong. At first she struggled against the series of "husbands" that were forced on her, but when all her efforts proved futile she adapted herself as best she could to her onerous duties. Nevertheless, she was continuously seeking a method of escape.

It was Betty, of course, who had authored the note in the bottle. She had been standing at her window, thinking with horror of the impending visit of a heavyweight wrestler called Selim Hammid Bey, who claimed to be in love with her, when she suddenly saw Lem Pitkin turn the corner and pass in front of the laundry. She had hastily written a note describing her predicament, and putting it into a bottle had tossed it into the street.

But, unfortunately, her action had not gone unobserved. One of Wu Fong's many servants had been carefully watching her through the keyhole, and had immediately carried the intelligence to his master, who had sent the enormous Chinaman after Lem with a knife.

Before I take up where I left off in my last chapter, there are several changes in Wu Fong's establishment which I would like to report. These changes seem significant to me, and while their bearing on this story may not be obvious, still I believe it does exist.

The depression hit Wu Fong as hard as it did more respectable merchants, and like them he decided that he was over-stocked. In order to cut down, he would have to specialize and could no longer run a "House of All Nations."

Wu Fong was a very shrewd man and a student of fashions. He saw that the trend was in the direction of home industry and home talent, and when the Hearst papers began their "Buy American" campaign he decided to get rid of all the foreigners in his employ and turn his establishment into an hundred per centum American place.

Although in 1928 it would have been exceedingly difficult for him to have obtained the necessary girls, by 1934 things were different. Many respectable families of genuine native stock had been reduced to extreme poverty and had thrown their female children on the open market.

He engaged Mr. Asa Goldstein to redecorate the house and that worthy designed a Pennsylvania Dutch, Old South, Log Cabin Pioneer, Victorian New York, Western Cattle Days, California Monterey, Indian, and Modern Girl series of interiors. In general the results were as follows:

Lena Haubengrauber from Perkiomen Creek, Bucks County, Pennsylvania. Her rooms were filled with painted pine furniture and decorated with slip ware, spatter ware, chalk ware and "Gaudy Dutch." Her simple farm dress was fashioned of bright gingham.

Alice Sweethorne from Paducah, Kentucky. Besides
many fine pieces of old Sheraton from Savannah, in her
suite there was a wonderful iron grille from Charleston
whose beauty of workmanship made every visitor gasp
with pleasure. She wore a ball gown of the Civil War
period.

Mary Judkins from Jugtown Hill, Arkansas. Her walls
were lined with oak puncheons chinked with mud. Her
mattress was stuffed with field corn and covered by a buffalo rope. There was real dirt on her floors. She was dressed
in homespun, butternut stained, and wore a pair of men's
boots.

Patricia Van Riis from Gramercy Park, Manhattan, New
York City. Her suite was done in the style known as
Biedermeier. The windows were draped with thirty yards
of white velvet apiece and the chandelier in her sitting room had over eight hundred crystal pendants attached to it. She was dressed like an early "Gibson Girl."

Powder River Rose from Carson's Store, Wyoming. Her
apartment was the replica of a ranch bunkhouse. Strewn
around it in well-calculated confusion were such miscel-
laneous articles as spurs, saddle blankets, straw, guitars,
quirts, pearl-handled revolvers, hayforks and playing cards.
She wore goatskin chaps, a silk blouse and a five-gallon hat
with a rattlesnake band.

Dolores O'Riely from Alta Vista, California. In order to
save money, Wu Fong had moved her into the suite that
had been occupied by Conchita, the Spanish girl. He
merely substituted a Mission chair for the horsehide one
with the steer-horn arms and called it "Monterey." Asa
Goldstein was very angry when he found out, but Wu
Fong refused to do anything more about it, because he
felt that she was bound to be a losing proposition. The
style, he said was not obviously enough American even in
its most authentic forms.

Princess Roan Fawn from Two Forks, Oklahoma Indian Reservation, Oklahoma. Her walls were papered with birch bark to make it look like a wigwam and she did business on the floor. Except for a necklace of wolf's teeth, she was naked under her bull's-eye blanket.

Miss Cobina Wiggs from Woodstock, Connecticut. She lived in one large room that was a combination of a locker in an athletic club and the office of a mechanical draughtsman. Strewn around were parts of an aeroplane, T-squares, callipers, golf clubs, books, gin bottles, hunting horns and paintings by modern masters. She had broad shoulders, no hips and very long legs. Her costume was an aviator's jumper complete with helmet attached. It was made of silver cloth and fitted very tightly.

Betty Prail from Ottsville, Vermont. Her furnishings and costume have already been described, and it should suffice to say here that they remained untouched.

These were not the only vital changes Wu Fong made in his establishment. He was as painstaking as a great artist, and in order to be as consistent as one he did away with the French cuisine and wines traditional to his business. Instead, he substituted an American kitchen and cellar.

When a client visited Lena Haubengrauber, it was possible for him to eat roast groundhog and drink Sam Thompson rye. While with Alice Sweethorne, he was served sow belly with grits and bourbon. In Mary Judkins' rooms he received, if he so desired, fried squirrel and corn liquor. In the suite occupied by Patricia Van Riis, lobster and champagne wine were the rule. The patrons of Powder River Rose usually ordered mountain oysters and washed them down with forty-rod. And so on down the list: while with Dolores O'Riely, tortillas and prune brandy from the Imperial Valley; while with Princess Roan Fawn, baked dog and firewater; while with Betty Prail, fish chowder and Jamaica rum. Finally, those who sought the favors of the "Modern Girl," Miss Cobina Wiggs, were regaled with tomato and lettuce sandwiches and gin.

19

The enormous Chinaman with the uplifted knife did not bring it down, because he had been struck by a sudden thought. While he debated the pros and cons of his idea over in his mind, the unsuspecting youth picked up the note Betty had thrown at him.

> "*Dear Mr. Pitkin—*" he read.
> "*I am held captive. Please save me.*
> *Your grateful friend,*
> *Elizabeth Prail.*"

When our hero had thoroughly digested the contents of the little missive, he turned to look for a policeman. It was this that made the Chinaman decide on a course of action. He dropped the knife, and with a skillful oriental trick that took our hero entirely by surprise pinned Lem's arms in such a way as to render him helpless.

He then whistled through his nose in coolie fashion. In obedience to this signal several more of Wu Fong's followers came running to his assistance. Although Lem struggled valiantly, he was overpowered and forced to enter the laundry.

Lem's captors dragged him into the presence of the sinister Wu Fong, who rubbed his hands gleefully as he inspected the poor lad.

"You have done well, Chin Lao Tse," he said, praising the man who had captured Lem.

"I demand to be set free!" expostulated our hero. "You have no right to keep me here."

But the crafty oriental ignored his protests and smiled inscrutably. He could well use a nice-looking American boy. That very night, he expected a visit from the Maharajah of Kanurani, whose tastes were notorious. Wu Fong congratulated himself; the gods were indeed good.

"Prepare him," said he in Chinese.

The poor lad was taken to a room that had been fitted out like a ship's cabin. The walls were paneled in teak, and there were sextants, compasses and other such gear in profusion. His captors then forced him to don a tight-fitting sailor suit. After warning him in no uncertain terms not to try to escape, they left him to his own devices.

Lem sat on the edge of a bunk that was built into one corner of the room with his head buried in his hands. He wondered what new ordeal fate had in store for him, but being unable to guess he thought of other things.

Would he lose his job if he failed to report to Mr. Hainey? Probably, yes. Where was his dear mother? Probably in the poorhouse, or begging from door to door, if she were not dead. Where was Mr. Whipple? Dead and buried in Potter's Field more than likely. And how could he get a message to Miss Prail?

Lem was still trying to solve this last problem when Chin Lao Tse, the man who had captured him, entered the room, carrying a savage-looking automatic in his hand.

"Listen, boy," he said menacingly, "see this gat? Well, if you don't behave I'll drill you clean."

Chin then proceeded to secrete himself in a closet. Before closing the door, he showed Lem that he intended to watch his every move through the keyhole.

The poor lad racked his brains, but could not imagine what was wanted of him. He was soon to find out, however.

There was a knock on the door and Wu Fong entered

followed by a little dark man whose hands were covered with jewels. It was the Maharajah of Kanurani.

"My, wath a pithy thailer boy," lisped the Indian prince with unfeigned delight.

"I'm extremely happy that he finds favor in your august eyes, excellency," said Wu Fong with a servile bow, after which he backed out of the room.

The Maharajah minced up to our hero, who was conscious only of the man in the closet, and put his arm around the lad's waist.

"Thom on, pithy boy, giff me a kith," he said with a leer that transfigured his otherwise unremarkable visage into a thing of evil.

A wave of disgust made Lem's hair stand on end. "Does he think me a girl?" the poor lad wondered. "No, he called me a boy at least twice."

Lem looked towards the closet for instructions. The man in that receptacle opened his door and poked his head out. Puckering up his lips, he rolled his eyes amorously, at the same time pointing at the Indian Prince.

When our hero realized what was expected of him, he turned pale with horror. He looked again at the Maharajah and what he saw of lust in that man's eyes made him almost swoon.

Fortunately for Lem, however, instead of swooning, he opened his mouth to scream. This was the only thing that could have saved him, for he spread his jaws too wide and his store teeth fell clattering to the carpet.

The Maharajah jumped away in disgust.

Then another lucky accident occurred. When Lem bent awkwardly to pick up his teeth, the glass eye that Mr. Hainey had given him popped from his head and smashed to smithereens on the floor.

This last was too much for the Maharajah of Kanurani.

He became enraged. Wu Fong had cheated him! What kind of a pretty boy was this that came apart so horribly?

Livid with anger, the Indian prince ran out of the room to demand his money back. After he had gotten it, he left the house, vowing never to return.

Wu Fong blamed the loss of the Maharajah's trade on Lem and was extremely vexed with the poor lad. He ordered his men to beat him roundly, strip him of his sailor suit, then throw him into the street with his clothes after him.

20

Lem gathered together his clothing and crawled into the areaway of a deserted house, where he donned his things. His first thought was to find a policeman.

As is usual in such circumstances, a guardian of the law was not immediately forthcoming and he had to go several miles before he found a "peeler."

"Officer," said our hero as best he could minus his oral equipment, "I want to lodge a complaint."

"Yes," said Patrolman Riley shortly, for the poor lad's appearance was far from prepossessing. The Chinaman had torn his clothing and his eye was gone as well as his teeth.

"I want you to summon reinforcements, then immediately arrest Wu Fong who is running a disorderly house under the guise of a laundry."

"Wu Fong is it that you want me to arrest? Why, you drunken fool, he's the biggest man in the district. Take my advice and get yourself a cup of black coffee, then go home and sleep it off."

"But I have positive proof that he's keeping a girl in his house against her will, and he did me physical violence."

"One more word out of you about my great good friend," said the officer, "and off you go to jail."

"But . . ." began Lem indignantly.

Officer Riley was a man of his word. He did not let the poor lad finish, but struck him a smart blow on the head with his truncheon, then took him by the collar and dragged him to the station house.

When Lem regained consciousness several hours later, he found himself in a cell. He quickly remembered what had happened to him and tried to think of a way in which to extricate himself from his difficulties. The first thing was to tell his story to some superior police officer or magistrate. But no matter how loudly he called, he was unable to attract the attention of anyone.

Not until the next day was he fed, and then a small man of the Jewish persuasion entered his cell.

"Have you any money?" said this member of the chosen people.

"Who are you?" countered Lem with another question.

"Me? I'm your lawyer, Seth Abromovitz, Esquire. Please answer my first question or I won't be able to handle your case properly."

"My case?" queried Lem in astonishment. "I've done nothing."

"Ignorance of the law is no defense," said Lawyer Abromovitz pompously.

"Of what am I accused?" asked the poor lad in confusion.

"Of several things. Disorderly conduct and assaulting a police officer, for one; of conspiring to overthrow the Government, for two; and last but not least, of using the glim racket to mulct storekeepers."

"But I didn't do any of these things," protested Lem.

"Listen, bud," said the lawyer, dropping all formality. "I'm not the judge, you don't have to lie to me. You're One-eyed Pitkin, the glim dropper, and you know it."

"It's true that I have but one eye, but . . ."

"But me no buts. This is a tough case. That is, unless you can grow an eye overnight in that hole in your mug."

"I am innocent," repeated Lem sadly.

"If that's the line you intend to take, I wouldn't be surprised if you got life. But tell me, didn't you go to the store of Hazelton Frères and make believe you lost your eye?"

"Yes," said Lem, "but I didn't take anything or do anything."

"Didn't you offer a reward of one thousand dollars for the return of your eye?"

"Yes, but . . ."

"Again, but. Please don't but me no buts. Your accomplice went around the next day and made believe he had found a glass eye on the floor of the store. Mr. Hazelton said that he knew who it belonged to and asked him for the eye. He refused to give it up, saying that it looked like a very valuable eye to him and that if Mr. Hazelton would give him the address of the man who owned it, he would return the eye himself. Mr. Hazelton thought that he was going to lose all chances of collecting the thousand-dollar reward, so he offered the man a hundred dollars for the eye. After some bargaining your accomplice went out with two hundred and fifty dollars, and Mr. Hazelton is still waiting for you to come and claim your eye."

"I didn't know about all that or I wouldn't have taken the job even if I was starving," said Lem. "I was told that it was a promotion idea for a glass eye company."

"O.K., son, but I'll have to think up a little better story. Before I begin thinking, how much money have you?"

"I worked three weeks and was paid thirty dollars a week. I have ninety dollars in a savings bank."

"That's not much. This conference is going to cost you one hundred dollars with ten per cent off for cash or ninety dollars. Hand it over."

"I don't want you as my lawyer," said Lem.

"That's all right with me; but come through with the dough for this conference."

"I don't owe you anything. I didn't hire you."

"Oh, yeh, you one-eyed rat," said the lawyer, showing his true colors. "The courts appointed me and the courts will decide how much you owe me. Give me the ninety and we'll call it square. Otherwise I'll sue you."

"I'll give you nothing!" exclaimed Lem.

"Getting tough, eh? We'll soon see how tough you are. I'll tell my friend the district attorney and you'll get life."

With this last as a parting shot, Lawyer Abromovitz left our hero alone again in his cell.

21

Several days later the prosecuting attorney paid the poor lad a visit. Elisha Barnes was that official's name, and he appeared to be a rather good-natured, indolent gentleman.

"Well, son," he said, "so you're about to discover that crime doesn't pay. But, tell me, have you any money?"

"Ninety dollars," said Lem truthfully.

"That's very little, so I guess you'd better plead guilty."

"But I'm innocent," protested Lem. "Wu Fong . . ."

"Stop," interrupted Mr. Barnes, hurriedly. He had turned pale on hearing the Chinaman's name. "Take my advice and don't mention him around here."

"I'm innocent!" repeated Lem, a little desperately.

"So was Christ," said Mr. Barnes with a sigh, "and they nailed Him. However, I like you; I can see you're from New England and I'm a New Hampshire man myself. I want to help you. You've been indicted on three counts; suppose you plead guilty to one of the three and we forget the other two."

"But I'm innocent," repeated Lem again.

"Maybe, but you haven't got enough money to prove it, and besides you've got some very powerful enemies. Be sensible, plead guilty to the charge of disorderly conduct and take thirty days in the workhouse. I'll see that you don't get more. Well, what do you say?"

Our hero was silent.

"I'm giving you a fine break," Mr. Barnes went on. "If I wasn't too busy to prepare the state's case against you, I probably could get you sent away for at least fifteen years. But you see, elections are coming and I have to take part in the campaign. Besides I'm a busy man, what with this and what with that. . . . Do me a favor and maybe I can help you some time. If you make me prepare a case against you I'll get sore. I won't like you."

Lem finally agreed to do as the prosecuting attorney asked. Three days later he was sent to the workhouse for thirty days. The judge wanted to give him ninety, but Mr. Barnes lived up to his part of the bargain. He whispered something to the judge, who changed the term to the thirty days agreed upon.

A month later, when Lem was set free, he went directly to the savings bank for his ninety dollars. It was his intention to draw out the entire amount, so that he could get himself another set of false teeth and a glass eye. Without those things, he could not hope to get a job.

He presented his passbook at the paying teller's window. After a little wait, he was told that they could not give him his money because it had been attached by Seth Abromovitz. This was too much. It took all the manliness of our hero to suppress the tear that started to his good eye. With the faltering step of an old man, he stumbled out of the bank building.

Lem stood on the steps of the imposing edifice, and looked blankly at the swirling crowds that eddied past the great savings institution. Suddenly he felt a touch on his arm and a voice in his ear.

"Why so blue, duckie? How about a little fun?"

He turned mechanically and to his amazement saw that it was Betty Prail who had solicited him.

"You!" exclaimed both of the hometown friends together.

Anyone who had ever seen these two youngsters on their way home from church in Ottsville would have been struck by the great change that only a few years in the great world had made.

Miss Prail was rouged most obviously. She smelled of cheap perfume, and her dress revealed much too much of her figure. She was a woman of the streets, and an unsuccessful one at that.

As for our hero, Lemuel, minus an eye and all his teeth, he had acquired nothing but a pronounced stoop.

"How did you escape Wu Fong?" asked Lem.

"You helped me without knowing it," replied Betty. "He and his henchmen were so busy throwing you into the street that I was able to walk out of the house without anyone seeing me."

"I'm glad," said Lem.

The two young people were silent, and stood looking at each other. They both wanted to ask the same question, but they were embarrassed. Finally, they spoke at the same time.

"Have you . . ."

That was as far as they got. They both stopped to let the other finish. There was a long silence, for neither wanted to complete the question. Finally, however, they spoke again.

". . . any money?"

"No," said Lem and Betty answering the question together as they had asked it.

"I'm hungry," said Betty sadly. "I just wondered."

"I'm hungry, too," said Lem.

A policeman now approached. He had been watching them since they met.

"Get along, you rats," he said gruffly.

"I resent your talking that way to a lady," said Lem indignantly.

"What's that?" asked the officer lifting his club.

"We are both citizens of this country and you have no right to treat us in this manner," went on Lem fearlessly.

The patrolman was just about to bring his truncheon down on the lad's skull, when Betty interfered and dragged him away.

The two youngsters walked along without talking. They felt a little better together because misery loves company. Soon they found themselves in Central Park, where they sat down on a bench.

Lem sighed.

"What's the matter?" asked Betty sympathetically.

"I'm a failure," answered Lem with still another sigh.

"Why, Lemuel Pitkin, how you talk!" exclaimed Betty indignantly. "You're only seventeen going on eighteen and . . ."

"Well," interrupted Lem, a little ashamed of having admitted that he was discouraged. "I left Ottsville to make my fortune and so far I've been to jail twice and lost all my teeth and one eye."

"To make an omelette you have to break eggs," said Betty. "When you've lost both your eyes, you can talk. I read only the other day about a man who lost both of his eyes yet accumulated a fortune. I forget how, but he did. Then, too, think of Henry Ford. He was dead broke at forty and borrowed a thousand dollars from James Couzens; when he paid him back it had become thirty-eight million dollars. You're only seventeen and say you're a failure. Lem Pitkin, I'm surprised at you."

Betty continued to comfort and encourage Lem until it grew dark. With the departure of the sun, it also grew extremely cold.

From behind some shrubs that did not quite conceal him, a policeman began to eye the two young people suspiciously.

"I have nowhere to sleep," said Betty, shivering with cold.

"Nor have I," said Lem with a profound sigh.

"Let's go to the Grand Central Station," suggested Betty. "It's warm there, and I like to watch the people hurrying through. If we make believe we are waiting for a train, they won't chase us."

22

"It all seems like a dream to me, Mr. Whipple. This morning when I was set free from jail I thought I would probably starve, and here I am on my way to California to dig gold."

Yes, it was Lem, our hero, talking. He was sitting in the dining room of the "Fifth Avenue Special" *en route* to Chicago, where he and the party he was traveling with were to change to "The Chief," crack train of the Atchison, Topeka and Santa Fe, and continue on to the high Sierras.

With him in the dining room were Betty, Mr. Whipple and Jake Raven, and the four friends were in a cheerful mood as they ate the excellent food provided by the Pullman Company.

The explanation of how this had come about is quite simple. While Lem and Betty were warming themselves in the waiting room of the Grand Central Station, they had spied Mr. Whipple on line at one of the ticket booths. Lem had approached the ex-banker and had been greeted effusively by him, for he was indeed glad to see the boy. He was also glad to see Betty, whose father he had known before Mr. Prail's death in the fire.

After listening to Lem's account of the difficulties the two of them were in, he invited them to accompany him on his trip to California. It seemed that Mr. Whipple was going there with Jake Raven to dig gold from a mine that the redskin owned. With this money, he intended to finance the further activities of the National Revolutionary Party.

Lem was to help Mr. Whipple in the digging operations, while Betty was to keep house for the miners. The two young people jumped at this opportunity, as we can well imagine, and overwhelmed Mr. Whipple with their gratitude.

"In Chicago," said Shagpoke, when the dining car waiter had brought coffee, "we will have three hours and a half before 'The Chief' leaves for the Golden West. During that time, Lem, of course, will have to get himself a new set of store teeth and an eye, but I believe that the rest of us will still have time to pay a short visit to the World's Fair."

Mr. Whipple went on to describe the purpose of the fair, until, on a courteous signal from the head waiter, the little party was forced to leave their table and retire to their berths.

In the morning, when the train pulled into the depot, they disembarked. Lem was given some money to purchase the things he needed, while the others started immediately for the fair. He was to look for them on the grounds, if he got through in time.

Lem hurried as much as he could and managed quickly to select an eye and a set of teeth in a store devoted to that type of equipment. He then set out for the fair grounds.

As he was walking down Eleventh Street towards the North Entrance, he was accosted by a short, stout man, who wore a soft, black felt hat, the brim of which was slouched over his eyes. A full, brown beard concealed the lower part of his face.

"Excuse me," he said in a repressed tone of voice, "but I think you are the young man I am looking for."

"How is that?" asked Lem, instantly on his guard, for he did not intend to be snared by a sharper.

"Your name is Lemuel Pitkin, is it not?"

"It is, sir."

"I thought you answered the description given me."

"Given you by whom?" queried our hero.

"By Mr. Whipple, of course," was the surprising answer the stranger made.

"Why should he have given you a description of me?"

"So I could find you at the fair."

"But why, when I am to meet him at the depot in two hours from now?"

"An unfortunate accident has made it impossible for him to be there."

"An accident?"

"Exactly."

"What kind of an accident?"

"A very serious one, I am afraid. He was struck by a sightseeing bus and . . ."

"Killed!" cried Lem in dismay. "Tell me the truth, was he killed?"

"No, not exactly, but he was seriously injured, perhaps fatally. He was taken unconscious to a hospital. When he regained his senses, he asked for you and I was sent to fetch you to him. Miss Prail and Chief Raven are at his bedside."

Lem was so stunned by the dire news that it required some five minutes for him to recover sufficiently to gasp, "This is terrible!"

He asked the bearded stranger to take him to Mr. Whipple at once.

This was just what the man had counted on. "I have a car with me," he said with a bow. "Please enter it."

He then led our hero to a powerful limousine that was drawn up at the curb. Lem got in, and the chauffeur, who was wearing green goggles and a long linen duster, drove off at top speed.

All this seemed natural to the lad because of his agitated state of mind, and the rate at which the car traveled pleased him rather than otherwise, for he was anxious to get to Mr. Whipple's bedside.

The limousine passed rapidly under one elevated structure and then another. There were fruit vendors on the street corners and merchants peddling neckties. People moved to and fro on the sidewalks; cabs, trucks and private vehicles flitted past. The roar of the great city rose on every side, but Lem saw and heard nothing.

"Where was Mr. Whipple taken?" he asked presently.

"To the Lake Shore Hospital."

"And is this the quickest way there?"

"Most certainly."

With this the stranger lapsed into moody silence again.

Lem looked from the window of the limousine and saw that the cars and trucks were growing less in number. Soon they disappeared from the streets altogether. The people also became fewer till no more than an occasional pedestrian was to be observed and then only of the lowest type.

As the car approached an extremely disreputable neighborhood, the bearded stranger drew the shade of one of its two windows.

"Why did you do that?" demanded Lem.

"Because the sun hurts my eyes," he said as he deliberately drew the other shade, throwing the interior into
complete darkness.

These acts made Lem think that all was not quite as it
should be.

"I must have one or both of these shades up," he said,
reaching for the nearest one to raise it.

"And I say that they must both remain down," returned
the man in a low harsh voice.

"What do you mean, sir?"

A strong hand suddenly fastened in a grip of iron on
Lem's throat, and these words reached his ears:

"I mean, Lemuel Pitkin, that you are in the power of the
Third International."

23

Although thus suddenly attacked, Lem grappled with his
assailant, determined to sell his life as dearly as possible.

The lad had been one of the best athletes in the Ottsville
High School, and when aroused he was no mean adver-
sary, as the bearded man soon discovered. He tore at the
hand which was strangling him and succeeded in removing
it from his throat, but when he tried to cry out for help,
he discovered that the terrible pressure had robbed him of
his vocal powers.

Even if he had been able to cry out it would have been
useless for him to do so because the chauffeur was in the
plot. Without once looking behind, he stepped on his accel-
erator and turned sharply into a noisome, dark alley.

Lem struck out savagely and landed a stiff blow in his
opponent's face. That worthy uttered a fierce imprecation
but did not strike back. He was fumbling for something in
his pocket.

Lem struck again, and this time his hand caught in

the beard. It proved to be false and came away readily.

Although it was dark in the car, if you had been sitting in it, dear reader, you would have recognized our hero's assailant to be none other than the fat man in the Chesterfield overcoat. Lem, however, did not recognize him because he had never seen him before.

Suddenly, as he battled with the stranger, he felt something cold and hard against his forehead. It was a pistol.

"Now, you fascist whelp, I have you! If you so much as move a finger, I'll blow you to hell!"

These words were not spoken; they were snarled.

"What do you want of me?" Lem managed to gasp.

"You were going to dig gold with Mr. Whipple. Where is the mine located?"

"I don't know," said Lem, speaking the truth, for Shagpoke had kept secret their final destination.

"You do know, you damned bourgeois. Tell me or . . ."

He was interrupted by the wild scream of a siren. The car swerved and bucked wildly, then there was a terrific crash. Lem felt as though he were being whirled rapidly through a dark tunnel full of clanging bells. Everything went black, and the last thing he was conscious of was a sharp, stabbing pain in his left hand.

When the poor lad recovered consciousness, he found himself stretched out upon a sort of a cot and he realized that he was still being carried somewhere. Near his head sat a man in a white suit, who was calmly smoking a cigar. Lem knew he was no longer in the limousine, for he saw that the rear end of the conveyance was wide open and admitted a great deal of light and air.

"What happened?" he asked naturally enough.

"So you are coming around. eh?" said the man in the white suit. "Well, I guess you will get well all right."

"But what happened?"

"You were in a bad smash-up."

"A smash-up? . . . Where are you taking me?"

"Don't get excited and I'll answer your questions. The limousine in which you were riding was struck by a fire engine and demolished. The driver must have run off, for you were the only one we found at the wreck. This is the ambulance of the Lake Shore Hospital and you are being taken there."

Lem now understood what he had been through, and thanked God that he was still alive.

"I hope you are not a violinist," the interne added mysteriously.

"No, I don't play, but why?"

"Because your left hand was badly mangled and I had to remove a part of it. The thumb, to be explicit."

Lem sighed deeply, but being a brave lad he forced himself to think of other things.

"What hospital is this ambulance from did you say?"

"The Lake Shore."

"Do you know how a patient called Nathan Whipple is getting on? He was run over on the fair grounds by a sightseeing bus."

"We have no patient by that name."

"Are you certain?"

"Absolutely. I know every accident case in the hospital."

Of a sudden everything became clear to Lem. "Then he tricked me with a lie!" he cried.

"Who did?" asked the interne.

Lem ignored his question. "What time is it?" he demanded.

"One o'clock."

"I have still fifteen minutes to make the train. Stop and let me off, please."

The ambulance doctor stared at our hero and wondered if the lad had gone crazy.

"I must get off," repeated Lem frantically.

"As a private citizen you of course can do as you like, but I advise you to go to the hospital."

"No," said Lem, "please, I must get to the depot at once. I have to catch a train."

"Well, I certainly admire your pluck. By George, I have half a mind to help you."

"Do," begged Lem.

Without further argument, the interne told his driver to head for the depot at top speed and to ignore all traffic laws. After an exciting ride through the city, they arrived at their destination just as "The Chief" was about to pull out.

24

As Lem had suspected, Mr. Whipple and his other friends were safe on the train. When they saw his bandaged hand, they demanded an explanation and the poor lad told the story of his adventure with the agent of the Third International. They were astounded and angered, as well they might be.

"One day," Mr. Whipple said ominously, "heads will roll in the sand, bearded and unbearded alike."

The rest of the trip proved uneventful. There happened to be an excellent doctor on board and he had our hero's hand in fair shape by the time the train reached southern California.

After several days of travel on horseback, the little party arrived at the Yuba River in the high Sierra Mountains. It was on one of the tributaries of this river that Jake Raven's gold mine was located.

Next to the diggings was a log cabin, which the men of the party soon had in a livable condition. Mr. Whipple and Betty occupied it, while Lem and the redskin made their bed under the stars.

One evening, after a hard day's work at the mine, the four friends were sitting around a fire drinking coffee when a man appeared who might have sat for the photograph of a Western bad man without any alteration in his countenance or apparel.

He wore a red flannel shirt, pants of leather with the hair still on them and a Mexican sombrero. He had a bowie knife in his boot and displayed two pearl-handled revolvers very ostentatiously.

When he was about two rods away from the group, he hailed it.

"How are you, strangers?" he asked.

"Pretty comfortable," said Shagpoke. "How fare you?"

"You're a Yank, ain't you?" he asked as he dismounted from his horse.

"Yes, from Vermont. Where might your home be?"

"I'm from Pike County, Missouri," was the answer. "You've heard of Pike, hain't you?"

"I've heard of Missouri," said Mr. Whipple with a smile, "but I can't say as I ever heard of your particular county."

The man with the leather pants frowned.

"You must have been born in the woods not to have heard of Pike County," he said. "The smartest fighters come from there. I kin whip my weight in wildcats, am a match for a dozen Injuns to oncet, and can tackle a lion without flinchin'."

"Won't you stop and rest with us?" said Mr. Whipple politely.

"I don't care if I do," was the uncouth Missourian's rejoinder. "You don't happen to have a bottle of whisky with you, strangers?" he asked.

"No," said Lem.

The newcomer looked disappointed.

"I wish you had," he said. "I feel dry as a salt herring. What are you doing here?"

"Mining," said Mr. Whipple.

"Grubbin' in the ground," said the stranger with disgust. "That's no job for a gentleman."

This last was uttered in such a magnificent tone of disdain that everyone smiled. In his red shirt, coarse leather breeches and brown, not overclean skin, he certainly didn't look much like a gentleman in the conventional sense of the term.

"It's well enough to be a gentleman, if you've got money to fall back on," remarked Lem sensibly but not offensively.

"Is that personal?" demanded the Pike County man, scowling and half rising from the ground.

"It's personal to me," said Lem quietly.

"I accept the apology," said the Missourian fiercely. "But you'd better not rile me, stranger, for I'm powerful bad. You don't know me, you don't. I'm a rip-tail roarer and a ring-tail squealer, I am. I always kills the man what riles me."

After this last bloodthirsty declaration, the man from Pike County temporarily subsided. He partook quietly of the coffee and cake which Betty served him. Suddenly he flared up again.

"Hain't that an Injun?" he shouted, pointing at Jake Raven and reaching for his gun.

Lem stepped hastily in front of the redskin, while Shagpoke grabbed the ruffian's wrist.

"He's a good friend of ours," said Betty.

"I don't give a darn," said the ring-tail squealer. "Turn me loose and I'll massacree the danged aboriginee."

Jake Raven, however, could take care of himself. He pulled his own revolver and pointing it at the bad man said, "Rascal shut up or me kill um pronto quick."

At the sight of the Indian's drawn gun, the ruffian calmed down.

"All right," he said, "but it's my policy always to shoot

an Injun on sight. The only good Injun is a dead one, is what I alluz say."

Mr. Whipple sent Jake Raven away from the fire and there was a long silence, during which everyone stared at the cheery flames. Finally the man from Pike County again broke into speech, this time addressing Lem.

"How about a game of cards, sport?" he asked. With these words he drew a greasy pack out of his pocket and shuffled them with great skill.

"I have never played cards in my life," said our hero.

"Where was you raised?" demanded the Missourian contemptuously.

"Ottsville, State of Vermont," said Lem. "I don't know one card from another, and don't want to know."

In no way abashed, the Pike man said, "I'll larn you. How about a game of poker?"

Mr. Whipple spoke up. "We do not permit gambling in this camp," he said firmly.

"That's durn foolishness," said the stranger, whose object it was to victimize his new friends, being an expert gambler.

"Perhaps it is," said Mr. Whipple. "But that's our business."

"Look here, hombre," blustered the bully. "I reckon you don't realize who you're a-talking to. 'Tarnal death and massacreeation, I'm the rip-tail roarer, I am."

"You told us that before," said Mr. Whipple quietly.

"Blood and massacreeation, if I don't mean it, too," exclaimed the Missourian with a fierce scowl. "Do you know how I treated a man last week?"

"No," said Mr. Whipple, truthfully.

"We was ridin' together over in Almeda County. We'd met permiscuous, like we've met tonight. I was tellin' him how four b'ars attacked me to oncet, and how I fit 'em all single-handed, when he laughed and said he reckoned

I'd been drinkin' and seed double. If he'd a-know'd me better he wouldn't have done it."

"What did you do?" asked Betty in horror.

"What did I do, madam?" echoed the Pike County man ferociously. "I told him he didn't realize who he'd insulted. I told him I was a ring-tail squealer and a rip-tail roarer. I told him that he had to fight, and asked him how it would be. Foot and fist, or tooth and nail, or claw and mudscraper, or knife, gun and tommyhawk."

"Did he fight?" asked Lem.

"He had to."

"How did it come out?"

"I shot him through the heart," said the Missourian coldly. "His bones are bleachin' in the canyon where he fell."

25

The next day, the Pike County man lay on his blankets until about eleven o'clock in the morning. He only got up when Lem, Jake and Shagpoke returned from their work on the creek to eat lunch. They were surprised to see him still in camp, but said nothing out of politeness.

Although they did not know it, the Missourian had not been sleeping. He had been lying under a tree, thinking dirty thoughts as he watched Betty go about her household chores.

"I'm hungry," he announced with great truculence. "When do we eat?"

"Won't you share our lunch?" asked Mr. Whipple with a sarcastic smile that was completely lost on the uncouth fellow.

"Thank ye, stranger, I don't mind if I do," the Pike County man said. "My fodder give out just before I made your camp, and I hain't found a place to stock up."

He displayed such an appetite that Mr. Whipple regarded him with anxiety. The camp was short of provisions, and if the stranger kept eating like that he would have to take a trip into town that very afternoon for more food.

"You have a healthy appetite, my friend," Mr. Whipple said.

"I generally have," said the Pike man. "You'd orter keep some whisky to wash these vittles down with."

"We prefer coffee," said Lem.

"Coffee is for children, whisky for strong men," was the ring-tail squealer's rejoinder.

"I still prefer coffee," Lem said firmly.

"Bah!" said the other, disdainfully; "I'd as soon drink skim milk. Good whisky or cawn for me."

"The only thing I miss in this camp," said Mr. Whipple, "is baked beans and brown bread. Ever eat 'em, stranger?"

"No," said the Pike man, "none of your Yankee truck for me."

"What's your favorite food?" asked Lem with a smile.

"Sow teats and hominy, hoe cakes and forty-rod."

"Well," said Lem, "it depends on how you've been brought up. I like baked beans and brown bread and pumpkin pie. Ever eat pumpkin pie?"

"Yes."

"Like it?"

"I don't lay much on it."

Throughout this dialogue, the stranger ate enormous quantities of food and drank six or seven cups of coffee. Mr. Whipple realized that the damage was done and that he would have to go into the town of Yuba for a fresh supply of provisions.

Having finished three cans of pineapple, the Pike man became social over one of Mr. Whipple's cigars, which he had taken without so much as a "by-your-leave."

"Strangers," he said, "did you ever hear of the affair I had with Jack Scott?"

"No," said Mr. Whipple.

"Jack and me used to be a heap together. We went huntin' together, camped out for weeks together, and was like two brothers. One day we was a-ridin' out, when a deer started up about fifty yards ahead of us. We both raised our guns and shot at him. There was only one bullet into him, and I knowed it was mine."

"How did you know it?" asked Lem.

"Don't you get curious, stranger. I knowed it, and that was enough. But Jack said it was his. 'It's my deer,' he says, 'for you missed your shot.' 'Looka here, Jack,' says I, 'you're mistaken. You missed it. Don't you think I know my own bullet?' 'No, I don't,' says he. 'Jack,' says I calmly, 'don't talk that way. It's dangerous.' 'Do you think I'm afraid of you?' he says turnin' on me. 'Jack,' says I, 'don't provoke me. I kin whip my weight in wildcats.' 'You can't whip me,' he says. That was too much for me to stand. I'm the rip-tail roarer from Pike County, Missouri, and no man can insult me and live. 'Jack,' says I, 'we've been friends, but you've insulted me and you must pay with your life.' Then I up with my iron and shot him through the head."

"My, how cruel!" exclaimed Betty.

"I was sorry to do it, beautiful gal, for he was my best friend, but he disputed my word, and the man that does that has to make his will if he's got property."

No one said anything, so the Pike man continued to talk.

"You see," he said with a friendly smile. "I was brought up on fightin'. When I was a boy I could whip every boy in the school."

"That's why they call you a rip-tail roarer," said Mr. Whipple jokingly.

"You're right, pardner," said the Pike man complacently.

"What did you do when the teacher gave you a licking?" asked Mr. Whipple.

"What did I do?" yelled the Missourian with a demoniac laugh.

"Yes, what?" asked Mr. Whipple.

"Why, I shot him dead," said the Pike man briefly.

"My," said Mr. Whipple with a smile. "How many teachers did you shoot when you were a boy?"

"Only one. The rest heard of it and never dared touch me."

After this last statement, the desperado lay down under a tree to finish in comfort the cigar he had snatched from Mr. Whipple.

Seeing that he did not intend to move just yet, the others proceeded to go about their business. Lem and Jake Raven went to the mine, which was about a mile from the cabin. Shagpoke saddled his horse for the ride into town after a fresh stock of provisions. Betty occupied herself over the washtub.

Some time had elapsed, when Lem and Jake Raven decided that they would need dynamite to continue their operations. Lem was down at the bottom of the shaft, so the Indian was the one to go to camp for the explosives.

When Jake did not return after several hours, Lem began to worry about him. He remembered what the Pike man had said about his Indian policy and was afraid that that ruffian might have done Jake an injury.

Our hero decided to go back and see if everything was all right. When he entered the clearing in which the cabin stood, he was surprised to find the place deserted.

"Hi, Jake!" Lem shouted bewilderedly. "Hi, Jake Raven!"

There was no answer. Only the woods sent his words back to him in an echo almost as loud as his shout.

Suddenly, a scream rent the silence. Lem recognized the

voice of the screamer as Betty's, and ran quickly toward the cabin.

26

The door was locked. Lem hammered on it, but no one answered. He went to the woodpile to get an ax and there found Jake Raven lying on the ground. He had been shot through the chest. Hastily snatching up the ax Lem ran to the cabin. A few hearty blows and the door tumbled in.

In the half gloom of the cabin, Lem was horrified to see the Pike man busily tearing off Betty's sole remaining piece of underwear. She was struggling as best she could, but the ruffian from Missouri was too strong for her.

Lem raised the ax high over his head and started forward to interfere. He did not get very far because the ruffian had prepared for just such a contingency by setting an enormous bear trap inside the door.

Our hero stepped on the pan of the trap and its saw-toothed jaws closed with great force on the calf of his leg, cutting through his trousers, skin, flesh and halfway into the bone besides. He dropped in a heap, as though he had been shot through the brain.

At the sight of poor Lem weltering in his own blood, Betty fainted. In no way disturbed, the Missourian went coolly about his nefarious business and soon accomplished his purpose.

With the hapless girl in his arms he then left the cabin. Throwing her behind his saddle, he pressed his cruel spurs into his horse's sides and galloped off in the general direction of Mexico.

Once more the deep hush of the primeval forest descended on the little clearing, making peaceful what had been a scene of wild torment and savage villainy. A

squirrel began to chatter hysterically in a treetop and
from somewhere along the brook came the plash of a
rising trout. Birds sang.

Suddenly the birds were still. The squirrel fled from
the tree in which he had been gathering pine cones.
Something was moving behind the woodpile. Jake Raven
was not dead after all.

With all the stoical disregard of pain for which his
race is famous, the sorely wounded Indian crawled along
on his hands and knees. His progress was slow but sure.

Some three miles away was the boundary line of the
California Indian Reservation. Jake knew that there was
an encampment of his people close by the line and it was
to them that he was going for help.

After a long, tortuous struggle, he arrived at his destination, but his efforts had so weakened him that he
fainted dead away in the arms of the first redskin to reach
him. Not before, however, he had managed to mumble
the following words:

"White man shoot. Go camp quick. . . ."

Leaving Jake to the tender ministrations of the village
squaws, the warriors of the tribe assembled around the
wigwam of their chief to plan a course of action. Somewhere a tom-tom began to throb.

The chief's name was Israel Satinpenny. He had been to
Harvard and hated the white man with undying venom.
For many years now, he had been trying to get the
Indian nations to rise and drive the palefaces back to the
countries from which they had come, but so far he had
had little success. His people had grown soft and lost their
warlike ways. Perhaps, with the wanton wounding of Jake
Raven, his chance had come.

When the warriors had all gathered around his tent, he
appeared in full regalia and began a harangue.

"Red men!" he thundered. "The time has come to protest

in the name of the Indian peoples and to cry out against that abomination of abominations, the paleface.

"In our father's memory this was a fair, sweet land, where a man could hear his heart beat without wondering if what he heard wasn't an alarm clock, where a man could fill his nose with pleasant flower odors without finding that they came from a bottle. Need I speak of springs that had never known the tyranny of iron pipes? Of deer that had never tasted hay? Of wild ducks that had never been banded by the U.S. Department of Conservation?

"In return for the loss of these things, we accepted the white man's civilization, syphilis and the radio, tuberculosis and the cinema. We accepted his civilization because he himself believed in it. But now that he has begun to doubt, why should we continue to accept? His final gift to us is doubt, a soul-corroding doubt. He rotted this land in the name of progress, and now it is he himself who is rotting. The stench of his fear stinks in the nostrils of the great god Manitou.

"In what way is the white man wiser than the red? We lived here from time immemorial and everything was sweet and fresh. The paleface came and in his wisdom filled the sky with smoke and the rivers with refuse. What, in his wisdom, was he doing? I'll tell you. He was making clever cigarette lighters. He was making superb fountain pens. He was making paper bags, doorknobs, leatherette satchels. All the powers of water, air and earth he made to turn his wheels within wheels within wheels within wheels. They turned, sure enough, and the land was flooded with toilet paper, painted boxes to keep pins in, key rings, watch fobs, leatherette satchels.

"When the paleface controlled the things he manufactured, we red men could only wonder at and praise his ability to hide his vomit. But now all the secret places of the earth are full. Now even the Grand Canyon will no longer hold razor blades. Now the dam, O warriors, has broken and he is up to his neck in the articles of his manufacture.

"He has loused the continent up good. But is he trying to de-louse it? No, all his efforts go to keep on lousing up the joint. All that worries him is how he can go on making little painted boxes for pins, watch fobs, leatherette satchels.

"Don't mistake me, Indians. I'm no Rousseauistic philosopher. I know that you can't put the clock back. But there is one thing you can do. You can stop that clock. You can smash that clock.

"The time is ripe. Riot and profaneness, poverty and violence are everywhere. The gates of pandemonium are open and through the land stalk the gods Mapeeo and Suraniou.

"The day of vengeance is here. The star of the paleface is sinking and he knows it. Spengler has said so; Valéry has said so; thousands of his wise men proclaim it.

"O, brothers, this is the time to run upon his neck and the bosses of his armor. While he is sick and fainting, while he is dying of a surfeit of shoddy."

Wild yells for vengeance broke from the throats of the warriors. Shouting their new war cry of "Smash that clock!" they smeared themselves with bright paint and mounted their ponies. In every brave's hand was a tomahawk and between his teeth a scalping knife.

Before jumping on his own mustang, Chief Satinpenny ordered one of his lieutenants to the nearest telegraph office. From there he was to send code messages to all the Indian tribes in the United States, Canada and Mexico, ordering them to rise and slay.

With Satinpenny leading them, the warriors galloped

through the forest over the trail that Jake Raven had come. When they arrived at the cabin, they found Lem still fast in the unrelenting jaws of the bear trap.

"Yeehoieee!" screamed the chief, as he stooped over the recumbent form of the poor lad and tore the scalp from his head. Then brandishing his reeking trophy on high, he sprang on his pony and made for the nearest settlements, followed by his horde of blood-crazed savages.

An Indian boy remained behind with instructions to fire the cabin. Fortunately, he had no matches and tried to do it with two sticks, but no matter how hard he rubbed them together he alone grew warm.

With a curse unbecoming one of his few years, he left off to go swimming in the creek, first looting Lem's bloody head of its store teeth and glass eye.

27

A few hours later, Mr. Whipple rode on the scene with his load of provisions. The moment he entered the clearing he knew that something was wrong and hurried to the cabin. There he found Lem with his leg still in the bear trap.

He bent over the unconscious form of the poor, mutilated lad and was happy to discover that his heart still beat. He tried desperately to release the trap, but failed, and was forced to carry Lem out of the cabin with it dangling from his leg.

Placing our hero across the pommel of his saddle, he galloped all that night, arriving at the county hospital the next morning. Lem was immediately admitted to the ward, where the good doctors began their long fight to save the lad's life. They triumphed, but not before they had found it necessary to remove his leg at the knee.

With the disappearance of Jake Raven, there was no use in Mr. Whipple's returning to the mine, so he remained near Lem, visiting the poor boy every day. Once he brought him an orange to eat, another time some simple wild flowers which he himself had gathered.

Lem's convalescence was a long one. Before it was over all of Shagpoke's funds were spent, and the ex-President was forced to work in a livery stable in order to keep body and soul together. When our hero left the hospital, he joined him there.

At first Lem had some difficulty in using the wooden leg with which the hospital authorities had equipped him. Practice, however, makes perfect, and in time he was able to help Mr. Whipple clean the stalls and curry the horses.

It goes without saying that the two friends were not satisfied to remain hostlers. They both searched for more suitable employment, but there was none to be had.

Shagpoke's mind was quick and fertile. One day, as he watched Lem show his scalped skull for the twentieth time, he was struck by an idea. Why not get a tent and exhibit his young friend as the last man to have been scalped by the Indians and the sole survivor of the Yuba River massacre?

Our hero was not very enthusiastic about the plan, but Mr. Whipple finally managed to convince him that it was the only way in which they could hope to escape from their drudgery in the livery stable. He promised Lem that as soon as they had accumulated a little money they would abandon the tent show and enter some other business.

Out of an old piece of tarpaulin they fashioned a rough tent. Mr. Whipple then obtained a crate of cheap kerosene lighters from a dealer in pedlar's supplies. With this meager equipment they took to the open road.

Their method of work was very simple. When they arrived at the outskirts of a likely town, they set up their tent. Lem hid himself inside it, while Mr. Whipple beat furiously on the bottom of a tin can with a stick.

In a short while, he was surrounded by a crowd eager to know what the noise was about. After describing the merits of his kerosene lighters, he made his audience a "dual" offer. For the same ten cents, they could both obtain a cigarette lighter and enter the tent where they would see the sole survivor of the Yuba River massacre, getting a close view of his freshly scalped skull.

Business was not as good as they had thought it would be. Although Mr. Whipple was an excellent salesman, the people they encountered had very little money to spend and could not afford to gratify their curiosity no matter how much it was aroused.

One day, after many weary months on the road, the two friends were about to set up their tent, when a small boy volunteered the information that there was a much bigger show being given free at the local opera house. Realizing that it would be futile for them to try to compete with this other attraction, they decided to visit it.

There were bills posted on every fence, and the two friends stopped to read one of them.

FREE   FREE   FREE

Chamber of American Horrors
Animate and Inanimate
Hideosities
also
Chief Jake Raven

COME ONE   COME ALL

S. Snodgrasse
Mgr.

FREE   FREE   FREE

Delighted to discover that their red-skinned friend was still alive, they set out to find him. He was coming down the steps of the opera house just as they arrived there, and his joy on seeing them was very great. He insisted on their accompanying him to a restaurant.

Over his coffee, Jake explained that after being shot by the man from Pike County, he had crawled to the Indian encampment. There his wounds had been healed by the use of certain medicaments secret to the squaws of his tribe. It was this same elixir that he was now selling in conjunction with the "Chamber of American Horrors."

Lem in his turn told how he had been scalped and how Mr. Whipple had arrived just in time to carry him to the hospital. After listening sympathetically to the lad's story, Jake expressed his anger in no uncertain terms. He condemned Chief Satinpenny for being a hothead, and assured Lem and Mr. Whipple that the respectable members of the tribe frowned on Satinpenny's activities.

Although Mr. Whipple believed Jake, he was not satisfied that the Indian rising was as simple as it seemed. "Where," he asked the friendly redskin, "had Satinpenny obtained the machine guns and whisky needed to keep his warriors in the field?"

Jake was unable to answer this question, and Mr. Whipple smiled as though he knew a great deal more than he was prepared to divulge at this time.

28

"I remember your administration very well," said Sylvanus Snodgrasse to Mr. Whipple. "It will be an honor to have you and your young friend, whom I also know and admire, in my employ."

"Thank you," said both Shagpoke and Lem together.

"You will spend today rehearsing your roles and tomorrow you will appear in the pageant."

It was through the good offices of Jake Raven that the above interview was made possible. Realizing how poor they were, he had suggested that the two friends abandon their own little show and obtain positions in the one with which he was traveling.

As soon as Shagpoke and Lem left the manager's office, an inner door opened and through it entered a certain man. If they had seen him and had known who he was, they would have been greatly surprised. Moreover, they would not have been quite so happy over their new jobs.

This stranger was none other than the fat man in the Chesterfield overcoat, Operative 6348XM, or Comrade Z as he was known at a different address. His presence in Snodgrasse's office is explained by the fact that the "Chamber of American Horrors, Animate and Inanimate Hideosities," although it appeared to be a museum, was in reality a bureau for disseminating propaganda of the most subversive nature. It had been created and financed to this end by the same groups that employed the fat man.

Snodgrasse had become one of their agents because of his inability to sell his "poems." Like many another "poet," he blamed his literary failure on the American public instead of on his own lack of talent, and his desire for revolution was really a desire for revenge. Furthermore, having lost faith in himself, he thought it his duty to undermine the nation's faith in itself.

As its name promised, the show was divided into two parts, "animate" and "inanimate." Let us first briefly consider the latter, which consisted of innumerable objects culled from the popular art of the country and of an equally large number of manufactured articles of the kind detested so heartily by Chief Satinpenny.

("Can this be a coincidence?" Mr. Whipple was later to ask.)

The hall which led to the main room of the "inanimate" exhibit was lined with sculptures in plaster. Among the most striking of these was a Venus de Milo with a clock in her abdomen, a copy of Power's "Greek Slave" with elastic bandages on all her joints, A Hercules wearing a small, compact truss.

In the center of the principal salon was a gigantic hemorrhoid that was lit from within by electric lights. To give the effect of throbbing pain, these lights went on and off.

All was not medical, however. Along the walls were tables on which were displayed collections of objects whose distinction lay in the great skill with which their materials had been disguised. Paper had been made to look like wood, wood like rubber, rubber like steel, steel like cheese, cheese like glass, and, finally, glass like paper.

Other tables carried instruments whose purposes were dual and sometimes triple or even sextuple. Among the most ingenious were pencil sharpeners that could also be used as earpicks, can openers as hair brushes. Then, too, there was a large variety of objects whose real uses had been cleverly camouflaged. The visitor saw flower pots that were really victrolas, revolvers that held candy, candy that held collar buttons and so forth.

The "animate" part of the show took place in the auditorium of the opera house. It was called "The Pageant of America or A Curse on Columbus," and consisted of a series of short sketches in which Quakers were shown being branded, Indians brutalized and cheated, Negroes sold, children sweated to death. Snodgrasse tried to make obvious the relationship between these sketches and the "inanimate" exhibit by a little speech in which he claimed

that the former had resulted in the latter. His arguments
were not very convincing, however.

The "pageant" culminated in a small playlet which I
will attempt to set down from memory. When the curtain
rises, the audience sees the comfortable parlor of a typical
American home. An old, white-haired grandmother is
knitting near the fire while the three small sons of her
dead daughter play together on the floor. From a radio in
the corner comes a rich, melodic voice.

Radio: "The Indefatigable Investment Company of Wall
Street wishes its unseen audience all happiness, health
and wealth, especially the latter. Widows, orphans, cripples,
are you getting a large enough return on your capital? Is
the money left by your departed ones bringing you all that
they desired you to have in the way of comforts? Write or
telephone . . ."

Here the stage becomes dark for a few seconds. When
the lights are bright again, we hear the same voice, but
see that this time it comes from a sleek, young salesman.
He is talking to the old grandmother. The impression
given is that of a snake and a bird. The old lady is the
bird, of course.

Sleek Salesman: "Dear Madam, in South America lies
the fair, fertile land of Iguania. It is a marvelous country,
rich in minerals and oil. For five thousand dollars—yes,
Madam, I'm advising you to sell all your Liberty Bonds
—you will get ten of our Gold Iguanians, which yield
seventeen per centum per annum. These bonds are se-
cured by a first mortgage on all the natural resources of
Iguania."

Grandmother: "But I . . ."

Sleek Salesman: "You will have to act fast, as we have
only a limited number of Gold Iguanians left. The ones
I am offering you are part of a series set aside by our
company especially for widows and orphans. It was neces-

sary for us to do this because otherwise the big banks and mortgage companies would have snatched up the entire issue."

Grandmother: "But I . . ."

The Three Small Sons: "Goo, goo. . . ."

Sleek Salesman: "Think of these kiddies, Madam. Soon they will be ready for college. They will want Brooks suits and banjos and fur coats like the other boys. How will you feel when you have to refuse them these things because of your stubbornness?"

Here the curtain falls for a change of scene. It rises again on a busy street. The old grandmother is seen lying in the gutter with her head pillowed against the curb. Around her are arranged her three grandchildren, all very evidently dead of starvation.

Grandmother (feebly to the people who hurry past): "We are starving. Bread . . . bread . . ."

No one pays any attention to her and she dies.

An idle breeze plays mischievously with the rags draping the four corpses. Suddenly it whirls aloft several sheets of highly engraved paper, one of which is blown across the path of two gentlemen in silk hats, on whose vests huge dollar signs are embroidered. They are evidently millionaires.

First Millionaire (picking up engraved paper): "Hey, Bill, isn't this one of your Iguanian Gold Bonds?" (He laughs.)

Second Millionaire (echoing his companion's laughter): "Sure enough. That's from the special issue for widows and orphans. I got them out in 1928 and they sold like hot cakes. (He turns the bond over in his hands, admiring it.) I'll tell you one thing, George, it certainly pays to do a good printing job."

Laughing heartily, the two millionaires move along the street. In their way lie the four dead bodies and they almost trip over them. They exit cursing the street cleaning department for its negligence.

29

The "Chamber of American Horrors, Animate and Inanimate Hideosities," reached Detroit about a month after the two friends had joined it. It was while they were playing there that Lem questioned Mr. Whipple about the show. He was especially disturbed by the scene in which the millionaires stepped on the dead children.

"In the first place," Mr. Whipple said, in reply to Lem's questions, "the grandmother didn't have to buy the bonds unless she wanted to. Secondly, the whole piece is made ridiculous by the fact that no one can die in the streets. The authorities won't stand for it."

"But," said Lem, "I thought you were against the capitalists?"

"Not all capitalists," answered Shagpoke. "The distinction must be made between bad capitalists and good capitalists, between the parasites and the creators. I am against the parasitical international bankers, but not the creative American capitalists, like Henry Ford for example."

"Are not capitalists who step on the faces of dead children bad?"

"Even if they are," replied Shagpoke, "it is very wrong to show the public scenes of that sort. I object to them because they tend to foment bad feeling between the classes."

"I see," said Lem.

"What I am getting at," Mr. Whipple went on, "is that Capital and Labor must be taught to work together for the general good of the country. Both must be made to drop the materialistic struggle for higher wages on the one hand and bigger profits on the other. Both must be made to realize that the only struggle worthy of Americans is the idealistic one of their country against its enemies, England, Japan, Russia, Rome and Jerusalem. Always remember, my boy, that class war is civil war, and will destroy us."

"Shouldn't we then try to dissuade Mr. Snodgrasse from continuing with his show?" asked Lem innocently.

"No," replied Shagpoke. "If we try to he will merely get rid of us. Rather must we bide our time until a good opportunity presents itself, then denounce him for what he is, and his show likewise. Here, in Detroit, there are too many Jews, Catholics and members of unions. Unless I am greatly mistaken, however, we will shortly turn south. When we get to some really American town, we will act."

Mr. Whipple was right in his surmise. After playing a few more Midwestern cities, Snodgrasse headed his company south along the Mississippi River, finally arriving in the town of Beulah for a one-night stand.

"Now is the time for us to act," announced Mr. Whipple in a hoarse whisper to Lem, when he had obtained a good look at the inhabitants of Beulah. "Follow me."

Our hero accompanied Shagpoke to the town barber shop, which was run by one Keely Jefferson, a fervent Southerner of the old school. Mr. Whipple took the master barber to one side. After a whispered colloquy, he agreed to arrange a meeting of the town's citizens for Shagpoke to address.

By five o'clock that same evening, all the inhabitants of Beulah who were not colored, Jewish or Catholic assembled under a famous tree from whose every branch a Negro had dangled at one time or other. They stood together, almost a thousand strong, drinking Coca-Colas and joking with their friends. Although every third citizen carried either a rope or a gun, their cheerful manner belied the seriousness of the occasion.

Mr. Jefferson mounted a box to introduce Mr. Whipple. "Fellow townsmen, Southerners, Protestants, Americans," he began. "You have been called here to listen to the words of Shagpoke Whipple, one of the few Yanks whom we of the South can trust and respect. He ain't no nigger-lover, he don't give a damn for Jewish culture, and he knows the fine Italian hand of the Pope when he sees it. Mr. Whipple . . ."

Shagpoke mounted the box which Mr. Jefferson vacated and waited for the cheering to subside. He began by placing his hand on his heart. "I love the South," he announced. "I love her because her women are beautiful and chaste, her men brave and gallant, and her fields warm and fruitful. But there is one thing that I love more than the South . . . my country, these United States."

The cheers which greeted this avowal were even wilder and hoarser than those that had gone before it. Mr. Whipple held up his hand for silence, but it was fully five minutes before his audience would let him continue.

"Thank you," he cried happily, much moved by the enthusiasm of his hearers. "I know that your shouts rise from the bottom of your honest, fearless hearts. And I am grateful because I also know that you are cheering, not me, but the land we love so well.

"However, this is not a time or place for flowery speeches, this is a time for action. There is an enemy in our midst, who, by boring from within, undermines our institutions and threatens our freedom. Neither hot lead nor cold steel are his weapons, but insidious propaganda. He strives by it to set brother against brother, those who have not against those who have.

"You stand here now, under this heroic tree, like the free men that you are, but tomorrow you will become the slaves of Socialists and Bolsheviks. Your sweethearts and wives will become the common property of foreigners to maul and mouth at their leisure. Your shops will be torn from you and you will be driven from your farms. In return you will be thrown a stinking, slave's crust with Russian labels.

"Is the spirit of Jubal Early and Francis Marion then so dead that you can only crouch and howl like hound dogs? Have you forgotten Jefferson Davis?

"No?

"Then let those of you who remember your ancestors strike down Sylvanus Snodgrasse, that foul conspirator, that viper in the bosom of the body politic. Let those . . ."

Before Mr. Whipple had quite finished his little talk, the crowd ran off in all directions, shouting "Lynch him! Lynch him!" although a good three-quarters of its members did not know whom it was they were supposed to lynch. This fact did not bother them, however. They considered their lack of knowledge an advantage rather than a hindrance, for it gave them a great deal of leeway in their choice of a victim.

Those of the mob who were better informed made for the opera house where the "Chamber of American Horrors" was quartered. Snodgrasse, however, was nowhere to be found. He had been warned and had taken to his heels. Feeling that they ought to hang somebody, the crowd put a rope around Jake Raven's neck because of his dark complexion. They then fired the building.

Another section of Shagpoke's audience, made up mostly of older men, had somehow gotten the impression that the South had again seceded from the Union. Perhaps this had come about through their hearing Shagpoke mention the

names of Jubal Early, Francis Marion and Jefferson Davis
They ran up the Confederate flag on the courthouse pole,
and prepared to die in its defense.

Other, more practical-minded citizens proceeded to rob
the bank and loot the principal stores, and to free all
their relatives who had the misfortune to be in jail.

As time went on, the riot grew more general in character. Barricades were thrown up in the streets. The heads
of Negroes were paraded on poles. A Jewish drummer was
nailed to the door of his hotel room. The housekeeper of
the local Catholic priest was raped.

30

Lem lost track of Mr. Whipple when the meeting broke
up, and was unable to find him again although he searched
everywhere. As he wandered around, he was shot at several
times, and it was only by the greatest of good luck that
he succeeded in escaping with his life.

He managed this by walking to the nearest town that had
a depot and there taking the first train bound northeast.
Unfortunately, all his money had been lost in the opera
house fire and he was unable to pay for a ticket. The
conductor, however, was a good-natured man. Seeing that
the lad had only one leg, he waited until the train slowed
down at a curve before throwing him off.

It was only a matter of twenty miles or so to the
nearest highway, and Lem contrived to hobble there before
dawn. Once on the highway, he was able to beg rides all the
way to New York City, arriving there some ten weeks
later.

Times had grown exceedingly hard with the inhabitants
of that once prosperous metropolis and Lem's ragged,
emaciated appearance caused no adverse comment. He

was able to submerge himself in the great army of unemployed.

Our hero differed from most of that army in several ways, however. For one thing, he bathed regularly. Each morning he took a cold plunge in the Central Park lake on whose shores he was living in a piano crate. Also, he visited daily all the employment agencies that were still open, refusing to be discouraged or grow bitter and become a carping critic of things as they are.

One day, when he timidly opened the door of the "Golden Gates Employment Bureau," he was greeted with a welcoming smile instead of the usual jeers and curses.

"My boy," exclaimed Mr. Gates, the proprietor, "we have obtained a position for you."

At this news, tears welled up in Lem's good eye and his throat was so choked with emotion that he could not speak.

Mr. Gates was surprised and nettled by the lad's silence, not realizing its cause. "It's the opportunity of a lifetime," he said chidingly. "You have heard of course of the great team of Riley and Robbins. They're billed wherever they play as 'Fifteen Minutes of Furious Fun with Belly Laffs Galore.' Well, Moe Riley is an old friend of mine. He came in here this morning and asked me to get him a 'stooge' for his act. He wanted a one-eyed man, and the minute he said that, I thought of you."

By now Lem had gained sufficient control over himself to thank Mr. Gates, and he did so profusely.

"You almost didn't get the job," Mr. Gates went on, when he had had enough of the mutilated boy's gratitude. "There was a guy in here who heard Moe Riley talking to me, and we had some time preventing him from poking out one of his eyes so that he could qualify for the job. We had to call a cop."

"Oh, that's too bad," said Lem sadly.

"But I told Riley that you also had a wooden leg, wore a toupee and store teeth, and he wouldn't think of hiring anybody but you."

When our hero reported to the Bijou Theater, where Riley and Robbins were playing, he was stopped at the stage door by the watchman, who was suspicious of his tattered clothes. He insisted on getting in, and the watchman finally agreed to take a message to the comedians. Soon afterwards, he was shown to their dressing room.

Lem stood in the doorway, fumbling with the piece of soiled cloth that served him as a cap, until the gales of laughter with which Riley and Robbins had greeted him subsided. Fortunately, it never struck the poor lad that he was the object of their merriment or he might have fled.

To be perfectly just, from a certain point of view, not a very civilized one it must be admitted, there was much to laugh at in our hero's appearance. Instead of merely having no hair like a man prematurely bald, the gray bone of his skull showed plainly where he had been scalped by Chief Satinpenny. Then, too, his wooden leg had been carved with initials, twined hearts and other innocent insignia by mischievous boys.

"You're a wow!" exclaimed the two comics in the argot of their profession. "You're a riot! You'll blow them out of the back of the house. Boy, oh boy, wait till the pus-pockets and fleapits get a load of you."

Although Lem did not understand their language, he was made exceedingly happy by the evident satisfaction he gave his employers. He thanked them effusively.

"Your salary will be twelve dollars a week," said Riley, who was the businessman of the team. "We wish we could pay you more, for you're worth more, but these are hard times in the theater."

Lem accepted without quibbling and they began at once

to rehearse him. His role was a simple one, with no spoken lines, and he was soon perfect in it. He made his debut on the stage that same night. When the curtain went up, he was discovered standing between the two comics and facing the audience. He was dressed in an old Prince Albert, many times too large for him, and his expression was one of extreme sobriety and dignity. At his feet was a large box the contents of which could not be seen by the audience.

Riley and Robbins wore striped blue flannel suits of the latest cut, white linen spats and pale gray derby hats. To accent further the contrast between themselves and their "stooge," they were very gay and lively. In their hands they carried newspapers rolled up into clubs.

As soon as the laughter caused by their appearance had died down, they began their "breezy crossfire of smart cracks."

Riley: "I say, my good man, who was that dame I saw you with last night?"

Robbins: "How could you see me last night? You were blind drunk."

Riley: "Hey, listen, you slob, that's not in the act and you know it."

Robbins: "Act? What act?"

Riley: "All right! All right! You're a great little kidder, but let's get down to business. I say to you: 'Who was that dame I saw you out with last night?' And you say: 'That was no dame, that was a damn.' "

Robbins: "So you're stealing my lines, eh?"

At this both actors turned on Lem and beat him violently over the head and body with their rolled-up newspapers. Their object was to knock off his toupee or to knock out his teeth and eye. When they had accomplished one or all of these goals, they stopped clubbing him. Then Lem, whose part it was not to move while he was being hit, bent over and with sober dignity took from the box at his feet, which contained a large assortment of false hair, teeth and eyes, whatever he needed to replace the things that had been knocked off or out.

The turn lasted about fifteen minutes and during this time Riley and Robbins told some twenty jokes, beating Lem ruthlessly at the end of each one. For a final curtain, they brought out an enormous wooden mallet labeled "The Works" and with it completely demolished our hero. His toupee flew off, his eye and teeth popped out, and his wooden leg was knocked into the audience.

At sight of the wooden leg, the presence of which they had not even suspected, the spectators were convulsed with joy. They laughed heartily until the curtain came down, and for some time afterwards.

Our hero's employers congratulated him on his success, and although he had a headache from their blows he was made quite happy by this. After all, he reasoned, with millions out of work he had no cause to complain.

One of Lem's duties was to purchase newspapers and out of them fashion the clubs used to beat him. When the performance was over, he was given the papers to read. They formed his only relaxation, for his meager salary made more complicated amusements impossible.

The mental reactions of the poor lad had been slowed up considerably by the hardships he had suffered, and it was a heart-rending sight to watch him as he bent over a paper to spell out the headlines. More than this he could not manage.

"PRESIDENT CLOSES BANKS FOR GOOD," he read one night. He sighed profoundly. Not because he had again lost the few dollars he had saved, which he had, but because it made him think of Mr. Whipple and the Rat River National Bank. He spent the rest of the night wondering what had become of his old friend.

Some weeks later he was to find out. "WHIPPLE DE-
MANDS DICTATORSHIP," he read. "LEATHER SHIRTS RIOT IN
SOUTH." Then, in rapid succession, came other headlines
announcing victories for Mr. Whipple's National Revolutionary Party. The South and West, Lem learned, were
solidly behind his movement and he was marching on
Chicago.

31

One day a stranger came to the theater to see Lem. He
addressed our hero as Commander Pitkin and said that he
was Storm Trooper Zachary Coates.

Lem made him welcome and asked eagerly for news of
Mr. Whipple. He was told that that very night Shagpoke
would be in the city. Mr. Coates then went on to explain
that because of its large foreign population New York was
still holding out against the National Revolutionary Party.

"But tonight," he said, "this city will be filled with
thousands of 'Leather Shirts' from upstate and an attempt
will be made to take it over."

While talking he stared hard at our hero. Apparently
satisfied with what he saw, he saluted briskly and said, "As
one of the original members of the party, you are being
asked to cooperate."

"I'll be glad to do anything I can to help," Lem replied.

"Good! Mr. Whipple will be happy to hear that, for he
counted on you."

"I am something of a cripple," Lem added with a brave
smile. "I may not be able to do much."

"We of the party know how your wounds were acquired.
In fact one of our prime purposes is to prevent the
youth of this country from being tortured as you were
tortured. Let me add, Commander Pitkin, that in my
humble opinion you are well on your way to being rec-

ognized as one of the martyrs of our cause." Here he saluted Lem once more.

Lem was embarrassed by the man's praise and hurriedly changed the subject. "What are Mr. Whipple's orders?" he asked.

"Tonight, wherever large crowds gather, in the parks, theaters, subways, a member of our party will make a speech. Scattered among his listeners will be numerous 'Leather Shirts' in plain clothes, who will aid the speaker stir up the patriotic fury of the crowd. When this fury reaches its proper height, a march on the City Hall will be ordered. There a monster mass meeting will be held which Mr. Whipple will address. He will demand and get control of the city."

"It sounds splendid," said Lem. "I suppose you want me to make a speech in this theater?"

"Yes, exactly."

"I would if I could," replied Lem, "but I'm afraid I can't. I have never made a speech in my life. You see, I'm not a real actor but only a 'stooge.' And besides, Riley and Robbins wouldn't like it if I tried to interrupt their act."

"Don't worry about those gentlemen." Mr. Coates said with a smile. "They will be taken care of. As for your other reason, I have a speech in my pocket that was written expressly for you by Mr. Whipple. I have come here to rehearse you in it."

Zachary Coates reached into his pocket and brought out a sheaf of papers. "Read this through first," he said firmly, "then we will begin to study it."

That night Lem walked out on the stage alone. Although he was not wearing his stage costume, but the dress uniform of the "Leather Shirts," the audience knew from the program that he was a comedian and roared with laughter.

This unexpected reception destroyed what little self-assurance the poor lad had and for a minute it looked as though he were going to run. Fortunately, however, the orchestra leader, who was a member of Mr. Whipple's organization, had his wits about him and made his men play the national anthem. The audience stopped laughing and rose soberly to its feet.

In all that multitude one man alone failed to stand up. He was our old friend, the fat fellow in the Chesterfield overcoat. Secreted behind the curtains of a box, he crouched low in his chair and fondled an automatic pistol. He was again wearing a false beard.

When the orchestra had finished playing, the audience reseated itself and Lem prepared to make his speech.

"I am a clown," he began, "but there are times when even clowns must grow serious. This is such a time. I . . ."

Lem got no further. A shot rang out and he fell dead, drilled through the heart by an assassin's bullet.

Little else remains to be told, but before closing this book there is one last scene which I must describe.

It is Pitkin's Birthday, a national holiday, and the youth of America is parading down Fifth Avenue in his honor. They are a hundred thousand strong. On every boy's head is a coonskin hat complete with jaunty tail, and on every shoulder rests a squirrel rifle.

Hear what they are singing. It is *The Lemuel Pitkin Song*.

"Who dares?"—this was L. Pitkin's cry,
  As striding on the Bijou stage he came—
"Surge out with me in Shagpoke's name,
  For him to live, for him to die!"
A million hands flung up reply,
  A million voices answered, "I!"

Chorus

A million hearts for Pitkin, oh!
To do and die with Pitkin, oh!
To live and fight with Pitkin, oh!
Marching for Pitkin.

The youths pass the reviewing stand and from it Mr. Whipple proudly returns their salute. The years have dealt but lightly with him. His back is still as straight as ever and his gray eyes have not lost their keenness.

But who is the little lady in black next to the dictator? Can it be the Widow Pitkin? Yes, it is she. She is crying, for with a mother glory can never take the place of a beloved child. To her it seems like only yesterday that Lawyer Slemp threw Lem into the open cellar.

And next to the Widow Pitkin stands still another woman. This one is young and beautiful, yet her eyes too are full of tears. Let us look closer, for there is something vaguely familiar about her. It is Betty Prail. She seems to have some official position, and when we ask, a bystander tells us that she is Mr. Whipple's secretary.

The marchers have massed themselves in front of the reviewing stand and Mr. Whipple is going to address them.

"Why are we celebrating this day above other days?" he asked his hearers in a voice of thunder. "What made Lemuel Pitkin great? Let us examine his life.

"First we see him as a small boy, light of foot, fishing for bullheads in the Rat River of Vermont. Later, he attends the Ottsville High School, where he is captain of the nine and an excellent outfielder. Then, he leaves for the big city to make his fortune. All this is in the honorable tradition of his country and its people, and he has the right to expect certain rewards.

"Jail is his first reward. Poverty his second. Violence is his third. Death is his last.

"Simple was his pilgrimage and brief, yet a thousand years hence, no story, no tragedy, no epic poem will be filled with greater wonder, or be followed by mankind with deeper feeling, than that which tells of the life and death of Lemuel Pitkin.

"But I have not answered the question. Why is Lemuel Pitkin great? Why does the martyr move in triumph and the nation rise up at every stage of his coming? Why are cities and states his pallbearers?

"Because, although dead, yet he speaks.

"Of what is it that he speaks? Of the right of every American boy to go into the world and there receive fair play and a chance to make his fortune by industry and probity without being laughed at or conspired against by sophisticated aliens.

"Alas, Lemuel Pitkin himself did not have this chance, but instead was dismantled by the enemy. His teeth were pulled out. His eye was gouged from his head. His thumb was removed. His scalp was torn away. His leg was cut off. And, finally, he was shot through the heart.

"But he did not live or die in vain. Through his martyrdom the National Revolutionary Party triumphed, and by that triumph this country was delivered from sophistication, Marxism and International Capitalism. Through the National Revolution its people were purged of alien diseases and America became again American."

"Hail the Martyrdom in the Bijou Theater!" roar Shagpoke's youthful hearers when he is finished.

"Hail, Lemuel Pitkin!"

"All hail, the American Boy!"

1 9 3 9

T*he Day of the Locust*

For LAURA

1

Around quitting time, Tod Hackett heard a great din on the road outside his office. The groan of leather mingled with the jangle of iron and over all beat the tattoo of a thousand hooves. He hurried to the window.

An army of cavalry and foot was passing. It moved like a mob; its lines broken, as though fleeing from some terrible defeat. The dolmans of the hussars, the heavy shakos of the guards, Hanoverian light horse, with their flat leather caps and flowing red plumes, were all jumbled together in bobbing disorder. Behind the cavalry came the infantry, a wild sea of waving sabretaches, sloped muskets, crossed shoulder belts and swinging cartridge boxes. Tod recognized the scarlet infantry of England with their white shoulder pads, the black infantry of the Duke of Brunswick, the French grenadiers with their enormous white gaiters, the Scotch with bare knees under plaid skirts.

While he watched, a little fat man, wearing a cork sun-helmet, polo shirt and knickers, darted around the corner of the building in pursuit of the army.

"Stage Nine—you bastards—Stage Nine!" he screamed through a small megaphone.

The cavalry put spur to their horses and the infantry broke into a dogtrot. The little man in the cork hat ran after them, shaking his fist and cursing.

Tod watched until they had disappeared behind half a Mississippi steamboat, then put away his pencils and drawing board, and left the office. On the sidewalk outside the studio he stood for a moment trying to decide whether to walk home or take a streetcar. He had been in Hollywood less than three months and still found it a very exciting place, but he was lazy and didn't like to walk. He decided to take the streetcar as far as Vine Street and walk the rest of the way.

A talent scout for National Films had brought Tod to the Coast after seeing some of his drawings in an exhibit of undergraduate work at the Yale School of Fine Arts. He had been hired by telegram. If the scout had met Tod, he probably wouldn't have sent him to Hollywood to learn set and costume designing. His large, sprawling body, his slow blue eyes and sloppy grin made him seem completely without talent, almost doltish in fact.

Yes, despite his appearance, he was really a very complicated young man with a whole set of personalities, one inside the other like a nest of Chinese boxes. And "The

Burning of Los Angeles," a picture he was soon to paint, definitely proved he had talent.

He left the car at Vine Street. As he walked along, he examined the evening crowd. A great many of the people wore sports clothes which were not really sports clothes. Their sweaters, knickers, slacks, blue flannel jackets with brass buttons were fancy dress. The fat lady in the yachting cap was going shopping, not boating; the man in the Norfolk jacket and Tyrolean hat was returning, not from a mountain, but an insurance office; and the girl in slacks and sneaks with a bandanna around her head had just left a switchboard, not a tennis court.

Scattered among these masquerades were people of a different type. Their clothing was somber and badly cut, bought from mail-order houses. While the others moved rapidly, darting into stores and cocktail bars, they loitered on the corners or stood with their backs to the shop windows and stared at everyone who passed. When their stare was returned, their eyes filled with hatred. At this time Tod knew very little about them except that they had come to California to die.

He was determined to learn much more. They were the people he felt he must paint. He would never again do a fat red barn, old stone wall or sturdy Nantucket fisherman. From the moment he had seen them, he had known that, despite his race, training and heritage, neither Winslow Homer nor Thomas Ryder could be his masters and he turned to Goya and Daumier.

He had learned this just in time. During his last year in art school, he had begun to think that he might give up painting completely. The pleasures he received from the problems of composition and color had decreased as his facility had increased and he had realized that he was going the way of all his classmates, toward illustration or mere handsomeness. When the Hollywood job had come along, he had grabbed it despite the arguments of his friends who were certain that he was selling out and would never paint again.

He reached the end of Vine Street and began the climb into Pinyon Canyon. Night had started to fall.

The edges of the trees burned with a pale violet light and their centers gradually turned from deep purple to black. The same violet piping, like a Neon tube, outlined the tops of the ugly, hump-backed hills and they were almost beautiful.

But not even the soft wash of dusk could help the houses. Only dynamite would be of any use against the Mexican ranch houses, Samoan huts, Mediterranean villas, Egyptian and Japanese temples, Swiss chalets, Tudor cottages, and every possible combination of these styles that lined the slopes of the canyon.

When he noticed that they were all of plaster, lath and paper, he was charitable and blamed their shape on the materials used. Steel, stone and brick curb a builder's fancy a little, forcing him to distribute his stresses and weights and to keep his corners plumb, but plaster and paper know no law, not even that of gravity.

On the corner of La Huerta Road was a miniature Rhine castle with tarpaper turrets pierced for archers. Next to it was a little highly colored shack with domes and minarets out of the *Arabian Nights*. Again he was charitable. Both houses were comic, but he didn't laugh. Their desire to startle was so eager and guileless.

It is hard to laugh at the need for beauty and romance, no matter how tasteless, even horrible, the results of that need are. But it is easy to sigh. Few things are sadder than the truly monstrous.

2

The house he lived in was a nondescript affair called the San Bernardino Arms. It was an oblong three stories high, the back and sides of which were of plain, unpainted stucco, broken by even rows of unadorned windows. The façade was the color of diluted mustard and its windows, all double, were framed by pink Moorish columns which supported turnip-shaped lintels.

His room was on the third floor, but he paused for a moment on the landing of the second. It was on that floor that Faye Greener lived, in 208. When someone laughed in one of the apartments he started guiltily and continued upstairs.

As he opened his door a card fluttered to the floor. "Honest Abe Kusich," it said in large type, then underneath in smaller italics were several endorsements, printed to look like press notices.

"*. . . the Lloyds of Hollywood*"—*Stanley Rose.*

"*Abe's word is better than Morgan's bonds*"—*Gail Brenshaw.*

On the other side was a penciled message:

"Kingpin fourth, Solitair sixth. You can make some real dough on those nags."

After opening the window, he took off his jacket and lay down on the bed. Through the window he could see a square of enameled sky and a spray of eucalyptus. A light breeze stirred its long, narrow leaves, making them show first their green side, then their silver one.

He began to think of "Honest Abe Kusich" in order not to think of Faye Greener. He felt comfortable and wanted to remain that way.

Abe was an important figure in a set of lithographs called "The Dancers" on which Tod was working. He was one of the dancers. Faye Greener was another and her father, Harry, still another. They changed with each plate, but the group of uneasy people who formed their audience remained the same. They stood staring at the performers in just the way that they stared at the masqueraders on Vine Street. It was their stare that drove Abe and the others to spin crazily and leap into the air with twisted backs like hooked trout.

Despite the sincere indignation that Abe's grotesque depravity aroused in him, he welcomed his company. The little man excited him and in that way made him feel certain of his need to paint.

He had first met Abe when he was living on Ivar Street, in a hotel called the Chateau Mirabella. Another name for Ivar Street was "Lysol Alley," and the Chateau was mainly inhabited by hustlers, their managers, trainers and advance agents.

In the morning its halls reeked of antiseptic. Tod didn't like this odor. Moreover, the rent was high because it included police protection, a service for which he had no need. He wanted to move, but inertia and the fact that he didn't know where to go kept him in the Chateau until he met Abe. The meeting was accidental.

He was on the way to his room late one night when he saw what he supposed was a pile of soiled laundry lying in front of the door across the hall from his own. Just as he was passing it, the bundle moved and made a peculiar noise. He struck a match, thinking it might be a dog wrapped in a blanket. When the light flared up, he saw it was a tiny man.

The match went out and he hastily lit another. It was a male dwarf rolled up in a woman's flannel bathrobe. The round thing at the end was his slightly hydrocephalic head. A slow, choked snore bubbled from it.

The hall was cold and draughty. Tod decided to wake the man and stirred him with his toe. He groaned and opened his eyes.

"You oughtn't to sleep there."

"The hell you say," said the dwarf, closing his eyes again.

"You'll catch cold."

This friendly observation angered the little man still more.

"I want my clothes!" he bellowed.

The bottom of the door next to which he was lying filled with light. Tod decided to take a chance and knock. A few seconds later a woman opened it part way.

"What the hell do you want?" she demanded.

"There's a friend of yours out here who . . ."

Neither of them let him finish.

"So what!" she barked, slamming the door.

"Give me my clothes, you bitch!" roared the dwarf.

She opened the door again and began to hurl things into the hall. A jacket and trousers, a shirt, socks, shoes and underwear, a tie and hat followed each other through the air in rapid succession. With each article went a special curse.

Tod whistled with amazement.

"Some gal!"

"You bet," said the dwarf. "A lollapalooza—all slut and a yard wide."

He laughed at his own joke, using a high-pitched cackle more dwarflike than anything that had come from him so far, then struggled to his feet and arranged the voluminous robe so that he could walk without tripping. Tod helped him gather his scattered clothing.

"Say, mister," he asked, "could I dress in your place?"

Tod let him into his bathroom. While waiting for him to reappear, he couldn't help imagining what had happened in the woman's apartment. He began to feel sorry for having interfered. But when the dwarf came out wearing his hat, Tod felt better.

The little man's hat fixed almost everything. That year Tyrolean hats were being worn a great deal along Hollywood Boulevard and the dwarf's was a fine specimen. It was the proper magic green color and had a high, conical crown. There should have been a brass buckle on the front, but otherwise it was quite perfect.

The rest of his outfit didn't go well with the hat. Instead of shoes with long points and a leather apron, he wore a blue, double-breasted suit and a black shirt with a yellow tie. Instead of a crooked thorn stick, he carried a rolled copy of the *Daily Running Horse*.

"That's what I get for fooling with four-bit broads," he said by way of greeting.

Tod nodded and tried to concentrate on the green hat. His ready acquiescence seemed to irritate the little man.

"No quiff can give Abe Kusich the fingeroo and get away with it," he said bitterly. "Not when I can get her leg broke for twenty bucks and I got twenty."

He took out a thick billfold and shook it at Tod.

"So she thinks she can give me the fingeroo, hah? Well, let me tell . . ."

Tod broke in hastily.

"You're right, Mr. Kusich."

The dwarf came over to where Tod was sitting and for a moment Tod thought he was going to climb into his lap, but he only asked his name and shook hands. The little man had a powerful grip.

"Let me tell you something, Hackett, if you hadn't come along, I'da broke in the door. That dame thinks she can give me the fingeroo, but she's got another thinkola coming. But thanks anyway."

"Forget it."

"I don't forget nothing. I remember. I remember those who do me dirt and those who do me favors."

He wrinkled his brow and was silent for a moment.

"Listen," he finally said, "seeing as you helped me, I got to return it. I don't want anybody going around saying Abe Kusich owes him anything. So I'll tell you what. I'll give you a good one for the fifth at Caliente. You put a fiver on its nose and it'll get you twenty smackeroos. What I'm telling you is strictly correct."

Tod didn't know how to answer and his hesitation offended the little man.

"Would I give you a bum steer?" he demanded, scowling. "Would I?"

Tod walked toward the door to get rid of him.

"No," he said.

"Then why won't you bet, hah?"

"What's the name of the horse?" Tod asked, hoping to calm him.

The dwarf had followed him to the door, pulling the bathrobe after him by one sleeve. Hat and all, he came to a foot below Tod's belt.

"Tragopan. He's a certain, sure winner. I know the guy who owns him and he gave me the office."

"Is he a Greek?" Tod asked.

He was being pleasant in order to hide the attempt he was making to maneuver the dwarf through the door.

"Yeh, he's a Greek. Do you know him?"

"No."

"No?"

"No," said Tod with finality.

"Keep your drawers on," ordered the dwarf, "all I want to know is how you know he's a Greek if you don't know him?"

His eyes narrowed with suspicion and he clenched his fists.

Tod smiled to placate him.

"I just guessed it."

"You did?"

The dwarf hunched his shoulders as though he were going to pull a gun or throw a punch. Tod backed off and tried to explain.

"I guessed he was a Greek because Tragopan is a Greek word that means pheasant."

The dwarf was far from satisfied.

"How do you know what it means? You ain't a Greek?"

"No, but I know a few Greek words."

"So you're a wise guy, hah, a know-it-all."

He took a short step forward, moving on his toes, and Tod got set to block a punch.

"A college man, hah? Well, let me tell . . ."

His foot caught in the wrapper and he fell forward on his hands. He forgot Tod and cursed the bathrobe, then got started on the woman again.

"So she thinks she can give me the fingeroo."

He kept poking himself in the chest with his thumbs.

"Who gave her forty bucks for an abortion? Who? And another ten to go to the country for a rest that time. To a ranch I sent her. And who got her fiddle out of hock that time in Santa Monica? Who?"

"That's right," Tod said, getting ready to give him a quick shove through the door.

But he didn't have to shove him. The little man suddenly darted out of the room and ran down the hall, dragging the bathrobe after him.

A few days later, Tod went into a stationary store on Vine Street to buy a magazine. While he was looking through the rack, he felt a tug at the bottom of his jacket. It was Abe Kusich, the dwarf, again.

"How's things?" he demanded.

Tod was surprised to find that he was just as truculent

as he had been the other night. Later, when he got to know
him better, he discovered that Abe's pugnacity was often a
joke. When he used it on his friends, they played with him
like one does with a growling puppy, staving off his mad
rushes and then baiting him to rush again.

"Fair enough," Tod said, "but I think I'll move."

He had spent most of Sunday looking for a place to live
and was full of the subject. The moment he mentioned it,
however, he knew that he had made a mistake. He tried to
end the matter by turning away, but the little man blocked
him. He evidently considered himself an expert on the
housing situation. After naming and discarding a dozen
possibilities without a word from Tod, he finally hit on the
San Bernardino Arms.

"That's the place for you, the San Berdoo. I live there,
so I ought to know. The owner's strictly from hunger.
Come on, I'll get you fixed up swell."

"I don't know, I . . ." Tod began.

The dwarf bridled instantly, and appeared to be mor-
tally offended.

"I suppose it ain't good enough for you. Well, let me tell
you something, you . . ."

Tod allowed himself to be bullied and went with the
dwarf to Pinyon Canyon. The rooms in the San Berdoo
were small and not very clean. He rented one without hesitation, however, when he saw Faye Greener in the hall.

3

Tod had fallen asleep. When he woke again, it was after
eight o'clock. He took a bath and shaved, then dressed in
front of the bureau mirror. He tried to watch his fingers
as he fixed his collar and tie, but his eyes kept straying to
the photograph that was pushed into the upper corner of
the frame.

It was a picture of Faye Greener, a still from a two-reel farce in which she had worked as an extra. She had given him the photograph willingly enough, had even auto-graphed it in a large, wild hand, "Affectionately yours, Faye Greener," but she refused his friendship, or, rather, insisted on keeping it impersonal. She had told him why. He had nothing to offer her, neither money nor looks, and she could only love a handsome man and would only let a wealthy man love her. Tod was a "good-hearted man," and she liked "good-hearted men," but only as friends. She wasn't hard-boiled. It was just that she put love on a special plane, where a man without money or looks couldn't move.

Tod grunted with annoyance as he turned to the photo-graph. In it she was wearing a harem costume, full Turk-ish trousers, breastplates and a monkey jacket, and lay stretched out on a silken divan. One hand held a beer bottle and the other a pewter stein.

He had gone all the way to Glendale to see her in that movie. It was about an American drummer who gets lost in the seraglio of a Damascus merchant and has a lot of fun with the female inmates. Faye played one of the dancing girls. She had only one line to speak, "Oh, Mr. Smith!" and spoke it badly.

She was a tall girl with wide, straight shoulders and long, swordlike legs. Her neck was long, too, and columnar. Her face was much fuller than the rest of her body would lead you to expect and much larger. It was a moon face, wide at the cheek bones and narrow at chin and brow. She wore her "platinum" hair long, letting it fall almost to her shoulders in back, but kept it away from her face and ears with a narrow blue ribbon that went under it and was tied on top of her head with a little bow.

She was supposed to look drunk and she did, but not with alcohol. She lay stretched out on the divan with her arms and legs spread, as though welcoming a lover, and her lips were parted in a heavy, sullen smile. She was supposed to look inviting, but the invitation wasn't to pleasure.

Tod lit a cigarette and inhaled with a nervous gasp. He started to fool with his tie again, but had to go back to the photograph.

Her invitation wasn't to pleasure, but to struggle, hard and sharp, closer to murder than to love. If you threw yourself on her, it would be like throwing yourself from the parapet of a skyscraper. You would do it with a scream. You couldn't expect to rise again. Your teeth would be driven into your skull like nails into a pine board and your back would be broken. You wouldn't even have time to sweat or close your eyes.

He managed to laugh at his language, but it wasn't a real laugh and nothing was destroyed by it.

If she would only let him, he would be glad to throw himself, no matter what the cost. But she wouldn't have him. She didn't love him and he couldn't further her career. She wasn't sentimental and she had no need for tenderness, even if he were capable of it.

When he had finished dressing, he hurried out of the room. He had promised to go to a party at Claude Estee's.

4

Claude was a successful screen writer who lived in a big house that was an exact reproduction of the old Dupuy mansion near Biloxi, Mississippi. When Tod came up the walk between the boxwood hedges, he greeted him from the enormous, two-story porch by doing the impersonation that went with the Southern colonial architecture. He teetered back and forth on his heels like a Civil War colonel and made believe he had a large belly.

He had no belly at all. He was a dried-up little man

with the rubbed features and stooped shoulders of a postal clerk. The shiny mohair coat and nondescript trousers of that official would have become him, but he was dressed, as always, elaborately. In the buttonhole of his brown jacket was a lemon flower. His trousers were of reddish Harris tweed with a hound tooth check and on his feet were a pair of magnificent, rust-colored blüchers. His shirt was ivory flannel and his knitted tie a red that was almost black.

While Tod mounted the steps to reach his outstretched hand, he shouted to the butler.

"Here, you black rascal! A mint julep."

A Chinese servant came running with a Scotch and soda.

After talking to Tod for a moment, Claude started him in the direction of Alice, his wife, who was at the other end of the porch.

"Don't run off," he whispered. "We're going to a sporting house."

Alice was sitting in a wicker swing with a woman named Mrs. Joan Schwartzen. When she asked him if he was playing any tennis, Mrs. Schwartzen interrupted her.

"How silly, batting an inoffensive ball across something that ought to be used to catch fish on account of millions are starving for a bite of herring."

"Joan's a female tennis champ," Alice explained.

Mrs. Schwartzen was a big girl with large hands and feet and square, bony shoulders. She had a pretty, eighteen-year-old face and a thirty-five-year-old neck that was veined and sinewy. Her deep sunburn, ruby colored with a slight blue tint, kept the contrast between her face and neck from being too startling.

"Well, I wish we were going to a brothel this minute," she said. "I adore them."

She turned to Tod and fluttered her eyelids.

"Don't you, Mr. Hackett?"

"That's right, Joan darling," Alice answered for him. "Nothing like a bagnio to set a fellow up. Hair of the dog that bit you."

"How dare you insult me!"

She stood up and took Tod's arm.

"Convoy me over there."

She pointed to the group of men with whom Claude was standing.

"For God's sake, convoy her," Alice said. "She thinks they're telling dirty stories."

Mrs. Schwartzen pushed right among them, dragging Tod after her.

"Are you talking smut?" she asked. "I adore smut."

They all laughed politely.

"No, shop," said someone.

"I don't believe it. I can tell from the beast in your voices. Go ahead, do say something obscene."

This time no one laughed.

Tod tried to disengage her arm, but she kept a firm grip on it. There was a moment of awkward silence, then the man she had interrupted tried to make a fresh start.

"The picture business is too humble," he said. "We ought to resent people like Coombes."

"That's right," said another man. "Guys like that come out here, make a lot of money, grouse all the time about the place, flop on their assignments, then go back East and tell dialect stories about producers they've never met."

"My God," Mrs. Schwartzen said to Tod in a loud, stagey whisper, "they *are* talking shop."

"Let's look for the man with the drinks," Tod said.

"No. Take me into the garden. Have you seen what's in the swimming pool?"

She pulled him along.

The air of the garden was heavy with the odor of

mimosa and honeysuckle. Through a slit in the blue serge sky poked a grained moon that looked like an enormous bone button. A little flagstone path, made narrow by its border of oleander, led to the edge of the sunken pool. On the bottom, near the deep end, he could see a heavy, black mass of some kind.

"What is it?" he asked.

She kicked a switch that was hidden at the base of a shrub and a row of submerged floodlights illuminated the green water. The thing was a dead horse, or, rather, a life-size, realistic reproduction of one. Its legs stuck up stiff and straight and it had an enormous, distended belly. Its hammerhead lay twisted to one side and from its mouth, which was set in an agonized grin, hung a heavy, black tongue.

"Isn't it marvelous!" exclaimed Mrs. Schwartzen, clapping her hands and jumping up and down excitedly like a little girl.

"What's it made of?"

"Then you weren't fooled? How impolite! It's rubber, of course. It cost lots of money."

"But why?"

"To amuse. We were looking at the pool one day and somebody, Jerry Appis, I think, said that it needed a dead horse on the bottom, so Alice got one. Don't you think it looks cute?"

"Very."

"You're just an old meanie. Think how happy the Estees must feel, showing it to people and listening to their merriment and their oh's and ah's of unconfined delight."

She stood on the edge of the pool and "ohed and ahed" rapidly several times in succession.

"Is it still there?" someone called.

Tod turned and saw two women and a man coming down the path.

"I think its belly's going to burst," Mrs. Schwartzen shouted to them gleefully.

"Goody," said the man, hurrying to look.

"But it's only full of air," said one of the women.

Mrs. Schwartzen made believe she was going to cry.

"You're just like that mean Mr. Hackett. You just won't let me cherish my illusions."

Tod was halfway to the house when she called after him. He waved but kept going.

The men with Claude were still talking shop.

"But how are you going to get rid of the illiterate mockies that run it? They've got a strangle hold on the industry. Maybe they're intellectual stumblebums, but they're damn good businessmen. Or at least they know how to go into receivership and come up with a gold watch in their teeth."

"They ought to put some of the millions they make back into the business again. Like Rockefeller does with his Foundation. People used to hate the Rockefellers, but now instead of hollering about their ill-gotten oil dough, everybody praises them for what the Foundation does. It's a swell stunt and pictures could do the same thing. Have a Cinema Foundation and make contributions to Science and Art. You know, give the racket a front."

Tod took Claude to one side to say good night, but he wouldn't let him go. He led him into the library and mixed two double Scotches. They sat down on the couch facing the fireplace.

"You haven't been to Audrey Jenning's place?" Claude asked.

"No, but I've heard tell of it."

"Then you've got to come along."

"I don't like pro-sport."

"We won't indulge in any. We're just going to see a movie."

"I get depressed."

"Not at Jenning's you won't. She makes vice attractive by skillful packaging. Her dive's a triumph of industrial design."

Tod liked to hear him talk. He was master of an involved comic rhetoric that permitted him to express his moral indignation and still keep his reputation for worldliness and wit.

Tod fed him another lead. "I don't care how much cellophane she wraps it in," he said—"nautch joints are depressing, like all places for deposit, banks, mail boxes, tombs, vending machines."

"Love is like a vending machine, eh? Not bad. You insert a coin and press home the lever. There's some mechanical activity inside the bowels of the device. You receive a small sweet, frown at yourself in the dirty mirror, adjust your hat, take a firm grip on your umbrella and walk away, trying to look as though nothing had happened. It's good, but it's not for pictures."

Tod played straight again.

"That's not it. I've been chasing a girl and it's like carrying something a little too large to conceal in your pocket, like a briefcase or a small valise. It's uncomfortable."

"I know, I know. It's always uncomfortable. First your right hand gets tired, then your left. You put the valise down and sit on it, but people are surprised and stop to stare at you, so you move on. You hide it behind a tree and hurry away, but someone finds it and runs after you to return it. It's a small valise when you leave home in the morning, cheap and with a bad handle, but by evening it's a trunk with brass corners and many foreign labels. I know. It's good, but it won't film. You've got to remember your audience. What about the barber in Purdue? He's been cutting hair all day and he's tired. He doesn't want to see some dope carrying a valise or fooling with a nickel machine. What the barber wants is amour and glamor."

The last part was for himself and he sighed heavily. He was about to begin again when the Chinese servant came in and said that the others were ready to leave for Mrs. Jenning's.

5

They started out in several cars. Tod rode in the front of the one Claude drove and as they went down Sunset Boulevard he described Mrs. Jenning for him. She had been a fairly prominent actress in the days of silent films, but sound made it impossible for her to get work. Instead of becoming an extra or a bit player like many other old stars, she had shown excellent business sense and had opened a callhouse. She wasn't vicious. Far from it. She ran her business just as other women run lending libraries, shrewdly and with taste.

None of the girls lived on the premises. You telephoned and she sent a girl over. The charge was thirty dollars for a single night of sport and Mrs. Jenning kept fifteen of it. Some people might think that fifty per cent is a high brokerage fee, but she really earned every cent of it. There was a big overhead. She maintained a beautiful house for the girls to wait in and a car and a chauffeur to deliver them to the clients.

Then, too, she had to move in the kind of society where she could make the right contacts. After all, not every man can afford thirty dollars. She permitted her girls to service only men of wealth and position, not to say taste and discretion. She was so particular that she insisted on meeting the prospective sportsman before servicing him. She had often said, and truthfully, that she would not let a girl of hers go to a man with whom she herself would not be willing to sleep.

And she was really cultured. All the most distinguished visitors considered it quite a lark to meet her. They were disappointed, however, when they discovered how refined she was. They wanted to talk about certain lively matters of universal interest, but she insisted on discussing Gertrude Stein and Juan Gris. No matter how hard the distinguished visitor tried, and some had been known to go to really great lengths, he could never find a flaw in her refinement or make a breach in her culture.

Claude was still using his peculiar rhetoric on Mrs. Jenning when she came to the door of her house to greet them.

"It's so nice to see you again," she said. "I was telling Mrs. Prince at tea only yesterday—the Estees are my favorite couple."

She was a handsome woman, smooth and buttery, with fair hair and a red complexion.

She led them into a small drawing room whose color scheme was violet, gray and rose. The Venetian blinds were rose, as was the ceiling, and the walls were covered with a pale gray paper that had a tiny, widely spaced flower design in violet. On one wall hung a silver screen, the kind that rolls up, and against the opposite wall, on each side of a cherrywood table, was a row of chairs covered with rose and gray, glazed chintz bound in violet piping. There was a small projection machine on the table and a young man in evening dress was fumbling with it.

She waved them to their seats. A waiter then came in and asked what they wanted to drink. When their orders had been taken and filled, she flipped the light switch and the young man started his machine. It whirred merrily, but he had trouble in getting it focused.

"What are we going to see first?" Mrs. Schwartzen asked.

"*Le Predicament de Marie.*"

"That sounds ducky."

"It's charming, utterly charming," said Mrs. Jenning.

"Yes," said the cameraman, who was still having trouble. "I love *Le Predicament de Marie*. It has a marvelous quality that is too exciting."

There was a long delay, during which he fussed desperately with his machine. Mrs. Schwartzen started to whistle and stamp her feet and the others joined in. They imitated a rowdy audience in the days of the nickelodeon.

"Get a move on, slow poke."

"What's your hurry? Here's your hat."

"Get a horse!"

"Get out and get under!"

The young man finally found the screen with his light beam and the film began.

LE PREDICAMENT DE MARIE

ou

LA BONNE DISTRAITE

Marie, the "bonne," was a buxom young girl in a tight-fitting black silk uniform with very short skirts. On her head was a tiny lace cap. In the first scene, she was shown serving dinner to a middle-class family in an oak-paneled dining room full of heavy, carved furniture. The family was very respectable and consisted of a bearded, frock-coated father, a mother with a whalebone collar and a cameo brooch, a tall, thin son with a long mustache and almost no chin and a little girl wearing a large bow in her hair and a crucifix on a gold chain around her neck.

After some low comedy with father's beard and the soup, the actors settled down seriously to their theme. It was evident that while the whole family desired Marie, she only desired the young girl. Using his napkin to hide his activities, the old man pinched Marie, the son tried to look down the neck of her dress and the mother patted her knee. Marie, for her part, surreptitiously fondled the child.

The scene changed to Marie's room. She undressed and got into a chiffon negligee, leaving on only her black silk stockings and high-heeled shoes. She was making an elaborate night toilet when the child entered. Marie took her on her lap and started to kiss her. There was a knock on the door. Consternation. She hid the child in the closet and let in the bearded father. He was suspicious and she had to accept his advances. He was embracing her when there was another knock. Again consternation and tableau. This time it was the mustachioed son. Marie hid the father under the bed. No sooner had the son begun to grow warm than there was another knock. Marie made him climb into a large blanket chest. The new caller was the lady of the house. She, too, was just settling down to work when there was another knock.

Who could it be? A telegram? A policeman? Frantically Marie counted the different hiding places. The whole family was present. She tiptoed to the door and listened.

"Who can it be that wishes to enter now?" read the title card.

And there the machine stuck. The young man in evening dress became as frantic as Marie. When he got it running again, there was a flash of light and the film whizzed through the apparatus until it had all run out.

"I'm sorry, extremely," he said. "I'll have to rewind."

"It's a frameup," someone yelled.

"Fake!"

"Cheat!"

"The old teaser routine!"

They stamped their feet and whistled.

Under cover of the mock riot, Tod sneaked out. He wanted to get some fresh air. The waiter, whom he found loitering in the hall, showed him to the patio in back of the house.

On his return, he peeked into the different rooms. In one of them he found a large number of miniature dogs in a curio cabinet. There were glass pointers, silver beagles, porcelain schnauzers, stone dachshunds, aluminum bull-dogs, onyx whippets, china bassets, wooden spaniels. Every recognized breed was represented and almost every material that could be sculptured, cast or carved.

While he was admiring the little figures, he heard a girl singing. He thought he recognized her voice and peeked into the hall. It was Mary Dove, one of Faye Greener's best friends.

Perhaps Faye also worked for Mrs. Jenning. If so, for thirty dollars . . .

He went back to see the rest of the film.

6

Tod's hope that he could end his trouble by paying a small fee didn't last long. When he got Claude to ask Mrs. Jenning about Faye, that lady said she had never heard of the girl. Claude then asked her to inquire through Mary Dove. A few days later she phoned him to say there was nothing doing. The girl wasn't available.

Tod wasn't really disappointed. He didn't want Faye that way, not at least while he still had a chance some other way. Lately, he had begun to think he had a good one. Harry, her father, was sick and that gave him an excuse for hanging around their apartment. He ran errands and kept the old man company. To repay his kindness, she permitted him the intimacies of a family friend. He hoped to deepen her gratitude and make it serious.

Apart from this purpose, he was interested in Harry and enjoyed visiting him. The old man was a clown and Tod had all the painter's usual love of clowns. But what was more important, he felt that his clownship was a clue to the people who stared (a painter's clue, that is—a clue in the form of a symbol), just as Faye's dreams were another.

He sat near Harry's bed and listened to his stories by the hour. Forty years in vaudeville and burlesque had provided him with an infinite number of them. As he put it, his life had consisted of a lightning series of "nip-ups," "high-gruesomes," "flying-W's" and "hundred-and-eights" done to escape a barrage of "exploding stoves." An "exploding stove" was any catastrophe, natural or human, from a flood in Medicine Hat, Wyoming, to an angry policeman in Moose Factory, Ontario.

When Harry had first begun his stage career, he had probably restricted his clowning to the boards, but now he clowned continuously. It was his sole method of defense. Most people, he had discovered, won't go out of their way to punish a clown.

He used a set of elegant gestures to accent the comedy of his bent, hopeless figure and wore a special costume, dressing like a banker, a cheap, unconvincing, imitation banker. The costume consisted of a greasy derby with an unusually high crown, a wing collar and polka dot four-in-hand, a shiny double-breasted jacket and gray-striped trousers. His outfit fooled no one, but then he didn't intend it to fool anyone. His slyness was of a different sort.

On the stage he was a complete failure and knew it. Yet he claimed to have once come very close to success. To prove how close, he made Tod read an old clipping from the theatrical section of the Sunday *Times.*

"BEDRAGGLED HARLEQUIN," it was headed.

"The commedia del' arte is not dead, but lives on in

Brooklyn, or was living there last week on the stage of the
Oglethorpe Theatre in the person of one Harry Greener.
Mr. Greener is of a troupe called 'The Flying Lings,'
who, by the time this reaches you, have probably moved on
to Mystic, Connecticut, or some other place more fitting
than the borough of large families. If you have the time and
really love the theatre, by all means seek out the Lings
wherever they may be.

"Mr. Greener, the bedraggled Harlequin of our caption,
is not bedraggled but clean, neat and sweet when he first
comes on. By the time the Lings, four muscular Orientals,
finish with him, however, he is plenty bedraggled. He is
tattered and bloody, but still sweet.

"When Mr. Greener enters the trumpets are properly
silent. Mama Ling is spinning a plate on the end of a stick
held in her mouth, Papa Ling is doing cartwheels, Sister
Ling is juggling fans and Sonny Ling is hanging from the
proscenium arch by his pigtail. As he inspects his strenuous
colleagues, Mr. Greener tries to hide his confusion under
some much too obvious worldliness. He ventures to tickle
Sister and receives a powerful kick in the belly in return
for this innocent attention. Having been kicked, he is on
familiar ground and begins to tell a dull joke. Father Ling
sneaks up behind him and tosses him to Brother, who
looks the other way. Mr. Greener lands on the back of his
neck. He shows his mettle by finishing his dull story from a
recumbent position. When he stands up, the audience,
which failed to laugh at his joke, laughs at his limp, so he
continues lame for the rest of the act.

"Mr. Greener begins another story, even longer and
duller than his first. Just before he arrives at the gag line,
the orchestra blares loudly and drowns him out. He is very
patient and very brave. He begins again, but the orchestra
will not let him finish. The pain that almost, not quite,
thank God, crumples his stiff little figure would be un-

bearable if it were not obviously make-believe. It is gloriously funny.

"The finale is superb. While the Ling Family flies through the air, Mr. Greener, held to the ground by his sense of reality and his knowledge of gravitation, tries hard to make the audience think that he is neither surprised nor worried by the rocketing Orientals. It's familiar stuff, his hands signal, but his face denies this. As time goes on and no one is hurt, he regains his assurance. The acrobats ignore him, so he ignores the acrobats. His is the final victory; the applause is for him.

"My first thought was that some producer should put Mr. Greener into a big revue against a background of beautiful girls and glittering curtains. But my second was that this would be a mistake. I am afraid that Mr. Greener, like certain humble field plants which die when transferred to richer soil, had better be left to bloom in vaudeville against a background of ventriloquists and lady bicycle riders."

Harry had more than a dozen copies of this article, several on rag paper. After trying to get a job by inserting a small advertisement in *Variety* (". . . 'some producer should put Mr. Greener into a big revue . . .' The *Times*"), he had come to Hollywood, thinking to earn a living playing comedy bits in films. There proved to be little demand for his talents, however. As he himself put it, he "stank from hunger." To supplement his meager income from the studios, he peddled silver polish which he made in the bathroom of the apartment out of chalk, soap and yellow axle grease. When Faye wasn't at Central Casting, she took him around on his peddling trips in her Model T Ford. It was on their last expedition together that he had fallen sick.

It was on this trip that Faye acquired a new suitor by the name of Homer Simpson. About a week after Harry had taken to his bed, Tod met Homer for the first time. He was keeping the old man company when their conversation was interrupted by a light knock on the apartment door. Tod answered it and found a man standing in the hall with flowers for Faye and a bottle of port wine for her father.

Tod examined him eagerly. He didn't mean to be rude but at first glance this man seemed an exact model for the kind of person who comes to California to die, perfect in every detail down to fever eyes and unruly hands.

"My name is Homer Simpson," the man gasped, then shifted uneasily and patted his perfectly dry forehead with a folded handkerchief.

"Won't you come in?" Tod asked.

He shook his head heavily and thrust the wine and flowers at Tod. Before Tod could say anything, he had lumbered off.

Tod saw that he was mistaken. Homer Simpson was only physically the type. The men he meant were not shy.

He took the gifts in to Harry, who didn't seem at all surprised. He said Homer was one of his grateful customers.

"That Miracle Polish of mine sure does fetch 'em."

Later, when Faye came home and heard the story, she was very much amused. They both told Tod how they had happened to meet Homer, interrupting themselves and each other every few seconds to laugh.

The next thing Tod saw Homer staring at the apartment house from the shadow of a date palm on the opposite side of the street. He watched him for a few minutes, then called out a friendly greeting. Without replying, Homer ran away. On the next day and the one after, Tod again saw him lurking near the palm tree. He finally caught him by approaching the tree silently from the rear.

"Hello, Mr. Simpson," Tod said softly. "The Greeners were very grateful for your gift."

This time Simpson didn't move, perhaps because Tod had him backed against the tree.

"That's fine," he blurted out. "I was passing . . . I live up the street."

Tod managed to keep their conversation going for several minutes before he escaped again.

The next time Tod was able to approach him without the stalk. From then on, he responded very quickly to his advances. Sympathy, even of the most obvious sort, made him articulate, almost garrulous.

7

Tod was right about one thing at least. Like most of the people he was interested in, Homer was a Middle-Westerner. He came from a little town near Des Moines, Iowa, called Wayneville, where he had worked for twenty years in a hotel.

One day, while sitting in the park in the rain, he had caught cold and his cold developed into pneumonia. When he came out of the hospital, he found that the hotel had hired a new bookkeeper. They offered to take him on again, but his doctor advised him to go to California for a rest. The doctor had an authoritative manner, so Homer left Wayneville for the Coast.

After living for a week in a railroad hotel in Los Angeles, he rented a cottage in Pinyon Canyon. It was only the second house the real estate agent showed him, but he took it because he was tired and because the agent was a bully.

He rather liked the way the cottage was located. It was the last house in the canyon and the hills rose directly behind the garage. They were covered with lupines, Canterbury bells, poppies, and several varieties of large yellow daisy. There were also some scrub pines, Joshua and eucalyptus trees. The agent told him that he would see doves and plumed quail, but during all the time he lived there, he saw only a few large, black velvet spiders and a lizard. He grew very fond of the lizard.

The house was cheap because it was hard to rent. Most of the people who took cottages in that neighborhood wanted them to be "Spanish" and this one, so the agent claimed, was "Irish." Homer thought that the place looked kind of queer, but the agent insisted that it was cute.

The house was queer. It had an enormous and very crooked stone chimney, little dormer windows with big hoods and a thatched roof that came down very low on both sides of the front door. This door was of gumwood painted like fumed oak and it hung on enormous hinges. Although made by machine, the hinges had been carefully stamped to appear hand-forged. The same kind of care and skill had been used to make the roof thatching, which was not really straw but heavy fireproof paper colored and ribbed to look like straw.

The prevailing taste had been followed in the living room. It was "Spanish." The walls were pale orange flecked with pink and on them hung several silk armorial banners in red and gold. A big galleon stood on the mantelpiece. Its hull was plaster, its sails paper and its rigging wire. In the fireplace was a variety of cactus in gaily colored Mexican pots. Some of the plants were made of rubber and cork; others were real.

The room was lit by wall fixtures in the shape of galleons with pointed amber bulbs projecting from their decks. The table held a lamp with a paper shade, oiled to look like parchment, that had several more galleons painted on it. On each side of the windows red velvet draperies hung from black, double-headed spears.

The furniture consisted of a heavy couch that had fat monks for legs and was covered with faded red damask, and three swollen armchairs, also red. In the center of the room was a very long mahogany table. It was of the trestle type and studded with large-headed bronze nails. Beside each of the chairs was a small end table, the same color and design as the big one, but with a colored tile let into the top.

In the two small bedrooms still another style had been used. This the agent had called "New England." There was a spool bed made of iron grained like wood, a Windsor chair of the kind frequently seen in tea shops, and a Governor Winthrop dresser painted to look like unpainted pine. On the floor was a small hooked rug. On the wall facing the dresser was a colored etching of a snowbound Connecticut farmhouse, complete with wolf. Both of these rooms were exactly alike in every detail. Even the pictures were duplicates.

There was also a bathroom and a kitchen.

8

It took Homer only a few minutes to get settled in his new home. He unpacked his trunk, hung his two suits, both dark gray, in the closet of one of his bedrooms and put his shirts and underclothes into the dresser drawers. He made no attempt to rearrange the furniture.

After an aimless tour of the house and the yard, he sat down on the couch in the living room. He sat as though waiting for someone in the lobby of a hotel. He remained that way for almost half an hour without moving anything but his hands, then got up and went into the bedroom and sat down on the edge of the bed.

Although it was still early in the afternoon, he felt very

sleepy. He was afraid to stretch out and go to sleep. Not
because he had bad dreams, but because it was so hard for
him to wake again. When he fell asleep, he was always
afraid that he would never get up.

But his fear wasn't as strong as his need. He got his
alarm clock and set it for seven o'clock, then lay down
with it next to his ear. Two hours later, it seemed like
seconds to him, the alarm went off. The bell rang for a
full minute before he began to work laboriously toward
consciousness. The struggle was a hard one. He groaned.
His head trembled and his feet shot out. Finally his eyes
opened, then widened. Once more the victory was his.

He lay stretched out on the bed, collecting his senses
and testing the different parts of his body. Every part
was awake but his hands. They still slept. He was not
surprised. They demanded special attention, had always
demanded it. When he had been a child, he used to stick
pins into them and once had even thrust them into a fire.
Now he used only cold water.

He got out of bed in sections, like a poorly made auto-
maton, and carried his hands into the bathroom. He turned
on the cold water. When the basin was full, he plunged his
hands in up to the wrists. They lay quietly on the bottom
like a pair of strange aquatic animals. When they were
thoroughly chilled and began to crawl about, he lifted them
out and hid them in a towel.

He was cold. He ran hot water into the tub and began
to undress, fumbling with the buttons of his clothing as
though he were undressing a stranger. He was naked before
the tub was full enough to get in and he sat down on a stool
to wait. He kept his enormous hands folded quietly on his
belly. Although absolutely still, they seemed curbed rather
than resting.

Except for his hands, which belonged on a piece of
monumental sculpture, and his small head, he was well

proportioned. His muscles were large and round and he had a full, heavy chest. Yet there was something wrong. For all his size and shape, he looked neither strong nor fertile. He was like one of Picasso's great sterile athletes, who brood hopelessly on pink sand, staring at veined marble waves.

When the tub was full, he got in and sank down in the hot water. He grunted his comfort. But in another moment he would begin to remember, in just another moment. He tried to fool his memory by overwhelming it with tears and brought up the sobs that were always lurking uneasily in his chest. He cried softly at first, then harder. The sound he made was like that of a dog lapping gruel. He concentrated on how miserable and lonely he was, but it didn't work. The thing he was trying so desperately to avoid kept crowding into his mind.

One day when he was working in the hotel, a guest called Romola Martin had spoken to him in the elevator.

"Mr. Simpson, you're Mr. Simpson, the bookkeeper?"

"Yes."

"I'm in six-eleven."

She was small and childlike, with a quick, nervous manner. In her arms she coddled a package which obviously contained a square gin bottle.

"Yes," said Homer again, working against his natural instinct to be friendly. He knew that Miss Martin owed several weeks' rent and had heard the room clerk say she was a drunkard.

"Oh! . . ." the girl went on coquettishly, making obvious their difference in size, "I'm sorry you're worried about your bill, I . . ."

The intimacy of her tone embarrassed Homer.

"You'll have to speak to the manager," he rapped out, turning away.

He was trembling when he reached his office.

How bold the creature was! She was drunk, of course,

but not so drunk that she didn't know what she was doing. He hurriedly labeled his excitement disgust.

Soon afterwards the manager called and asked him to bring in Miss Martin's credit card. When he went into the manager's office, he found Miss Carlisle, the room clerk there. Homer listened to what the manager was saying to her.

"You roomed six-eleven?"

"I did, yes, sir."

"Why? She's obvious enough, isn't she?"

"Not when she's sober."

"Never mind that. We don't want her kind in this hotel."

"I'm sorry."

The manager turned to Homer and took the credit card he was holding.

"She owes thirty-one dollars," Homer said.

"She'll have to pay up and get out. I don't want her kind around here." He smiled. "Especially when they run up bills. Get her on the phone for me."

Homer asked the telephone operator for six-eleven and after a short time was told that the room didn't answer.

"She's in the house," he said. "I saw her in the elevator."

"I'll have the housekeeper look."

Homer was working on his books some minutes later when his phone rang. It was the manager again. He said that six-eleven had been reported in by the housekeeper and asked Homer to take her a bill.

"Tell her to pay up or get out," he said.

His first thought was to ask that Miss Carlisle be sent because he was busy, but he didn't dare to suggest it. While making out the bill, he began to realize how excited he was. It was terrifying. Little waves of sensation moved along his nerves and the base of his tongue tingled.

When he got off at the sixth floor, he felt almost gay.

His step was buoyant and he had completely forgotten his troublesome hands. He stopped at six-eleven and made as though to knock, then suddenly took fright and lowered his fist without touching the door.

He couldn't go through with it. They would have to send Miss Carlisle.

The housekeeper, who had been watching from the end of the hall, came up before he could escape.

"She doesn't answer," Homer said hurriedly.

"Did you knock hard enough? That slut is in there." Before Homer could reply, she pounded on the door.

"Open up!" she shouted.

Homer heard someone move inside, then the door opened a few inches.

"Who is it, please?" a light voice asked.

"Mr. Simpson, the bookkeeper," he gasped.

"Come in, please."

The door opened a little wider and Homer went in without daring to look around at the housekeeper. He stumbled to the center of the room and stopped. At first he was conscious only of the heavy odor of alcohol and stale tobacco, but then underneath he smelled a metallic perfume. His eyes moved in a slow circle. On the floor was a litter of clothing, newspapers, magazines, and bottles. Miss Martin was huddled up on a corner of the bed. She was wearing a man's black silk dressing gown with light blue cuffs and lapel facings. Her close-cropped hair was the color and texture of straw and she looked like a little boy. Her youthfulness was heightened by her blue button eyes, pink button nose and red button mouth.

Homer was too busy with his growing excitement to speak or even think. He closed his eyes to tend it better, nursing carefully what he felt. He had to be careful, for if he went too fast, it might wither and then he would be cold again. It continued to grow.

"Go away, please, I'm drunk," Miss Martin said.

Homer neither moved nor spoke.

She suddenly began to sob. The coarse, broken sounds she made seemed to come from her stomach. She buried her face in her hands and pounded the floor with her feet.

Homer's feelings were so intense that his head bobbed stiffly on his neck like that of a toy Chinese dragon.

"I'm broke. I haven't any money. I haven't a dime. I'm broke, I tell you."

Homer pulled out his wallet and moved on the girl as though to strike her with it.

She cowered away from him and her sobs grew stronger.

He dropped the wallet in her lap and stood over her, not knowing what else to do. When she saw the wallet, she smiled, but continued sobbing.

"Sit down," she said.

He sat down on the bed beside her.

"You strange man," she said coyly. "I could kiss you for being so nice."

He caught her in his arms and hugged her. His suddenness frightened her and she tried to pull away, but he held on and began awkwardly to caress her. He was completely unconscious of what he was doing. He knew only that what he felt was marvelously sweet and that he had to make the sweetness carry through to the poor, sobbing woman.

Miss Martin's sobs grew less and soon stopped altogether. He could feel her fidget and gather strength.

The telephone rang.

"Don't answer it," she said, beginning to sob once more.

He pushed her away gently and stumbled to the telephone. It was Miss Carlisle.

"Are you all right?" she asked, "or shall we send for the cops?"

"All right," he said, hanging up.

It was all over. He couldn't go back to the bed.

Miss Martin laughed at his look of acute distress.

"Bring the gin, you enormous cow," she shouted gaily. "It's under the table."

He saw her stretch herself out in a way that couldn't be mistaken. He ran out of the room.

Now in California, he was crying because he had never seen Miss Martin again. The next day the manager had told him that he had done a good job and that she had paid up and checked out.

Homer tried to find her. There were two other hotels in Wayneville, small run-down houses, and he inquired at both of them. He also asked in the few rooming places, but with no success. She had left town.

He settled back into his regular routine, working ten hours, eating two, sleeping the rest. Then he caught cold and had been advised to come to California. He could easily afford not to work for a while. His father had left him about six thousand dollars and during the twenty years he had kept books in the hotel, he had saved at least ten more.

9

He got out of the tub, dried himself hurriedly with a rough towel, then went into the bedroom to dress. He felt even more stupid and washed out than usual. It was always like that. His emotions surged up in an enormous wave, curving and rearing, higher and higher, until it seemed as though the wave must carry everything before it. But the crash never came. Something always happened at the very top of the crest and the wave collapsed to run back like water down a drain, leaving, at the most, only the refuse of feeling.

It took him a long time to get all his clothing on. He stopped to rest after each garment with a desperation far out of proportion to the effort involved.

There was nothing to eat in the house and he had to go down to Hollywood Boulevard for food. He thought of waiting until morning, but then, although he was not hungry, decided against waiting. It was only eight o'clock and the trip would kill some time. If he just sat around, the temptation to go to sleep again would become irresistible.

The night was warm and very still. He started down hill, walking on the outer edge of the pavement. He hurried between lamp-posts, where the shadows were heaviest, and came to a full stop for a moment at every circle of light. By the time he reached the boulevard, he was fighting the desire to run. He stopped for several minutes on the corner to get his bearings. As he stood there, poised for flight, his fear made him seem almost graceful.

When several other people passed without paying any attention to him, he quieted down. He adjusted the collar of his coat and prepared to cross the street. Before he could take two steps someone called to him.

"Hey, you, mister."

It was a beggar who had spotted him from the shadow of a doorway. With the infallible instinct of his kind, he knew that Homer would be easy.

"Can you spare a nickel?"

"No," Homer said without conviction.

The beggar laughed and repeated his question, threateningly.

"A nickel, mister!"

He poked his hand into Homer's face.

Homer fumbled in his change pocket and dropped several coins on the sidewalk. While the man scrambled for them, he made his escape across the street.

The SunGold Market into which he turned was a large, brilliantly lit place. All the fixtures were chromium and the floors and walls were lined with white tile. Colored spotlights played on the showcases and counters, heightening the natural hues of the different foods. The oranges were bathed in red, the lemons in yellow, the fish in pale green, the steaks in rose and the eggs in ivory.

Homer went directly to the canned goods department and bought a can of mushroom soup and another of sardines. These and a half a pound of soda crackers would be enough for his supper.

Out on the street again with his parcel, he started to walk home. When he reached the corner that led to Pinyon Canyon and saw how steep and black the hill looked, he turned back along the lighted boulevard. He thought of waiting until someone else started up the hill, but finally took a taxicab.

10

Although Homer had nothing to do but prepare his scanty meals, he was not bored. Except for the Romola Martin incident and perhaps one or two other widely spaced events, the forty years of his life had been entirely without variety or excitement. As a bookkeeper, he had worked mechanically, totaling figures and making entries with the same impersonal detachment that he now opened cans of soup and made his bed.

Someone watching him go about his little cottage might have thought him sleep-walking or partially blind. His hands seemed to have a life and a will of their own. It was they who pulled the sheets tight and shaped the pillows.

One day, while opening a can of salmon for lunch, his thumb received a nasty cut. Although the wound must have hurt, the calm, slightly querulous expression he usually wore did not change. The wounded hand writhed about on the kitchen table until it was carried to the sink by its mate and bathed tenderly in hot water.

When not keeping house, he sat in the back yard, called the patio by the real estate agent, in an old broken deck chair. He went out to it immediately after breakfast to bake himself in the sun. In one of the closets he had found a tattered book and he held it in his lap without looking at it.

There was a much better view to be had in any direction other than the one he faced. By moving his chair in a quarter circle he could have seen a large part of the canyon twisting down to the city below. He never thought of making this shift. From where he sat, he saw the closed door of the garage and a patch of its shabby, tarpaper roof. In the foreground was a sooty, brick incinerator and a pile of rusty cans. A little to the right of them were the remains of a cactus garden in which a few ragged, tortured plants still survived.

One of these, a clump of thick, paddlelike blades, covered with ugly needles, was in bloom. From the tip of several of its topmost blades protruded a bright yellow flower, somewhat like a thistle blossom but coarser. No matter how hard the wind blew, its petals never trembled.

A lizard lived in a hole near the base of this plant. It was about five inches long and had a wedge-shaped head from which darted a fine, forked tongue. It earned a hard living catching the flies that strayed over to the cactus from the pile of cans.

The lizard was self-conscious and irritable, and Homer found it very amusing to watch. Whenever one of its elaborate stalks were foiled, it would shift about uneasily on its short legs and puff out its throat. Its coloring matched the cactus perfectly, but when it moved over to the cans where the flies were thick, it stood out very plainly. It would sit on the cactus by the hour without moving, then become impatient and start for the cans. The flies would spot it immediately and after several misses, it would sneak back sheepishly to its original post.

Homer was on the side of the flies. Whenever one of them, swinging too widely, would pass the cactus, he prayed silently for it to keep on going or turn back. If it lighted, he watched the lizard begin its stalk and held his breath until it had killed, hoping all the while that something would warn the fly. But no matter how much he wanted the fly to escape, he never thought of interfering, and was careful not to budge or make the slightest noise. Occasionally the lizard would miscalculate. When that happened Homer would laugh happily.

Between the sun, the lizard and the house, he was fairly well occupied. But whether he was happy or not it is hard to say. Probably he was neither, just as a plant is neither. He had memories to disturb him and a plant hasn't, but after the first bad night his memories were quiet.

11

He had been living this way for almost a month, when, one day, just as he was about to prepare his lunch, the door bell rang. He opened it and found a man standing on the step with a sample case in one hand and a derby hat in the other. Homer hurriedly shut the door again.

The bell continued to ring. He put his head out of the window nearest the door to order the fellow away, but the man bowed very politely and begged for a drink of water. Homer saw that he was old and tired and thought that he looked harmless. He got a bottle of water from the icebox, then opened the door and asked him in.

"The name, sir, is Harry Greener," the man announced in sing-song, stressing every other syllable.

Homer handed him a glass of water. He swallowed it quickly, then poured himself another.

"Much obliged," he said with an elaborate bow. "That was indeed refreshing."

Homer was astonished when he bowed again, did several quick jig steps, then let his derby hat roll down his arm. It fell to the floor. He stooped to retrieve it, straightening up with a jerk as though he had been kicked, then rubbed the seat of his trousers ruefully.

Homer understood that this was to amuse, so he laughed.

Harry thanked him by bowing again, but something went wrong. The exertion had been too much for him. His face blanched and he fumbled with his collar.

"A momentary indisposition," he murmured, wondering himself whether he was acting or sick.

"Sit down," Homer said.

But Harry wasn't through with his performance. He assumed a gallant smile and took a few unsteady steps toward the couch, then tripped himself. He examined the carpet indignantly, made believe he had found the object that had tripped him and kicked it away. He then limped to the couch and sat down with a whistling sigh like air escaping from a toy balloon.

Homer poured more water. Harry tried to stand up, but Homer pressed him back and made him drink sitting. He drank this glass as he had the other two, in quick gulps, then wiped his mouth with his handkerchief, imitating a man with a big mustache who had just drunk a glass of foamy beer.

"You are indeed kind, sir," he said. "Never fear, some day I'll repay you a thousandfold."

Homer clucked.

From his pocket Harry brought out a small can and held it out for him to take.

"Compliments of the house," he announced. "'Tis a box

of Miracle Solvent, the modern polish par excellence, the polish without peer or parallel, used by all the movie stars . . ."

He broke off his spiel with a trilling laugh.

Homer took the can.

"Thank you," he said, trying to appear grateful. "How much is it?"

"The ordinary price, the retail price, is fifty cents, but you can have it for the extraordinary price of a quarter, the wholesale price, the price I pay at the factory."

"A quarter?" asked Homer, habit for the moment having got the better of his timidity. "I can buy one twice that size for a quarter in the store."

Harry knew his man.

"Take it, take it for nothing," he said contemptuously.

Homer was tricked into protesting.

"I guess maybe this is a much better polish."

"No," said Harry, as though he were spurning a bribe. "Keep your money. I don't want it."

He laughed, this time bitterly.

Homer pulled out some change and offered it.

"Take it, please. You need it, I'm sure. I'll have two cans."

Harry had his man where he wanted him. He began to practice a variety of laughs, all of them theatrical, like a musician tuning up before a concert. He finally found the right one and let himself go. It was a victim's laugh.

"Please stop," Homer said.

But Harry couldn't stop. He was really sick. The last block that held him poised over the runway of self-pity had been knocked away and he was sliding down the chute, gaining momentum all the time. He jumped to his feet and began doing Harry Greener, poor Harry, honest Harry, well-meaning, humble, deserving, a good husband, a model father, a faithful Christian, a loyal friend.

Homer didn't appreciate the performance in the least. He was terrified and wondered whether to phone the police. But he did nothing. He just held up his hand for Harry to stop.

At the end of his pantomime, Harry stood with his head thrown back, clutching his throat, as though waiting for the curtain to fall. Homer poured him still another glass of water. But Harry wasn't finished. He bowed, sweeping his hat to his heart, then began again. He didn't get very far this time and had to gasp painfully for breath. Suddenly, like a mechanical toy that had been over-wound, something snapped inside of him and he began to spin through his entire repertoire. The effort was purely muscular, like the dance of a paralytic. He jigged, juggled his hat, made believe he had been kicked, tripped, and shook hands with himself. He went through it all in one dizzy spasm, then reeled to the couch and collapsed.

He lay on the couch with his eyes closed and his chest heaving. He was even more surprised than Homer. He had put on his performance four or five times already that day and nothing like this had happened. He was really sick.

"You've had a fit," Homer said when Harry opened his eyes.

As the minutes passed, Harry began to feel better and his confidence returned. He pushed all thought of sickness out of his mind and even went so far as to congratulate himself on having given the finest performance of his career. He should be able to get five dollars out of the big dope who was leaning over him.

"Have you any spirits in the house?" he asked weakly.

The grocer had sent Homer a bottle of port wine on approval and he went to get it. He filled a tumbler half full and handed it to Harry, who drank it in small sips, making the faces that usually go with medicine.

Speaking slowly, as though in great pain, he then asked Homer to bring in his sample case.

"It's on the doorstep. Somebody might steal it. The greater part of my small capital is invested in those cans of polish."

When Homer stepped outside to obey, he saw a girl near the curb. It was Faye Greener. She was looking at the house.

"Is my father in there?" she called out.

"Mr. Greener?"

She stamped her foot.

"Tell him to get a move on, damn it. I don't want to stay here all day."

"He's sick."

The girl turned away without giving any sign that she either heard or cared.

Homer took the sample case back into the house with him. He found Harry pouring himself another drink.

"Pretty fair stuff," he said, smacking his lips over it. "Pretty fair, all right, all right. Might I be so bold as to ask what you pay for a . . ."

Homer cut him short. He didn't approve of people who drank and wanted to get rid of him.

"Your daughter's outside," he said with as much firmness as he could muster. "She wants you."

Harry collapsed on the couch and began to breathe heavily. He was acting again.

"Don't tell her," he gasped. "Don't tell her how sick her old daddy is. She must never know."

Homer was shocked by his hypocrisy.

"You're better," he said as coldly as he could. "Why don't you go home?"

Harry smiled to show how offended and hurt he was by the heartless attitude of his host. When Homer said nothing, his smile became one expressing boundless courage. He got carefully to his feet, stood erect for a minute, then began to sway weakly and tumbled back on the couch.

"I'm faint," he groaned.

Once again he was surprised and frightened. He was faint.

"Get my daughter," he gasped.

Homer found her standing at the curb with her back to the house. When he called her, she whirled and came running toward him. He watched her for a second, then went in, leaving the door unlatched.

Faye burst into the room. She ignored Homer and went straight to the couch.

"Now what in hell's the matter?" she exploded.

"Darling daughter," he said. "I have been badly taken, and this gentleman has been kind enough to let me rest for a moment."

"He had a fit or something," Homer said.

She whirled around on him so suddenly that he was startled.

"How do you do?" she said, holding her hand forward and high up.

He shook it gingerly.

"Charmed," she said, when he mumbled something.

She spun around once more.

"It's my heart," Harry said. "I can't stand up."

The little performance he put on to sell polish was familiar to her and she knew that this wasn't part of it. When she turned to face Homer again, she looked quite tragic. Her head, instead of being held far back, now drooped forward.

"Please let him rest there," she said.

"Yes, of course."

Homer motioned her toward a chair, then got her a

match for her cigarette. He tried not to stare at her, but his good manners were wasted. Faye enjoyed being stared at.

He thought her extremely beautiful, but what affected him still more was her vitality. She was taut and vibrant. She was as shiny as a new spoon.

Although she was seventeen, she was dressed like a child of twelve in a white cotton dress with a blue sailor collar. Her long legs were bare and she had blue sandals on her feet.

"I'm so sorry," she said when Homer looked at her father again.

He made a motion with his hand to show that it was nothing.

"He has a vile heart, poor dear," she went on. "I've begged and begged him to go to a specialist, but you men are all alike."

"Yes, he ought to go to a doctor," Homer said.

Her odd mannerisms and artificial voice puzzled him. "What time is it?" she asked.

"About one o'clock."

She stood up suddenly and buried both her hands in her hair at the sides of her head, making it bunch at the top in a shiny ball.

"Oh," she gasped prettily, "and I had a luncheon date."

Still holding her hair, she turned at the waist without moving her legs, so that her snug dress twisted even tighter and Homer could see her dainty, arched ribs and little, dimpled belly. This elaborate gesture, like all her others, was so completely meaningless, almost formal, that she seemed a dancer rather than an affected actress.

"Do you like salmon salad?" Homer ventured to ask.

"Salmon sal-ahde?"

She seemed to be repeating the question to her stomach. The answer was yes.

"With plenty of mayonnaise, huh? I adore it."

"I was going to have some for lunch. I'll finish making it."

"Let me help."

They looked at Harry, who appeared to be asleep, then went into the kitchen. While he opened a can of salmon, she climbed on a chair and straddled it with her arms folded across the top of its back and rested her chin on her arms. Whenever he looked at her, she smiled intimately and tossed her pale, glittering hair first forward, then back.

Homer was excited and his hands worked quickly. He soon had a large bowl of salad ready. He set the table with his best cloth and his best silver and china.

"It makes me hungry just to look," she said.

The way she said this seemed to mean that it was Homer who made her hungry and he beamed at her. But before he had a chance to sit down, she was already eating. She buttered a slice of bread, covered the butter with sugar and took a big bite. Then she quickly smeared a gob of mayonnaise on the salmon and went to work. Just as he was about to sit down, she asked for something to drink. He poured her a glass of milk and stood watching her like a waiter. He was unaware of her rudeness.

As soon as she had gobbled up her salad, he brought her a large red apple. She ate the fruit more slowly, nibbling daintily, her smallest finger curled away from the rest of her hand. When she had finished it, she went back to the living room and Homer followed her.

Harry still lay as they had left him, stretched out on the sofa. The heavy noon-day sun hit directly on his face, beating down on him like a club. He hardly felt its blows, however. He was busy with the stabbing pain in his chest. He was so busy with himself that he had even stopped trying to plan how to get money out of the big dope.

Homer drew the window curtain to shade his face.

Harry didn't even notice. He was thinking about death. Faye bent over him. He saw, from under his partially closed eyelids, that she expected him to make a reassuring gesture. He refused. He examined the tragic expression that she had assumed and didn't like it. In a serious moment like this, her ham sorrow was insulting.

"Speak to me, Daddy," she begged.

She was baiting him without being aware of it.

"What the hell is this," he snarled, "a Tom show?"

His sudden fury scared her and she straightened up with a jerk. He didn't want to laugh, but a short bark escaped before he could stop it. He waited anxiously to see what would happen. When it didn't hurt he laughed again. He kept on, timidly at first, then with growing assurance. He laughed with his eyes closed and the sweat pouring down his brow. Faye knew only one way to stop him and that was to do something he hated as much as she hated his laughter. She began to sing.

> "*Jeepers Creepers!*
> *Where'd ya get those peepers?* . . ."

She trucked, jerking her buttocks and shaking her head from side to side.

Homer was amazed. He felt that the scene he was witnessing had been rehearsed. He was right. Their bitterest quarrels often took this form; he laughing, she singing.

> "*Jeepers Creepers!*
> *Where'd ya get those eyes?*
> *Gosh, all git up!*
> *How'd they get so lit up?*
> *Gosh all git* . . ."

When Harry stopped, she stopped and flung herself into a chair. But Harry was only gathering strength for a final

effort. He began again. This new laugh was not critical;
it was horrible. When she was a child, he used to punish
her with it. It was his masterpiece. There was a director
who always called on him to give it when he was shooting
a scene in an insane asylum or a haunted castle.

It began with a sharp, metallic crackle, like burning
sticks, then gradually increased in volume until it became
a rapid bark, then fell away again to an obscene chuckle.
After a slight pause, it climbed until it was the nicker of a
horse, then still higher to become a machinelike screech.

Faye listened helplessly with her head cocked on one
side. Suddenly, she too laughed, not willingly, but fighting
the sound.

"You bastard!" she yelled.

She leaped to the couch, grabbed him by the shoulders
and tried to shake him quiet.

He kept laughing.

Homer moved as though he meant to pull her away,
but he lost courage and was afraid to touch her. She was
so naked under her skimpy dress.

"Miss Greener," he pleaded, making his big hands dance
at the end of his arms. "Please, please . . ."

Harry couldn't stop laughing now. He pressed his belly
with his hands, but the noise poured out of him. It had
begun to hurt again.

Swinging her hand as though it held a hammer, she
brought her fist down hard on his mouth. She hit him
only once. He relaxed and was quiet.

"I had to do it," she said to Homer when he took her
arm and led her away.

He guided her to a chair in the kitchen and shut the
door. She continued to sob for a long time. He stood behind her chair, helplessly, watching the rhythmical heave
of her shoulders. Several times his hands moved forward
to comfort her, but he succeeded in curbing them.

When she was through crying, he handed her a napkin and she dried her face. The cloth was badly stained by her rouge and mascara.

"I've spoilt it," she said, keeping her face averted. "I'm very sorry."

"It was dirty," Homer said.

She took a compact from her pocket and looked at herself in its tiny mirror.

"I'm a fright."

She asked if she could use the bathroom and he showed her where it was. He then tiptoed into the living room to see Harry. The old man's breathing was noisy but regular and he seemed to be sleeping quietly. Homer put a cushion under his head without disturbing him and went back into the kitchen. He lit the stove and put the coffeepot on the flame, then sat down to wait for the girl to return. He heard her go into the living room. A few seconds later she came into the kitchen.

She hesitated apologetically in the doorway.

"Won't you have some coffee?"

Without waiting for her to reply, he poured a cup and moved the sugar and cream so that she could reach them.

"I had to do it," she said. "I just had to."

"That's all right."

To show her that it wasn't necessary to apologize, he busied himself at the sink.

"No, I had to," she insisted. "He laughs that way just to drive me wild. I can't stand it. I simply can't."

"Yes."

"He's crazy. We Greeners are all crazy."

She made this last statement as though there were merit in being crazy.

"He's pretty sick," Homer said, apologizing for her. "Maybe he had a sunstroke."

"No, he's crazy."

He put a plate of gingersnaps on the table and she ate them with her second cup of coffee. The dainty crunching sound she made chewing fascinated him.

When she remained quiet for several minutes, he turned from the sink to see if anything was wrong. She was smoking a cigarette and seemed lost in thought.

He tried to be gay.

"What are you thinking?" he said awkwardly, then felt foolish.

She sighed to show how dark and foreboding her thoughts were, but didn't reply.

"I'll bet you would like some candy," Homer said. "There isn't any in the house, but I could call the drugstore and they'd send it right over. Or some ice cream?"

"No, thanks, please."

"It's no trouble."

"My father isn't really a peddler," she said, abruptly. "He's an actor. I'm an actress. My mother was also an actress, a dancer. The theatre is in our blood."

"I haven't seen many shows. I . . ."

He broke off because he saw that she wasn't interested.

"I'm going to be a star some day," she announced as though daring him to contradict her.

"I'm sure you . . ."

"It's my life. It's the only thing in the whole world that I want."

"It's good to know what you want. I used to be a bookkeeper in a hotel, but . . ."

"If I'm not, I'll commit suicide."

She stood up and put her hands to her hair, opened her eyes wide and frowned.

"I don't go to shows very often," he apologized, pushing the gingersnaps toward her. "The lights hurt my eyes."

She laughed and took a cracker.

"I'll get fat."

"Oh, no."

"They say fat women are going to be popular next year. Do you think so? I don't. It's just publicity for Mae West."

He agreed with her.

She talked on and on, endlessly, about herself and about the picture business. He watched her, but didn't listen, and whenever she repeated a question in order to get a reply, he nodded his head without saying anything.

His hands began to bother him. He rubbed them against the edge of the table to relieve their itch, but it only stimulated them. When he clasped them behind his back, the strain became intolerable. They were hot and swollen. Using the dishes as an excuse, he held them under the cold water tap of the sink.

Faye was still talking when Harry appeared in the doorway. He leaned weakly against the door jamb. His nose was very red, but the rest of his face was drained white and he seemed to have grown too small for his clothing. He was smiling, however.

To Homer's amazement, they greeted each other as though nothing had happened.

"You okay now, Pop?"

"Fine and dandy, baby. Right as rain, fit as a fiddle and lively as a flea, as the feller says."

The nasal twang he used in imitation of a country yokel made Homer smile.

"Do you want something to eat?" he asked. "A glass of milk, maybe?"

"I could do with a snack."

Faye helped him over to the table. He tried to disguise how weak he was by doing an exaggerated Negro shuffle.

Homer opened a can of sardines and sliced some bread. Harry smacked his lips over the food, but ate slowly and with an effort.

"That hit the spot, all righty right," he said when he had finished.

He leaned back and fished a crumpled cigar butt out of his vest pocket. Faye lit it for him and he playfully blew a puff of smoke in her face.

"We'd better go, Daddy," she said.

"In a jiffy, child."

He turned to Homer.

"Nice place you've got here. Married?"

Faye tried to interfere.

"Dad!"

He ignored her.

"Bachelor, eh?"

"Yes."

"Well, well, a young fellow like you."

"I'm here for my health," Homer found it necessary to say.

"Don't answer his questions," Faye broke in.

"Now, now, daughter, I'm just being friendly like. I don't mean no harm."

He was still using an exaggerated backwoods accent. He spat dry into an imaginary spittoon and made believe he was shifting a cud of tobacco from cheek to cheek.

Homer thought his mimicry funny.

"I'd be lonesome and scared living alone in a big house like this," Harry went on. "Don't you ever get lonesome?"

Homer looked at Faye for his answer. She was frowning with annoyance.

"No," he said, to prevent Harry from repeating the uncomfortable question.

"No? Well, that's fine."

He blew several smoke rings at the ceiling and watched their behavior judiciously.

"Did you ever think of taking boarders?" he asked.

"Some nice, sociable folks, I mean. It'll bring in a little extra money and make things more homey."

Homer was indignant, but underneath his indignation lurked another idea, a very exciting one. He didn't know what to say.

Faye misunderstood his agitation.

"Cut it out, Dad," she exclaimed before Homer could reply. "You've been a big enough nuisance already."

"Just chinning," he protested innocently. "Just chewing the fat."

"Well, then, let's get going," she snapped.

"There's plenty of time," Homer said.

He wanted to add something stronger, but didn't have the courage. His hands were braver. When Faye shook good-bye, they clutched and refused to let go.

Faye laughed at their warm insistence.

"Thanks a million, Mr. Simpson," she said. "You've been very kind. Thanks for the lunch and for helping Daddy."

"We're very grateful," Harry chimed in. "You've done a Christian deed this day. God will reward you."

He had suddenly become very pious.

"Please look us up," Faye said. "We live close-by in the San Berdoo Apartments, about five blocks down the canyon. It's the big yellow house."

When Harry stood, he had to lean against the table for support. Faye and Homer each took him by the arm and helped him into the street. Homer held him erect, while Faye went to get their Ford which was parked across the street.

"We're forgetting your order of Miracle Salve," Harry said, "the polish without peer or parallel."

Homer found a dollar and slipped it into his hand. He hid the money quickly and tried to become businesslike.

"I'll leave the goods tomorrow."

"Yes, that'll be fine," Homer said. "I really need some silver polish."

Harry was angry because it hurt him to be patronized by a sucker. He made an attempt to re-establish what he considered to be their proper relationship by bowing ironically, but didn't get very far with the gesture and began to fumble with his Adam's apple. Homer helped him into the car and he slumped down in the seat beside Faye.

They drove off. She turned to wave, but Harry didn't even look back.

12

Homer spent the rest of the afternoon in the broken deck chair. The lizard was on the cactus, but he took little interest in its hunting. His hands kept his thoughts busy. They trembled and jerked, as though troubled by dreams. To hold them still, he clasped them together. Their fingers twined like a tangle of thighs in miniature. He snatched them apart and sat on them.

When the days passed and he couldn't forget Faye, he began to grow frightened. He somehow knew that his only defense was chastity, that it served him, like the shell of a tortoise, as both spine and armor. He couldn't shed it even in thought. If he did, he would be destroyed.

He was right. There are men who can lust with parts of themselves. Only their brain or their hearts burn and then not completely. There are others, still more fortunate, who are like the filaments of an incandescent lamp. They burn fiercely, yet nothing is destroyed. But in Homer's case it would be like dropping a spark into a barn full of hay. He had escaped in the Romola Martin incident, but he wouldn't escape again. Then, for one thing, he had had his job in the hotel, a daily all-day task that protected him by tiring him, but now he had nothing.

His thoughts frightened him and he bolted into the house, hoping to leave them behind like a hat. He ran into his bedroom and threw himself down on the bed. He was simple enough to believe that people don't think while asleep.

In his troubled state, even this delusion was denied him and he was unable to fall asleep. He closed his eyes and tried to make himself drowsy. The approach to sleep which had once been automatic had somehow become a long, shining tunnel. Sleep was at the far end of it, a soft bit of shadow in the hard glare. He couldn't run, only crawl toward the black patch. Just as he was about to give up, habit came to his rescue. It collapsed the shining tunnel and hurled him into the shadow.

When he awoke it was without a struggle. He tried to fall asleep once more, but this time couldn't even find the tunnel. He was thoroughly awake. He tried to think of how very tired he was, but he wasn't tired. He felt more alive than he had at any time since Romola Martin.

Outside a few birds still sang intermittently, starting and breaking off, as though sorry to acknowledge the end of another day. He thought that he heard the lisp of silk against silk, but it was only the wind playing in the trees. How empty the house was! He tried to fill it by singing.

"Oh, say can you see,
By the dawn's early light . . ."

It was the only song he knew. He thought of buying a victrola or a radio. He knew, however, that he would buy neither. This fact made him very sad. It was a pleasant sadness, very sweet and calm.

But he couldn't let well enough alone. He was impatient

and began to prod at his sadness, hoping to make it acute
and so still more pleasant. He had been getting pamphlets
in the mail from a travel bureau and he thought of the
trips he would never take. Mexico was only a few hundred
miles away. Boats left daily for Hawaii.

His sadness turned to anguish before he knew it and
became sour. He was miserable again. He began to cry.

Only those who still have hope can benefit from tears.
When they finish, they feel better. But to those without
hope, like Homer, whose anguish is basic and permanent,
no good comes from crying. Nothing changes for them.
They usually know this, but still can't help crying.

Homer was lucky. He cried himself to sleep.

But he awoke again in the morning with Faye uppermost in his mind. He bathed, ate breakfast and sat in his
deck chair. In the afternoon, he decided to go for a walk.
There was only one way for him to go and that led past
the San Bernardino Apartments.

Some time during his long sleep he had given up the
battle. When he came to the apartment house, he peered
into the amber-lit hallway and read the Greener card on
the letter box, then turned and went home. On the next
night, he repeated the trip, carrying a gift of flowers and
wine.

13

Harry Greener's condition didn't improve. He remained
in bed, staring at the ceiling with his hands folded on his
chest.

Tod went to see him almost every night. There were
usually other guests. Sometimes Abe Kusich, sometimes
Anna and Annabelle Lee, a sister act of the nineteen-tens,
more often the four Gingos, a family of performing
Eskimos from Point Barrow, Alaska.

If Harry were asleep or there were visitors, Faye usually invited Tod into her room for a talk. His interest in her grew despite the things she said and he continued to find her very exciting. Had any other girl been so affected, he would have thought her intolerable. Faye's affectations, however, were so completely artificial that he found them charming.

Being with her was like being backstage during an amateurish, ridiculous play. From in front, the stupid lines and grotesque situations would have made him squirm with annoyance, but because he saw the perspiring stage-hands and the wires that held up the tawdry summerhouse with its tangle of paper flowers, he accepted everything and was anxious for it to succeed.

He found still another way to excuse her. He believed that while she often recognized the falseness of an attitude, she persisted in it because she didn't know how to be simpler or more honest. She was an actress who had learned from bad models in a bad school.

Yet Faye did have some critical ability, almost enough to recognize the ridiculous. He had often seen her laugh at herself. What was more, he had even seen her laugh at her dreams.

One evening they talked about what she did with herself when she wasn't working as an extra. She told him that she often spent the whole day making up stories. She laughed as she said it. When he questioned her, she described her method quite willingly.

She would get some music on the radio, then lie down on her bed and shut her eyes. She had a large assortment of stories to choose from. After getting herself in the right mood, she would go over them in her mind, as though they were a pack of cards, discarding one after another until she found the one that suited. On some days, she would run through the whole pack without making a choice. When that happened, she would either go to Vine Street for an ice cream soda or, if she was broke, thumb over the pack again and force herself to choose.

While she admitted that her method was too mechanical for the best results and that it was better to slip into a dream naturally, she said that any dream was better than no dream and beggars couldn't be choosers. She hadn't exactly said this, but he was able to understand it from what she did say. He thought it important that she smiled while telling him, not with embarrassment, but critically. However, her critical powers ended there. She only smiled at the mechanics.

The first time he had ever heard one of her dreams was late at night in her bedroom. About half an hour earlier, she had knocked on his door and had asked him to come and help her with Harry because she thought he was dying. His noisy breathing, which she had taken for the death rattle, had awakened her and she was badly frightened. Tod put on his bathrobe and followed her downstairs. When he got to the apartment, Harry had managed to clear his throat and his breathing had become quiet again.

She invited him into her room for a smoke. She sat on the bed and he sat beside her. She was wearing an old beach robe of white toweling over her pajamas and it was very becoming.

He wanted to beg her for a kiss but was afraid, not because she would refuse, but because she would insist on making it meaningless. To flatter her, he commented on her appearance. He did a bad job of it. He was incapable of direct flattery and got bogged down in a much too roundabout observation. She didn't listen and he broke off feeling like an idiot.

"I've got a swell idea," she said suddenly. "An idea how we can make some real money."

He made another attempt to flatter her. This time by assuming an attitude of serious interest.

"You're educated," she said. "Well, I've got some swell ideas for pictures. All you got to do is write them up and then we'll sell them to the studios."

He agreed and she described her plan. It was very vague until she came to what she considered would be its results, then she went into concrete details. As soon as they had sold one story, she would give him another. They would make loads and loads of money. Of course she wouldn't give up acting, even if she was a big success as a writer, because acting was her life.

He realized as she went on that she was manufacturing another dream to add to her already very thick pack. When she finally got through spending the money, he asked her to tell him the idea he was to "write up," keeping all trace of irony out of his voice.

On the wall of the room beyond the foot of her bed was a large photograph that must have once been used in the lobby of a theatre to advertise a Tarzan picture. It showed a beautiful young man with magnificent muscles, wearing only a narrow loin cloth, who was ardently squeezing a slim girl in a torn riding habit. They stood in a jungle clearing and all around the pair writhed great vines loaded with fat orchids. When she told her story, he knew that this photograph had a lot to do with inspiring it.

A young girl is cruising on her father's yacht in the South Seas. She is engaged to marry a Russian count, who is tall, thin and old, but with beautiful manners. He is on the yacht, too, and keeps begging her to name the day. But she is spoiled and won't do it. Maybe she became engaged to him in order to spite another man. She becomes interested in a young sailor who is far below her in station, but very handsome. She flirts with him because she is bored. The sailor refuses to be toyed with no matter how

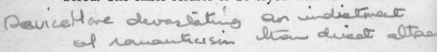

much money she's got and tells her that he only takes orders from the captain and to go back to her foreigner. She gets sore as hell and threatens to have him fired, but he only laughs at her. How can he be fired in the middle of the ocean? She falls in love with him, although maybe she doesn't realize it herself, because he is the first man who has ever said no to one of her whims and because he is so handsome. Then there is a big storm and the yacht is wrecked near an island. Everybody is drowned, but she manages to swim to shore. She makes herself a hut of boughs and lives on fish and fruit. It's the tropics. One morning, while she is bathing naked in a brook, a big snake grabs her. She struggles but the snake is too strong for her and it looks like curtains. But the sailor, who has been watching her from behind some bushes, leaps to her rescue. He fights the snake for her and wins.

Tod was to go on from there. He asked her how she thought the picture should end, but she seemed to have lost interest. He insisted on hearing, however.

"Well, he marries her, of course, and they're rescued. First they're rescued and then they're married, I mean. Maybe he turns out to be a rich boy who is being a sailor just for the adventure of it, or something like that. You can work it out easy enough."

"It's sure-fire," Tod said earnestly, staring at her wet lips and the tiny point of her tongue which she kept moving between them.

"I've got just hundreds and hundreds more."

He didn't say anything and her manner changed. While telling the story, she had been full of surface animation and her hands and face were alive with little illustrative grimaces and gestures. But now her excitement narrowed and became deeper and its play internal. He guessed that she must be thumbing over her pack and that she would soon select another card to show him.

[handwritten top margin: 2nd para — strikes with destructive staccato force, power increased by contrast, create feeling of latent violence.]

[handwritten left margin: language vivid to direct first para by real / Sensuous language too full intended / lang. of naive "romance" pulp magazine erotic ethos suggest porny.]

He had often seen her like this, but had never before understood it. All these little stories, these little daydreams of hers, were what gave such extraordinary color and mystery to her movements. She seemed always to be struggling in their soft grasp as though she were trying to run in a swamp. As he watched her, he felt sure that her lips must taste of blood and salt and that there must be a delicious weakness in her legs. His impulse wasn't to aid her to get free, but to throw her down in the soft, warm mud and to keep her there.

He expressed some of his desire by a grunt. If he only had the courage to throw himself on her. Nothing less violent than rape would do. The sensation he felt was like that he got when holding an egg in his hand. Not that she was fragile or even seemed fragile. It wasn't that. It was her completeness, her egglike self-sufficiency, that made him want to crush her.

But he did nothing and she began to talk again.

"I've got another swell idea that I want to tell you. Maybe you had better write this one up first. It's a backstage story and they're making a lot of them this year."

She told him about a young chorus girl who gets her big chance when the star of the show falls sick. It was a familiar version of the Cinderella theme, but her technique was much different from the one she had used for the South Sea tale. Although the events she described were miraculous, her description of them was realistic. The effect was similar to that obtained by the artists of the Middle Ages, who, when doing a subject like the raising of Lazarus from the dead or Christ walking on water, were careful to keep all the details intensely realistic. She, like them, seemed to think that fantasy could be made plausible by a humdrum technique.

"I like that one, too," he said when she had finished.

"Think them over and do the one that has the best chance."

She was dismissing him and if he didn't act at once the opportunity would be gone. He started to lean toward her, but she caught his meaning and stood up. She took his arm with affectionate brusqueness—they were now business partners—and guided him to the door.

In the hall, when she thanked him for coming down and apologized for having disturbed him, he tried again. She seemed to melt a little and he reached for her. She kissed him willingly enough, but when he tried to extend the caress, she tore free.

"Whoa there, palsy-walsy," she laughed. "Mamma spank."

He started for the stairs.

"Good-bye now," she called after him, then laughed again.

He barely heard her. He was thinking of the drawings he had made of her and of the new one he would do as soon as he got to his room.

In "The Burning of Los Angeles" Faye is the naked girl in the left foreground being chased by the group of men and women who have separated from the main body of the mob. One of the women is about to hurl a rock at her to bring her down. She is running with her eyes closed and a strange half-smile on her lips. Despite the dreamy repose of her face, her body is straining to hurl her along at top speed. The only explanation for this contrast is that she is enjoying the release that wild flight gives in much the same way that a game bird must when, after hiding for several tense minutes, it bursts from cover in complete, unthinking panic.

14

Tod had other and more successful rivals than Homer Simpson. One of the most important was a young man called Earle Shoop.

Earle was a cowboy from a small town in Arizona. He worked occasionally in horse-operas and spent the rest of his time in front of a saddlery store on Sunset Boulevard. In the window of this store was an enormous Mexican saddle covered with carved silver, and around it was arranged a large collection of torture instruments. Among other things there were fancy, braided quirts, spurs with great spiked wheels, and double bits that looked as though they could break a horse's jaw without trouble. Across the back of the window ran a low shelf on which was a row of boots, some black, some red and some a pale yellow. All of the boots had scalloped tops and very high heels.

Earle always stood with his back to the window, his eyes fixed on a sign on the roof of a one-story building across the street that read: "Malted Milks Too Thick For A Straw." Regularly, twice every hour, he pulled a sack of tobacco and a sheaf of papers from his shirt pocket and rolled a cigarette. Then he tightened the cloth of his trousers by lifting his knee and struck a match along the underside of his thigh.

He was over six feet tall. The big Stetson hat he wore added five inches more to his height and the heels of his boots still another three. His polelike appearance was further exaggerated by the narrowness of his shoulders and by his lack of either hips or buttocks. The years he had spent in the saddle had not made him bowlegged. In fact his legs were so straight that his dungarees, bleached very light blue by the sun and much washing, hung down without a wrinkle, as though they were empty.

Tod could see why Faye thought him handsome. He had a two-dimensional face that a talented child might have drawn with a ruler and a compass. His chin was perfectly round and his eyes, which were wide apart, were also round. His thin mouth ran at right angles to his straight, perpendicular nose. His reddish tan complexion was the same color from hairline to throat, as though washed in by an expert, and it completed his resemblance to a mechanical drawing.

Tod had told Faye that Earle was a dull fool. She agreed laughing, but then said that he was "criminally handsome," an expression she had picked up in the chatter column of a trade paper.

Meeting her on the stairs one night, Tod asked if she would go to dinner with him.

"I can't. I've got a date. But you can come along."

"With Earle?"

"Yes, with Earle," she repeated, mimicking his annoyance.

"No, thanks."

She misunderstood, perhaps on purpose, and said, "He'll treat this time."

Earle was always broke and whenever Tod went with them he was the one who paid.

"That isn't it, and you damn well know it."

"Oh, isn't it?" she asked archly, then, absolutely sure of herself, added, "Meet us at Hodge's around five."

Hodge's was the saddlery store. When Tod got there, he found Earle Shoop at his usual post, just standing and just looking at the sign across the street. He had on his ten-gallon hat and his high-heeled boots. Neatly folded over his left arm was a dark gray jacket. His shirt was navy-blue cotton with large polka dots, each the size of a dime. The sleeves of his shirt were not rolled, but pulled to the middle of his forearm and held there by a pair of fancy, rose armbands. His hands were the same clean reddish tan as his face.

"Lo, thar," was the way he returned Tod's salute.

Tod found his Western accent amusing. The first time he had heard it, he had replied, "Lo, thar, stranger," and had been surprised to discover that Earle didn't know he was being kidded. Even when Tod talked about "cayuses," "mean hombres" and "rustlers," Earle took him seriously.

"Howdy, partner," Tod said.

Next to Earle was another Westerner in a big hat and boots, sitting on his heels and chewing vigorously on a little twig. Close behind him was a battered paper valise held together by heavy rope tied with professional-looking knots.

Soon after Tod arrived a third man came along. He made a thorough examination of the merchandise in the window, then turned and began to stare across the street like the other two.

He was middle-aged and looked like an exercise boy from a racing stable. His face was completely covered with a fine mesh of wrinkles, as though he had been sleeping with it pressed against a roll of rabbit wire. He was very shabby and had probably sold his big hat, but he still had his boots.

"Lo, boys," he said.

"Lo, Hink," said the man with the paper valise.

Tod didn't know whether he was included in the greeting, but took a chance and replied.

"Howdy."

Hink prodded the valise with his toe.

"Goin' some place, Calvin?" he asked.

"Azusa, there's a rodeo."

"Who's running it?"

"A fellow calls himself 'Badlands Jack.' "

"That grifter! . . . You goin', Earle?"

"Nope."

"I gotta eat," said Calvin.

Hink carefully considered all the information he had received before speaking again.

"Mono's makin' a new Buck Stevens," he said. "Will Ferris told me they'd use more than forty riders."

Calvin turned and looked up at Earle.

"Still got the piebald vest?" he asked slyly.

"Why?"

"It'll cinch you a job as a road agent."

Tod understood that this was a joke of some sort because Calvin and Hink chuckled and slapped their thighs loudly while Earle frowned.

There was another long silence, then Calvin spoke again.

"Ain't your old man still got some cows?" he asked Earle.

But Earle was wary this time and refused to answer.

Calvin winked at Tod, slowly and elaborately, contorting one whole side of his face.

"That's right, Earle," Hink said. "Your old man's still got some stock. Why don't you go home?"

They couldn't get a rise out of Earle, so Calvin answered the question.

"He dassint. He got caught in a sheep car with a pair of rubber boots on."

It was another joke. Calvin and Hink slapped their thighs and laughed, but Tod could see that they were waiting for something else. Earle, suddenly, without even shifting his weight, shot his foot out and kicked Calvin solidly in the rump. This was the real point of the joke. They were delighted by Earle's fury. Tod also laughed. The way Earle had gone from apathy to action without the usual transition was funny. The seriousness of his violence was even funnier.

A little while later, Faye drove by in her battered Ford

touring car and pulled into the curb some twenty feet away. Calvin and Hink waved, but Earle didn't budge. He took his time, as befitted his dignity. Not until she tooted her horn did he move. Tod followed a short distance behind him.

"Hi, cowboy," said Faye gaily.

"Lo, honey," he drawled, removing his hat carefully and replacing it with even greater care.

Faye smiled at Tod and motioned for them both to climb in. Tod got in the back. Earle unfolded the jacket he was carrying, slapped it a few times to remove the wrinkles, then put it on and adjusted its collar and shaped the roll of its lapels. He then climbed in beside Faye.

She started the car with a jerk. When she reached LaBrea, she turned right to Hollywood Boulevard and then left along it. Tod could see that she was watching Earle out of the corner of her eye and that he was preparing to speak.

"Get going," she said, trying to hurry him. "What is it?"

"Looka here, honey, I ain't got any dough for supper."

She was very much put out.

"But I told Tod we'd treat him. He's treated us enough times."

"That's all right," Tod interposed. "Next time'll do. I've got plenty of money."

"No, damn it," she said without looking around. "I'm sick of it."

She pulled into the curb and slammed on the brakes.

"It's always the same story," she said to Earle.

He adjusted his hat, his collar and his sleeves, then spoke. "We've got some grub at camp."

"Beans, I suppose."

"Nope."

She prodded him.

"Well, what've you got?"

"Mig and me's set some traps."

Faye laughed.

"Rat traps, eh? We're going to eat rats."

Earle didn't say anything.

"Listen, you big, strong, silent dope," she said, "either make sense, or God damn it, get out of this car."

"They're quail traps," he said without the slightest change in his wooden, formal manner.

She ignored his explanation.

"Talking to you is like pulling teeth. You wear me out."

Tod knew that there was no hope for him in this quarrel. He had heard it all before.

"I didn't mean nothing," Earle said. "I was only funning. I wouldn't feed you rats."

She slammed off the emergency brake and started the car again. At Zacarias Street, she turned into the hills. After climbing steadily for a quarter of a mile, she reached a dirt road and followed it to its end. They all climbed out, Earle helping Faye.

"Give me a kiss," she said, smiling her forgiveness.

He took his hat off ceremoniously and placed it on the hood of the car, then wrapped his long arms around her. They paid no attention to Tod, who was standing off to one side watching them. He saw Earle close his eyes and pucker up his lips like a little boy. But there was nothing boyish about what he did to her. When she had had as much as she wanted, she pushed him away.

"You, too?" she called gaily to Tod, who had turned his back.

"Oh, some other time," he replied, imitating her casualness.

She laughed, then took out a compact and began to fix her mouth. When she was ready, they started along a little path that was a continuation of the dirt road. Earle led, Faye came next and Tod brought up the rear.

It was full spring. The path ran along the bottom of a narrow canyon and wherever weeds could get a purchase in its steep banks they flowered in purple, blue and yellow. Orange poppies bordered the path. Their petals were wrinkled like crepe and their leaves were heavy with talcumlike dust.

They climbed until they reached another canyon. This one was sterile, but its bare ground and jagged rocks were even more brilliantly colored than the flowers of the first. The path was silver, grained with streaks of rose-gray, and the walls of the canyon were turquoise, mauve, chocolate and lavender. The air itself was vibrant pink.

They stopped to watch a humming bird chase a blue jay. The jay flashed by squawking with its tiny enemy on its tail like a ruby bullet. The gaudy birds burst the colored air into a thousand glittering particles like metal confetti.

When they came out of this canyon, they saw below them a little green valley thick with trees, mostly eucalyptus, with here and there a poplar and one enormous black live-oak. Sliding and stumbling down a dry wash, they made for the valley.

Tod saw a man watching their approach from the edge of the wood. Faye also saw him and waved.

"Hi, Mig!" she shouted.

"Chinita!" he called back.

She ran the last ten yards of the slope and the man caught her in his arms.

He was toffee-colored with large Armenian eyes and pouting black lips. His head was a mass of tight, ordered curls. He wore a long-haired sweater, called a "gorilla" in and around Los Angeles, with nothing under it. His soiled duck trousers were held up by a red bandanna handkerchief. On his feet were a pair of tattered tennis sneakers.

They moved on to the camp which was located in a clearing in the center of the wood. It consisted of little more than a ramshackle hut patched with tin signs that had been stolen from the highway and a stove without legs or bottom set on some rocks. Near the hut was a row of chicken coops.

Earle started a fire under the stove while Faye sat down on a box and watched him. Tod went over to look at the chickens. There was one old hen and a half a dozen game cocks. A great deal of pains had been taken in making the coops, which were of grooved boards, carefully matched and joined. Their floors were freshly spread with peat moss.

The Mexican came over and began to talk about the cocks. He was very proud of them.

"That's Hermano, five times winner. He's one of Street's Butcher Boys. Pepe and El Negro are still stags. I fight them next week in San Pedro. That's Villa, he's a blinker, but still good. And that one's Zapata, twice winner, a Tassel Dom he is. And that's Jujutla. My champ."

He opened the coop and lifted the bird out for Tod.

"A murderer is what the guy is. Speedy and how!"

The cock's plumage was green, bronze and copper. Its beak was lemon and its legs orange.

"He's beautiful," Tod said.

"I'll say."

Mig tossed the bird back into the coop and they went back to join the others at the fire.

"When do we eat?" Faye asked.

Miguel tested the stove by spitting on it. He next found a large iron skillet and began to scour it with sand. Earle gave Faye a knife and some potatoes to peel, then picked up a burlap sack.

"I'll get the birds," he said.

Tod went along with him. They followed a narrow path

that looked as though it had been used by sheep until they came to a tiny field covered with high, tufted grass. Earle stopped behind a gum bush and held up his hand to warn Tod.

A mocking bird was singing near by. Its song was like pebbles being dropped one by one from a height into a pool of water. Then a quail began to call, using two soft guttural notes. Another quail answered and the birds talked back and forth. Their call was not like the cheerful whistle of the Eastern bobwhite. It was full of melancholy and weariness, yet marvelously sweet. Still another quail joined the duet. This one called from near the center of the field. It was a trapped bird, but the sound it made had no anxiety in it, only sadness, impersonal and without hope.

When Earle was satisfied that no one was there to spy on his poaching, he went to the trap. It was a wire basket about the size of a washtub with a small door in the top. He stooped over and began to fumble with the door. Five birds ran wildly along the inner edge and threw themselves at the wire. One of them, a cock, had a dainty plume on his head that curled forward almost to his beak.

Earle caught the birds one at a time and pulled their heads off before dropping them into his sack. Then he started back. As he walked along, he held the sack under his left arm. He lifted the birds out with his right hand and plucked them one at a time. Their feathers fell to the ground, point first, weighed down by the tiny drop of blood that trembled on the tips of their quills.

The sun went down before they reached the camp again. It grew chilly and Tod was glad of the fire. Faye shared her seat on the box with him and they both leaned forward into the heat.

Mig brought a jug of tequila from the hut. He filled a peanut butter jar for Faye and passed the jug to Tod.

The liquor smelled like rotten fruit, but he liked the taste. When he had had enough, Earle took it and then Miguel. They continued to pass it from hand to hand.

Earle tried to show Faye how plump the game was, but she wouldn't look. He gutted the birds, then began cutting them into quarters with a pair of heavy tin shears. Faye held her hands over her ears in order not to hear the soft click made by the blades as they cut through flesh and bone. Earle wiped the pieces with a rag and dropped them into the skillet where a large piece of lard was already sputtering.

For all her squeamishness, Faye ate as heartily as the men did. There was no coffee and they finished with tequila. They smoked and kept the jug moving. Faye tossed away the peanut butter jar and drank like the others, throwing her head back and tilting the jug.

Tod could sense her growing excitement. The box on which they were sitting was so small that their backs touched and he could feel how hot she was and how restless. Her neck and face had turned from ivory to rose. She kept reaching for his cigarettes.

Earle's features were hidden in the shadow of his big hat, but the Mexican sat full in the light of the fire. His skin glowed and the oil in his black curls sparkled. He kept smiling at Faye in a manner that Tod didn't like. The more he drank, the less he liked it.

Faye kept crowding Tod, so he left the box to sit on the ground where he could watch her better. She was smiling back at the Mexican. She seemed to know what he was thinking and to be thinking the same thing. Earle, too, became aware of what was passing between them. Tod heard him curse softly and saw him lean forward into the light and pick up a thick piece of firewood.

Mig laughed guiltily and began to sing.

"Las palmeras lloran por tu ausencia,
Las laguna se seco—ay!
La cerca de alambre que estaba en
El patio tambien se cayo!"

His voice was a plaintive tenor and it turned the revolutionary song into a sentimental lament, sweet and cloying. Faye joined in when he began another stanza. She didn't know the words, but she was able to carry the melody and to harmonize.

"Pues mi madre las cuidaba, ay!
Toditito se acabo—ay!"

Their voices touched in the thin, still air to form a minor chord and it was as though their bodies had touched. The song was transformed again. The melody remained the same, but the rhythm broke and its beat became ragged. It was a rumba now.

Earle shifted uneasily and played with his stick. Tod saw her look at him and saw that she was afraid, but instead of becoming wary, she grew still more reckless. She took a long pull at the jug and stood up. She put one hand on each of her buttocks and began to dance.

Mig seemed to have completely forgotten Earle. He clapped his hands, cupping them to make a hollow, drum-like sound, and put all he felt into his voice. He had changed to a more fitting song.

"Tony's wife,
The boys in Havana love Tony's wife . . ."

Faye had her hands clasped behind her head now and she rolled her hips to the broken beat. She was doing the "bump."

*"Tony's wife,
They're fightin' their duels about Tony's
      wife . . ."*

Perhaps Tod had been mistaken about Earle. He was
using his club on the back of the skillet, using it to bang
out the rhythm.

The Mexican stood up, still singing, and joined her in
the dance. They approached each other with short mincing
steps. She held her skirt up and out with her thumbs and
forefingers and he did the same with his trousers. They
met head on, blue-black against palegold, and used their
heads to pivot, then danced back to back with their buttocks touching, their knees bent and wide apart. While
Faye shook her breasts and her head, holding the rest of
her body rigid, he struck the soft ground heavily with his
feet and circled her. They faced each other again and
made believe they were cradling their behinds in a shawl.

Earle pounded the skillet harder and harder until it
rang like an anvil. Suddenly he, too, jumped up and
began to dance. He did a crude hoe-down. He leaped into
the air and knocked his heels together. He whooped. But
he couldn't become part of their dance. Its rhythm was like
a smooth glass wall between him and the dancers. No
matter how loudly he whooped or threw himself around, he
was unable to disturb the precision with which they retreated and advanced, separated and came together again.

Tod saw the blow before it fell. He saw Earle raise his
stick and bring it down on the Mexican's head. He heard
the crack and saw the Mexican go to his knees still dancing, his body unwilling or unable to acknowledge the interruption.

Faye had her back to Mig when he fell, but she didn't
turn to look. She ran. She flashed by Tod. He reached

for her ankle to pull her down, but missed. He scrambled
to his feet and ran after her.

If he caught her now, she wouldn't escape. He could
hear her on the hill a little way ahead of him. He shouted
to her, a deep, agonized bellow, like that a hound makes
when it strikes a fresh line after hours of cold trailing.
Already he could feel how it would be when he pulled her
to the ground.

But the going was heavy and the stones and sand moved
under his feet. He fell prone with his face in a clump of
wild mustard that smelled of the rain and sun, clean, fresh
and sharp. He rolled over on his back and stared up at
the sky. The violent exercise had driven most of the heat
out of his blood, but enough remained to make him tingle
pleasantly. He felt comfortably relaxed, even happy.

Somewhere farther up the hill a bird began to sing. He
listened. At first the low rich music sounded like water
dripping on something hollow, the bottom of a silver pot
perhaps, then like a stick dragged slowly over the strings
of a harp. He lay quietly, listening.

When the bird grew silent, he made an effort to put
Faye out of his mind and began to think about the series
of cartoons he was making for his canvas of Los Angeles
on fire. He was going to show the city burning at high
noon, so that the flames would have to compete with the
desert sun and thereby appear less fearful, more like
bright flags flying from roofs and windows than a terrible
holocaust. He wanted the city to have quite a gala air as
it burned, to appear almost gay. And the people who set
it on fire would be a holiday crowd.

The bird began to sing again. When it stopped, Faye
was forgotten and he only wondered if he weren't exagger-
ating the importance of the people who come to California
to die. Maybe they weren't really desperate enough to set
a single city on fire, let alone the whole country. Maybe

they were only the pick of America's madmen and not at all typical of the rest of the land.

He told himself that it didn't make any difference because he was an artist, not a prophet. His work would not be judged by the accuracy with which it foretold a future event but by its merit as painting. Nevertheless, he refused to give up the role of Jeremiah. He changed "pick of America's madmen" to "cream" and felt almost certain that the milk from which it had been skimmed was just as rich in violence. The Angelenos would be first, but their comrades all over the country would follow. There would be civil war.

He was amused by the strong feeling of satisfaction this dire conclusion gave him. Were all prophets of doom and destruction such happy men?

He stood up without trying to answer. When he reached the dirt road at the top of the canyon Faye and the car were gone.

15

"She went to the pictures with that Simpson guy," Harry told him when he called to see her the next night.

He sat down to wait for her. The old man was very ill and lay on the bed with extreme care as though it were a narrow shelf from which he might fall if he moved.

"What are they making on your lot?" he asked slowly, rolling his eyes toward Tod without budging his head.

" 'Manifest Destiny,' 'Sweet and Low Down,' 'Waterloo,' 'The Great Divide,' Begging Your . . .' "

" 'The Great Divide'—" Harry said, interrupting eagerly. "I remember that vehicle."

Tod realized he shouldn't have got him started, but there was nothing he could do about it now. He had to let him run down like a clock.

"When it opened I was playing the Irving in a little number called 'Enter Two Gents,' a trifle, but entertainment, real entertainment. I played a Jew comic, a Ben Welch effect, derby and big pants—'Pat, dey hoffered me a chob in de Heagle Laundreh' . . . 'Faith now, Ikey, and did you take it?' . . . 'No, who vants to vash heagles?' Joe Parvos played straight for me in a cop's suit. Well, the night 'The Great Divide' opened, Joe was laying up with a whisker in the old Fifth Avenue when the stove exploded. It was the broad's husband who blew the whistle. He was . . ."

He hadn't run down. He had stopped and was squeezing his left side with both hands.

Tod leaned over anxiously.

"Some water?"

Harry framed the word "no" with his lips, then groaned skillfully. It was a second-act curtain groan, so phony that Tod had to hide a smile. And yet, the old man's pallor hadn't come from a box.

Harry groaned again, modulating from pain to exhaustion, then closed his eyes. Tod saw how skillfully he got the maximum effect out of his agonized profile by using the pillow to set it off. He also noticed that Harry, like many actors, had very little back or top to his head. It was almost all face, like a mask, with deep furrows between the eyes, across the forehead and on either side of the nose and mouth, plowed there by years of broad grinning and heavy frowning. Because of them, he could never express anything either subtly or exactly. They wouldn't permit degrees of feeling, only the furthest degree.

Tod began to wonder if it might not be true that actors suffer less than other people. He thought about this for a while, then decided that he was wrong. Feeling is of the heart and nerves and the crudeness of its expression has nothing to do with its intensity. Harry suffered as keenly as anyone, despite the theatricality of his groans and grimaces.

He seemed to enjoy suffering. But not all kinds, certainly not sickness. Like many people, he only enjoyed the sort that was self-inflicted. His favorite method was to bare his soul to strangers in barrooms. He would make believe he was drunk, and stumble over to where some strangers were sitting. He usually began by reciting a poem.

"Let me sit down for a moment,
I have a stone in my shoe.
I was once blithe and happy,
I was once young like you."

If his audience shouted, "scram, bum!" he only smiled humbly and went on with his act.

"Have pity, folks, on my gray hair . . ."

The bartender or someone else had to stop him by force, otherwise he would go on no matter what was said to him. Once he got started everyone in the bar usually listened, for he gave a great performance. He roared and whispered, commanded and cajoled. He imitated the whimper of a little girl crying for her vanished mother, as well as the different dialects of the many cruel managers he had known. He even did the off-stage noises, twittering like birds to herald the dawn of Love and yelping like a pack of bloodhounds when describing how an Evil Fate ever pursued him.

He made his audience see him start out in his youth to play Shakespeare in the auditorium of the Cambridge Latin School, full of glorious dreams, burning with ambi-

tion. Follow him, as still a mere stripling, he starved in a
Broadway rooming house, an idealist who desired only to
share his art with the world. Stand with him, as, in the
prime of manhood, he married a beautiful dancer, a head-
liner on the Gus Sun time. Be close behind him as, one night,
he returned home unexpectedly to find her in the arms of a
head usher. Forgive, as he forgave, out of the goodness of
his heart and the greatness of his love. Then laugh, tasting
the bitter gall, when the very next night he found her in
the arms of a booking agent. Again he forgave her and
again she sinned. Even then he didn't cast her out, no,
though she jeered, mocked and even struck him repeatedly
with an umbrella. But she ran off with a foreigner, a
swarthy magician fellow. Behind she left memories and
their baby daughter. He made his audience shadow him
still as misfortune followed misfortune and, a middle-aged
man, he haunted the booking offices, only a ghost of his
former self. He who had hoped to play Hamlet, Lear,
Othello, must needs become the Co. in an act called Nat
Plumstone & Co., light quips and breezy patter. He made
them dog his dragging feet as, an aged and trembling old
man, he . . .

Faye came in quietly. Tod started to greet her, but she
put her finger to her lips for him to be silent and motioned toward the bed.

The old man was asleep. Tod thought his worn, dry
skin looked like eroded ground. The few beads of sweat
that glistened on his forehead and temples carried no
promise of relief. It might rot, like rain that comes too late
to a field, but could never refresh.

They both tiptoed out of the room.

In the hall he asked if she had had a good time with
Homer.

"That dope!" she exclaimed, making a wry face. "He's
strictly home-cooking."

Tod started to ask some more questions, but she dismissed him with a curt, "I'm tired, honey."

16

The next afternoon, Tod was on his way upstairs when he saw a crowd in front of the door to the Greeners' apartment. They were excited and talked in whispers.

"What's happened?" he asked.

"Harry's dead."

He tried the door of the apartment. It wasn't locked, so he went in. The corpse lay stretched out on the bed, completely covered with a blanket. From Faye's room came the sound of crying. He knocked softly on her door. She opened it for him, then turned without saying a word, and stumbled to her bed. She was sobbing into a face towel.

He stood in the doorway, without knowing what to do or say. Finally, he went over to the bed and tried to comfort her. He patted her shoulder.

"You poor kid."

She was wearing a tattered, black lace negligee that had large rents in it. When he leaned over her, he noticed that her skin gave off a warm, sweet odor, like that of buckwheat in flower.

He turned away and lit a cigarette. There was a knock on the door. When he opened it, Mary Dove rushed past him to take Faye in her arms.

Mary also told Faye to be brave. She phrased it differently than he had done, however, and made it sound a lot more convincing.

"Show some guts, kid. Come on now, show some guts."

Faye shoved her away and stood up. She took a few wild steps, then sat down on the bed again.

"I killed him," she groaned.

Mary and he both denied this emphatically.

"I killed him, I tell you! I did! I did!"

She began to call herself names. Mary wanted to stop her, but Tod told her not to. Faye had begun to act and he felt that if they didn't interfere she would manage an escape for herself.

"She'll talk herself quiet," he said.

In a voice heavy with self-accusation, she began to tell what had happened. She had come home from the studio and found Harry in bed. She asked him how he was, but didn't wait for an answer. Instead, she turned her back on him to examine herself in the wall mirror. While fixing her face, she told him that she had seen Ben Murphy and that Ben had said if Harry were feeling better he might be able to use him in a Bowery sequence. She had been surprised when he didn't shout as he always did when Ben's name was mentioned. He was jealous of Ben and always shouted, "To hell with that bastard; I knew him when he cleaned spittoons in a nigger barroom."

She realized that he must be pretty sick. She didn't turn around because she noticed what looked like the beginning of a pimple. It was only a speck of dirt and she wiped it off, but then she had to do her face all over again. While she was working at it, she told him that she could get a job as a dress extra if she had a new evening gown. Just to kid him, she looked tough and said, "If you can't buy me an evening gown, I'll find someone who can."

When he didn't say anything, she got sore and began to sing, "Jeepers Creepers." He didn't tell her to shut up, so she knew something must be wrong. She ran over to the couch. He was dead.

As soon as she had finished telling all this, she began to sob in a lower key, almost a coo, and rocked herself back and forth.

"Poor papa . . . Poor darling . . ."

The fun they used to have together when she was little. No matter how hard up he was, he always bought her dolls and candy, and no matter how tired, he always played with her. She used to ride piggy-back and they would roll on the floor and laugh and laugh.

Mary's sobs made Faye speed up her own and they both began to get out of hand.

There was a knock on the door. Tod answered it and found Mrs. Johnson, the janitress. Faye shook her head for him not to let her in.

"Come back later," Tod said.

He shut the door in her face. A minute later it opened again and Mrs. Johnson entered boldly. She had used a pass-key.

"Get out," he said.

She tried to push past him, but he held her until Faye told him to let her go.

He disliked Mrs. Johnson intensely. She was an officious, bustling woman with a face like a baked apple, soft and blotched. Later he found out that her hobby was funerals. Her preoccupation with them wasn't morbid; it was formal. She was interested in the arrangement of the flowers, the order of the procession, the clothing and deportment of the mourners.

She went straight to Faye and stopped her sobs with a firm, "Now, Miss Greener."

There was so much authority in her voice and manner that she succeeded where Mary and Tod had failed.

Faye looked up at her respectfully.

"First, my dear," Mrs. Johnson said, counting one with the thumb of her right hand on the index finger of her left, "first, I want you to understand that my sole desire in this matter is to help you."

She looked hard at Mary, then at Tod.

"I don't get anything out of it, and it's just a lot of trouble."

"Yes," Faye said.

"All right. There are several things I have to know, if I'm to help you. Did the deceased leave any money or insurance?"

"No."

"Have you any money?"

"No."

"Can you borrow any?"

"I don't think so."

Mrs. Johnson sighed.

"Then the city will have to bury him."

Faye didn't comment.

"Don't you understand, child, the city will have to bury him in a pauper's grave?"

She put so much contempt into "city" and horror into "pauper" that Faye flushed and began to sob again.

Mrs. Johnson made as though to walk out, even took several steps in the direction of the door, then changed her mind and came back.

"How much does a funeral cost?" Faye asked.

"Two hundred dollars. But you can pay on the installment plan—fifty dollars down and twenty-five a month."

Mary and Tod both spoke together.

"I'll get the money."

"I've got some."

"That's fine," Mrs. Johnson said. "You'll need at least fifty more for incidental expenses. I'll go ahead and take care of everything. Mr. Holsepp will bury your father. He'll do it right."

She shook hands with Faye, as though she were congratulating her, and hurried out of the room.

Mrs. Johnson's little business talk had apparently done Faye some good. Her lips were set and her eyes dry.

"Don't worry," Tod said. "I can raise the money."

"No, thanks," she said.

Mary opened her purse and took out a roll of bills.

"Here's some."

"No," she said, pushing it away.

She sat thinking for a while, then went to the dressing table and began to fix her tear-stained face. She wore a hard smile as she worked. Suddenly she turned, lipstick in air, and spoke to Mary.

"Can you get me into Mrs. Jenning's?"

"What for?" Tod demanded. "I'll get the money."

Both girls ignored him.

"Sure," said Mary, "you ought to done that long ago. It's a soft touch."

Faye laughed.

"I was saving it."

The change that had come over both of them startled Tod. They had suddenly become very tough.

"For a punkola like that Earle. Get smart, girlie, and lay off the cheapies. Let him ride a horse, he's a cowboy, ain't he?"

They laughed shrilly and went into the bathroom with their arms around each other.

Tod thought he understood their sudden change to slang. It made them feel worldly and realistic, and so more able to cope with serious things.

He knocked on the bathroom door.

"What do *you* want?" Faye called out.

"Listen, kid," he said, trying to imitate them. "Why go on the turf? I can get the dough."

"Oh, yeah! No, thanks," Faye said.

"But listen . . ." he began again.

"Go peddle your tripe!" Mary shouted.

17

On the day of Harry's funeral Tod was drunk. He hadn't seen Faye since she went off with Mary Dove, but he knew that he was certain to find her at the undertaking parlor and he wanted to have the courage to quarrel with her. He started drinking at lunch. When he got to Holsepp's in the late afternoon, he had passed the brave state and was well into the ugly one.

He found Harry in his box, waiting to be wheeled out for exhibition in the adjoining chapel. The casket was open and the old man looked quite snug. Drawn up to a little below his shoulders and folded back to show its fancy lining was an ivory satin coverlet. Under his head was a tiny lace cushion. He was wearing a Tuxedo, or at least had on a black bow tie with his stiff shirt and wing collar. His face had been newly shaved, his eyebrows shaped and plucked and his lips and cheeks rouged. He looked like the interlocutor in a minstrel show.

Tod bowed his head as though in silent prayer when he heard someone come in. He recognized Mrs. Johnson's voice and turned carefully to face her. He caught her eye and nodded, but she ignored him. She was busy with a man in a badly fitting frock coat.

"It's the principle of the thing," she scolded. "Your estimate said bronze. Those handles ain't bronze and you know it."

"But I asked Miss Greener," whined the man. "She okayed them."

"I don't care. I'm surprised at you, trying to save a few dollars by fobbing off a set of cheap gun-metal handles on the poor child."

Tod didn't wait for the undertaker to answer. He had seen Faye pass the door on the arm of one of the Lee sisters. When he caught up with her, he didn't know what to say. She misunderstood his agitation and was touched. She sobbed a little for him.

She had never looked more beautiful. She was wearing a new, very tight black dress and her platinum hair was tucked up in a shining bun under a black straw sailor. Ever so often, she carried a tiny lace handkerchief to 'her eyes and made it flutter there for a moment. But all he could think of was that she had earned the money for her outfit on her back.

She grew uneasy under his stare and started to edge away. He caught her arm.

"May I speak with you for a minute, alone?"

Miss Lee took the hint and left.

"What is it?" Faye asked.

"Not here," he whispered, making mystery out of his uncertainty.

He led her along the hall until he found an empty showroom. On the walls were framed photographs of important funerals and on little stands and tables were samples of coffin materials, and models of tombstones and mausoleums.

Not knowing what to say, he accented his awkwardness, playing the inoffensive fool.

She smiled and became almost friendly.

"Give out, you big dope."

"A kiss . . ."

"Sure, baby," she laughed, "only don't muss me." They pecked at each other.

She tried to get away, but he held her. She became annoyed and demanded an explanation. He searched his head for one. It wasn't his head he should have searched, however.

She was leaning toward him, drooping slightly, but not from fatigue. He had seen young birches droop like that at midday when they are over-heavy with sun.

"You're drunk," she said, pushing him away.

"Please," he begged.

"Le'go, you bastard."

Raging at him, she was still beautiful. That was because her beauty was structural like a tree's, not a quality of her mind or heart. Perhaps even whoring couldn't damage it for that reason, only age or accident or disease.

In a minute she would scream for help. He had to say something. She wouldn't understand the aesthetic argument and with what values could he back up the moral one? The economic didn't make sense either. Whoring certainly paid. Half of the customer's thirty dollars. Say ten men a week.

She kicked at his shins, but he held on to her. Suddenly he began to talk. He had found an argument. Disease would destroy her beauty. He shouted at her like a Y.M.C.A. lecturer on sex hygiene.

She stopped struggling and held her head down, sobbing fitfully. When he was through, he let go of her arms and she bolted from the room. He groped his way to a carved, marble coffin.

He was still sitting there when a young man in a black jacket and gray striped trousers came in.

"Are you here for the Greener funeral?"

Tod stood up and nodded vaguely.

"The services are beginning," the man said, then opened a little casket covered with grosgrain satin and took out a dust cloth. Tod watched him go around the showroom wiping off the samples.

"Services have probably started," the man repeated with a wave at the door.

Tod understood this time and left. The only exit he could find led through the chapel. The moment he entered it, Mrs. Johnson caught him and directed him to a seat.

He wanted badly to get away, but it was impossible to do so without making a scene.

Faye was sitting in the front row of benches, facing the pulpit. She had the Lee sisters on one side and Mary Dove and Abe Kusich on the other. Behind them sat the tenants of the San Berdoo, occupying about six rows. Tod was alone in the seventh. After him were several empty rows and then a scattering of men and women who looked very much out of place.

He turned in order not to see Faye's jerking shoulders and examined the people in the last rows. He knew their kind. While not torch-bearers themselves, they would run behind the fire and do a great deal of the shouting. They had come to see Harry buried, hoping for a dramatic incident of some sort, hoping at least for one of the mourners to be led weeping hysterically from the chapel. It seemed to Tod that they stared back at him with an expression of vicious, acrid boredom that trembled on the edge of violence. When they began to mutter among themselves, he half-turned and watched them out of the corner of his eyes.

An old woman with a face pulled out of shape by badly-fitting store teeth came in and whispered to a man sucking on the handle of a home-made walking stick. He passed her message along and they all stood up and went out hurriedly. Tod guessed that some star had been seen going into a restaurant by one of their scouts. If so, they would wait outside the place for hours until the star came out again or the police drove them away.

The Gingo family arrived soon after they had left. The Gingos were Eskimos who had been brought to Hollywood to make retakes for a picture about polar exploration. Although it had been released long ago, they refused to return to Alaska. They liked Hollywood.

Harry had been a good friend of theirs and had eaten

with them quite regularly, sharing the smoked salmon, white fish, marinated and maatjes herrings they bought at Jewish delicatessen stores. He also shared the great quantities of cheap brandy they mixed with hot water and salt butter and drank out of tin cups.

Mama and Papa Gingo, trailed by their son, moved down the center aisle of the chapel, bowing and waving to everyone, until they reached the front row. Here they gathered around Faye and shook hands with her, each one in turn. Mrs. Johnson tried to make them go to one of the back rows, but they ignored her orders and sat down in front.

The overhead lights of the chapel were suddenly dimmed. Simultaneously other lights went on behind imitation stained-glass windows which hung on the fake oak-paneled walls. There was a moment of hushed silence, broken only by Faye's sobs, then an electric organ started to play a recording of one of Bach's chorales, "Come Redeemer, Our Saviour."

Tod recognized the music. His mother often played a piano adaptation of it on Sundays at home. It very politely asked Christ to come, in clear and honest tones with just the proper amount of supplication. The God it invited was not the King of Kings, but a shy and gentle Christ, a maiden surrounded by maidens, and the invitation was to a lawn fete, not to the home of some weary, suffering sinner. It didn't plead; it urged with infinite grace and delicacy, almost as though it were afraid of frightening the prospective guest.

So far as Tod could tell, no one was listening to the music. Faye was sobbing and the others seemed busy inside themselves. Bach politely serenading Christ was not for them.

The music would soon change its tone and grow exciting. He wondered if that would make any difference. Already the bass was beginning to throb. He noticed that it made the Eskimos uneasy. As the bass gained in power and began to dominate the treble, he heard Papa Gingo grunt with pleasure. Mama caught Mrs. Johnson eyeing him, and put her fat hand on the back of his head to keep him quiet.

"Now come, O our Saviour," the music begged. Gone was its diffidence and no longer was it polite. Its struggle with the bass had changed it. Even a hint of a threat crept in and a little impatience. Of doubt, however, he could not detect the slightest trace.

If there was a hint of a threat, he thought, just a hint, and a tiny bit of impatience, could Bach be blamed? After all, when he wrote this music, the world had already been waiting for its lover more than seventeen hundred years. But the music changed again and both threat and impatience disappeared. The treble soared free and triumphant and the bass no longer struggled to keep it down. It had become a rich accompaniment. "Come or don't come," the music seemed to say, "I love you and my love is enough." It was a simple statement of fact, neither cry nor serenade, made without arrogance or humility.

Perhaps Christ heard. If He did, He gave no sign. The attendants heard, for it was their cue to trundle on Harry in his box. Mrs. Johnson followed close behind and saw to it that the casket was properly placed. She raised her hand and Bach was silenced in the middle of a phrase.

"Will those of you who wish to view the deceased before the sermon please step forward?" she called out.

Only the Gingos stood up immediately. They made for the coffin in a group. Mrs. Johnson held them back and motioned for Faye to look first. Supported by Mary Dove and the Lee girls, she took a quick peek, increased the tempo of her sobs for a moment, then hurried back to the bench.

The Gingos had their chance next. They leaned over the coffin and told each other something in a series of thick, explosive gutturals. When they tried to take another look, Mrs. Johnson herded them firmly to their seats.

The dwarf sidled up to the box, made a play with his handkerchief and retreated. When no one followed him, Mrs. Johnson lost patience, seeming to take what she understood as a lack of interest for a personal insult.

"Those who wish to view the remains of the late Mr. Greener must do so at once," she barked.

There was a little stir, but no one stood up.

"You, Mrs. Gail," she finally said, looking directly at the person named. "How about you? Don't you want a last look? Soon all that remains of your neighbor will be buried forever."

There was no getting out of it. Mrs. Gail moved down the aisle, trailed by several others.

Tod used them to cover his escape.

18

Faye moved out of the San Berdoo the day after the funeral. Tod didn't know where she had gone and was getting up the courage to call Mrs. Jenning when he saw her from the window of his office. She was dressed in the costume of a Napoleonic vivandière. By the time he got the window open, she had almost turned the corner of the building. He shouted for her to wait. She waved, but when he got downstairs she was gone.

From her dress, he was sure that she was working in the picture called "Waterloo." He asked a studio policeman where the company was shooting and was told on the back lot. He started toward it at once. A platoon of cuirassiers, big men mounted on gigantic horses, went by. He knew that they must be headed for the same set and followed them. They broke into a gallop and he was soon outdistanced.

The sun was very hot. His eyes and throat were choked with the dust thrown up by the horses' hooves and his head throbbed. The only bit of shade he could find was under an ocean liner made of painted canvas with real lifeboats hanging from its davits. He stood in its narrow shadow for a while, then went on toward a great forty-foot papier mâché sphinx that loomed up in the distance. He had to cross a desert to reach it, a desert that was continually being made larger by a fleet of trucks dumping white sand. He had gone only a few feet when a man with a megaphone ordered him off.

He skirted the desert, making a wide turn to the right, and came to a Western street with a plank sidewalk. On the porch of the "Last Chance Saloon" was a rocking chair. He sat down on it and lit a cigarette.

From there he could see a jungle compound with a water buffalo tethered to the side of a conical grass hut. Every few seconds the animal groaned musically. Suddenly an Arab charged by on a white stallion. He shouted at the man, but got no answer. A little while later he saw a truck with a load of snow and several malamute dogs. He shouted again. The driver shouted something back, but didn't stop.

Throwing away his cigarette, he went through the swinging doors of the saloon. There was no back to the building and he found himself in a Paris street. He followed it to its end, coming out in a Romanesque courtyard. He heard voices a short distance away and went toward them. On a lawn of fiber, a group of men and women in riding costume were picnicking. They were eating cardboard food in front of a cellophane waterfall. He started toward them to ask his way, but was stopped by a man who scowled and held up a sign—"Quiet, Please, We're Shooting."

When Tod took another step forward, the man shook his fist threateningly.

Next he came to a small pond with large celluloid swans floating on it. Across one end was a bridge with a sign that read, "To Kamp Komfit." He crossed the bridge and followed a little path that ended at a Greek temple dedicated to Eros. The god himself lay face downward in a pile of old newspapers and bottles.

From the steps of the temple, he could see in the distance a road lined with Lombardy poplars. It was the one on which he had lost the cuirassiers. He pushed his way through a tangle of briars, old flats and iron junk, skirting the skeleton of a Zeppelin, a bamboo stockade, an adobe fort, the wooden horse of Troy, a flight of baroque palace stairs that started in a bed of weeds and ended against the branches of an oak, part of the Fourteenth Street elevated station, a Dutch windmill, the bones of a dinosaur, the upper half of the Merrimac, a corner of a Mayan temple, until he finally reached the road.

He was out of breath. He sat down under one of the poplars on a rock made of brown plaster and took off his jacket. There was a cool breeze blowing and he soon felt more comfortable.

He had lately begun to think not only of Goya and Daumier but also of certain Italian artists of the seventeenth and eighteenth centuries, of Salvator Rosa, Francesco Guardi and Monsu Desiderio, the painters of Decay and Mystery. Looking downhill now, he could see compositions that might have actually been arranged from the Calabrian work of Rosa. There were partially demolished buildings and broken monuments, half-hidden by great, tortured trees, whose exposed roots writhed dramatically in the arid ground, and by shrubs that carried, not flowers or berries, but armories of spikes, hooks and swords.

For Guardi and Desiderio there were bridges which

bridged nothing, sculpture in trees, palaces that seemed of marble until a whole stone portico began to flap in the light breeze. And there were figures as well. A hundred yards from where Tod was sitting a man in a derby hat leaned drowsily against the gilded poop of a Venetian barque and peeled an apple. Still farther on, a charwoman on a stepladder was scrubbing with soap and water the face of a Buddha thirty feet high.

He left the road and climbed across the spine of the hill to look down on the other side. From there he could see a ten-acre field of cockleburs spotted with clumps of sunflowers and wild gum. In the center of the field was a gigantic pile of sets, flats and props. While he watched, a ten-ton truck added another load to it. This was the final dumping ground. He thought of Janvier's "Sargasso Sea." Just as that imaginary body of water was a history of civilization in the form of a marine junkyard, the studio lot was one in the form of a dream dump. A Sargasso of the imagination! And the dump grew continually, for there wasn't a dream afloat somewhere which wouldn't sooner or later turn up on it, having first been made photographic by plaster, canvas, lath and paint. Many boats sink and never reach the Sargasso, but no dream ever entirely disappears. Somewhere it troubles some unfortunate person and some day, when that person has been sufficiently troubled, it will be reproduced on the lot.

When he saw a red glare in the sky and heard the rumble of cannon, he knew it must be Waterloo. From around a bend in the road trotted several cavalry regiments. They wore casques and chest armor of black cardboard and carried long horse pistols in their saddle holsters. They were Victor Hugo's soldiers. He had worked on some of the drawings for their uniforms himself, following carefully the descriptions in "Les Miserables."

He went in the direction they took. Before long he was

passed by the men of Lefebvre-Desnouttes, followed by a regiment of gendarmes d'élite, several companies of chasseurs of the guard and a flying detachment of Rimbaud's lancers.

They must be moving up for the disastrous attack on La Haite Santée. He hadn't read the scenario and wondered if it had rained yesterday. Would Grouchy or Bulcher arrive? Grotenstein, the producer, might have changed it.

The sound of cannon was becoming louder all the time and the red fan in the sky more intense. He could smell the sweet, pungent odor of blank powder. It might be over before he could get there. He started to run. When he topped a rise after a sharp bend in the road, he found a great plain below him covered with early nineteenth-century troops, wearing all the gay and elaborate uniforms that used to please him so much when he was a child and spent long hours looking at the soldiers in an old dictionary. At the far end of the field, he could see an enormous hump around which the English and their allies were gathered. It was Mont St. Jean and they were getting ready to defend it gallantly. It wasn't quite finished, however, and swarmed with grips, property men, set dressers, carpenters and painters.

Tod stood near a eucalyptus tree to watch, concealing himself behind a sign that read, " 'Waterloo'—A Charles H. Grotenstein Production." Nearby a youth in a carefully torn horse guard's uniform was being rehearsed in his lines by one of the assistant directors.

"Vive l'Empereur!" the young man shouted, then clutched his breast and fell forward dead. The assistant director was a hard man to please and made him do it over and over again.

In the center of the plain, the battle was going ahead briskly. Things looked tough for the British and their allies.

The Prince of Orange commanding the center, Hill the right and Picton the left wing, were being pressed hard by the veteran French. The desperate and intrepid Prince was in an especially bad spot. Tod heard him cry hoarsely above the din of battle, shouting to the Hollande-Belgians, "Nassau! Brunswick! Never retreat!" Nevertheless, the retreat began. Hill, too, fell back. The French killed General Picton with a ball through the head and he returned to his dressing room. Alten was put to the sword and also retired. The colors of the Lunenberg battalion, borne by a prince of the family of Deux-Ponts, were captured by a famous child star in the uniform of a Parisian drummer boy. The Scotch Greys were destroyed and went to change into another uniform. Ponsonby's heavy dragoons were also cut to ribbons. Mr. Grotenstein would have a large bill to pay at the Western Costume Company.

Neither Napoleon nor Wellington was to be seen. In Wellington's absence, one of the assistant directors, a Mr. Crane, was in command of the allies. He reinforced his center with one of Chasse's brigades and one of Wincke's. He supported these with infantry from Brunswick, Welsh foot, Devon yeomanry and Hanoverian light horse with oblong leather caps and flowing plumes of horsehair.

For the French, a man in a checked cap ordered Milhaud's cuirassiers to carry Mont St. Jean. With their sabers in their teeth and their pistols in their hands, they charged. It was a fearful sight.

The man in the checked cap was making a fatal error. Mont St. Jean was unfinished. The paint was not yet dry and all the struts were not in place. Because of the thickness of the cannon smoke, he had failed to see that the hill was still being worked on by property men, grips and carpenters.

It was the classic mistake, Tod realized, the same one Napoleon had made. Then it had been wrong for a different reason. The Emperor had ordered the cuirassiers to charge Mont St. Jean not knowing that a deep ditch was hidden at its foot to trap his heavy cavalry. The result had been disaster for the French; the beginning of the end.

This time the same mistake had a different outcome. Waterloo, instead of being the end of the Grand Army, resulted in a draw. Neither side won, and it would have to be fought over again the next day. Big losses, however, were sustained by the insurance company in workmen's compensation. The man in the checked cap was sent to the dog house by Mr. Grotenstein just as Napoleon was sent to St. Helena.

When the front rank of Milhaud's heavy division started up the slope of Mont St. Jean, the hill collapsed. The noise was terrific. Nails screamed with agony as they pulled out of joists. The sound of ripping canvas was like that of little children whimpering. Lath and scantling snapped as though they were brittle bones. The whole hill folded like an enormous umbrella and covered Napoleon's army with painted cloth.

It turned into a route. The victors of Bersina, Leipsic, Austerlitz, fled like schoolboys who had broken a pane of glass. "Sauve qui peut!" they cried, or, rather, "Scram!"

The armies of England and her allies were too deep in scenery to flee. They had to wait for the carpenters and ambulances to come up. The men of the gallant Seventy-Fifth Highlanders were lifted out of the wreck with block and tackle. They were carted off by the stretcher-bearers, still clinging bravely to their claymores.

19

Tod got a lift back to his office in a studio car. He had to ride on the running board because the seats were occupied by two Walloon grenadiers and four Swabian foot. One of the infantrymen had a broken leg, the other extras were only scratched and bruised. They were quite happy about their wounds. They were certain to receive several extra days' pay, and the man with the broken leg thought he might get as much as five hundred dollars.

When Tod arrived at his office, he found Faye waiting to see him. She hadn't been in the battle. At the last moment, the director had decided not to use any vivandières.

To his surprise, she greeted him with warm friendliness. Nevertheless, he tried to apologize for his behavior in the funeral parlor. He had hardly started before she interrupted him. She wasn't angry, but grateful for his lecture on venereal disease. It had brought her to her senses.

She had still another surprise for him. She was living in Homer Simpson's house. The arrangement was a business one. Homer had agreed to board and dress her until she became a star. They were keeping a record of every cent he spent and as soon as she clicked in pictures, she would pay him back with six per cent interest. To make it absolutely legal, they were going to have a lawyer draw up a contract.

She pressed Tod for an opinion and he said it was a splendid idea. She thanked him and invited him to dinner for the next night.

After she had gone, he wondered what living with her would do to Homer. He thought it might straighten him out. He fooled himself into believing this with an image, as though a man were a piece of iron to be heated and then straightened with hammer blows. He should have known better, for if anyone ever lacked malleability Homer did.

He continued to make this mistake when he had dinner with them. Faye seemed very happy, talking about charge accounts and stupid sales clerks. Homer had a flower in his buttonhole, wore carpet slippers and beamed at her continually.

After they had eaten, while Homer was in the kitchen washing dishes, Tod got her to tell him what they did with themselves all day. She said that they lived quietly and that she was glad because she was tired of excitement. All she wanted was a career. Homer did the housework and she was getting a real rest. Daddy's long sickness had tired her out completely. Homer liked to do housework and anyway he wouldn't let her go into the kitchen because of her hands.

"Protecting his investment," Tod said.

"Yes," she replied seriously, "they have to be beautiful."

They had breakfast around ten, she went on. Homer brought it to her in bed. He took a housekeeping magazine and fixed the tray like the pictures in it. While she bathed and dressed, he cleaned the house. Then they went downtown to the stores and she bought all sorts of things, mostly clothes. They didn't eat lunch on account of her figure, but usually had dinner out and went to the movies.

"Then, ice cream sodas," Homer finished for her, as he came out of the kitchen.

Faye laughed and excused herself. They were going to a picture and she wanted to change her dress. When she had left, Homer suggested that they get some air in the patio. He made Tod take the deck chair while he sat on an upturned orange crate.

If he had been careful and had acted decently, Tod couldn't help thinking, she might be living with him. He was at least better looking than Homer. But then there was her other prerequisite. Homer had an income and lived in a house, while he earned thirty dollars a week and lived in a furnished room.

The happy grin on Homer's face made him feel ashamed

of himself. He was being unfair. Homer was a humble, grateful man who would never laugh at her, who was incapable of laughing at anything. Because of this great quality, she could live with him on what she considered a much higher plane.

"What's the matter?" Homer asked softly, laying one of his heavy hands on Tod's knee.

"Nothing. Why?"

Tod moved so that the hand slipped off.

"You were making faces."

"I was thinking of something."

"Oh," Homer said sympathetically.

Tod couldn't resist asking an ugly question.

"When are you two getting married?"

Homer looked hurt.

"Didn't Faye tell about us?"

"Yes, sort of."

"It's a business arrangement."

"Yes?"

To make Tod believe it, he poured out a long, disjointed argument, the one he must have used on himself. He even went further than the business part and claimed that they were doing it for poor Harry's sake. Faye had nothing left in the world except her career and she must succeed for her daddy's sake. The reason she wasn't a star was because she didn't have the right clothes. He had money and believed in her talent, so it was only natural for them to enter into a business arrangement. Did Tod know a good lawyer?

It was a rhetorical question, but would become a real one, painfully insistent, if Tod smiled. He frowned. That was wrong, too.

"We must see a lawyer this week and have papers drawn up."

His eagerness was pathetic. Tod wanted to help him,

but didn't know what to say. He was still fumbling for an answer when they heard a woman shouting from the hill behind the garage.

"Adore! Adore!"

She had a high soprano voice, very clear and pure.

"What a funny name," Tod said, glad to change the subject.

"Maybe it's a foreigner," Homer said.

The woman came into the yard from around the corner of the garage. She was eager and plump and very American.

"Have you seen my little boy?" she asked, making a gesture of helplessness. "Adore's such a wanderer."

Homer surprised Tod by standing up and smiling at the woman. Faye had certainly helped his timidity.

"Is your son lost?" Homer said.

"Oh, no—just hiding to tease me."

She held out her hand.

"We're neighbors. I'm Maybelle Loomis."

"Glad to know you, ma'am. I'm Homer Simpson and this is Mr. Hackett."

Tod also shook hands with her.

"Have you been living here long?" she asked.

"No. I've just come from the East," Homer said.

"Oh, have you? I've been here ever since Mr. Loomis passed on six years ago. I'm an old settler."

"You like it then?" Tod asked.

"Like California?" she laughed at the idea that anyone might not like it. "Why, it's a paradise on earth!"

"Yes," Homer agreed gravely.

"And anyway," she went on, "I have to live here on account of Adore."

"Is he sick?"

"Oh, no. On account of his career. His agent calls him the biggest little attraction in Hollywood."

She spoke so vehemently that Homer flinched.

"He's in the movies?" Tod asked.

"I'll say," she snapped.

Homer tried to placate her.

"That's very nice."

"If it weren't for favoritism," she said bitterly, "he'd be a star. It ain't talent. It's pull. What's Shirley Temple got that he ain't got?"

"Why, I don't know," Homer mumbled.

She ignored this and let out a fearful bellow.

"Adore! Adore!"

Tod had seen her kind around the studio. She was one of that army of women who drag their children from casting office to casting office and sit for hours, weeks, months, waiting for a chance to show what Junior can do. Some of them are very poor, but no matter how poor, they always manage to scrape together enough money, often by making great sacrifices, to send their children to one of the innumerable talent schools.

"Adore!" she yelled once more, then laughed and became a friendly housewife again, a chubby little person with dimples in her fat cheeks and fat elbows.

"Have you any children, Mr. Simpson?" she asked.

"No," he replied, blushing.

"You're lucky—they're a nuisance."

She laughed to show that she didn't really mean it and called her child again.

"Adore . . . Oh, Adore . . ."

Her next question surprised them both.

"Who do you follow?"

"What?" said Tod.

"I mean—in the Search for Health, along the Road of Life?"

They both gaped at her.

"I'm a raw-foodist, myself," she said. "Dr. Pierce is our

leader. You must have seen his ads—'Know-All Pierce-All.' "

"Oh, yes," Tod said, "you're vegetarians."

She laughed at his ignorance.

"Far from it. We're much stricter. Vegetarians eat cooked vegetables. We eat only raw ones. Death comes from eating dead things."

Neither Tod nor Homer found anything to say.

"Adore," she began again. "Adore . . ."

This time there was an answer from around the corner of the garage.

"Here I am, mama."

A minute later, a little boy appeared dragging behind him a small sailboat on wheels. He was about eight years old, with a pale, peaked face and a large, troubled forehead. He had great staring eyes. His eyebrows had been plucked and shaped carefully. Except for his Buster Brown collar, he was dressed like a man, in long trousers, vest and jacket.

He tried to kiss his mother, but she fended him off and pulled at his clothes, straightening and arranging them with savage little tugs.

"Adore," she said sternly, "I want you to meet Mr. Simpson, our neighbor."

Turning like a soldier at the command of a drill sergeant, he walked up to Homer and grasped his hand.

"A pleasure, sir," he said, bowing stiffly with his heels together.

"That's the way they do it in Europe," Mrs. Loomis beamed. "Isn't he cute?"

"What a pretty sailboat!" Homer said, trying to be friendly.

Both mother and son ignored his comment. She pointed to Tod, and the child repeated his bow and heel-click.

"Well, we've got to go," she said.

Tod watched the child, who was standing a little to one side of his mother and making faces at Homer. He rolled his eyes back in his head so that only the whites showed and twisted his lips in a snarl.

Mrs. Loomis noticed Tod's glance and turned sharply. When she saw what Adore was doing, she yanked him by the arm, jerking him clear off the ground.

"Adore!" she yelled.

To Tod she said apologetically, "He thinks he's the Frankenstein monster."

She picked the boy up, hugging and kissing him ardently. Then she set him down again and fixed his rumpled clothing.

"Won't Adore sing something for us?" Tod asked.

"No," the little boy said sharply.

"Adore," his mother scolded, "sing at once."

"That's all right, if he doesn't feel like it," Homer said.

But Mrs. Loomis was determined to have him sing. She could never permit him to refuse an audience.

"Sing, Adore," she repeated with quiet menace. "Sing 'Mama Doan Wan' No Peas.'"

His shoulders twitched as though they already felt the strap. He tilted his straw sailor over one eye, buttoned up his jacket and did a little strut, then began:

"Mama doan wan' no peas,
An' rice, an' cocoanut oil,
Just a bottle of brandy handy all the day.
Mama doan wan' no peas,
Mama doan wan' no cocoanut oil."

His singing voice was deep and rough and he used the broken groan of the blues singer quite expertly. He moved his body only a little, against rather than in time with the music. The gestures he made with his hands were extremely suggestive.

"Mama doan wan't no gin,
Because gin do make her sin,
Mama doan wan' no glass of gin,
Because it boun' to make her sin,
An' keep her hot and bothered all the day."

He seemed to know what the words meant, or at least his body and his voice seemed to know. When he came to the final chorus, his buttocks writhed and his voice carried a top-heavy load of sexual pain.

Tod and Homer applauded. Adore grabbed the string of his sailboat and circled the yard. He was imitating a tugboat. He tooted several times, then ran off.

"He's just a baby," Mrs. Loomis said proudly, "but he's got loads of talent."

Tod and Homer agreed.

She saw that he was gone again and left hurriedly. They could hear her calling in the brush back of the garage.

"Adore! Adore . . ."

"That's a funny woman," Tod said.

Homer sighed.

"I guess it's hard to get a start in pictures. But Faye is awfully pretty."

Tod agreed. She appeared a moment later in a new flower print dress and picture hat and it was his turn to sigh. She was much more than pretty. She posed, quivering and balanced, on the doorstep and looked down at the two men in the patio. She was smiling, a subtle half-smile uncontaminated by thought. She looked just born, everything moist and fresh, volatile and perfumed. Tod suddenly became very conscious of his dull, insensitive feet bound in dead skin and of his hands, sticky and thick, holding a heavy, rough felt hat.

He tried to get out of going to the pictures with them, but couldn't. Sitting next to her in the dark proved the ordeal he expected it to be. Her self-sufficiency made him squirm and the desire to break its smooth surface with a blow, or at least a sudden obscene gesture, became irresistible.

He began to wonder if he himself didn't suffer from the ingrained, morbid apathy he liked to draw in others. Maybe he could only be galvanized into sensibility and that was why he was chasing Faye.

He left hurriedly, without saying good-bye. He had decided to stop running after her. It was an easy decision to make, but a hard one to carry out. In order to manage it, he fell back on one of the oldest tricks in the very full bag of the intellectual. After all, he told himself, he had drawn her enough times. He shut the portfolio that held the drawings he had made of her, tied it with a string, and put it away in his trunk.

It was a childish trick, hardly worthy of a primitive witch doctor, yet it worked. He was able to avoid her for several months. During this time, he took his pad and pencils on a continuous hunt for other models. He spent his nights at the different Hollywood churches, drawing the worshipers. He visited the "Church of Christ, Physical" where holiness was attained through the constant use of chestweights and spring grips; the "Church Invisible" where fortunes were told and the dead made to find lost objects; the "Tabernacle of the Third Coming" where a woman in male clothing preached the "Crusade Against Salt"; and the "Temple Moderne" under whose glass and chromium roof "Brain-Breathing, the Secret of the Aztecs" was taught.

As he watched these people writhe on the hard seats of their churches, he thought of how well Alessandro Magnasco would dramatize the contrast between their drained-out, feeble bodies and their wild, disordered minds. He would not satirize them as Hogarth or Daumier might, nor would he pity them. He would paint their fury with respect, appreciating its awful, anarchic power and aware that they had it in them to destroy civilization.

One Friday night in the "Tabernacle of the Third Coming," a man near Tod stood up to speak. Although his name most likely was Thompson or Johnson and his home town Sioux City, he had the same countersunk eyes, like the heads of burnished spikes, that a monk by Magnasco might have. He was probably just in from one of the colonies in the desert near Soboba Hot Springs where he had been conning over his soul on a diet of raw fruit and nuts. He was very angry. The message he had brought to the city was one that an illiterate anchorite might have given decadent Rome. It was a crazy jumble of dietary rules, economics and Biblical threats. He claimed to have seen the Tiger of Wrath stalking the walls of the citadel and the Jackal of Lust skulking in the shrubbery, and he connected these omens with "thirty dollars every Thursday" and meat eating.

Tod didn't laugh at the man's rhetoric. He knew it was unimportant. What mattered were his messianic rage and the emotional response of his hearers. They sprang to their feet, shaking their fists and shouting. On the altar someone began to beat a bass drum and soon the entire congregation was singing "Onward Christian Soldiers."

20

As time went on, the relationship between Faye and Homer began to change. She became bored with the life they were leading together and as her boredom deepened, she began to persecute him. At first she did it unconsciously, later maliciously.

Homer realized that the end was in sight even before she did. All he could do to prevent its coming was to increase his servility and his generosity. He waited on her hand and foot. He bought her a coat of summer ermine and a light blue Buick runabout.

His servility was like that of a cringing, clumsy dog, who is always anticipating a blow, welcoming it even, and in a way that makes overwhelming the desire to strike him. His generosity was still more irritating. It was so helpless and unselfish that it made her feel mean and cruel, no matter how hard she tried to be kind. And it was so bulky that she was unable to ignore it. She had to resent it. He was destroying himself, and although he didn't mean it that way, forcing her to accept the blame.

They had almost reached a final crisis when Tod saw them again. Late one night, just as he was preparing for bed, Homer knocked on his door and said that Faye was downstairs in the car and that they wanted him to go to a night club with them.

The outfit Homer wore was very funny. He had on loose blue linen slacks and a chocolate flannel jacket over a yellow polo shirt. Only a Negro could have worn it without looking ridiculous, and no one was ever less a Negro than Homer.

Tod drove with them to the "Cinderella Bar," a little stucco building in the shape of a lady's slipper, on Western Avenue. Its floor show consisted of female impersonators.

Faye was in a nasty mood. When the waiter took their order, she insisted on a champagne cocktail for Homer. He wanted coffee. The waiter brought both, but she made him take the coffee back.

Homer explained painstakingly, as he must have done many times, that he could not drink alcohol because it made him sick. Faye listened with mock patience. When he finished, she laughed and lifted the cocktail to his mouth.

"Drink it, damn you," she said.

She tilted the glass, but he didn't open his mouth and the liquor ran down his chin. He wiped himself, using the napkin without unfolding it.

Faye called the waiter again.

"He doesn't like champagne cocktails," she said. "Bring him brandy."

Homer shook his head.

"Please, Faye," he whimpered.

She held the brandy to his lips, moving the glass when he turned away.

"Come on, sport—bottoms up."

"Let him alone," Tod finally said.

She ignored him as though she hadn't even heard his protest. She was both furious and ashamed of herself. Her shame strengthened her fury and gave it a target.

"Come on, sport," she said savagely, "or mama'll spank."

She turned to Tod.

"I don't like people who won't drink. It isn't sociable. They feel superior and I don't like people who feel superior."

"I don't feel superior," Homer said.

"Oh, yes, you do. I'm drunk and you're sober and so you feel superior. Goddamned, stinking superior."

He opened his mouth to reply and she poured the brandy into it, then clapped her hand over his lips so that he couldn't spit it back. Some of it came out of his nose.

Still without unfolding the napkin, he wiped himself. Faye ordered another brandy. When it came, she held it to his lips again, but this time he took it and drank it himself, fighting the stuff down.

"That's the boy," Faye laughed. "Well done, sloppy-boppy."

Tod asked her to dance in order to give Homer a moment alone. When they reached the floor, she made an attempt to defend herself.

"That guy's superiority is driving me crazy."

"He loves you," Tod said.

"Yeah, I know, but he's such a slob."

She started to cry on his shoulder and he held her very tight. He took a long chance.

"Sleep with me."

"No, baby," she said sympathetically.

"Please, please . . . just once."

"I can't, honey. I don't love you."

"You worked for Mrs. Jenning. Make believe you're still working for her."

She didn't get angry.

"That was a mistake. And anyway, that was different. I only went on call enough times to pay for the funeral and besides those men were complete strangers. You know what I mean?"

"Yes. But please, darling. I'll never bother you again. I'll go east right after. Be kind."

"I can't."

"Why . . . ?"

"I just can't. I'm sorry, darling. I'm not a tease, but I can't like that."

"I love you."

"No, sweetheart, I can't."

They danced until the number finished without saying anything else. He was grateful to her for having behaved so well, for not having made him feel too ridiculous.

When they returned to the table, Homer was sitting exactly as they had left him. He held the folded napkin in one hand and the empty brandy glass in the other. His helplessness was extremely irritating.

"You're right about the brandy, Faye," Homer said. "It's swell! Whoopee!"

He made a little circular gesture with the hand that held the glass.

"I'd like a Scotch," Tod said.

"Me, too," Faye said.

Homer made another gallant attempt to get into the spirit of the evening.

"Garsoon," he called to the waiter, "more drinks."

He grinned at them anxiously. Faye burst out laughing and Homer did his best to laugh with her. When she stopped suddenly, he found himself laughing alone and turned his laugh into a cough, then hid the cough in his napkin.

She turned to Tod.

"What the devil can you do with a slob like that?"

The orchestra started and Tod was able to ignore her question. All three of them turned to watch a young man in a tight evening gown of red silk sing a lullaby.

"Little man, you're crying,
I know why you're blue,
Someone took your kiddycar away;
Better go to sleep now,
Little man, you've had a busy day . . ."

He had a soft, throbbing voice and his gestures were matronly, tender and aborted, a series of unconscious caresses. What he was doing was in no sense parody; it was too simple and too restrained. It wasn't even theatrical. This dark young man with his thin, hairless arms and soft, rounded shoulders, who rocked an imaginary cradle as he crooned, was really a woman.

When he had finished, there was a great deal of applause. The young man shook himself and became an actor again. He tripped on his train, as though he weren't used to it, lifted his skirts to show he was wearing Paris garters, then strode off swinging his shoulders. His imitation of a man was awkward and obscene.

Homer and Tod applauded him.

"I hate fairies," Faye said.

"All women do."

Tod meant it as a joke, but Faye was angry.

"They're dirty," she said.

He started to say something else, but Faye had turned to Homer again. She seemed unable to resist nagging him. This time she pinched his arm until he gave a little squeak.

"Do you know what a fairy is?" she demanded.

"Yes," he said hesitatingly.

"All right, then," she barked. "Give out! What's a fairy?"

Homer twisted uneasily, as though he already felt the ruler on his behind, and looked imploring at Tod, who tried to help him by forming the word "homo" with his lips.

"Momo," Homer said.

Faye burst out laughing. But his hurt look made it impossible not to relent, so she patted his shoulder.

"What a hick," she said.

He grinned gratefully and signaled the waiter to bring another round of drinks.

The orchestra began to play and a man came over to ask Faye to dance. Without saying a word to Homer, she followed him to the floor.

"Who's that?" Homer asked, chasing them with his eyes.

Tod made believe he knew and said that he had often seen him around the San Berdoo. His explanation satisfied Homer, but at the same time set him to thinking of something else. Tod could almost see him shaping a question in his head.

"Do you know Earle Shoop?" Homer finally asked.

"Yes."

Homer then poured out a long, confused story about a dirty black hen. He kept referring to the hen again and again, as though it were the one thing he couldn't stand

about Earle and the Mexican. For a man who was incapable of hatred, he managed to draw a pretty horrible picture of the bird.

"You never saw such a disgusting thing, the way it
squats and turns its head. The roosters have torn all the
feathers off its neck and made its comb all bloody and it
has scabby feet covered with warts and it cackles so nasty
when they drop it into the pen."

"Who drops it into what pen?"

"The Mexican."

"Miguel?"

"Yes. He's almost as bad as his hen."

"You've been to their camp?"

"Camp?"

"In the mountains?"

"No. They're living in the garage. Faye asked me if I
minded if a friend of hers lived in the garage for a while
because he was broke. But I didn't know about the chickens or the Mexican. . . . Lots of people are out of work
nowadays."

"Why don't you throw them out?"

"They're broke and they have no place to go. It isn't
very comfortable living in a garage."

"But if they don't behave?"

"It's just that hen. I don't mind the roosters, they're
pretty, but that dirty hen. She shakes her dirty feathers
each time and clucks so nasty."

"You don't have to look at it."

"They do it every afternoon at the same time when I'm
usually sitting in the chair in the sun after I get back from
shopping with Faye and just before dinner. The Mexican
knows I don't like to see it so he tries to make me look just
for spite. I go into the house, but he taps on the windows
and calls me to come out and watch. I don't call that fun.
Some people have funny ideas of what's fun."

"What's Faye say?"

"She doesn't mind the hen. She says it's only natural."

Then, in case Tod should mistake this for criticism, he told him what a fine, wholesome child she was. Tod agreed, but brought him back to the subject.

"If I were you," he said, "I'd report the chickens to the police. You have to have a permit to keep chickens in the city. I'd do something and damned quick."

Homer avoided a direct answer.

"I wouldn't touch that thing for all the money in the world. She's all over scabs and almost naked. She looks like a buzzard. She eats meat. I saw her one time eating some meat that the Mexican got out of the garbage can. He feeds the roosters grain but the hen eats garbage and he keeps her in a dirty box."

"If I were you, I'd throw those bastards out and their birds with them."

"No, they're nice enough young fellows, just down on their luck, like a lot of people these days, you know. It's just that hen . . ."

He shook his head wearily, as though he could smell and taste her.

Faye was coming back. Homer saw that Tod was going to speak to her about Earle and the Mexican and signaled desperately for him not to do it. She, however, caught him at it and was curious.

"What have you guys been chinning about?"

"You, darling," Tod said. "Homer has a t.l. for you."

"Tell me, Homer."

"No, first you tell me one."

"Well, the man I just danced with asked me if you were a movie big shot."

Tod saw that Homer was unable to think of a return compliment so he spoke for him.

"I said you were the most beautiful girl in the place."

"Yes," Homer agreed. "That's what Tod said."

"I don't believe it. Tod hates me. And anyway, I caught you telling him to keep quiet. You were shushing him."

She laughed.

"I bet I know what you were talking about." She mimicked Homer's excited disgust. " 'That dirty black hen, she's all over scabs and almost naked.' "

Homer laughed apologetically, but Tod was angry.

"What's the idea of keeping those guys in the garage?" he demanded.

"What the hell is it your business?" she replied, but not with real anger. She was amused.

"Homer enjoys their company. Don't you, sloppy-boppy?"

"I told Tod they were nice fellows just down on their luck like a lot of people these days. There's an awful lot of unemployment going around."

"That's right," she said. "If they go, I go."

Tod had guessed as much. He realized there was no use in saying anything. Homer was again signaling for him to keep quiet.

For some reason or other, Faye suddenly became ashamed of herself. She apologized to Tod by offering to dance with him again, flirting as she suggested it. Tod refused.

She broke the silence that followed by a eulogy of Miguel's game chickens, which was really meant to be an excuse for herself. She described what marvelous fighters the birds were, how much Miguel loved them and what good care he took of them.

Homer agreed enthusiastically. Tod remained silent. She asked him if he had ever seen a cock fight and invited him to the garage for the next night. A man from San Diego was coming north with his birds to pit them against Miguel's.

When she turned to Homer again, he leaned away as though she were going to hit him. She flushed with shame at this and looked at Tod to see if he had noticed. The rest of the evening, she tried to be nice to Homer. She even touched him a little, straightening his collar and patting his hair smooth. He beamed happily.

21

When Tod told Claude Estee about the cock fight, he wanted to go with him. They drove to Homer's place together.

It was one of those blue and lavender nights when the luminous color seems to have been blown over the scene with an air brush. Even the darkest shadows held some purple.

A car stood in the driveway of the garage with its headlights on. They could see several men in the corner of the building and could hear their voices. Someone laughed, using only two notes, ha-ha and ha-ha, over and over again.

Tod stepped ahead to make himself known, in case they were taking precautions against the police. When he entered the light, Abe Kusich and Miguel greeted him, but Earle didn't.

"The fights are off," Abe said. "That stinkola from Diego didn't get here."

Claude came up and Tod introduced him to the three men. The dwarf was arrogant, Miguel gracious and Earle his usual wooden, surly self.

Most of the garage floor had been converted into a pit, an oval space about nine feet long and seven or eight wide. It was floored with an old carpet and walled by a low, ragged fence made of odd pieces of lath and wire. Faye's coupe stood in the driveway, placed so that its headlights flooded the arena.

Claude and Tod followed Abe out of the glare and sat down with him on an old trunk in the back of the garage. Earle and Miguel came in and squatted on their heels facing them. They were both wearing blue denims, polka-dot shirts, big hats and high-heeled boots. They looked very handsome and picturesque.

They sat smoking silently, all of them calm except the dwarf, who was fidgety. Although he had plenty of room, he suddenly gave Tod a shove.

"Get over, lard-ass," he snarled.

Tod moved, crowding against Claude, without saying anything. Earle laughed at Tod rather than the dwarf, but the dwarf turned on him anyway.

"Why, you punkola! Who you laughing at?"

"You," Earle said.

"That so, hah? Well, listen to me, you pee-hole bandit, for two cents I'd knock you out of them prop boots."

Earle reached into his shirt pocket and threw a coin on the ground.

"There's a nickel," he said.

The dwarf started to get off the trunk, but Tod caught him by the collar. He didn't try to get loose, but leaned forward against his coat, like a terrier in a harness, and wagged his great head from side to side.

"Go on," he sputtered, "you fugitive from the Western Costume Company, you . . . you louse in a fright-wig, you."

Earle would have been much less angry if he could have thought of a snappy comeback. He mumbled something about a half-pint bastard, then spat. He hit the instep of the dwarf's shoe with a big gob of spittle.

"Nice shot," Miguel said.

This was apparently enough for Earle to consider himself the winner, for he smiled and became quiet. The dwarf slapped Tod's hand away from his collar with a curse and settled down on the trunk again.

"He ought to wear gaffs," Miguel said.

"I don't need them for a punk like that."

They all laughed and everything was fine again.

Abe leaned across Tod to speak to Claude.

"It would have been a swell main," he said. "There was more than a dozen guys here before you come and some of them with real dough. I was going to make book."

He took out his wallet and gave him one of his business cards.

"It was in the bag," Miguel said. "I got five birds that would of won easy and two sure losers. We would of made a killing."

"I've never seen a chicken fight," Claude said. "In fact, I've never even seen a game chicken."

Miguel offered to show him one of his birds and left to get it. Tod went down to the car for the bottle of whiskey they had left in a side pocket. When he got back, Miguel was holding Jujutala in the light. They all examined the bird.

Miguel held the cock firmly with both hands, somewhat in the manner that a basketball is held for an underhand toss. The bird had short, oval wings and a heart-shaped tail that stood at right angles to its body. It had a triangular head, like a snake's, terminating in a slightly curved beak, thick at the base and fine at the point. All its feathers were so tight and hard that they looked as though they had been varnished. They had been thinned out for fighting and the lines of its body, which was like a truncated wedge, stood out plainly. From between Miguel's fingers dangled its long, bright orange legs and its slightly darker feet with their horn nails.

"Juju was bred by John R. Bowes of Lindale, Texas,"

Miguel said proudly. "He's a six times winner. I give fifty dollars and a shotgun for him."

"He's a nice bird," the dwarf said grudgingly, "but looks ain't everything."

Claude took out his wallet.

"I'd like to see him fight," he said. "Suppose you sell me one of your other birds and I put it against him."

Miguel thought a while and looked at Earle, who told him to go ahead.

"I've got a bird I'll sell you for fifteen bucks," he said.

The dwarf interfered.

"Let me pick the bird."

"Oh, I don't care," Claude said, "I just want to see a fight. Here's your fifteen."

Earle took the money and Miguel told him to get Hermano, the big red.

"That red'll go over eight pounds," he said, "while Juju won't go more than six."

Earle came back carrying a large rooster that had a silver shawl. He looked like an ordinary barnyard fowl.

When the dwarf saw him, he became indignant.

"What do you call that, a goose?"

"That's one of Street's Butcher Boys," Miguel said.

"I wouldn't bait a hook with him," the dwarf said.

"You don't have to bet," Earle mumbled.

The dwarf eyed the bird and the bird eyed him. He turned to Claude.

"Let me handle him for you, mister," he said.

Miguel spoke quickly.

"Earle'll do it. He knows the cock."

The dwarf exploded at this.

"It's a frame-up!" he yelled.

He tried to take the red, but Earle held the bird high in the air out of the little man's reach.

Miguel opened the trunk and took out a small wooden

box, the kind chessmen are kept in. It was full of curved gaffs, small squares of chamois with holes in their centers and bits of waxed string like that used by a shoemaker.

They crowded around to watch him arm Juju. First he wiped the short stubs on the cock's legs to make sure they were clean and then placed a leather square over one of them so that the stub came through the hole. He then fitted a gaff over it and fastened it with a bit of the soft string, wrapping very carefully. He did the same to the other leg.

When he had finished, Earle started on the big red.

"That's a bird with lots of cojones," Miguel said. "He's won plenty fights. He don't look fast maybe, but he's fast all right and he packs an awful wallop."

"Strictly for the cook stove, if you ask me," the dwarf said.

Earle took out a pair of shears and started to lighten the red's plumage. The dwarf watched him cut away most of the bird's tail, but when he began to work on the breast, he caught his hand.

"Leave him be!" he barked. "You'll kill him fast that way. He needs that stuff for protection."

He turned to Claude again.

"Please, mister, let me handle him."

"Make him buy a share in the bird," Miguel said.

Claude laughed and motioned for Earle to give Abe the bird. Earle didn't want to and looked meaningly at Miguel.

The dwarf began to dance with rage.

"You're trying to cold-deck us!" he screamed.

"Aw, give it to him," Miguel said.

The little man tucked the bird under his left arm so that his hands were free and began to look over the gaffs in the box. They were all the same length, three inches, but some had more pronounced curves than the others. He selected a pair and explained his strategy to Claude.

"He's going to do most of his fighting on his back. This pair'll hit right that way. If he could get over the other bird, I wouldn't use them."

He got down on his knees and honed the gaffs on the cement floor until they were like needles.

"Have we a chance?" Tod asked.

"You can't ever tell," he said, shaking his extra large head. "He feels almost like a dead bird."

After adjusting the gaffs with great care, he looked the bird over, stretching its wings and blowing its feathers in order to see its skin.

"The comb ain't bright enough for fighting condition," he said, pinching it, "but he looks strong. He may have been a good one once."

He held the bird in the light and looked at its head. When Miguel saw him examining its beak, he told him anxiously to quit stalling. But the dwarf paid no attention and went on muttering to himself. He motioned for Tod and Claude to look.

"What'd I tell you!" he said, puffing with indignation. "We've been cold-decked."

He pointed to a hair line running across the top of the bird's beak.

"That's not a crack," Miguel protested, "it's just a mark."

He reached for the bird as though to rub its beak and the bird pecked savagely at him. This pleased the dwarf.

"We'll fight," he said, "but we won't bet."

Earle was to referee. He took a piece of chalk and drew three lines in the center of the pit, a long one in the middle and two shorter ones parallel to it and about three feet away.

"Pit your cocks," he called.

"No, bill them first," the dwarf protested.

He and Miguel stood at arm's length and thrust their birds together to anger them. Juju caught the big red by the comb and held on viciously until Miguel jerked him away. The red, who had been rather apathetic, came to life and the dwarf had trouble holding him. The two men thrust their birds together again, and again Juju caught the red's comb. The big cock became frantic with rage and struggled to get at the smaller bird.

"We're ready," the dwarf said.

He and Miguel climbed into the pit and set their birds down on the short lines so that they faced each other. They held them by the tails and waited for Earle to give the signal to let go.

"Pit them," he ordered.

The dwarf had been watching Earle's lips and he had his bird off first, but Juju rose straight in the air and sank one spur in the red's breast. It went through the feathers into the flesh. The red turned with the gaff still stuck in him and pecked twice at his opponent's head.

They separated the birds and held them to the lines again.

"Pit 'em!" Earle shouted.

Again Juju got above the other bird, but this time he missed with his spurs. The red tried to get above him, but couldn't. He was too clumsy and heavy to fight in the air. Juju climbed again, cutting and hitting so rapidly that his legs were a golden blur. The red met him by going back on his tail and hooking upward like a cat. Juju landed again and again. He broke one of the red's wings, then practically severed a leg.

"Handle them," Earle called.

When the dwarf gathered the red up, its neck had begun to droop and it was a mass of blood and matted feathers. The little man moaned over the bird, then set to work. He spit into its gaping beak and took the comb between his lips and sucked the blood back into it. The red began to regain its fury, but not its strength. Its

beak closed and its neck straightened. The dwarf smoothed
and shaped its plumage. He could no nothing to help the
broken wing or the dangling leg.

"Pit 'em," Earle said.

The dwarf insisted that the birds be put down beak to
beak on the center line, so that the red would not have to
move to get at his opponent. Miguel agreed.

The red was very gallant. When Abe let go of its tail,
it made a great effort to get off the ground and meet Juju
in the air, but it could only thrust with one leg and fell
over on its side. Juju sailed above it, half turned and
came down on its back, driving in both spurs. The red
twisted free, throwing Juju, and made a terrific effort to
hook with its good leg, but fell sideways again.

Before Juju could get into the air, the red managed to
drive a hard blow with its beak to Juju's head. This slowed
the smaller bird down and he fought on the ground. In the
pecking match, the red's greater weight and strength
evened up for his lack of a leg and a wing. He managed
to give as good as he got. But suddenly his cracked beak
broke off, leaving only the lower half. A large bubble of
blood rose where the beak had been. The red didn't retreat
an inch, but made a great effort to get into the air once
more. Using its one leg skillfully, it managed to rise six or
seven inches from the ground, not enough, however, to get
its spurs into play. Juju went up with him and got well
above, then drove both gaffs into the red's breast. Again
one of the steel needles stuck.

"Handle them," Earle shouted.

Miguel freed his bird and gave the other back to the
dwarf. Abe, moaning softly, smoothed its feathers and
licked its eyes clean, then took its whole head in his
mouth. The red was finished, however. It couldn't even
hold its neck straight. The dwarf blew away the feathers
from under its tail and pressed the lips of its vent together

hard. When that didn't seem to help, he inserted his little finger and scratched the bird's testicles. It fluttered and made a gallant effort to straighten its neck.

"Pit birds."

Once more the red tried to rise with Juju, pushing hard with its remaining leg, but it only spun crazily. Juju rose, but missed. The red thrust weakly with its broken bill. Juju went into the air again and this time drove a gaff through one of the red's eyes into its brain. The red fell over stone dead.

The dwarf groaned with anguish, but no one else said anything. Juju pecked at the dead bird's remaining eye.

"Take off that stinking cannibal!" the dwarf screamed.

Miguel laughed, then caught Juju and removed its gaffs. Earle did the same for the red. He handled the dead cock gently and with respect.

Tod passed the whiskey.

22

They were well on their way to getting drunk when Homer came out to the garage. He gave a little start when he saw the dead chicken sprawled on the carpet. He shook hands with Claude after Tod introduced him, and with Abe Kusich, then made a little set speech about everybody coming in for a drink. They trooped after him.

Faye greeted them at the door. She was wearing a pair of green silk lounging pajamas and green mules with large pompons and very high heels. The top three buttons of her jacket were open and a good deal of her chest was exposed but nothing of her breasts; not because they were small, but because they were placed wide apart and their thrust was upward and outward.

She gave Tod her hand and patted the dwarf on the top of the head. They were old friends. In acknowledging

Homer's awkward introduction of Claude, she was very much the lady. It was her favorite role and she assumed it whenever she met a new man, especially if he were someone whose affluence was obvious.

"Charmed to have you," she trilled.

The dwarf laughed at her.

In a voice stiff with hauteur, she then ordered Homer into the kitchen for soda, ice and glasses.

"A swell layout," announced the dwarf, putting on the hat he had taken off in the doorway.

He climbed into one of the big Spanish chairs, using his knees and hands to do it, and sat on the edge with his feet dangling. He looked like a ventriloquist's dummy.

Earle and Miguel had remained behind to wash up. When they came in, Faye welcomed them with stilted condescension.

"How do you do, boys? The refreshments will be along in a jiffy. But perhaps you prefer a liqueur, Miguel?"

"No, mum," he said, a little startled. "I'll have what the others have."

He followed Earle across the room to the couch. Both of them took long, wooden steps, as though they weren't used to being in a house. They sat down gingerly with their backs straight, their big hats on their knees and their hands under their hats. They had combed their hair before leaving the garage and their small round heads glistened prettily.

Homer took the drinks around on a small tray.

They all made a show of manners, all but the dwarf, that is, who remained as arrogant as ever. He even commented on the quality of the whiskey. As soon as everyone had been served, Homer sat down.

Faye alone remained standing. She was completely self-possessed despite their stares. She stood with one hip thrown out and her hand on it. From where Claude was sitting he could follow the charming line of her spine as it swooped into her buttocks, which were like a heart upside down.

He gave a low whistle of admiration and everyone agreed by moving uneasily or laughing.

"My dear," she said to Homer, "perhaps some of the men would like cigars?"

He was surprised and mumbled something about there being no cigars in the house but that he would go to the store for them if . . . Having to say all this made him unhappy and he took the whiskey around again. He poured very generous shots.

"That's a becoming shade of green," Tod said.

Faye peacocked for them all.

"I thought maybe it was a little gaudy . . . vulgar, you know."

"No," Claude said enthusiastically, "it's stunning."

She repaid him for his compliment by smiling in a peculiar, secret way and running her tongue over her lips. It was one of her most characteristic gestures and very effective. It seemed to promise all sorts of undefined intimacies, yet it was really as simple and automatic as the word thanks. She used it to reward anyone for anything, no matter how unimportant.

Claude made the same mistake Tod had often made and jumped to his feet.

"Won't you sit here?" he said, waving gallantly at his chair.

She accepted by repeating the secret smile and the tongue caress. Claude bowed, but then, realizing that everyone was watching him, added a little mock flourish to make himself less ridiculous. Tod joined them, then Earle and Miguel came over. Claude did the courting while the others stood by and stared at her.

"Do you work in pictures, Mr. Estee?" she asked.

"Yes. You're in pictures, of course?"

Everyone was aware of the begging note in his voice, but no one smiled. They didn't blame him. It was almost impossible to keep that note out when talking to her. Men used it just to say good morning.

"Not exactly, but I hope to be," she said. "I've worked as an extra, but I haven't had a real chance yet. I expect to get one soon. All I ask is a chance. Acting is in my blood. We Greeners, you know, were all theatre people from away back."

"Yes. I . . ."

She didn't let Claude finish, but he didn't care.

"Not musicals, but real dramas. Of course, maybe light comedies at first. All I ask is a chance. I've been buying a lot of clothes lately to make myself one. I don't believe in luck. Luck is just hard work, they say, and I'm willing to work as hard as anybody."

"You have a delightful voice and you handle it well," he said.

He couldn't help it. Having once seen her secret smile and the things that accompanied it, he wanted to make her repeat it again and again.

"I'd like to do a show on Broadway," she continued. "That's the way to get a start nowadays. They won't talk to you unless you've had stage experience."

She went on and on, telling him how careers are made in the movies and how she intended to make hers. It was all nonsense. She mixed bits of badly understood advice from the trade papers with other bits out of the fan magazines and compared these with the legends that surround the activities of screen stars and executives. Without any noticeable transition, possibilities became probabilities and wound up as inevitabilities. At first she occasionally stopped and waited for Claude to chorus a hearty agreement, but when she had a good start, all her questions were rhetorical and the stream of words rippled on without a break.

None of them really heard her. They were all too busy watching her smile, laugh, shiver, whisper, grow indignant, cross and uncross her legs, stick out her tongue, widen and narrow her eyes, toss her head so that her platinum hair splashed against the red plush of the chair back. The strange thing about her gestures and expressions was that they didn't really illustrate what she was saying. They were almost pure. It was as though her body recognized how foolish her words were and tried to excite her hearers into being uncritical. It worked that night; no one even thought of laughing at her. The only move they made was to narrow their circle about her.

Tod stood on the outer edge, watching her through the opening between Earle and the Mexican. When he felt a light tap on his shoulder, he knew it was Homer, but didn't turn. When the tap was repeated, he shrugged the hand away. A few minutes later, he heard a shoe squeak behind him and turned to see Homer tiptoeing off. He reached a chair safely and sank into it with a sigh. He put his heavy hands on the knees, one on each, and stared for a while at their backs. He felt Tod's eyes on him and looked up and smiled.

His smile annoyed Tod. It was one of those irritating smiles that seem to say: "My friend, what can you know of suffering?" There was something very patronizing and superior about it, and intolerably snobbish.

He felt hot and a little sick. He turned his back on Homer and went out the front door. His indignant exit wasn't very successful. He wobbled quite badly and when he reached the sidewalk, he had to sit down on the curb with his back against a date palm.

From where he was sitting, he couldn't see the city in the valley below the canyon, but he could see the reflection of its lights, which hung in the sky above it like a batik parasol. The unlighted part of the sky at the edge of the parasol was a deep black with hardly a trace of blue.

Homer followed him out of the house and stood standing behind him, afraid to approach. He might have sneaked away without Tod's knowing it, if he had not suddenly looked down and seen his shadow.

"Hello," he said.

He motioned for Homer to join him on the curb.

"You'll catch cold," Homer said.

Tod understood his protest. He made it because he wanted to be certain that his company was really welcome. Nevertheless, Tod refused to repeat the invitation. He didn't even turn to look at him again. He was sure he was wearing his long-suffering smile and didn't want to see it.

He wondered why all his sympathy had turned to malice. Because of Faye? It was impossible for him to admit it. Because he was unable to do anything to help him? This reason was a more comfortable one, but he dismissed it with even less consideration. He had never set himself up as a healer.

Homer was looking the other way, at the house, watching the parlor window. He cocked his head to one side when someone laughed. The four short sounds, ha-ha and again ha-ha, distinct musical notes, were made by the dwarf.

"You could learn from him," Tod said.

"What?" Homer asked, turning to look at him.

"Let it go."

His impatience both hurt and puzzled Homer. He saw that and motioned for him to sit down, this time emphatically.

Homer obeyed. He did a poor job of squatting and hurt himself. He sat nursing his knee.

"What is it?" Tod finally said, making an attempt to be kind.

"Nothing, Tod, nothing."

He was grateful and increased his smile. Tod couldn't help seeing all its annoying attributes, resignation, kindliness, and humility.

They sat quietly, Homer with his heavy shoulders hunched and the sweet grin on his face, Tod frowning, his back pressed hard against the palm tree. In the house the radio was playing and its blare filled the street.

They sat for a long time without speaking. Several times Homer started to tell Tod something but he didn't seem able to get the words out. Tod refused to help him with a question.

His big hands left his lap, where they had been playing "here's the church and here the steeple," and hid in his armpits. They remained there for a moment, then slid under his thighs. A moment later they were back in his lap. The right hand cracked the joints of the left, one by one, then the left did the same service for the right. They seemed easier for a moment, but not for long. They started "here's the church" again, going through the entire performance and ending with the joint manipulation as before. He started a third time, but catching Tod's eyes, he stopped and trapped his hands between his knees.

It was the most complicated tic Tod had ever seen. What made it particularly horrible was its precision. It wasn't pantomime, as he had first thought, but manual ballet.

When Tod saw the hands start to crawl out again, he exploded.

"For Christ's sake!"

The hands struggled to get free, but Homer clamped his knees shut and held them.

"I'm sorry," he said.

"Oh, all right."

"But I can't help it, Tod. I have to do it three times."

"Okay with me."

He turned his back on him.

Faye started to sing and her voice poured into the street.

"Dreamed about a reefer five feet long
Not too mild and not too strong,
You'll be high, but not for long,
If you're a viper—a vi-paah."

Instead of her usual swing delivery, she was using a lugubrious one, wailing the tune as though it were a dirge. At the end of every stanza, she shifted to an added minor.

"I'm the queen of everything,
Gotta be high before I can swing,
Light a tea and let it be,
If you're a viper—a vi-paah."

"She sings very pretty," Homer said.

"She's drunk."

"I don't know what to do, Tod," Homer complained. "She's drinking an awful lot lately. It's that Earle. We used to have a lot of fun before he came, but now we don't have any fun any more since he started to hang around."

"Why don't you get rid of him?"

"I was thinking about what you said about the license to keep chickens."

Tod understood what he wanted.

"I'll report them to the Board of Health tomorrow."

Homer thanked him, then insisted on explaining in detail why he couldn't do it himself.

"But that'll only get rid of the Mexican," Tod said. "You'll have to throw Earle out yourself."

"Maybe he'll go with his friend?"

Tod knew that Homer was begging him to agree so that he could go on hoping, but he refused.

"Not a chance. You'll have to throw him out."

Homer accepted this with his brave, sweet smile.

"Maybe . . ."

"Tell Faye to do it," Tod said.

"Oh, I can't."

"Why the hell not? It's your house."

"Don't be mad at me, Toddie."

"All right, Homie, I'm not mad at you."

Faye's voice came through the open window.

"And when your throat gets dry,
You know you're high,
If you're a viper."

The others harmonized on the last word, repeating it.

"Vi-paah . . ."

"Toddie," Homer began, "if . . ."

"Stop calling me Toddie, for Christ's sake!"

Homer didn't understand. He took Tod's hand.

"I didn't mean nothing. Back home we call . . ."

Tod couldn't stand his trembling signals of affection. He tore free with a jerk.

"Oh, but, Toddie, I . . ."

"She's a whore!"

He heard Homer grunt, then heard his knees creak as he struggled to his feet.

Faye's voice came pouring through the window, a reedy wail that broke in the middle with a husky catch.

"High, high, high, high, when you're high,
Everything is dandy,
Truck on down to the candy store,
Bust your conk on peppermint candy!
Then you know your body's sent,
Don't care if you don't pay rent,
Sky is high and so am I,
If you're a viper—a vi-paah."

23

When Tod went back into the house, he found Earle, Abe Kusich and Claude standing together in a tight group, watching Faye dance with Miguel. She and the Mexican were doing a slow tango to music from the phonograph. He held her very tight, one of his legs thrust between hers, and they swayed together in long spirals that broke rhythmically at the top of each curve into a dip. All the buttons on her lounging pajamas were open and the arm he had around her waist was inside her clothes.

Tod stood watching the dancers from the doorway for a moment, then went to a little table on which the whiskey bottle was. He poured himself a quarter of a tumblerful, tossed it off, then poured another drink. Carrying the glass, he went over to Claude and the others. They paid no attention to him; their heads moved only to follow the dancers, like the gallery at a tennis match.

"Did you see Homer?" Tod asked, touching Claude's arm.

Claude didn't turn, but the dwarf did. He spoke as though hypnotized.

"What a quiff! What a quiff!"

Tod left them and went to look for Homer. He wasn't in the kitchen, so he tried the bedrooms. One of them was locked. He knocked lightly, waited, then repeated the knock. There was no answer, but he thought he heard someone move. He looked through the keyhole. **The room** was pitch dark.

"Homer," he called softly.

He heard the bed creak, then Homer replied.

"Who is it?"

"It's me—Toddie."

He used the diminutive with perfect seriousness.

"Go away, please," Homer said.

"Let me in for a minute. I want to explain something."

"No," Homer said, "go away, please."

Tod went back to the living room. The phonograph record had been changed to a fox-trot and Earle was now dancing with Faye. He had both his arms around her in a bear hug and they were stumbling all over the room, bumping into the walls and furniture. Faye, her head thrown back, was laughing wildly. Earle had both eyes shut tight.

Miguel and Claude were also laughing, but not the dwarf. He stood with his fists clenched and his chin stuck out. When he couldn't stand any more of it, he ran after the dancers to cut in. He caught Earle by the seat of his trousers.

"Le'me dance," he barked.

Earle turned his head, looking down at the dwarf from over his shoulder.

"Git! G'wan, git!"

Faye and Earle had come to a halt with their arms around each other. When the dwarf lowered his head like a goat and tried to push between them, she reached down and tweaked his nose.

"Le'me dance," he bellowed.

They tried to start again, but Abe wouldn't let them. He had his hands between them and was trying frantically to pull them apart. When that wouldn't work, he kicked Earle sharply in the shins. Earle kicked back and his boot landed in the little man's stomach, knocking him flat on his back. Everyone laughed.

The dwarf struggled to his feet and stood with his head lowered like a tiny ram. Just as Faye and Earle started to dance again, he charged between Earle's legs and dug upward with both hands. Earle screamed with pain, and tried to get at him. He screamed again, then groaned and started to sink to the floor, tearing Faye's silk pajamas on his way down.

Miguel grabbed Abe by the throat. The dwarf let go his hold and Earle sank to the floor. Lifting the little man free, Miguel shifted his grip to his ankles and dashed him against the wall, like a man killing a rabbit against a tree. He swung the dwarf back to slam him again, but Tod caught his arm. Then Claude grabbed the dwarf and together they pulled him away from the Mexican.

He was unconscious. They carried him into the kitchen and held him under the cold water. He came to quickly and began to curse. When they saw he was all right, they went back to the living room.

Miguel was helping Earle over to the couch. All the tan had drained from his face and it was covered with sweat. Miguel loosened his trousers while Claude took off his necktie and opened his collar.

Faye and Tod watched from the side.

"Look," she said, "my new pajamas are ruined."

One of the sleeves had been pulled almost off and her shoulder stuck through it. The trousers were also torn. While he stared at her, she undid the top of the trousers and stepped out of them. She was wearing tight black lace drawers. Tod took a step toward her and hesitated. She threw the pajama bottoms over her arm, turned slowly and walked toward the door.

"Faye," Tod gasped.

She stopped and smiled at him.

"I'm going to bed," she said. "Get that little guy out of here."

Claude came over and took Tod by the arm.

"Let's blow," he said.

Tod nodded.

"We'd better take the homunculus with us or he's liable to murder the whole household."

Tod nodded again and followed him into the kitchen. They found the dwarf holding a big piece of ice to the side of his head.

"There's some lump where that greaser slammed me."

He made them finger and admire it.

"Let's go home," Claude said.

"No," said the dwarf, "let's go see some girls. I'm just getting started."

"To hell with that," snapped Tod. "Come on."

He pushed the dwarf toward the door.

"Take your hands off, punk!" roared the little man.

Claude stepped between them.

"Easy there, citizen," he said.

"All right, but no shoving."

He strutted out and they followed.

Earle still lay stretched on the couch. He had his eyes closed and was holding himself below the stomach with both hands. Miguel wasn't there.

Abe chuckled, wagging his big head gleefully.

"I fixed that buckeroo."

Out on the sidewalk he tried again to get them to go with him.

"Come on, you guys—we'll have some fun."

"I'm going home," Claude said.

They went with the dwarf to his car and watched him climb in behind the wheel. He had special extensions on the clutch and brake so that he could reach them with his tiny feet.

"Come to town?"

"No, thanks," Claude said politely.

"Then to hell with you!"

That was his farewell. He let out the brake and the car rolled away.

24

Tod woke up the next morning with a splitting headache. He called the studio to say he wouldn't be in and remained in bed until noon, then went downtown for breakfast. After several cups of hot tea, he felt a little better and decided to visit Homer. He still wanted to apologize.

Climbing the hill to Pinyon Canyon made his head throb and he was relieved when no one answered his repeated knocks. As he started away, he saw one of the curtains move and went back to knock once more. There was still no answer.

He went around to the garage. Faye's car was gone and so were the game chickens. He went to the back of the house and knocked on the kitchen door. Somehow the silence seemed too complete. He tried the handle and found that the door wasn't locked. He shouted hello a few times, as a warning, then went through the kitchen into the living room.

The red velvet curtains were all drawn tight, but he could see Homer sitting on the couch and staring at the backs of his hands which were cupped over his knees. He wore an old-fashioned cotton nightgown and his feet were bare.

"Just get up?"

Homer neither moved nor replied.

Tod tried again.

"Some party!"

He knew it was stupid to be hearty, but he didn't know what else to be.

"Boy, have I got a hang-over," he went on, even going so far as to attempt a chuckle.

Homer paid absolutely no attention to him.

The room was just as they had left it the night before. Tables and chairs were overturned and the smashed picture lay where it had fallen. To give himself a reason for staying, he began to tidy up. He righted the chairs, straightened the carpet and picked up the cigarette butts that littered the floor. He also threw aside the curtains and opened a window.

"There, that's better, isn't it?" he asked cheerfully.

Homer looked up for a second, then down at his hands again. Tod saw that he was coming out of his stupor.

"Want some coffee?" he asked.

He lifted his hands from his knees and hid them in his armpits, clamping them tight, but didn't answer.

"Some hot coffee—what do you say?"

He took his hands from under his arms and sat on them. After waiting a little while he shook his head no, slowly, heavily, like a dog with a foxtail in its ear.

"I'll make some."

Tod went to the kitchen and put the pot on the stove. While it was boiling, he took a peek into Faye's room. It had been stripped. All the dresser drawers were pulled out and there were empty boxes all over the floor. A broken flask of perfume lay in the middle of the carpet and the place reeked of gardenia.

When the coffee was ready, he poured two cups and carried them into the living room on a tray. He found Homer just as he had left him, sitting on his hands. He moved a small table close to him and put the tray on it.

"I brought a cup for myself, too," he said. "Come on—drink it while it's hot."

Tod lifted a cup and held it out, but when he saw that he was going to speak, he put it down and waited.

"I'm going back to Wayneville," Homer said.

"A swell idea—great!"

He pushed the coffee at him again. Homer ignored it. He gulped several times, trying to swallow something that was stuck in his throat, then began to sob. He cried without covering his face or bending his head. The sound was like an ax chopping pine, a heavy, hollow, chunking noise. It was repeated rhythmically but without accent. There was no progress in it. Each chunk was exactly like the one that preceded. It would never reach a climax.

Tod realized that there was no use trying to stop him. Only a very stupid man would have the courage to try to do it. He went to the farthest corner of the room and waited.

Just as he was about to light a second cigarette, Homer called him.

"Tod!"

"I'm here, Homer."

He hurried over to the couch again.

Homer was still crying, but he suddenly stopped even more abruptly than he had started.

"Yes, Homer?" Tod asked encouragingly.

"She's left."

"Yes, I know. Drink some coffee."

"She's left."

Tod knew that he put a great deal of faith in sayings, so he tried one.

"Good riddance to bad rubbish."

"She left before I got up," he said.

"What the hell do you care? You're going back to Wayneville."

"You shouldn't curse," Homer said with the same lunatic calm.

"I'm sorry," Tod mumbled.

The word "sorry" was like dynamite set off under a dam. Language leaped out of Homer in a muddy, twisting torrent. At first, Tod thought it would do him a lot of good to pour out in this way. But he was wrong. The lake behind the dam replenished itself too fast. The more he talked the greater the pressure grew because the flood was circular and ran back behind the dam again.

After going on continuously for about twenty minutes, he stopped in the middle of a sentence. He leaned back, closed his eyes and seemed to fall asleep. Tod put a cushion under his head. After watching him for a while, he went back to the kitchen.

He sat down and tried to make sense out of what Homer had told him. A great deal of it was gibberish. Some of it, however, wasn't. He hit on a key that helped when he realized that a lot of it wasn't jumbled so much as timeless. The words went behind each other instead of after. What he had taken for long strings were really one thick word and not a sentence. In the same way several sentences were simultaneous and not a paragraph. Using this key, he was able to arrange a part of what he had heard so that it made the usual kind of sense.

After Tod had hurt him by saying that nasty thing about Faye, Homer ran around to the back of the house and let himself in through the kitchen, then went to peek into the parlor. He wasn't angry with Tod, just surprised and upset because Tod was a nice boy. From the hall that led into the parlor he could see everybody having a good time and he was glad because it was kind of dull for Faye living with an old man like him. It made her restless. No one noticed him peeking there and he was glad because he didn't feel much like joining the fun, although he liked to watch people enjoy themselves. Faye was dancing with Mr. Estee and they made a nice pair. She seemed happy. Her face shone like always when she was happy. Next she danced with Earle. He didn't like that because of the way he held her. He couldn't see what she saw in that fellow. He just wasn't nice, that's all. He had mean eyes. In the hotel business they used to watch out for fellows like that and never gave them credit because they would jump their bills. Maybe he couldn't get a job because nobody would trust him, although it was true as Faye said that a lot of people were out of work nowadays. Standing there peeking at the party, enjoying the laughing and singing, he saw Earle catch Faye and bend her back and kiss her and everybody laughed although you could see Faye didn't like it because she slapped his face. Earle didn't care, he just kissed her again, a long nasty one. She got away from him and ran toward the door where he was standing. He tried to hide, but she caught him. Although he didn't say anything, she said he was nasty spying on her and wouldn't listen when he tried to explain. She went into her room and he followed to tell about the peeking, but she carried on awful and cursed him some more as she put red on her lips. Then she knocked over the perfume. That made her twice as mad. He tried to explain but she wouldn't listen and just went on calling him all sorts of dirty things. So he went to his room and got undressed and tried to go to sleep. Then Tod woke him up and wanted to come in and talk. He wasn't angry, but didn't feel like talking just then, all he wanted to do was go to sleep. Tod went away and no sooner had he climbed back into bed when there was some awful screaming and banging. He was afraid to go out and see and he thought of calling the police, but he was scared to go in the hall where the phone was so he started to get dressed to climb out of the window and go for help because it sounded like murder but before he finished putting his shoes on, he heard Tod talking to Faye and he figured that it must be all right or she wouldn't be laughing so he got undressed and went back to bed again. He couldn't fall asleep wondering what had happened, so when the house was quiet, he took a chance and knocked on Faye's door to find out. Faye let him in. She was curled up in bed like a little girl. She called him daddy and kissed him and said that she wasn't angry at him at all. She said there had been a fight but nobody got hurt much and for him to go back to bed and that they would talk more in the morning. He went back like she said and fell asleep, but he woke up again as it was just breaking daylight. At first he wondered why he was up because when he once fell asleep, usually he didn't get up before the alarm clock rang. He knew that something had happened, but he didn't know what until he heard a noise in Faye's room. It was a moan and he thought he was dreaming, but he heard it again. Sure enough, Faye was moaning all right. He thought she must be sick. She moaned again like in pain. He got out of bed and went to her door and knocked and asked if she was sick. She didn't answer and the moaning stopped so he went back to bed. A little later, she moaned again so he got out of bed, thinking she might want the hot water bottle or some aspirin and a drink of water or something and knocked on her door again, only meaning to help her. She heard him and said something. He didn't understand what but he thought she meant for him to go in. Lots of times when she had a headache he brought her an aspirin and a glass of water in the middle of the night. The door wasn't locked. You'd have thought she would have locked the door because the Mexican was in bed with her, both of them naked and she had her arms around him. Faye saw him and pulled the sheets over her head without saying anything. He didn't know what to do, so he backed out of the room and closed the door. He was standing in the hall, trying to figure out what to do, feeling so ashamed, when Earle appeared with his boots in his hand. He must have been sleeping in the parlor. He wanted to know what the trouble was. "Faye's sick," he said, "and I'm getting her a glass of water." But then Faye moaned again and Earle heard it. He pushed open the door. Faye screamed. He could hear Earl and Miguel cursing each other and fighting. He was afraid to call the police on account of Faye and didn't know what to do. Faye kept on screaming. When he opened the door again, Miguel fell out with Earle on top of him and both of them tearing at each other. He ran inside the room and locked the door. She had the sheets over her head, screaming. He could hear Earle and Miguel fighting in the hall and then he couldn't hear them any more. She kept the sheets over her head. He tried to talk to her but she wouldn't answer. He sat down on a chair to guard her in case Earle and Miguel came back, but they didn't and after a while she pulled the sheets away from her face and told him to get out. She pulled the sheets over her face again when he answered, so then he waited a little longer and again she told him to get out without letting him see her face. He couldn't hear either Miguel or Earle. He opened the door and looked out. They were gone. He locked the doors and windows and went to his room and lay down on his bed. Before he knew it he fell asleep and when he woke up she was gone. All he could find was Earle's boots in the hall. He threw them out the back and this morning they were gone.

25

Tod went into the living room to see how Homer was getting on. He was still on the couch, but had changed his position. He had curled his big body into a ball. His knees were drawn up almost to his chin, his elbows were tucked in close and his hands were against his chest. But he wasn't relaxed. Some inner force of nerve and muscle was straining to make the ball tighter and still tighter. He was like a steel spring which has been freed of its function in a machine and allowed to use all its strength centripetally. While part of a machine the pull of the spring had been used against other and stronger forces, but now, free at last, it was striving to attain the shape of its original coil.

Original coil . . . In a book of abnormal psychology borrowed from the college library, he had once seen a picture of a woman sleeping in a net hammock whose posture was much like Homer's. "Uterine Flight," or something like that, had been the caption under the photograph. The woman had been sleeping in the hammock without changing her position, that of the foetus in the womb, for a great many years. The doctors of the insane asylum had been able to awaken her for only short periods of time and those months apart.

He sat down to smoke a cigarette and wondered what he ought to do. Call a doctor? But after all Homer had been awake most of the night and was exhausted. The doctor would shake him a few times and he would yawn and ask what the matter was. He could try to wake him up himself. But hadn't he been enough of a pest already? He was so much better off asleep, even if it was a case of "Uterine Flight."

What a perfect escape the return to the womb was. Better by far than Religion or Art or the South Sea Islands. It was so snug and warm there, and the feeding was automatic. Everything perfect in that hotel. No wonder the memory of those accommodations lingered in the blood and nerves of everyone. It was dark, yes, but what a warm, rich darkness. The grave wasn't in it. No wonder one fought so desperately against being evicted when the nine months' lease was up.

Tod crushed his cigarette. He was hungry and wanted his dinner, also a double Scotch and soda. After he had eaten, he would come back and see how Homer was. If he was still asleep, he would try to wake him. If he couldn't, he might call a doctor.

He took another look at him, then tiptoed out of the cottage, shutting the door carefully.

26

Tod didn't go directly to dinner. He went first to Hodge's saddlery store thinking he might be able to find out something about Earle and through him about Faye. Calvin was standing there with a wrinkled Indian who had long hair held by a bead strap around his forehead. Hanging over the Indian's chest was a sandwich board that read—

TUTTLE'S TRADING POST

for

GENUINE RELICS OF THE OLD WEST

Beads, Silver, Jewelry, Moccasins,

Dolls, Toys, Rare Books, Postcards.

TAKE BACK A SOUVENIR

from

TUTTLE'S TRADING POST

Calvin was always friendly.

" 'Lo, thar," he called out, when Tod came up.

"Meet the chief," he added, grinning. "Chief Kiss-My-Towkus."

The Indian laughed heartily at the joke.

"You gotta live," he said.

"Earle been around today?" Tod asked.

"Yop. Went by an hour ago."

"We were at a party last night and I . . ."

Calvin broke in by hitting his thigh a wallop with the flat of his palm.

"That must've been some shindig to hear Earle tell it. Eh, Skookum?"

"Vas you dere, Sharley?" the Indian agreed, showing the black inside of his mouth, purple tongue and broken orange teeth.

"I heard there was a fight after I left."

Calvin smacked his thigh again.

"Sure musta been. Earle get himself two black eyes, lulus."

"That's what comes of palling up with a dirty greaser," said the Indian excitedly.

He and Calvin got into a long argument about Mexicans. The Indian said that they were all bad. Calvin claimed he had known quite a few good ones in his time. When the Indian cited the case of the Hermanos brothers who had killed a lonely prospector for half a dollar, Calvin countered with a long tale about a man called Tomas Lopez who shared his last pint of water with a stranger when they both were lost in the desert.

Tod tried to get the conversation back to what interested him.

"Mexicans are very good with women," he said.

"Better with horses," said the Indian. "I remember one time along the Brazos, I . . ."

Tod tried again.

"They fought over Earle's girl, didn't they?"

"Not to hear him tell it," Calvin said. "He claims it was dough—claims the Mex robbed him while he was sleeping."

"The dirty, thievin' rat," said the Indian, spitting.

"He claims he's all washed up with that bitch," Calvin went on. "Yes, siree, that's his story, to hear him tell it."

Tod had enough.

"So long," he said.

"Glad to meet you," said the Indian.

"Don't take any wooden nickels," Calvin shouted after him.

Tod wondered if she had gone with Miguel. He thought it more likely that she would go back to work for Mrs. Jenning. But either way she would come out all right. Nothing could hurt her. She was like a cork. No matter how rough the sea got, she would go dancing over the same waves that sank iron ships and tore away piers of reinforced concrete. He pictured her riding a tremendous sea. Wave after wave reared its ton on ton of solid water and crashed down only to have her spin gaily away.

When he arrived at Musso Frank's restaurant, he ordered a steak and a double Scotch. The drink came first and he sipped it with his inner eye still on the spinning cork.

It was a very pretty cork, gilt with a glittering fragment of mirror set in its top. The sea in which it danced was beautiful, green in the trough of the waves and silver at their tips. But for all their moondriven power, they could do no more than net the bright cork for a moment in a spume of intricate lace. Finally it was set down on a strange shore where a savage with pork-sausage fingers and a pimpled butt picked it up and hugged it to his sagging belly. Tod recognized the fortunate man; he was one of Mrs. Jenning's customers.

The waiter brought his order and paused with bent back for him to comment. In vain. Tod was far too busy to inspect the steak.

"Satisfactory, sir?" asked the waiter.

Tod waved him away with a gesture more often used on flies. The waiter disappeared. Tod tried the same gesture on what he felt, but the driving itch refused to go. If only he had the courage to wait for her some night and hit her with a bottle and rape her.

He knew what it would be like lurking in the dark in a vacant lot, waiting for her. Whatever that bird was that sang at night in California would be bursting its heart in theatrical runs and quavers and the chill night air would smell of spice pink. She would drive up, turn the motor off, look up at the stars, so that her breasts reared, then toss her head and sigh. She would throw the ignition keys into her purse and snap it shut, then get out of the car. The long step she took would make her tight dress pull up so that an inch of glowing flesh would show above her black stocking. As he approached carefully, she would be pulling her dress down, smoothing it nicely over her hips.

"Faye, Faye, just a minute," he would call.

"Why, Tod, hello."

She would hold her hand out to him at the end of her long arm that swooped so gracefully to join her curving shoulder.

"You scared me!"

She would look like a deer on the edge of the road when a truck comes unexpectedly around a bend.

He could feel the cold bottle he held behind his back and the forward step he would take to bring . . .

"Is there anything wrong with it, sir?"

The fly-like waiter had come back. Tod waved at him, but this time the man continued to hover.

"Perhaps you would like me to take it back, sir?"

"No, no."

"Thank you, sir."

But he didn't leave. He waited to make sure that the

customer was really going to eat. Tod picked up his knife and cut a piece. Not until he had also put some boiled potato in his mouth did the man leave.

Tod tried to start the rape going again, but he couldn't feel the bottle as he raised it to strike. He had to give it up.

The waiter came back. Tod looked at the steak. It was a very good one, but he wasn't hungry any more.

"A check, please."

"No dessert, sir?"

"No, thank you, just a check."

"Check it is, sir," the man said brightly as he fumbled for his pad and pencil.

27

When Tod reached the street, he saw a dozen great violet shafts of light moving across the evening sky in wide crazy sweeps. Whenever one of the fiery columns reached the lowest point of its arc, it lit for a moment the rose-colored domes and delicate minarets of Kahn's Persian Palace Theatre. The purpose of this display was to signal the world premiere of a new picture.

Turning his back on the searchlights, he started in the opposite direction, toward Homer's place. Before he had gone very far, he saw a clock that read a quarter past six and changed his mind about going back just yet. He might as well let the poor fellow sleep for another hour and kill some time by looking at the crowds.

When still a block from the theatre, he saw an enormous electric sign that hung over the middle of the street. In letters ten feet high he read that—

"MR. KAHN A PLEASURE DOME DECREED"

Although it was still several hours before the celebrities would arrive, thousands of people had already gathered.

They stood facing the theatre with their backs toward the gutter in a thick line hundreds of feet long. A big squad of policemen was trying to keep a lane open between the front rank of the crowd and the façade of the theatre.

Tod entered the lane while the policeman guarding it was busy with a woman whose parcel had torn open, dropping oranges all over the place. Another policeman shouted for him to get the hell across the street, but he took a chance and kept going. They had enough to do without chasing him. He noticed how worried they looked and how careful they tried to be. If they had to arrest some-one, they joked good-naturedly with the culprit, making light of it until they got him around the corner, then they whaled him with their clubs. Only so long as the man was actually part of the crowd did they have to be gentle.

Tod had walked only a short distance along the narrow lane when he began to get frightened. People shouted, commenting on his hat, his carriage, and his clothing. There was a continuous roar of catcalls, laughter and yells, pierced occasionally by a scream. The scream was usually followed by a sudden movement in the dense mass and part of it would surge forward wherever the police line was weakest. As soon as that part was rammed back, the bulge would pop out somewhere else.

The police force would have to be doubled when the stars started to arrive. At the sight of their heroes and heroines, the crowd would turn demoniac. Some little gesture, either too pleasing or too offensive, would start it moving and then nothing but machine guns would stop it. Individually the purpose of its members might simply be to get a souvenir, but collectively it would grab and rend.

A young man with a portable microphone was describing the scene. His rapid, hysterical voice was like that of a revivalist preacher whipping his congregation toward the ecstasy of fits.

"What a crowd, folks! What a crowd! There must be ten thousand excited, screaming fans outside Kahn's Persian tonight. The police can't hold them. Here, listen to them roar."

. He held the microphone out and those near it obligingly roared for him.

"Did you hear it? It's a bedlam, folks. A veritable bedlam! What excitement! Of all the premières I've attended, this is the most . . . the most . . . stupendous, folks. Can the police hold them? Can they? It doesn't look so, folks . . ."

Another squad of police came charging up. The sergeant pleaded with the announcer to stand further back so the people couldn't hear him His men threw themselves at the crowd. It allowed itself to be hustled and shoved out of habit and because it lacked an objective. It tolerated the police, just as a bull elephant does when he allows a small boy to drive him with a light stick.

Tod could see very few people who looked tough, nor could he see any working men. The crowd was made up of the lower middle classes, every other person one of his torchbearers.

Just as he came near the end of the lane, it closed in front of him with a heave, and he had to fight his way through. Someone knocked his hat off and when he stooped to pick it up, someone kicked him. He whirled around angrily and found himself surrounded by people who were laughing at him. He knew enough to laugh with them. The crowd became sympathetic. A stout woman slapped him on the back, while a man handed him his hat, first brushing it carefully with his sleeve. Still another man shouted for a way to be cleared.

By a great deal of pushing and squirming, always trying to look as though he were enjoying himself, Tod finally managed to break into the open. After rearranging his clothes, he went over to a parking lot and sat down on the low retaining wall that ran along the front of it.

New groups, whole families, kept arriving. He could see a change come over them as soon as they had become part of the crowd. Until they reached the line, they looked diffident, almost furtive, but the moment they had become part of it, they turned arrogant and pugnacious. It was a mistake to think them harmless curiosity seekers. They were savage and bitter, especially the middle-aged and the old, and had been made so by boredom and disappointment.

All their lives they had slaved at some kind of dull, heavy labor, behind desks and counters, in the fields and at tedious machines of all sorts, saving their pennies and dreaming of the leisure that would be theirs when they had enough. Finally that day came. They could draw a weekly income of ten or fifteen dollars. Where else should they go but California, the land of sunshine and oranges?

Once there, they discover that sunshine isn't enough. They get tired of oranges, even of avocado pears and passion fruit. Nothing happens. They don't know what to do with their time. They haven't the mental equipment for leisure, the money nor the physical equipment for pleasure. Did they slave so long just to go to an occasional Iowa picnic? What else is there? They watch the waves come in at Venice. There wasn't any ocean where most of them came from, but after you've seen one wave, you've seen them all. The same is true of the airplanes at Glendale. If only a plane would crash once in a while so that they could watch the passengers being consumed in a "holocaust of flame," as the newspapers put it. But the planes never crash.

Their boredom becomes more and more terrible. They realize that they've been tricked and burn with resentment. Every day of their lives they read the newspapers and

Need to understand
orgies alternatively
fulfilled in passing
(their capacity for natur...)

went to the movies. Both fed them on lynchings, murder,
sex crimes, explosions, wrecks, love nests, fires, miracles,
revolutions, war. This daily diet made sophisticates of
them. The sun is a joke. Oranges can't titillate their jaded
palates. Nothing can ever be violent enough to make taut
their slack minds and bodies. They have been cheated
and betrayed. They have slaved and saved for nothing.

powerful
short
terminal
sentences

Tod stood up. During the ten minutes he had been
sitting on the wall, the crowd had grown thirty feet and he
was afraid that his escape might be cut off if he loitered
much longer. He crossed to the other side of the street
and started back.

He was trying to figure what to do if he were unable to
wake Homer when, suddenly he saw his head bobbing
above the crowd. He hurried toward him. From his appearance, it was evident that there was something definitely
wrong.

Homer walked more than ever like a badly made autom-
aton and his features were set in a rigid, mechanical grin.
He had his trousers on over his nightgown and part of it
hung out of his open fly. In both of his hands were suitcases.
With each step, he lurched to one side then the other,
using the suitcases for balance weights.

Tod stopped directly in front of him, blocking his way.
"Where're you going?"

"Wayneville," he replied, using an extraordinary amount
of jaw movement to get out this single word.

"That's fine. But you can't walk to the station from here.
It's in Los Angeles."

Homer tried to get around him, but he caught his arm.
"We'll get a taxi. I'll go with you."

The cabs were all being routed around the block because
of the preview. He explained this to Homer and tried to get
him to walk to the corner.

"Come on, we're sure to get one on the next street."

e.g. at best's emotional involvement
& intellectual detachment.
Root of his intensity - violent imagery

413

Once Tod got him into a cab, he intended to tell the driver to go to the nearest hospital. But Homer wouldn't budge, no matter how hard he yanked and pleaded. People stopped to watch them, others turned their heads curiously. He decided to leave him and get a cab.

"I'll come right back," he said.

He couldn't tell from either Homer's eyes or expression whether he heard, for they both were empty of everything, even annoyance. At the corner he looked around and saw that Homer had started to cross the street, moving blindly. Brakes screeched and twice he was almost run over, but he didn't swerve or hurry. He moved in a straight diagonal. When he reached the other curb, he tried to get on the sidewalk at a point where the crowd was very thick and was shoved violently back. He made another attempt and this time a policeman grabbed him by the back of the neck and hustled him to the end of the line. When the policeman let go of him, he kept on walking as though nothing had happened.

Tod tried to get over to him, but was unable to cross until the traffic lights changed. When he reached the other side, he found Homer sitting on a bench, fifty or sixty feet from the outskirts of the crowd.

He put his arm around Homer's shoulder and suggested that they walk a few blocks further. When Homer didn't answer, he reached over to pick up one of the valises. Homer held on to it.

"I'll carry it for you," he said, tugging gently.

"Thief!"

Before Homer could repeat the shout, he jumped away. It would be extremely embarrassing if Homer shouted thief in front of a cop. He thought of phoning for an ambulance. But then, after all, how could he be sure that Homer was crazy? He was sitting quietly on the bench, minding his own business.

Tod decided to wait, then try again to get him into a cab. The crowd was growing in size all the time, but it would be at least half an hour before it over-ran the bench. Before that happened, he would think of some plan. He moved a short distance away and stood with his back to a store window so that he could watch Homer without attracting attention.

About ten feet from where Homer was sitting grew a large eucalyptus tree and behind the trunk of the tree was a little boy. Tod saw him peer around it with great caution, then suddenly jerk his head back. A minute later he repeated the maneuver. At first Tod thought he was playing hide and seek, then noticed that he had a string in his hand which was attached to an old purse that lay in front of Homer's bench. Every once in a while the child would jerk the string, making the purse hop like a sluggish toad. Its torn lining hung from its iron mouth like a furry tongue and a few uncertain flies hovered over it.

Tod knew the game the child was playing. He used to play it himself when he was small. If Homer reached to pick up the purse, thinking there was money in it, he would yank it away and scream with laughter.

When Tod went over to the tree, he was surprised to discover that it was Adore Loomis, the kid who lived across the street from Homer. Tod tried to chase him, but he dodged around the tree, thumbing his nose. He gave up and went back to his original position. The moment he left, Adore got busy with his purse again. Homer wasn't paying any attention to the child, so Tod decided to let him alone.

Mrs. Loomis must be somewhere in the crowd, he thought. Tonight when she found Adore, she would give him a hiding. He had torn the pocket of his jacket and his Buster Brown collar was smeared with grease.

Adore had a nasty temper. The completeness with which

Homer ignored both him and his pocketbook made him frantic. He gave up dancing it at the end of the string and approached the bench on tiptoes, making ferocious faces, yet ready to run at Homer's first move. He stopped when about four feet away and stuck his tongue out. Homer ignored him. He took another step forward and ran through a series of insulting gestures.

If Tod had known that the boy held a stone in his hand, he would have interfered. But he felt sure that Homer wouldn't hurt the child and was waiting to see if he wouldn't move because of his pestering. When Adore raised his arm, it was too late. The stone hit Homer in the face. The boy turned to flee, but tripped and fell. Before he could scramble away, Homer landed on his back with both feet, then jumped again.

Tod yelled for him to stop and tried to yank him away. He shoved Tod and went on using his heels. Tod hit him as hard as he could, first in the belly, then in the face. He ignored the blows and continued to stamp on the boy. Tod hit him again and again, then threw both arms around him and tried to pull him off. He couldn't budge him. He was like a stone column.

The next thing Tod knew, he was torn loose from Homer and sent to his knees by a blow in the back of the head that spun him sideways. The crowd in front of the theatre had charged. He was surrounded by churning legs and feet. He pulled himself erect by grabbing a man's coat, then let himself be carried along backwards in a long, curving swoop. He saw Homer rise above the mass for a moment, shoved against the sky, his jaw hanging as though he wanted to scream but couldn't. A hand reached up and caught him by his open mouth and pulled him forward and down.

There was another dizzy rush. Tod closed his eyes and fought to keep upright. He was jostled about in a hacking cross surf of shoulders and backs, carried rapidly in one direction and then in the opposite. He kept pushing and hitting out at the people around him, trying to face in the direction he was going. Being carried backwards terrified him.

Using the eucalyptus tree as a landmark, he tried to work toward it by slipping sideways against the tide, pushing hard when carried away from it and riding the current when it moved toward his objective. He was within only a few feet of the tree when a sudden, driving rush carried him far past it. He struggled desperately for a moment, then gave up and let himself be swept along. He was the spearhead of a flying wedge when it collided with a mass going in the opposite direction. The impact turned him around. As the two forces ground against each other, he was turned again and again, like a grain between millstones. This didn't stop until he became part of the opposing force. The pressure continued to increase until he thought he must collapse. He was slowly being pushed into the air. Although relief for his cracking ribs could be gotten by continuing to rise, he fought to keep his feet on the ground. Not being able to touch was an even more dreadful sensation than being carried backwards.

There was another rush, shorter this time, and he found himself in a dead spot where the pressure was less and equal. He became conscious of a terrible pain in his left leg, just above the ankle, and tried to work it into a more comfortable position. He couldn't turn his body, but managed to get his head around. A very skinny boy, wearing a Western Union cap, had his back wedged against his shoulder. The pain continued to grow and his whole leg as high as the groin throbbed. He finally got his left arm free and took the back of the boy's neck in his fingers. He twisted as hard as he could. The boy began to jump up and down in his clothes. He managed to straighten his elbow, by pushing at the back of the boy's head, and so turn half-way around and free his leg. The pain didn't grow less.

There was another wild surge forward that ended in another dead spot. He now faced a young girl who was sobbing steadily. Her silk print dress had been torn down the front and her tiny brassiere hung from one strap. He tried by pressing back to give her room, but she moved with him every time he moved. Now and then, she would jerk violently and he wondered if she was going to have a fit. One of her thighs was between his legs. He struggled to get free of her, but she clung to him, moving with him and pressing against him.

She turned her head and said, "Stop, stop," to someone behind her.

He saw what the trouble was. An old man, wearing a Panama hat and horn-rimmed glasses, was hugging her. He had one of his hands inside her dress and was biting her neck.

Tod freed his right arm with a heave, reached over the girl and brought his fist down on the man's head. He couldn't hit very hard but managed to knock the man's hat off, also his glasses. The man tried to bury his face in the girl's shoulder, but Tod grabbed one of his ears and yanked. They started to move again. Tod held on to the ear as long as he could hoping that it would come away in his hand. The girl managed to twist under his arm. A piece of her dress tore, but she was free of her attacker.

Another spasm passed through the mob and he was carried toward the curb. He fought toward a lamp-post, but he was swept by before he could grasp it. He saw another man catch the girl with the torn dress. She screamed for help. He tried to get to her, but was carried in the opposite direction. This rush also ended in a dead spot. Here his neighbors were all shorter than he was. He turned his head upward toward the sky and tried to pull some fresh air into his aching lungs, but it was all heavily tainted with sweat.

In this part of the mob no one was hysterical. In fact, most of the people seemed to be enjoying themselves. Near him was a stout woman with a man pressing hard against her from in front. His chin was on her shoulder, and his arms were around her. She paid no attention to him and went on talking to the woman at her side.

"The first thing I knew," Tod heard her say, "there was a rush and I was in the middle."

"Yeah. Somebody hollered, 'Here comes Gary Cooper,' and then wham!"

"That ain't it," said a little man wearing a cloth cap and pullover sweater. "This is a riot you're in."

"Yeah," said a third woman, whose snaky gray hair was hanging over her face and shoulders. "A pervert attacked a child."

"He ought to be lynched."

Everybody agreed vehemently.

"I come from St. Louis," announced the stout woman, "and we had one of them pervert fellers in our neighborhood once. He ripped up a girl with a pair of scissors."

"He must have been crazy," said the man in the cap. "What kind of fun is that?"

Everybody laughed. The stout woman spoke to the man who was hugging her.

"Hey, you," she said. "I ain't no pillow."

The man smiled beatifically but didn't move. She laughed, making no effort to get out of his embrace.

"A fresh guy," she said.

The other woman laughed.

"Yeah," she said, "this is a regular free-for-all."

The man in the cap and sweater thought there was another laugh in his comment about the pervert.

"Ripping up a girl with scissors. That's the wrong tool."

He was right. They laughed even louder than the first time.

"You'd a done it different, eh, kid?" said a young man with a kidney-shaped head and waxed mustaches.

The two women laughed. This encouraged the man in the cap and he reached over and pinched the stout woman's friend. She squealed.

"Lay off that," she said good-naturedly.

"I was shoved," he said.

An ambulance siren screamed in the street. Its wailing moan started the crowd moving again and Tod was carried along in a slow, steady push. He closed his eyes and tried to protect his throbbing leg. This time, when the movement ended, he found himself with his back to the theatre wall. He kept his eyes closed and stood on his good leg. After what seemed like hours, the pack began to loosen and move again with a churning motion. It gathered momentum and rushed. He rode it until he was slammed against the base of an iron rail which fenced the driveway of the theatre from the street. He had the wind knocked out of him by the impact, but managed to cling to the rail. He held on desperately, fighting to keep from being sucked back. A woman caught him around the waist and tried to hang on. She was sobbing rhythmically. Tod felt his fingers slipping from the rail and kicked backwards as hard as he could. The woman let go.

Despite the agony in his leg, he was able to think clearly about his picture, "The Burning of Los Angeles." After his quarrel with Faye, he had worked on it continually to escape tormenting himself, and the way to it in his mind had become almost automatic.

As he stood on his good leg, clinging desperately to the iron rail, he could see all the rough charcoal strokes with which he had blocked it out on the big canvas. Across the top, parallel with the frame, he had drawn the burning city, a great bonfire of architectural styles, ranging from Egyptian to Cape Cod colonial. Through the center, winding from left to right, was a long hill street and down it, spilling into the middle foreground, came the mob carrying baseball bats and torches. For the faces of its members, he was using the innumerable sketches he had made of the people who come to California to die; the cultists of all sorts, economic as well as religious, the wave, airplane, funeral and preview watchers—all those poor devils who can only be stirred by the promise of miracles and then only to violence. A super "Dr. Know-All Pierce-All" had made the necessary promise and they were marching behind his banner in a great united front of screwballs and screwboxes to purify the land. No longer bored, they sang and danced joyously in the red light of the flames.

In the lower foreground, men and women fled wildly before the vanguard of the crusading mob. Among them were Faye, Harry, Homer, Claude and himself. Faye ran proudly, throwing her knees high. Harry stumbled along behind her, holding on to his beloved derby hat with both hands. Homer seemed to be falling out of the canvas, his face half-asleep, his big hands clawing the air in anguished pantomime. Claude turned his head as he ran to thumb his nose at his pursuers. Tod himself picked up a small stone to throw before continuing his flight.

He had almost forgotten both his leg and his predicament, and to make his escape still more complete he stood on a chair and worked at the flames in an upper corner of the canvas, modeling the tongues of fire so that they licked even more avidly at a corinthian column that held up the palmleaf roof of a nutburger stand.

He had finished one flame and was starting on another when he was brought back by someone shouting in his ear. He opened his eyes and saw a policeman trying to reach him from behind the rail to which he was clinging. He let go with his left hand and raised his arm. The policeman caught him by the wrist, but couldn't lift him. Tod was afraid to let go until another man came to aid the policeman and caught him by the back of his jacket. He let go of the rail and they hauled him up and over it.

When they saw that he couldn't stand, they let him down easily to the ground. He was in the theatre driveway. On the curb next to him sat a woman crying into her skirt. Along the wall were groups of other disheveled people. At the end of the driveway was an ambulance. A policeman asked him if he wanted to go to the hospital. He shook his head no. He then offered him a lift home. Tod had the presence of mind to give Claude's address.

He was carried through the exit to the back street and lifted into a police car. The siren began to scream and at first he thought he was making the noise himself. He felt his lips with his hands. They were clamped tight. He knew then it was the siren. For some reason this made him laugh and he began to imitate the siren as loud as he could.